CAMERON UNSCRIPTED

Durango Street Theatre – Book 6

Emily Mims

ALSO BY EMILY MIMS

Durango Street Theatre
Vivi's Leading Man
Maggie's Starring Role
Wade's Dangerous Debut
Jessica's Hero
Letti's Second Act

The Smoky Blues series
Mist
Smoke
Evergreen
Indigo
Emerald
Mistletoe
Violet
Ruby
Amethyst
Noelle

The Texas Hill Country series
Solomon's Choice
After the Heartbreak
A Gift of Trust
Daughter of Valor
Welcome Home
Unexpected Assets
Never and Always
A Gift of Hope
Once, Again

Other Romances

Season of Enchantment
A Dangerous Attraction
For the Thrill of It All

Boroughs
Publishing Group

www.**BOROUGHSPUBLISHINGGROUP**.com

CAMERON UNSCRIPTED

ISBN 978-1-953810-37-3

To the staff and volunteers at the Woodlawn Theatre who have kept the faith and reached out to the community during this time of crisis.

Thank you for the Facebook posts and virtual performances designed to put a smile on our faces.

Thank you for this summer's Virtual Academy and Camp.

Thank you for the upcoming virtual cast reunions.

Thank you for keeping a smile on your face and a song in your heart.

It means more than you will ever know.

ACKNOWLEDGMENTS

As always, this book was not written in a vacuum. I would like to express my sincere thanks to Woodlawn Theatre Board Chairman Melissa Gonzales, and Executive and Artistic Director Chris Rodriguez for their valuable input into this story. They made what they do come alive and I hope I've made it come equally alive for my readers.

I would also like to thank my beta readers Roy Bartels and Edwin Floyd for their nitpicky beta reads (their description, not mine). My editor for her spot-on editing, and her insight into a world unfamiliar to me, and the Boroughs Art Department for another knock-'em-out-of-the-park cover.

My heartfelt thanks to all the gay parents who were willing to talk to me about the unique challenges facing them in the 2020s. Moms and dads, you rock!

CAMERON UNSCRIPTED

Chapter One

Josh leaned against the back wall and watched the second act of the Durango Street Theatre's production of *South Pacific.* One more performance after this they'd put the production to bed and start gearing up for *Peter Pan,* which would run during the holiday season.

The *Peter Pan* cast had already been chosen, and according to guest director Damon Ortega, Letti Aldrete's colleague from the local community college, rehearsals had already begun. The show was taking shape nicely.

As executive director of the theater, Josh's first choice to direct had been Letti—a longtime troupe member, director, and badass. But pregnancy at forty was kicking her badassness, and her soon-to-be husband persuaded her that her health and the baby's were more important than a theater production. Kevin was right, of course, but it brought home the kind of sacrifices they'd be making for the next twenty years or so. Josh couldn't imagine why Letti, who'd already raised one family with her ex, would want to do it again. But she was thrilled, and that was all that mattered.

That kind of sacrifice was the last thing he wanted in his life.

Not that it would ever be an issue for him. He was unattached, and he planned to stay that way. A family was not on his horizon in any way, shape, or form.

Thank god.

He turned his attention back to the production. Kevin's Joseph Cable had blown off Liat, and Letti had delivered Bloody Mary's "You stingy bastard" line. It was time for Cameron Heiser's Emile LeBecque to sing "This Nearly was Mine," the heart-wrenching lament of lost love. This was Cameron's best scene in the play. His character's heartbreak over losing Nellie prompted him to put his life on the line in the allied cause.

Josh stared up at the stage, taking in every one of Cameron's gestures while listening to every note. He was glad the theater was dark. Otherwise, the lust and longing he kept hidden from the world would be evident for everyone to see.

He'd been lusting after Cameron Heiser for a long time. Three and a half years ago, Josh had gotten bitten by the Cameron bug. The man topped six feet by a couple of inches and had the kind of lean and rangy body Josh had always admired. The sport coats and dress pants he usually wore as president of Heiser Steel emphasized the breadth of his shoulders, but did little to showcase his fantastic body, which was evident in his welding clothes he'd worn a few times to rehearsals. Cameron still liked to get his hand dirty, and in a tight tee and work jeans, every delectable inch of his delicious body could be seen and appreciated, which made Josh want to get his hands all kinds of dirty.

Thick ash-blond hair framed Cameron's long, thin face, stark with prominent cheekbones, and bright blue eyes. His wide mouth was made for kissing, and a whole lot of other things Josh had featured in his fantasies. The biggest plus: Cameron was gay. Though he wasn't especially open about it.

The song ended and the stage went dark for a scene change. A few more scenes and the show would be over. The cast would shake hands with the audience, and then take off their costumes. Most of them would head down the street to Thirties, the deco bar that had become the unofficial hangout for the Durango twenty-somethings in the cast and crew.

After a meteoric rise in the San Antonio theater world, at twenty-five Josh had been hired as the executive director of the Durango. As chairman of the board, Cameron was Josh's boss, and more than ten years older than him.

At the time, Josh thought Cameron possessed a worldliness and sophistication Josh could only aspire to someday. In the last few years he'd garnered confidence with his experience. He wasn't a gauche kid anymore. There was no reason he and Cameron couldn't get together.

Josh had a front row seat to see an age gap didn't have to be a big deal. Wade Baxter and Owen Aldrete were fifteen years apart and it didn't seem to affect their relationship. Letti's soon-to-be husband was twenty-five to her forty.

If it didn't matter for those two couples, it shouldn't matter for him and Cameron.

Not that he was looking for anything permanent, but he was tired of lusting after Cameron from afar. He wanted to get up close and personal. Sweaty.

He didn't think it was his imagination: Cameron wanted the same thing with him.

He'd decided to make his move tonight. It would be subtle, but gay men in San Antonio were used to subtle. As far as they'd come societally, this wasn't LA.

Josh was thinking about the potential the evening to come held when his phone vibrated in his pocket. He started to ignore the buzz and let the call go to voice mail. But something, he wasn't sure what, prompted him to look at the screen and he frowned. *Bubbe*. Clara Goldstein had turned ninety-one last month and was never up past eight at night. Something was wrong.

He jogged to the lobby and tried to catch the call but was too late. He hit the call button and got her on the third try. "Are you all right?"

"I'm fine, Joshie. Fine."

But she didn't sound fine. Her German accent was thicker than usual, a surefire tell that she was stressed. Plus, she sounded weary. "What is it?" he demanded.

She hesitated for a moment. "It's Miriam. She and the kids drove in a few minutes ago. She needs to talk to us."

Josh frowned. That wasn't so unusual. San Marcos was only a forty-five-minute drive, and Miriam brought her children for a visit often enough, though not usually on a Saturday night. Now that he thought about it, she hadn't come in a couple of months.

Plus, he could tell *Bubbe* was upset about something.

"Just…just come, Joshie." *Bubbe*'s voice broke. "We'll talk when you get here." His grandmother disconnected.

Something was definitely *wrong*. If he hurried, he could make it to her place in fifteen minutes.

He shot off a text to Rachel to cover for him greeting the audience. He took one more peek in the theater and looked at Cameron wistfully.

So much for seducing his favorite fantasy.

Tonight, family came first.

He jogged around the building to the large parking lot in the back. The air was cool this long after sunset in early November, so he left the top up on his vintage Miata as he slid into the tiny red car, parked next to Cameron's lovingly restored Shelby Mustang.

Cameron's father had driven it first and given it to his son as a graduation gift when Cameron had gotten his MBA from Wharton. Josh and Cameron had joked more than once about taking them to the drag strip for a race, but they were both a little too fond of their beloved classics to do that.

Besides, the Mustang would leave the Miata in the dust and they both knew it.

Josh had more important things to do this evening than think about drag racing. Such as why Miriam had driven in tonight, and why *Bubbe* was so rattled.

Not that Miriam hadn't given her grandmother a few things to be rattled about over the years. She'd gone off the rails a while back, taking up with country and western bass player Jimmy Joe McDonald out of somewhere in North Texas. Jimmy Joe was into Shiner Bok and dive bars, and *Bubbe* had nearly died when Miriam eloped with him after the pregnancy test came back positive. Those two practically had a knock-down drag-out over the marriage. "I don't care if you are pregnant," *Bubbe* had railed. "He's…he's not—"

"I *know* he's not Jewish. But I love him and he's the baby's father," Miriam shot back. "It's done. We're married. Get over it."

Sadly, it hadn't taken long for Jimmy Joe to show his true colors. Miriam made the best of it anyway, juggling first Jackson and then Beth while getting her degrees and then a coveted teaching position at Texas State University. Much to the fury of her small-town in-laws, she trained the children carefully in the ways of the family's heritage and faith, and refused to move closer to the McDonalds' small Panhandle town after Jimmy Joe had been stabbed to death in a bar fight.

But Miriam wouldn't move back to San Antonio either, insisting she needed a few miles between her and *Bubbe*. "We're too much alike," she'd said when Josh asked her about it. "Besides, I'm a tenured professor and haven't turned thirty yet. Why would I go off and leave that?"

While *Bubbe* loved Miriam with all her heart, she'd never quite forgiven her for her early rebellion and still took issue with her refusal to move back to San Antonio. There was still some strain between them, and more than once Josh found himself trying to bridge the gap between their opposing viewpoints. At the same time, they loved one another with a fierce intensity. Josh loved them both the same way.

Despite the inevitable sibling squabbles, he and Miriam always had one another's backs. He'd been there for her when her marriage had gone sour. She'd had his back when he came out of the closet. She was his sister, and she was also his best friend.

Which was why he was scared to damn death at whatever was going down with her.

Traffic this late was light, and the drive across town to *Bubbe*'s large home in historic Monte Vista only took a few minutes. Josh pulled into the driveway all the way to the side portico and parked behind Miriam's spanking new crossover. He looked at the massive house and shook his head.

Why *Bubbe* continued to live here was anybody's guess. It was big and drafty, and wasn't particularly handicapped accessible, which made it difficult for her to negotiate using her walker. But she'd lived in the house for almost sixty years and raised her only son as well as her two grandchildren here. She wouldn't hear of moving elsewhere.

"It's where I raised my family," she protested. "It's where Saul and I made a home. It's where my memories are. I'm not leaving, Joshie. Not until they carry me out in a body bag."

The side door was unlocked and he could hear the low murmur of voices coming from the breakfast room off the kitchen. Half-empty cartons of moo goo gai pan and fried rice emitted what would normally be an enticing aroma, but was anything but appealing tonight. A sense of foreboding swept over him.

Something was absolutely wrong. He took a deep breath and steeled himself. He didn't know what he was going to find when he walked into the breakfast room. Whatever it was, he was sure it was going to suck.

He plastered a smile on his face and strolled through the recently remodeled kitchen to the spacious breakfast room that looked out onto the huge terrace and swimming pool, which lay beyond it.

Bubbe sat in her usual chair facing the windows. She was wrapped in a fluffy pink robe and had on no makeup, which was not the norm for his fashion-conscious, elegant grandmother.

Miriam had gravitated to her old spot across the table and between them sat Miriam's children, Jackson and Beth. He tried to smile at them, but his gaze kept returning to the brightly patterned scarf tied around Miriam's head framing her pale, thin face.

The scarf wasn't a fashion statement.

There were no brown curls sticking out. The scarf lay too close to her head. There was no hair beneath it.

Oh shit. Shit, shit, shit.

Josh swallowed and forced a smile. He wouldn't let on that the sight his sister presented, and all it meant, knocked him on his ass. Instead he moved across the room and threw his arms around Miriam's thin shoulders. "It's good to see you, pain in the butt."

Miriam rose from her chair and gave him a huge hug, her body waifish under the stylish jeans and sweater. "It's good to see you too, nuisance. You're looking fine. I take it *South Pacific* went well."

"It was great. Awesome. Best ever."

"Never gonna sell pants with *Bubbe*, huh?"

Bubbe lifted her chin. "In my dreams, apparently."

It was a running joke between him and Miriam. His grandmother owned Goldstein's, the premier men's clothing stores in San Antonio. His grandfather and his father had made it no secret that they wanted him to be part of the family business. For years they had nagged him to give up the "theater nonsense," but Josh ignored them and held firm on his life choice.

Bubbe had been disappointed by his decision too, but chose to take it more graciously than she had Miriam's choices, even after his father and grandfather died, which left her to run the stores by herself.

"My managers are doing fine," *Bubbe* said dryly.

"They're doing a fantastic job of it. Better than I ever would," Josh stated. He released Miriam and she sat down.

"Joshie, get some supper. There's plenty left," *Bubbe* ordered. The thought of food turned his stomach, but he dished up a little of the moo goo gai pan and sat down at his usual place beside his grandmother.

Miriam and his grandmother didn't appear all that hungry either, but the kids eagerly cleaned their plates. Jackson, the eight-year-old, had grown in the couple of months since Josh had seen him. The boy was the image of Jimmy Joe. The same dark hair, the same vivid blue eyes, the same cheekbones and jawline as his Scots-Irish father. He would be a babe magnet someday.

Beth, who had turned six in the summer, looked more like Miriam and Josh, with curly brown hair and gray eyes passed down from Saul Goldstein to his son and grandchildren, and now to Beth. The little girl looked at her mother. "Mommy threw up this morning," she said solemnly. "She does that a lot."

"Hush, Beth," Miriam murmured.

Bubbe looked at Miriam sharply. "You've been sick a lot?"

"Later," Miriam said firmly, cutting a look at the children.

Bubbe's lips firmed, but she said nothing else.

The child said no more as well and conversation faltered. Questions Josh longed to ask bounced around in his head. Like how sick Miriam was, how long had she been ill, whether she would get better. But mostly *why*. Why hadn't she leveled with them earlier? Why she hadn't let them know until now? Not a discussion to have in front of the children.

By the time they were finished eating, the children were visibly flagging. "I know this is unexpected, but is it okay if we spend the night? I don't really feel like driving back."

"Of course," Josh and *Bubbe* said in unison. *Like she had to ask?*

"Then let me put the kids to bed and we'll talk," Miriam said. "*Bubbe*, which bedrooms do you want me to use?"

"The usual. Jackson in Joshie's old room. You and Beth in your old room and the guest room next door." *Bubbe* pulled her walker close. "Joshie and I will load the dishwasher."

"You stay put. I'll take care of it," Josh said quickly.

Miriam disappeared with the children. Josh waited until he heard them go upstairs before turning to his grandmother. "What's going on?"

"You know as much as I do. She rang the doorbell at seven forty-five and said we needed to talk and to please call you. It's obvious she's not well."

Josh stood and started gathering up the dirty dishes. "Clearly. I guess she'll fill us in when she comes down."

He loaded the dishwasher and put away the leftover food. *Bubbe* waited for him and Miriam in the sunroom adjacent to the breakfast area. Josh joined her and they waited none too patiently for Miriam's return.

It seemed like forever, but it was probably only fifteen minutes before Miriam joined them. She collapsed onto the sofa and shut her eyes for a moment. "I'm so tired."

"It's no wonder, if you're as sick as I think you are," *Bubbe* said tartly. "What's going on and how sick are you?"

Miriam sat up straighter and looked from Josh to *Bubbe*. "I won't sugarcoat it. I have ovarian cancer. It had already spread by the time it was diagnosed. The ultrasound was conclusive. It's all over. Short of a miracle, and that's what it would be, I'm terminal."

Bubbe's face contorted. Josh felt a blanket of numbness cover him. He'd already figured things were bad, but having it spelled out made it horribly, frighteningly real. "How much time do they think you have left?" he asked softly.

Her shoulders twitched. "One month. Maybe two."

"One month? Two? *Shayna madela,* why didn't you tell us?"

"Oh, *Bubbe,* I didn't want it to be true. I wanted a miracle. I prayed for one, but it didn't come." Tears filled her eyes and she looked down at her hands. "I started a leave of absence today. I would have resigned outright, but by burning my vacation and sick leave there'll be that much more in my pension fund for the kids' educations. I'm too sick to work." She wiped the tears from her eyes. "I'm too sick to take care of my children."

"You put them in the car and drove here?" Josh asked. "I would've come and gotten y'all."

"In that toy car you drive? I'd like to see that." She smiled through her tears.

"He could have driven mine," *Bubbe* said imperiously. "You will, of course, close up your house and stay here. Joshie and I can help you with the children."

Miriam looked relieved. "Thank you." She looked from *Bubbe* to Josh. "Later. I'll need your help with them later." Her face firmed and she raised her chin. "I want them to grow up with my family. Not the McDonalds. I don't want those people anywhere near my children."

Josh and his grandmother looked at one another as they each absorbed the reality of the situation. Miriam wanted her family to raise her children. But Miriam had practically no family left. His grandparents had lost everyone in the Holocaust. Josh's mother had run off with her boyfriend to a *kibbutz* in Israel when Josh was a baby, and his maternal grandparents were long gone. Josh's grandfather had passed some time back, and his father died from an untimely coronary when Josh was in college. The only Goldsteins left were him, *Bubbe*, Miriam, and her children.

Josh sucked in his breath and hoped his dismay wasn't obvious.

His sister was asking him and his ninety-one-year-old grandmother to raise her children.

Knowing what he did about the McDonald family, he and *Bubbe* would do as Miriam asked. Hell, he'd fight to keep those children with them.

God in heaven, how is he going to raise two kids?

Chapter Two

Cameron took the hand of his leading lady and ran to the front of the stage, bowing low before the whistling, stomping, clapping audience. The crowd had been on their feet since the cast had come out to take their bows, their enthusiasm escalating as first the ensemble, then the sailors and nurses, and then the featured players came out to bow and curtsy.

As they had every night of the performance, the audience gave Letti a good five minutes of whistles and cheers for rocking the role of Bloody Mary. Letti smiled hugely and accepted their accolades, pale under her makeup and visibly relieved the production was almost over. Her baby daddy, and soon-to-be husband, Kevin, playing Joseph, and Sophie Aldrete as Liat received appreciative applause as well.

Cameron's smile was wide and genuine as he and leading lady Sasha Fontenot bowed to their enthusiastic fans. It had been like this every night of *South Pacific*. A part of him was sorry the production was finishing tomorrow afternoon, but the part that was looking forty in the face and had his family's business to run was glad the show was over. He needed to go back to the interesting, fulfilling, but less intense role of serving as chairman of the board of the Durango Street Theatre.

Josh and Cameron were the public faces of the Durango, and it didn't hurt he was a child of San Antonio old money and privilege. Cam knew every deep pocket in town and had no problem getting them to donate to the theater.

Cameron took his bows and followed Sasha and the rest of the cast up the side aisle into the lobby. The house was packed, which meant it would be a good thirty or forty minutes before they'd finished glad-handing with their well-wishers. He positioned himself between Sasha and Letti. On a good day Sasha was aloof and withdrawn, and on a bad day, she was downright uncommunicative.

Frequently, he needed to step in and pour on the charm for her admirers. He'd wondered about Sasha from the day she walked in the theater. She was breathtakingly talented and put on the performance of a lifetime every time she took to the boards, but was completely closed off otherwise. She never joined them at Thirties, but she was a genuine jewel of a singer and performer. Cameron hoped she'd grace their stage again.

He glanced over at Letti, who was smiling graciously and chatting with one of their newer patrons. She was as outgoing and charming as they came, but she'd almost passed out twice shaking hands, and the men in the cast made it a point that one of them be on one side while Kevin was at her other.

She was forty and pregnant after raising two children to near adulthood. Sure, the relationship made sense. Letti defined hot and Kevin was sex on a stick. What Cameron couldn't understand was why they were both so damned happy about the pregnancy.

Kevin was going to be walking a squalling infant all night while he was in law school. Letti would be over sixty before the kid got out of college. Cam shuddered. Forty years of rearing children. It was beyond him why someone would want to do that.

It sounded like the definition of hell.

They finished greeting the audience and went back to the dressing rooms to change. Sasha did her usual disappearing act, and Kevin spirited Letti away as soon as she was dressed. After he washed off his stage makeup, Cam changed into jeans and a polo then headed for the parking lot and the prized Shelby his father gave him. His feelings toward Tripp Heiser were mixed, but the love with which the car was given wasn't lost on him.

He was almost to the car when his phone rang with his mother's ringtone. He looked at the screen and frowned. Betsy Heiser almost never called past eight in the evening and it was after ten. He clicked on the phone and winced at the piercing screams of a baby crying in the background. "Mom? What's wrong?"

"Nothing, really. I'm going to have to beg off on brunch tomorrow morning." Once a month he and his mother had a late breakfast together at a small deli in the middle of Alamo Heights, the tony suburb where he and Vivi had grown up, and where his mother still lived. "I hate to cancel this late, but Julie's been crying since three this afternoon and it doesn't look like it's ending any time soon. Vivi and Miguel are both at their wits' end. I said I'd come over and spell them for a bit."

Cam made a face. "She's three months old. I thought babies were supposed to be over colic by three months."

"Tell you what. You come over and explain that to her." He could hear the amusement in his mother's voice. "Seriously, the doctor said not to worry. It's almost always gone by four months and always by six. By then she'll be teething and fussing about that. I wish I knew something that would make her feel better. I don't know what to do. Neither of you had colic. You would both be back to sleep by the time your bottles were empty."

"Has Vivi asked Miguel's mother if she knows anything?"

"Juliana's as mystified as the rest of us. We'll tough it out. Okay, baby girl. Mimi has you. It's gonna be fine, little one."

His lips twitched into a smile. "Mimi, huh? Whatever happened to good old Granny?"

"You have to be kidding." His mother's voice dripped icicles. "Do I look like a Granny to you?"

He had to admit, she didn't. The society wife turned professional fundraiser looked like anything but a Granny. "Actually, Mimi is so you." Despite being an airhead when it came to money, his mother had been the best mom ever, and was crushing it as a grandmother.

"Thanks, Cam. We'll try for next week."

Jesus, Mary, and Joseph why would anybody want that? he asked himself as he got in his car. Not that he wasn't glad for his sister. She was on cloud nine. But her pregnancy hadn't been a walk in the park, and now they were coping with colic, sleepless nights, and a helpless infant dependent on them for everything, who would eventually turn into a *teenager.*

Not on Cam's agenda, that was for sure. Sure, he made a few clucking noises over Julie, held her a few minutes, and handed her back to one of her parents. Then he returned to his recently purchased loft in Southtown, complete with new furniture and unobstructed views of downtown San Antonio.

He'd continue the life he led, working late, or all day Saturday or Sunday, without worrying about kids' sports teams, playdates, and birthday parties. He'd continue to enjoy quiet evenings dining in fine restaurants with good wine. He'd continue to travel whenever he got the urge to go to exotic destinations, or European cities. He'd date whoever he damn well pleased and not worry about whether his stud of the month was a nice guy around the kids.

In the unlikely event he found "The One," they could pour out their love to one another. That would be more than enough for him.

Besides, it wasn't fair to the children. He lived in San Antonio not New York City.

The rare times the topic came up, his father would say things like, "I mean, think about it, Cam. Your kids will be the kids on the block with 'those' parents. Your kids will be the ones whose family gets whispered about. Who in his right mind would put a child through that? Gay men have no business trying to raise a family."

The unspoken *You have no business trying to raise a family* hung in the air, but was never said. Tripp would never admit out loud what was an open family secret: his only son was gay.

He sat for a minute and watched as some of the actors drifted toward their cars and others headed down the street, most likely to Thirties. The parking place next his car was empty, but he could've sworn Josh Goldstein's Miata had been parked there when Cam drove in earlier. Now that he thought about it, he hadn't seen Josh after the show, and he usually stayed on closing weekend, greeting their patrons along with the cast. Josh always accompanied the cast and crew to Thirties. Everyone enjoyed his wry sense of humor.

He was also as sexy as hell with thick, curling brown hair he never could quite tame, a well-muscled body, and a face worthy of a Michelangelo painting. Chiseled cheekbones and chin, lush, full lips, and soulful gray eyes. He wasn't a particularly big man, maybe five nine, but he carried himself with authority. He always seemed bigger than he was. Then there was the megawatt smile that'd never been sent Cam's way, but he'd watched Josh work a room and use that smile like a velvet weapon.

Every once in a while, Cam thought there might be something between them, but it seemed more wishful thinking than reality.

He moved his car closer to the bar. He'd had enough exercise today and was tired after wrestling all day with a heavy iron gate he was custom welding, and after a full day's work, doing the show. His best chance to connect with Josh was at Thirties.

At the theater they assumed their roles of board chairman and executive director, which should put the kibosh to anything personal, but wouldn't necessarily. After all, this was the theater world. Unlike the tight-assed environment of business, in which Cameron lived in most of the time, the theater was looser, less bound by PC.

It would be better if Josh made the first move, since, theoretically, Cameron was his employer. But if Josh didn't make the first move, Cameron was more than willing to take the lead. The only problem he could foresee was the inevitable chatter it was bound to generate. Gossip spread faster than wildfire at the theater, and the tongue-wagging would jump out of the theater in less than an hour.

As much as he hated being talked about, he wasn't going to let that stop him. He doubted Josh would either.

Cam entered the busy bar, told the hostess he was with the Durango crowd, and was ushered to their usual spot in the back, an alcove, which was marginally separated from the main room. Artistic director Rachel Castillo motioned him to a booth she was sharing with Owen Aldrete and Wade Baxter, who'd defied the odds, fallen in love, and were happy.

Cameron ordered his usual Pino Grigio and looked around the room. "I thought Josh was at the theater earlier this evening. Did he go home early?"

"He left, but not to go home. *Bubbe* called during the second act," Rachel volunteered. "Some kind of emergency. I hope everything's all right."

"He didn't say what was wrong?"

"Nope. He said he had to leave and was gone."

Cam took a deep breath. Damn. He'd been so sure tonight would be the night Josh would make his move. There'd be other nights, he reminded himself. There'd be plenty of chances for the two of them to connect in the weeks to come.

Unless he had imagined the sidelong glances Josh had sent his way. He knew damned well he hadn't imagined those glances. Josh was as hot for him as he was for Josh.

The question was when they would act on it, and which one of them would make the first move.

***

Josh yawned as he filled his favorite insulated mug with hot, black coffee. Today was going to be a long one. After he'd gotten damned little sleep the night before, he still had to go to the Durango for the Sunday afternoon performance. He'd spent most of the night thinking about Miriam's bombshell and what it meant for his future. His emotions alternating between heart-wrenching grief and virulent anger.

Why her? Hadn't their family suffered enough loss? She deserved to be happy, and her children deserved to have their mother at least until they reached adulthood.

Shit.

He understood why she wanted him to raise her children, he really did, but his lifestyle was going to take a one-eighty and he didn't want to sound like a selfish prick, but resented the hell out of it.

With too many thoughts and heavy emotions weighing on him, he'd tossed and turned until almost dawn, only to be awakened a couple hours later by a call from *Bubbe*. "I told Miriam a white lie and said you'd called and asked her to brunch. I want you to talk to her and find out what's going on."

"I think we know what's going on," he'd stated the obvious.

"Not really. She was too tired to say much, and you ran out of here like a scalded cat," *Bubbe* said dryly. "You need to talk to her, Joshie. Really talk to her. You need to make plans. Especially if she has as little time as she says she does."

Bubbe was right. One month or two, he had damned little time to make the changes in his life he needed to become a father.

Tamping down another wave of sorrow—he'd cried off and on through the night—he showered, letting his hair curl naturally rather than trying to comb it into anything resembling a style. He lathered up his face and made quick work of shaving his thick, fast-growing beard. He did a speedy search through his wardrobe. He might not have gone into the family business, but weekends and summers at Goldstein's had taught him a thing or two about dressing well. He paired slim-cut black jeans with a red dress shirt and a casual jacket in deference to the cool front that had blown in late last night. He wouldn't have time to change and the outfit should get him through brunch and Sunday afternoon at the theater.

He fed and walked Pepper, the long-legged chihuahua mix he'd adopted as a puppy last year, and locked up the two-bedroom Craftsman he'd recently purchased in the Deco District in part for its charm, but mostly for its proximity to the theater. The streets were almost deserted this early on a Sunday, and he made it to his grandmother's in no time at all.

Despite the early hour, the Goldstein household was in full swing. Ella Marsh, *Bubbe*'s cook/housekeeper/aide, was in the kitchen making pancakes, and *Bubbe* was sitting with the children at the breakfast table.

His grandmother was dressed in a fashionable pantsuit from her favorite boutique, and her face was carefully made up for the day. The children were happily digging into stacks of pancakes. Josh looked at the pancakes ruefully. "Those look so good," he said longingly.

Bubbe shrugged. "Take Miriam someplace that serves them."

"Nah. I think I'd rather go someplace where they make a decent bagel," Miriam said as she strode into the room. "Is that place on Broadway still there? The bagel shops in San Marcos aren't all that great."

"No, but there are others that are as good as the one used to be on Broadway. The best one's over in Alamo Heights. That work for you?" Josh smiled at his sister.

Miriam smiled back. "It does." She leaned over and kissed her children. "You two behave for *Bubbe* and Ella. When Uncle Josh and I get back, maybe we can go to the zoo or one of the museums. If I feel like it," she added under her breath.

The children murmured their agreement and went back to eating. Josh escorted Miriam to his car. She looked better this morning. She had a bit of color in her cheeks, but was still way too thin and pale. His sister had learned from *Bubbe* all about dressing well, and was attractively decked out in ripped-in-the-right-place jeans, a chunky sweater, and a colorful head scarf. God help the day either of them left the house looking less than perfect.

Shit. That day was coming for Miriam, all too soon.

He opened the door and helped her inside. "*Bubbe*'s cotillion lessons kicking in?" she teased. "Opening the car door for a lady?"

"Don't get to do that too often, considering my dates," he joked.

Miriam snickered. "Good point."

Traffic had picked up some but was still light, and they made good time to the deli. Miriam took a deep breath. "I love bagels so much. It must be something genetic."

"That, and 'cause *Bubbe* and *Zayde* served them to us three or four times a week," Josh reminded her of something they knew and cherished. "They loved a good bagel like nobody's business."

"It was a shame they couldn't get the ones like they make in New York City."

"You know, you can get them shipped next day," Josh said. "From lots of places in New York."

"Still, it's not like buying them fresh," Miriam muttered before they placed their orders at the counter. They sat at a table in the back, each with a toasted sesame bagel smothered by a healthy schmear of cream cheese. Miriam had thin slices of lox on hers. They ate in silence for a few minutes while Josh tried to figure out how to bring up what was weighing so heavily on his mind. Miriam finally pushed her plate away and wiped her lips with a paper napkin. "Okay. Spill. What does *Bubbe* want you to discuss with me?"

Josh looked at her in surprise. "How did—"

"C'mon. Like I don't know she put you up to this."

"Busted." He shrugged. "She's worried, and I got questions. I was going to wait a couple of days, but we might as well go ahead and talk."

"Okay." Miriam took a deep breath. "There's no point in worrying, at least not about me. I'm dying. I know I'm dying. As much as is humanly possible, I've come to terms with it. My only concern is who is going to take care of my children after I'm gone. I've given it a lot of thought. I want that to be you, Josh. You and, however much she can, *Bubbe*."

"Okay. I can do that." Josh hoped his uncertainty didn't show.

No such luck. "You don't sound too thrilled."

"No, what I'm not thrilled about is losing my big sister. Neither of us has any control over the inevitable, and that sucks. You can't fault me that."

"Believe me." She reached across the table and grabbed his hand. Her fingers felt bony and fragile. "If I had it in my power to change things, I would. This is one of those things money can't buy. You know, it's a stupid thought, but when I got my diagnosis, I said to myself, if Paul McCartney, who has more money than God, couldn't save Linda, I shouldn't feel so bad our family's money can't save me." She shrugged. "I hate that I'm sick, Josh. I hate that I'm leaving my kids. I hate leaving them with you is going to fuck up your life big-time, but I have no choice but to ask you. They have other family—"

"You can stop right there." Josh held up his hand. "They're my blood. My family. There are precious few of us. I wouldn't want anyone else raising *my* niece and nephew. Especially not your former in-laws."

Miriam looked relieved. "You get it, then."

"Of course, I do. It's not that I don't want to take the kids, but I'm scared shitless. I'm young and single, and don't know the first thing about raising children. What if I mess them up?"

Miriam tried and failed to stifle a laugh. "You're not gonna mess them up. Without sounding too maudlin, they're going to be messed up plenty losing their mother. You're the person in their life who'll provide stability and continuity. The fact you're even worried about it tells me you won't be messing up anybody. Not intentionally. Besides, the kids love you, and children feed off love. You love them back, and they'll forgive you anything." She took a breath. "They love you a lot more than they love any of their father's people."

"As much money as the McDonald grandparents have spent on them?"

"Money to try to cover for how they really feel about the kids. Jackson and Beth aren't stupid. They know they're not really part of that family, and they know damn well why."

Josh ground his teeth. "Fuck 'em."

"That about covers it."

"So tell me about Jackson and Beth."

"You know them, Josh."

"I don't know them well enough to raise them. I need to know more. Stuff about them you know and I don't. Stuff I need to know when I'm dealing with them. Tell me how I go about being a good father."

She squeezed his fingers and smiled. "Jackson tries to come on like a tough kid." She rolled her eyes. "But inside he's a marshmallow. Very sensitive. Only he doesn't want anyone else to know."

"And Beth?" he prompted.

"A princess with a bulging wardrobe and an AK-47." Miriam laughed. "She's a girly-girl with the heart of a warrior."

"Like you were."

"Fiercer than I ever thought about being. It kills me, knowing I don't get to raise them." Her eyes began to fill.

"It kills me too." He leaned forward. "Every time I'll look at them, I'll see you." He sat back and tried to steer them back to information sharing.

He asked about clothes, food, school, doctors, discipline, and guidance. She did her best to give him what he needed to know, but he could tell, her heart was breaking with every explanation.

He could tell she was getting tired, and they walked back to the car. They'd barely scratched the surface, and he didn't feel any more ready to raise the children than he had before, but he'd be damned if he let on.

"So was talking to me any help?" she asked as he started the engine.

"Absolutely," he said with more confidence than he felt. "Please believe me when I tell you, I'll raise them the best way I know how."

This sucked so huge, he couldn't process it. Miriam didn't ask to get sick. She didn't ask to die and leave a couple of kids with no parents. He might be scrambling on the inside, but he'd be damned if he let her see anything but his strength.

By the time he dropped her back at *Bubbe*'s and headed home for a folder he'd forgotten to take with him, he was drained. He pulled into his driveway and raised the Miata's top before turning off the engine. Damn. The little car was the first thing that would have to go. He could hardly put both kids and a week's worth of groceries in the tiny two-seater.

He stood in the driveway for a minute, staring at the car and picturing a crossover sitting in its place.

Well, hell.

He shrugged and let himself in the house. He glanced around the stylishly retro Craftsman furnished in Art Deco and Danish Modern. They couldn't stay here. The house was too small for him and two children, and in this neighborhood, the schools were iffy. His heart sank as he considered his options. It was either a bigger house in the Deco District with hefty private school tuition, or a cookie-cutter three-two in a suburban school district.

Pepper greeted him with yelps of joy and wagged his tail eagerly. At least he already had a dog. The kids would love Pepper, and Pepper would love them.

He didn't want to talk about this with Miriam, and frankly, there was no need. He and *Bubbe* had covered the McDonald family topic plenty. He'd never entrust the kids with any McDonald.

Jackson and Beth were Jewish, which stuck in the McDonalds' craw like a two by four. They knew nothing of Jewish heritage, of the Goldstein family history, or the cultural connection the children had with Jews worldwide. They didn't and wouldn't because they were flagrant anti-Semites.

Bubbe was too old to raise another family. He was it. The only family member who could provide what those children needed. Time to suck it up, buttercup. He'd change houses, change cars, and learn to shop for little girl clothes. He'd find the right school, and provide the loving guidance his sister always had while teaching them who they were. He would be the best parent he knew how to be.

He found the folder he needed sitting on top of a picture he'd taken a year or so ago with his most recent lover. He stared down at the image of him and Stuart in Cozumel with their arms around one another. The relationship had been casual, and they'd broken up not long afterward. But it gave him pause.

Stuart hadn't been into children, and had come out and said so. Stuart's attitude wasn't unusual. While a few of the men in his circle were married or parenting solo, most of them were unattached. They weren't looking for permanent relationships or families. They weren't interested in crossovers or mortgages in good school districts. They weren't into afternoons at the zoo, or family-style restaurants, or nailing down a babysitter so they could go out on the town.

They weren't interested in parenting, and they weren't into men who were.

When it came to finding your forever, they weren't going to look twice at a partner who came as a package deal.

He wondered if any available man out there would.

Josh shook his head and pushed aside the thought. He had too much to worry about to angst over his love life. His beloved sister was dying, and he was about to become a father.

He had to worry about a house, a vehicle, a babysitter, and being there for two young children who were about to lose the only parent they had.

The last thing he had time for was wondering what taking on the children was going to do to his love life. Their needs came first. Not whether he got laid any time in the near future.

He could worry about his love life later.

Much, much later.

Chapter Three

Cameron sat at the head of the table and looked around at his assembled board members, some of whom were smiling at him encouragingly and others who were giving him the stink eye. "We don't need to expand the Academy right now," Jen Acevedo insisted. "We barely have the room or the resources to house the kids we're already serving." Jen was a local pediatrician and longtime benefactor of the theater, having sent all three of her children to the Academy at one time or another.

"I think we need to expand," Byron Summerset argued. "We have a waiting list a mile long of children who desperately want to be part of our program. Josh, have you talked to Jessica about this? How does she feel about expanding the Academy?"

Everyone turned to look at Josh, who was staring off into space. Cameron gave him a minute. "Josh?" he asked quietly, then more insistently when he didn't answer the first time.

Josh blinked and looked around the table at the gazes trained on him. "Oh. Sorry. What was the question?"

"I asked how Jessica feels about expanding the Academy at this time." Byron looked a little impatient.

"She and I haven't discussed it recently," Josh said frankly. "The last time we talked was before we added classes in the elementary and middle school curricula."

"What was her feeling then?" Cameron prompted.

"That if we expand the high school level as well, we would have to scare up more studio space, or utilize space that is being used for adult rehearsal or storage."

"We can't sacrifice adult rehearsal space," Vivi Abonce said quickly. "We're squeezed as it is." She looked around the table. "If you're serious about expanding the Academy, *and* willing to rent commercial storage space for the larger props, I can talk to Miguel about turning that big back storage room into more Academy space."

Cameron glanced over at his sister. Her husband owned the theater and rented it to the Durango for a dollar a year. "Is Miguel willing to invest yet more money in this place?"

Vivi bit her lip. "I can't sit here and commit Miguel's money or his construction crews without talking to him first. Why don't you let us talk about it and get back to you?"

The board agreed that was reasonable. The next item on the agenda was a proposed switch to a different concession stand vendor, which was quickly approved when Josh gave them a figure in savings. Again, he seemed distant and distracted. He was no longer gracing Cameron with the occasional discreet appreciative glance.

Cameron wondered what the hell was going on.

He hoped the young hottie hadn't changed his mind. He'd planned to make his move this afternoon after the board meeting. He'd ask Josh out, maybe for dinner at that new place in the Pearl he'd been wanting to try. Nothing heavy. A simple dinner and conversation where they could get to know one another better.

Perhaps explore the attraction that they both were feeling.

The board meeting dragged on for another hour. Josh took off like a shot while the rest of the board lingered for another fifteen minutes, gathering up their papers and shooting the breeze. He thought he heard Josh's name mentioned once or twice across the room but didn't think too much of it. Josh was an integral part of the theater and it would be natural that his name would come up in discussion. A smile played around his lips. He wondered how much more often it would come up if Josh took him up on his invitation. He'd bet his favorite soldering iron they would barely be to the front door of the restaurant before someone back here was broadcasting the news.

But first he had to make that date. It had become clear in the last few days that Josh wasn't going to make the first move, so Cameron headed out and around to the office suites. Josh was nowhere to be seen, but Rachel and Maggie Gutierrez, their developmental director, were leaning over looking at something on Maggie's hand. "Come take a look," Rachel said. "Kirby surprised her with it last night."

"What is it? An engagement ring?"

Maggie laughed. She held out her hand to show off a stylish silver bangle. "Hardly. Kirby's been looking to move somewhere close to here and I've checked out a couple of town houses for him. The rent on his condo doubled and he's tired of fighting the traffic out north of the loop. It takes him forty-five minutes to get downtown. From this neighborhood he could do it in ten or less. I found him something nice and this is my thank you gift."

"Are you moving in with him?" Cameron asked.

"No, we're not ready for that," Maggie said quickly.

"Nothing wrong with taking it slow," Rachel murmured.

He nodded, hoping his relief didn't show. As far as he was concerned, the jury was still out on Kirby Martinez. He'd been a real ass on more than one occasion in the past. At the same time, he'd been instrumental in getting several generous grants for the theater, and for that Cameron was grateful. He glanced around. "Have any of you seen Josh floating around?"

Rachel and Maggie exchanged a look. "Uh, I think he had to go." Rachel looked at him hesitantly. It was a couple of hours before Josh usually left.

"Okay. No problem." Cameron smiled reassuringly. Josh provided plenty of value for the money they paid him. He could leave early if he needed to.

The women looked relieved. "We better get back to work," Rachel said as they disappeared into their respective offices.

Cameron's face fell. So much for making his move today.

He put his paperwork back in his own desk and was coming out of his office when Vivi wandered up. "Whatcha doin' back here? You're usually hot to get back to Heiser Steel," she teased.

"What are you doing still here? You're usually in a rush to get back to Princess Julie," he shot back with a smile.

"I'm making myself stay away to see if the new nanny can handle her. I need to get back to work, and you need me to come back, even though you're too much of a good brother to tell me so."

"You're coming back? Oh my god. Can I do a happy dance right here and now?"

"Dance away." Vivi laughed when he did a passable soft shoe down the hall. "But you never answered my question. Why are you still here?"

"I wanted to talk to Josh." He couldn't stop the sheepish smile that crept across his face.

Vivi looked at him with consternation. "Oh shit."

He felt his smile disappear. "Oh shit what?"

Vivi glanced around. There were sounds coming from the offices and a group of Academy parents chatting at the end of the hall. "You have a few minutes? We can walk down to the new coffee shop down the street. Or the Fruteria."

"Whatever."

Mystified, he followed Vivi out the door and down the street. The chill that had teased the city for most of the weekend was gone, and San Antonio was back to its usual Chamber of Commerce November delightful.

It was warm enough for the Fruteria, and both the tall, lanky Heisers treated themselves to *frescas con crema*, a wickedly delicious concoction of strawberries and freshly whipped cream. They sat down at the table and dug into the sinful midafternoon treats.

It wasn't until they were finished that Cameron repeated his question. "I said I wanted to talk to Josh and you said 'Oh shit.' Kinda wonder what prompted that."

"It wasn't that you wanted to talk to him. It was that you looked all sheepish. Like you wanted to talk to him about more than theater business."

"Give the lady a cigar. You nailed it, little sister. I was about to put the moves on him. Ask him out on a date."

Vivi's face fell. "That's what I was afraid of. Damn, damn, damn. I've wanted you to get your head out of your ass and ask him out for so long. Now you want to and your timing couldn't be any worse."

He felt his face fall. "Is he seeing someone else?" A sharp stab of jealousy shot through him.

"No, nothing like that. It's his sister. Miriam. She came home last week and told them she's dying. Josh is devastated."

"Aw, fuck. No. Not Miriam. The young widow with those pretty little kids? I've met her a few times. Lovely woman."

"Lovely and smart, and so accomplished. It's a waste."

"What's she got?"

"Ovarian cancer. Swift, silent, and deadly. Anyway, she's got a month left, maybe two. Josh is spending as much time as he can with her. He's distracted. Upset. Out of it. You saw him at the board meeting."

"I wondered what was going on."

"He's in a bad way, Cam. I doubt he's interested in anything right now, with you or any other man. All his time and energy are going to her." She smiled crookedly. "A couple of months ago I'd have laid bets he was as interested in you as you are in him. But not right now."

"Well, hell. Our timing does suck."

Vivi laid her hand on his arm. "It won't suck forever," she said. "The question is your attention span. Are you willing to give him a few months to get past her death when he's in a better place, or are you going to get tired of waiting and start looking around for somebody else?"

He looked at her indignantly. "My attention span's fine, thank you very much. I can wait a few months until he's ready. Why would you think I couldn't?"

Vivi's response was a raised eyebrow.

"All right. Maybe I used to be like that. I'd like to think I've matured, at least a little."

"Oh, you have. Hang in there. Your time with him will come."

Cameron ran his hand down the side of his face. "I wish I could do something to help him. I hurt for him as much as I hurt for her. He's gonna have to bury her. His only sister. Kind of like if I had to bury you."

"He's worse off than you would be. You have Mom and Aunt Katie. You'd have Miguel and Julie. All he has is his ninety-one-year-old grandmother and the children."

Who would most likely go live with her late husband's family, Cameron thought later as he drove home to his Southtown loft. Josh was going to miss them.

If memory served, Miriam's in-laws lived somewhere up in the Panhandle, in one of those towns where there was barely a blinking traffic light. Josh and his grandmother could get in the car and go see them on occasion. Or the kids could come here for a visit. It wasn't the end of the world. Far from it.

He was almost to his loft when his phone rang and Trevor Marquart flashed across the screen. He'd met Trevor years ago at a bar and they'd enjoyed a hot and heavy affair, which flamed up quickly and died down just as fast. They'd managed to remain good friends and when Trevor married the love of his life last year,

Cameron stood as his best man. "Yo, Trevor, what's up? Haven't heard from you in a while."

"Been busy. Got time to meet for breakfast tomorrow?"

They settled on a time and place and Cameron was waiting at the funky old coffee shop on the edge of Southtown when Trevor arrived the next morning. Trevor slid into the booth with a tired smile on his face. His friend had made partner at one of the most prestigious law firms in San Antonio and, as usual, was impeccably dressed for the part in a beautifully cut suit that cost the earth and an exquisite dress shirt of the finest cotton. A heavy gold wedding ring graced Trevor's hand and the requisite Rolex and gold cufflinks completed the look.

A small smile twitched around Cameron's lips. He'd bet his November take-home that the suit and high-dollar shirt were from Goldstein's.

"I took the liberty of ordering for both of us. I hope your usual is okay." Trevor loved the Texas Plate of *huevos rancheros* and spicy sausage. Cameron preferred simple scrambled eggs and bacon.

Trevor looked around the coffee shop with a rueful smile. "God, I miss this place. I miss this part of town, period." Southtown had become one of San Antonio's hippest neighborhoods, with its combination of historic old homes and chic, fashionable condos like Cameron's. A lovely neighborhood for singles and couples. It didn't work too well for raising a family, and Cameron had cringed when Trevor gave up his historic bungalow and moved out north of the loop to his husband's roomy, kid-friendly two-story.

"I can imagine," Cameron murmured. "Your offices are a few blocks away. You could sneak over here for lunch and a walk along the river every so often."

"Every so often is it?" Trevor said. "That's getting harder to do. Patrick's in the middle of coaching basketball season and not getting home these days until after seven. Guess who's cutting out of work at five on the dot to do the after-school chauffeuring routine."

Cameron's head snapped up. "Why are you having to do that? I thought Paul got his license and Patrick bought that old Crown Vic for the kids to use."

Trevor rolled his eyes. "The Crown Vic's in the body shop and Paul's on restriction. The little bastard got wasted last month and smashed it into Pat's crossover in the driveway. The crossover was two weeks in the body shop, and now the Crown Vic's there."

Cameron's mouth dropped open. "Paul got wasted? I thought the kid had more sense than that."

"A year ago I would've agreed. Now? Nothing any of them pull surprises me any longer."

"Color me stunned." Cameron sipped his coffee. "They seemed like such nice kids when you were dating. What happened?"

"I happened. At least that's what Denise said when she lied to Patrick about where she was the other night. She told us she was going to her friend's house to work on a school project, but she met her boyfriend and they spent the evening together at the local make-out spot. Got home after twelve on a school night. Patrick caught her sneaking in when the boy dropped her off."

"God, I hope making out was all she did."

"So do we."

"Why was her lying to her father your fault?"

"She says she doesn't like living with a couple of queers. She says she can't bring her friends home anymore because she'd have to explain us to them. She used that to justify lying to her dad about where she was. She didn't want her boyfriend to know she had a couple of gay men raising her. She said she'd rather live with her mother."

Cameron winced. "Is that a possibility?"

"Hell no. Her mother's back using and hasn't seen the kids in over a year. Patrick fought long and hard for custody and isn't about to give them up."

"Nor should he." Cameron was silent for a minute. "What about Austin?"

"The police gave him a ride home last Sunday. He and a couple of his friends were up on the roof of the elementary school. Thank god he wasn't doing anything destructive." Trevor threw up his hands. "We've taken them for counseling. It's not much help. We can all talk until we're blue in the face, but until the kids accept I'm a permanent part of their father's life, and decide to be okay with it, nothing's gonna change. From what I'm seeing, we're a damned long way from that."

"What about laying down the law?"

"That's pretty much happened. After the shit they've pulled the last couple of weeks, Patrick told them how it was going to be. We are together and married and that isn't changing because of them. We don't care if they liked the way things were. He offered them a choice. They can behave and make it easy on themselves or keep acting like shits and pay the consequences. Man, they really didn't like that." He shook his head. "I never dreamed when I married Patrick it was going to be so damned hard. Foolishly, I thought we'd be a family. Maybe not like *Modern Family*, but we'd be a family. Stupid, huh?"

You got that right. Cameron bit his lip and searched for the right words. "More like idealistic." He shrugged. "I don't know what to tell you. I could offer you platitudes and tell you it's all going to work out fine, but I don't know if it will. What you and Patrick have is special, extraordinary even, and it'd be a crying shame to let the kids destroy it. Besides, they won't be there forever. Five, six more years and they will all be away at college. You'll be broke, but the house will be blissfully quiet."

"If we don't strangle one of them before then." Trevor's smile was crooked. "Don't worry. We won't let the kids come between us. We waited too long to find one another to let that happen."

Cameron hoped to hell Patrick felt the same way. A lot of parents wouldn't. They would put their children's feelings, however misguided, before their own or those of their significant other. Cameron hoped Patrick would stick to his guns and continue to put his marriage first.

The waitress brought their plates and they dug in. Conversation turned to the upcoming city elections.

As Cameron drove to work, he thought about his conversation with Trevor. While he'd never say it to his friend or to Patrick, part of him felt sorry for the kids.

They'd lost their mother to her drugs, which was shitty enough, but then to have their father remarry—that's rough. Introducing anyone new into those kids' lives after all the trauma they'd endured would've been difficult. Over the years, Cameron had heard all sorts of stories about people remarrying and the kids acting out. That seemed to be universal.

Here in San Antonio, where being gay was accepted with open arms in certain circles—like the theater folks at the Durango—and tolerated by some of the population—as long as you didn't make them uncomfortable—for the most part, gay people were vilified by the rest of the citizenry.

Christ, he could imagine the ribbing the kids took. Teenagers didn't do well with different, and being gay and married in their little suburb, Trevor and Patrick were as different as it got. The kids didn't have the maturity to understand, though he was sure Patrick had talked to them at length. All they knew was having Trevor in their life made things a whole lot harder, and they reacted accordingly.

Cameron pulled into his parking space at Heiser Steel, folded his hands across the steering wheel, and thought for a minute. Thank goodness Miriam's children had other family they could go to. Josh and his grandmother were the last two people who had any business taking them. Short of a miracle, Clara Goldstein had maybe four or five years left, at most. Josh was a terrific man who was young, single, and gay. Not a good choice to raise those children.

What was going on with Patrick's kids was proof positive Cam was right.

Chapter Four

A cold December wind rattled the windows in *Bubbe*'s smaller guest bedroom as Josh yawned and turned over. He was tired down to his bones. Tired and heartsick. As he and *Bubbe* stood outside Miriam's hospital room yesterday afternoon, the doctors had said she had only days left.

Miriam's body was in the process of shutting down, and his courageous sister had insisted they let her go.

"No heroics," she'd insisted. "No more pain. I'm ready for whatever's coming." She was mostly unconscious now, and after a brief run by the theater—*Peter Pan* was in full swing and going well—he'd stayed at the hospital until the night nurse ran him out at midnight. He'd heard *Bubbe* and Ella leave the house a few minutes ago. They would spend the day with Miriam at the hospital while he spent Saturday with the children.

The children he was desperately trying to connect to without too much success, before he took them on full-time.

They were all trying. He'd spent lots of time with Jackson and Beth in the past, but it was always doing fun things, and there was never any discipline involved. Now he was the one telling them it was time to go to bed or to eat their vegetables. The kids were less than receptive.

"Mommy's the one who tells us that," Beth had snapped yesterday morning when he told her to eat her breakfast. "Not you."

He didn't know how to explain to her that her mother would never again be able to tell her to eat her breakfast.

He started to turn over, but he heard footsteps he thought were Jackson's heading toward the bathroom. So much for a few more minutes in bed. Rachel was covering him at the theater, so he was free to spend the day with the kids, and go to the hospital late in the afternoon, earlier if Ella called him to relieve her and *Bubbe*. His grandmother had no business wearing herself out, but he'd tried to tell her and it had fallen on deaf ears.

"I can rest after my sweet granddaughter, *mein eynikl,* is gone," she said firmly. "You need to spend time with the children."

Time to get up and the kids dressed. He'd spend the day with them. Only it wasn't that easy. Jackson announced he didn't have any clean clothes to wear. He did, but they were in the laundry room and it took Josh fifteen minutes to find them. Beth changed her clothes three times before she was willing to wear anything other than shorts. The only clean clothes he had left in his duffel were a pair of dress pants and a *Peter Pan* tee he'd brought home a couple of nights ago. Promising himself he'd make time to pick up more clothes at his place, he started a wash and asked the kids what they'd like to eat.

"Pancakes," Beth insisted.

"Naw. We've had those every morning this week," Jackson complained. "I want bagels."

Beth poked out her lip. "Bagels are for Jews. Uncle A.J. said so."

Josh flinched. "Beth, sweetie, you are Jewish."

"Oh. That's right. I guess bagels are all right then."

Damn those fuckin' McDonalds. What other shitty things had they said to his niece and nephew?

The wind gusted as he closed the front door. The sun was trying valiantly to peek through the clouds as Josh led them to the brand-new cherry red crossover sitting in the driveway. It wasn't a Miata, but at least it had a sunroof. The kids climbed into their car seats and Josh made sure they were buckled in. "What do you want to do today?" he asked as he backed out of the driveway.

"I wanna Christmas tree," Jackson said.

Josh started. A Christmas tree? Where had that come from?

"So do I," Beth piped up.

Josh glanced in the rearview mirror. "A Christmas tree? Tell me, have you ever had a Christmas tree before?"

They looked at one another. "Well, no," Beth admitted. "Not at our house. But Granny McDonald always has one, and she thinks we need one. Last Christmas she told Mommy so."

"Yeah, she and Mom had a big fight about it," Jackson shared. "Mom said we didn't have a tree because we don't do Christmas. Granny said it was criminal and Daddy wouldn't have wanted that for us. Then Mom said that Daddy knew Mom was Jewish when he married her and Granny said Daddy must have been out of his mind."

"So, if Granny thinks we need a Christmas tree, then maybe we do," Beth said helpfully.

Josh thought of *Bubbe*'s likely reaction to a Christmas tree and cringed. "Beth, if you didn't need a Christmas tree last year, you don't need one this year either."

"That's not fair," Beth wailed. "All our friends have a tree."

Josh sighed. Ah, the pleasures of being the only Jewish kids on the block. Having a tree wasn't their custom, and he wasn't going to pretend it was. Surely there was something he could do so the children didn't feel left out. *Bubbe* had already put her menorah in the window. He didn't think that was going to work.

Inspiration hit as he turned the corner on Main and passed a store selling arts and crafts from Mexico. "How about a *piñata*?" he asked, pointing to the brightly colored *piñatas* hanging from the porch. "Maybe a couple of them. They're pretty and fun, and you can put candy in them."

"It's not a tree," Beth protested.

"Beth, we're not gonna get a tree so you may as well give it up," Jackson said. "Let's take the *piñata*."

"Smart boy," Josh muttered.

Beth's glare could've melted a glacier.

The bagel place had a line out the door. Josh almost drove away, but the kids said they didn't mind waiting so they took their place in line. They had brought their iPads and were perfectly happy playing games as the line inched along. Josh fired off a quick text to *Bubbe* and Ella texted back: *No change – waiting for doctor.*

He was in the middle of going through a backlog of emails when he looked up and saw Cameron and his mother coming out of the deli. Betsy Heiser caught his eye and started toward them, Cameron on her heels. He eyed Josh's odd clothing combination and a smile played about his lips, but he had the grace to say nothing.

If Mrs. Heiser noticed his mismatched attire she chose to ignore it. She enveloped him in a swift hug. "Josh, sweetheart, it's good to see you."

He returned her hug. "It's so good to see you, Mrs. Heiser. How've you been?"

"Fine." She glanced at the children, still absorbed in their iPads. "How are you getting along?" she asked under her breath. "How are they doing?"

"We've all been better. I'm hanging in there for them." He looked at Beth and Jackson. "They don't realize."

"I'm sure they don't."

Josh extended his hand to Cameron. "Thanks for being patient with me this month."

Cameron's hand was firm as he grasped Josh's and a spark of electricity shot up his arm. "Absolutely. No problem. You do what you have to do and don't worry about it." His smile was warm and his expression concerned with a touch of interest. Nothing inappropriate, but enough for Josh to get the message.

Cameron was still interested in him.

"Thanks. It's a load off my mind."

Mrs. Heiser turned to the children. "How are you two doing this morning?"

The children looked up at her and smiled. "Hello. Are you a friend of Uncle Josh?" Jackson asked.

"We most certainly are. I'm Miss Betsy and this is Mr. Cameron. I've met you before but your names have kind of slipped my mind."

"I'm Beth, and this is Jackson." Beth looked up at them curiously. "Are you Jews?"

Josh felt himself blush. "I…uh…Beth—"

Betsy Heiser laughed gently. "No, Beth, we're not."

"Then why are you eating bagels? My Uncle A.J. says bagels are food for Jews."

Josh felt his face turning even redder. Where was a hole to crawl in when you needed one? He opened his mouth but Mrs. Heiser beat him to it. "Beth, let me tell you a little secret. Methodists like bagels, too."

"Oh. Okay. It was nice to meet you." Beth turned back to her iPad.

Mrs. Heiser turned to Josh. "She's delightful. They both are."

"Thanks. They're the light of *Bubbe*'s and my life. Right now we're all kind of feeling our way through this."

Cameron looked at the children with compassion. "I hope your *bubbe* gets to see them often."

That was an odd statement. *Bubbe* would get to see them all the time. He wondered about it for a couple of moments, but then Mrs. Heiser asked about *Peter Pan*, and he gave it no more thought.

They exchanged a few more pleasantries and the Heisers went on their way. Josh turned to watch them go. Specifically, he watched Cameron's ass as he walked away. He was dressed in his work clothes, and Josh loved those work clothes. Jeans that cupped his ass and clung to his muscular thighs, and a bright white tee stretched across strong, powerful shoulders.

Josh sighed.

Only a month ago he'd been planning to finally ask Cameron out. Then the bottom fell out of the Goldsteins' lives, and all thoughts of Cameron had disappeared. Only a month that felt like a million years. The attraction hadn't died, but he sure as hell wasn't in a position to do anything about it. Later. Maybe. After everything else in his life was squared away.

If Cameron was even interested at that point.

They finally made it to the head of the line. The kids were famished and he had the counter person toast a half dozen bagels, which they went through like buzz saws, despite a squabble or two over who got the everything bagel and who got the jalapeño cheese. He Googled *piñatas*, made a few phone calls, and found a couple of promising stores in the *barrio*. "You kids up for an adventure?" he asked.

"Yeah," they yelled, and he set the GPS for the first store. Which turned out to be a bust. The second store was better, but the *piñatas* were leftovers from Halloween or wise men and stars, which wouldn't amuse *Bubbe* in the least.

The kids were getting antsy, and Josh was beginning to regret the *piñata* idea when he pulled into the driveway of the third store, a dumpy little building deep on the West Side with dozens of piñatas hanging from hooks on the front porch. There were even more *piñatas* inside, and he and the kids spent nearly an hour poking through the merchandise and debating the pros and cons of each *piñata* before Jackson went with Captain America and Beth opted for an Elsa.

"What are you getting, Uncle Josh?" Beth asked, resisting his efforts to herd them to checkout.

"Sweetie, I don't need a *piñata*," he told her.

"But you do," Beth insisted.

"Especially since we can't have a Christmas tree," Jackson added. Josh looked down at the kids. Okay, why not?

They took another fifteen minutes looking at *piñatas* and he was about to settle for a traditional *burro* when a big blue parrot caught Jackson's eye. "How about this?" the boy asked.

Josh smiled. It was perfect.

They loaded the *piñatas* into the back—he would've never had room in the Miata—and they swung by Josh's place long enough for Josh to pack a bag with a week's worth of coordinated outfits. It was after two when he got the kids back to *Bubbe*'s.

They opted for peanut butter and jelly sandwiches. Josh didn't remember having a nonstop appetite when he was a kid, but these two ate like they'd been starved for years. He made a PB&J for himself and was surprised at how good it tasted. He hadn't eaten one in years and had forgotten how much he enjoyed them. He figured he was going to be revisiting a lot of things from his childhood that had fallen by the wayside.

"So where can we hang the *piñatas*?" Jackson asked eagerly.

"How about in your rooms?" Josh suggested.

"Not in there," Beth protested. "In the window. I want everybody to see them."

Josh eyed *Bubbe*'s elegant front room. "Hmm. I don't think *piñatas* are exactly going to fit in here. How about in the sunroom? They'd look really nice on that back shelf. That way we can see them all the time, not only when we're passing through the front of the house."

It took a little more persuading, but Beth finally agreed. The shelf was higher than Josh remembered, but there was a stepstool in the utility room. He went in search of the stool, and returned to the sunroom to find Beth and Jackson sitting cross-legged on the floor, looking at the *piñatas* sadly. "I miss Mommy," Beth practically wailed. She turned her anxious little face toward Jackson. "Is Mommy gonna die?"

"Yeah, she is," Jackson said sullenly. "I heard *Bubbe* tell Miss Ella Mom probably won't last another week." He scuffed his heel on the tile.

Beth's eyes widened. "What's gonna happen to us?"

"Dunno. Nobody wants us."

"Oh."

Josh felt tears well up in his eyes. "That's not true. *Bubbe* and I want you," he said as he stepped into the room. He sat down on the floor and put Beth in his lap and drew Jackson close. "Now, tell me why you think nobody wants you."

They were silent for a minute. "Uncle A.J. said so," Beth whispered.

Josh stiffened. "When did he say that?"

"Mommy took us up to see them. Right before we came here. I heard Uncle A.J. tell Aunt June he wasn't raising a couple of little kikes," Jackson said. He turned his wary gaze on Josh. "Are you sure you want us? That night we came and Mom said she wanted us to stay here, you had kind of an *oh shit* look on your face." When Josh opened his mouth to protest, Jackson said, Well, you did."

"Of course I had an *oh shit* look on my face," Josh said, deciding honesty was the best way to go. He would deal with the profanity later. "I was scared out of my mind. I still am. You and Beth are precious, wonderful kids, and I love you to pieces. I want you with all my heart. But I'm scared I'm gonna mess up. You deserve the best, and the thought of not being the best scares me."

Jackson didn't appear too relieved. "You've got nowhere to put us. Your house is really tiny."

"I know that. I put my house on the market, and have a realtor looking for a bigger one."

"What's a realtor?" Beth asked.

"It's somebody who finds houses for other people. I called her last week. She's looking for a house that's big enough so you can each have your own bedroom and Pepper can have a big backyard to run around in."

"Or we could stay here with *Bubbe*," Beth said.

"*Bubbe* and I talked about that. We could, but *Bubbe* doesn't like a lot of noise and she goes to bed really early," Josh explained. "She doesn't want a dog digging holes in her pretty backyard. We'd have to be quiet all the time, and I'd have to leave Pepper at Miss Rachel's and not bring him home."

"I don't want to leave Pepper with Miss Rachel. I like Pepper," Jackson said quickly.

"I do too. So as soon as we can, the three of us are moving into a new house that's perfect for us and we're bringing Pepper home."

He looked at Jackson. "Now why do you look like you still don't believe me? I got a new car you can fit in, didn't I? I'll get a house we can all fit in, too."

"You want us badly enough to get a new house?" Jackson asked. "You really, really want us?"

"You bet. I really, really want you." His tears spilled over at the enormous relief on the children's faces.

"Don't worry about messing up. We'll mess up too," Beth said as she hugged his neck.

Josh nodded and pulled them closer.

They got the *piñatas* placed on the shelf and admired their handiwork. It was cheating, big time, but he downloaded a Disney movie and collapsed on the sofa. He was exhausted from the day. The kids had worn him out.

And scared him to death.

He'd been honest with them. He didn't know the first thing about raising kids. If today was anything to go by, he wasn't all that wonderful at it. Moving was going to be a pain in the butt, but the more the children told him about the McDonald family, the more he was convinced taking them was the right thing to do. *Kikes*? A.J. McDonald deserved to be horsewhipped.

It was about seven when *the call* came. "Joshie, put the kids in the car and come," *Bubbe* instructed him. "They need to say their good-byes. Hurry."

The kids were already in their pajamas and Josh had showered and changed in anticipation of spending the evening at Miriam's bedside. He made quick work of putting on tennis shoes and coats. Saturday night traffic was heavy this close to Christmas, and Josh fumed and drummed his fingers on the steering wheel as they caught traffic jam after traffic jam.

They finally made it to the hospital parking garage and caught the shuttle from the garage to the big, imposing teaching hospital. They snaked through the warren of elevator rides and halls to Miriam's room, only to learn she'd been moved to the oncology ICU, which wasn't what she'd wanted. He backtracked to the oncology ICU, where they were stopped by an officious nurse who pointed to the children and shook her head. "No children in ICU. No exceptions."

"You'll make one tonight," Josh said firmly. He lowered his voice. "They're here to say their good-byes. Miriam McDonald. These are her children."

"Oh. All right then." He thought he caught a glimmer of compassion on her face. He took the children by the hand and they followed the nurse to a cubicle, where *Bubbe* and Ella were parked on uncomfortable-looking chairs next to the bed. *Bubbe* was holding Miriam's thin blue hand.

Miriam was hooked up to a mountain of machines that beeped, whooshed, and whistled. *Bubbe* looked at him and there was anger in her expression. "I told them she didn't want this and they did it anyway," she said through tight lips.

"Why?" Josh asked.

"No medical directive," Ella said. "They wouldn't take *Bubbe*'s word for it."

Miriam's eyes flickered and she moaned softly. "Babies," she breathed quietly.

Josh hoisted Beth into his arms. "I brought your babies." He held the child where Miriam could see her. "Say hello to your mommy, Beth," he said softly. "Tell her you love her."

"I love you, Mommy," Beth said. She looked at her mother with bewilderment. "Is Mommy gonna be okay?"

Josh looked at *Bubbe*, who looked back helplessly. Miriam looked up at Beth. "O-kay," she breathed. "Love you." She shut her eyes.

Josh set Beth on the floor and reached for Jackson. He lifted the boy so he could see his mother. "Jackson, tell your mom you love her."

Jackson looked down at Miriam. "I love you, Mom. I'll take care of Beth and be good for Uncle Josh."

Josh bit his lip and cursed the tears running down his cheeks. Miriam's eyes opened slightly and she nodded. "Love you, baby," she whispered. Her lids lowered as the monitor showed that her heartbeat had begun to slow and her breathing took on an odd pattern.

Josh stood for a minute holding Jackson until the nurse put her hand on his shoulder. "She's in the dying process now. You might want to take the children out to the waiting room."

He glanced at *Bubbe* and she nodded. "We'll wait for you there," he said as he shepherded the children out of the room. The nurse showed him to the waiting room and he sat down on a sofa and pulled Jackson close and put Beth on his lap. "She's dying, isn't she?" Jackson asked.

"She is. Do you want to go back in there with her?" Josh asked quietly. Maybe he shouldn't have been so quick to take the children away.

"No. I want to remember her alive," the boy said.

"Okay."

It seemed like forever, but it couldn't've been more than thirty minutes until *Bubbe* and Ella joined them. *Bubbe*'s face was drawn and her eyes were red. She looked every one of her ninety-one years and then some.

"She's gone," his grandmother said softly. *Bubbe* collapsed into a chair next to the sofa.

"Gone? When's she coming back?" Beth demanded. "When's my mommy coming back?" Her voice rose into a shriek. "She has to come back! *I want my mommy!*" She pounded Josh's chest with her fists. "*Mommmmeeeee!*" The child threw her arms around Josh's neck and wailed.

Jackson looked at Josh as his eyes filled with tears. "She doesn't understand, Uncle Josh. Mom's not coming back." The boy started to sob uncontrollably as well.

Josh gathered them as close as he could and looked to *Bubbe*. "Let them cry. Let them get it all out," she said as tears welled in her eyes. "Cry with them. They need to see that we're all hurting."

Josh nodded. He gathered them as close as he could and let them sob. Tears poured down his cheeks as he looked down at the heartbroken children.

Miriam, how do I do this? Can I really do justice to these precious kids of yours?

A pain twisted inside his chest, and he felt the actual ache of his heart breaking. He would miss his sister. Horribly. But he'd have to do his own grieving privately. Right now, he had to be here for two children whose hearts were breaking too.

The children's sobs turned to weeping, and Josh's tears never abated.

Beth raised her head. "Jackson said Mommy's gone. But that's not fair. I want Mommy."

"Beth, sweetheart, I know it's not fair. I know you want your mommy. I want your mommy too. But you know what? Your mommy's not really gone because she lives on in you." He patted her on her little chest. "As long as she lives within you, she's not really gone."

Jackson looked up at Josh with a tear-stained face. "Does she live on in me, too?"

"Oh yes. Absolutely. She lives on in you. She lives on in all of us who love her." He looked over at *Bubbe*. "Do I need to call the funeral home?"

"They did it at the nurses' station," *Bubbe* said. "Miriam and I made the preliminary arrangements last week."

"Do they understand our traditions? Do I need to spend the night with her body?" he asked, referring to the tradition of someone being with the body at all times until burial.

"No, they have a rabbi on call who performs that ritual. You'll need to go down and take care of the last-minute stuff. We also need to call the synagogue and tell Rabbi Feldman we need him tomorrow." Her lips trembled. "I guess I need to call her in-laws."

"I'll do that too," Josh said quickly. The less *Bubbe* had to deal with those jerks, the better.

They waited until the funeral home came for Miriam. Ella and *Bubbe* took the children so Josh could make the necessary phone calls. He called the rabbi first, and then some of *Bubbe*'s old friends. He texted Rachel to please share the sad news with the Durango crowd.

He couldn't put it off any longer. He scrolled down his contact list and put in the dreaded call to the McDonald family. Eloisa McDonald, Jimmy Joe's mother, reacted predictably. "I don't know how we're supposed to get down there by tomorrow afternoon," she said, sounding put-upon. "It could have waited until Monday or Tuesday."

"Actually, *we*," he made sure she heard the emphasis and its implications, "bury our dead within the first twenty-four hours," he said smoothly. "We'll certainly understand if you don't feel you can make it."

There was a pregnant pause. "We'll be there," she said before abruptly disconnecting.

What a piece of work.

It took longer than expected at the funeral home, and it was nearly one in the morning by the time Josh made it back to *Bubbe*'s. He'd expected the household to be asleep, but *Bubbe* was sitting by herself in the sunroom staring out at the moonlight playing across the surface of the swimming pool. "Shouldn't you be in bed?" he asked softly.

"I can't sleep." She turned to him tiredly. "Did you get everything taken care of?"

"The funeral's scheduled for two. We'll sit shiva for three days." She shook her head adamantly. "A whole week will wear you out and be too much for the kids," he said when she started to object. "Some of the ladies from the synagogue and Jennie Kirby's family have agreed to help us with serving at shiva. All you have to do is come downstairs."

"It's not quite that simple. We're going to honor our tradition. We'll sit the entire week. I'll do nothing less for my Miriam." She patted the sofa next to her. He sank down in the cushions and sighed. He knew she'd never go for it. "It took Ella awhile, but she finally got the children to bed about eleven." She looked at him solemnly. "It's not going to be easy raising Jackson and Beth."

"It scares the hell out of me. We didn't do so well today. I don't have the vaguest idea what to do with kids."

"You'll learn. Nobody's born knowing how to parent. You learn it as you go. I had to learn twice. Once when your father was born, and again at sixty-three when your father left a baby and a three-year-old in my care." She patted his hand. "Your *zayde* and I managed, and so will you."

"I'll have to make a lot of changes. I've got to sell my house and buy another. I have to decide what to do about school and find someone to watch them on theater nights and—"

"Joshie, take a breath. It will all get taken care of, one thing at a time." She squeezed his hand. "At least you already have a car and a dog."

"But do I have what it takes? *Bubbe*, I'm young, I'm single, I never thought I'd be a parent. I'm scared to death I'll mess them up. I love them so much. Those kids deserve better than me."

She took his hand. A single tear ran down her wrinkled cheek. "Joshie, you absolutely, positively have what it takes to do this. You'll be a wonderful father, and those kids are lucky to have you. I'm here to help you." *Bubbe*'s lips firmed. "It's going to cost you money, the changes you have to make. Don't be shy about asking for help. You and those babies are all I have left in this world, and I want to take care of you."

Josh swallowed his pride and nodded. "I will."

"Now, you need to go to bed. Sleep. Don't lie there and fret," she admonished. "Have faith, Joshie. Everything's gonna turn out fine."

Josh nodded. He hoped his grandmother, who was always right, was right about this.

Chapter Five

A cold rain blew in Cameron's face as he got out of Miguel's crossover in the parking lot of the funeral home. He handed Miguel and Vivienne their umbrellas and opened his own. "What a wretched day to have to bury her," he murmured as the three of them scurried toward the awning.

"A week before Christmas. God, this sucks," Vivi added. "At least they got it organized quickly. She died last night."

"That's their custom," Miguel reminded her.

"I wonder how the asshole in-laws felt about that. They would've had to come in from some little bumfuck town in the Panhandle." Vivi shook her head. "On the other hand, the way they feel about Miriam, I'd be surprised if they come at all."

"Come on. They can't be that bad," Cameron protested.

"Oh yeah, they are," Miguel and Vivi said in unison.

"Whatever." He stifled a shrug. Not his problem.

Cameron breathed a sigh of relief as they stepped into the warm, dry lobby of the funeral home. He looked around at the large crowd and was surprised at how many of Miriam's mourners he knew.

The Durango crowd was here in force. Surely, to support Josh and because Miriam had driven in to see every one of their productions. The business community was well represented. They had to've come out of respect for the Goldstein legacy, and to support Clara Goldstein. Many of those he didn't know were young enough to be current or former students, and there was a group in the corner that had the nerdy academic thing going. He, Vivi, and Miguel made the rounds as representatives of the Durango as well as Heiser Steel and Abonce Construction.

He wondered when the family, particularly Josh, would make an appearance. He hoped he would at least get to speak to him this afternoon. It was only yesterday he and his mother had run into Josh and the children at the deli. As the weeks went by, he'd wondered if the attraction had been all on his side. But there had been a definite zing yesterday when he'd taken Josh's hand, and he'd caught Josh discreetly checking out his ass when he and his mother walked away.

Yep. Josh was as interested as he was.

As sad as Miriam's death was, as hard on Josh as it had been, the worst of it was over. The children would go to live with the McDonald family. Josh would come back to work and his life would settle down. Sooner or later Josh would be ready for Cameron to make a move. Or to make one himself. The attraction was there. They had no reason not to act on it. *Smokin' hot affair, here we come.*

Who knew? It might even amount to something deeper. Josh was more than a pretty face and had a bangin' body. Cameron had seen a lot of Josh over the past few months to make him like and admire the man. The way he'd been there for his sister and grandmother. The way he'd stepped up to the plate with the children. Oh yeah. Josh was good for more than a few dates or a brief hot affair.

Josh was the kind of man Cameron had always wanted to have a permanent place in his life.

They signed the book and sat down in the chapel adorned only by a Star of David behind the simple casket. At precisely the stroke of two, the family, led by the elderly Clara Goldstein, filed into the chapel and sat down in the front two rows.

Josh followed his grandmother, holding the hands of a little boy about eight and a girl a couple of years younger. *Jackson and Beth McDonald.* Josh wore a yarmulke, and he and his grandmother, as well as the children, wore torn black ribbons pinned to their lapels. A couple about his age and an older couple filed in with them. Unlike Josh, the men were bare-headed and none of them wore a ribbon. All four of them looked uncomfortable.

They had to be the McDonalds.

Cameron looked at the McDonalds and breathed an inward sigh of relief. They looked like good people. The kind of people who would love the children and do right by them. The younger couple in particular. They were somewhere in their late thirties and had small-town wholesome written all over them. Josh and his grandmother would have nothing to worry about as far as the children were concerned. They could and would visit, but the heavy lifting wouldn't be on them. Josh could go on about his life and his grandmother could die in peace, knowing Jackson and Beth were in good hands.

Josh and he could get together and see where their mutual interest would take them.

The service was moving, with readings from Psalms and a touching eulogy by the rabbi. The congregation stood for a prayer delivered in Hebrew. Then the rabbi tried to hand what looked like a scroll of some kind to Mrs. Goldstein, but she shook her head and indicated that it should go to Josh. Vivi leaned over. "That's a *Yahrzeit* calendar. The Jewish people mark the days for years into the future when they should light candles for their beloved dead."

"How'd you know that?"

"David Ackerman. I learned a lot about Judaism when I was dating him."

Cameron nodded. Vivi had dated the guy for nearly two years during college. She'd learned a lot, all right. She'd learned that Tripp and Betsy Heiser did *not* want their daughter marrying into a Jewish family. They didn't care how well-respected and affluent they were. It turned out the Ackermans *really* didn't want their pride and joy married to a Methodist.

The last they'd heard, David was married to a nice Jewish girl out of St. Louis, and here sat Vivi with her C&E Catholic. He wondered if Mrs. Goldstein's dismay Miriam married a gentile was reserved for her granddaughter, or if it would extend to Josh as well.

Damn. He was getting ahead of himself. First they had to go out on a date.

He jerked his thoughts away from Josh's hot body and returned them to the funeral. The family stood and filed out. The pallbearers followed with the plain wooden casket, and the rabbi announced that those who chose to should reconvene to the graveside.

The rain had slacked off, so the three of them opted to walk the couple of hundred yards through the cemetery to the burial site. As they followed the narrow lane through the graves, Vivienne touched his elbow and gestured. "Daddy's grave is right over there. Maybe we can stop a minute before we leave."

Cameron swallowed the lump in his throat and nodded.

The cemetery was sectioned off by religion. The Jewish portion was set off to the right, with two rows of trees surrounding it. "A Jewish cemetery has physical boundaries that sets the cemetery off from its surroundings, making it holy for Jews," Vivi said. "The ground is consecrated for only Jewish burials."

Cam nodded as they approached the waiting tent. The back of the hearse was open. Josh was helping his grandmother from the limousine and into the tent covering Miriam's casket. The older McDonalds had Beth and Jackson in tow. The assembled crowd was somewhat smaller but still substantial as the rabbi stepped forward.

The service was brief. Prayers were recited, the casket was gently lowered, and Josh and his grandmother stepped forward. Josh helped Mrs. Goldstein shovel three spades of dirt into the grave, and Josh then shoveled three more. He stuck the shovel in the dirt and gestured to the younger McDonald to pick up the shovel. Looking uncertain, the younger man did the same and stuck the shovel back in the dirt.

The mourners lined up and one by one solemnly carried out the ritual. As Cameron stuck the shovel into the much lower pile of dirt, he caught Josh's eye. Josh looked at him with hope. Cameron nodded to himself. Josh was thinking ahead, and it seemed his thoughts were aligned with Cameron's.

Everyone arranged themselves into two lines. The family began walking through the line, stopping to speak briefly to those who had come. Most merely murmured a phrase in Hebrew or simply, "May God comfort you." When Josh and Mrs. Goldstein reached the three of them, Josh paused a moment. "*Bubbe*, I would like you to meet my boss, Cameron Heiser, and his sister and brother-in-law Vivi and Miguel Abonce. This is my grandmother, Clara Goldstein."

Mrs. Goldstein let go of her walker handle and extended her hand. "I'm so glad to meet the three of you. Joshie has spoken fondly of you so many times. I know you mean a lot to him, all of you."

As usual, Vivienne took the lead. "We are so delighted to meet you, Mrs. Goldstein. Josh has spoken often of you as well. We are so, so sorry for your family's loss." Cameron and Miguel murmured in agreement.

The old lady nodded regally. "Thank you. I still have my granddaughter's beautiful children. And Joshie." She reached for Josh's hand with fingers that were surprising steady. "I still have my Joshie by my side. My grandson is a good boy. The best. He'll do what this family needs for him to in the days ahead."

Cameron blinked. He wasn't sure what the old lady meant by that. But she was right. Josh would be there for her. "I'm sure he will," he said warmly. "Josh will be there for you. He's that kind of man."

Josh and his grandmother turned to the next in line and the three of them exchanged perfunctory handshakes with the McDonalds. They stepped back and waited patiently until the Goldsteins had made it to the end of the double line and the crowd began to disperse. Miguel turned to him and Vivi. "Do you still want to visit Tripp's grave?"

Cameron and Vivi nodded. Miguel took Vivi's hand and the three of them took the fork in the lane that would take them to the graves of four generations of the Heiser family. Tripp's was the most recent, the brass nameplate over his grave the shiniest. "We should've brought flowers," Vivienne murmured.

"Your mother will bring some out on Christmas," Miguel said. "She does every year."

"I wonder what she meant," Cameron murmured quietly.

"You wonder what who meant?" Miguel asked.

"Mrs. Goldstein. When she said Josh would do whatever the family needed him to do. Seems to me he's already done it. Seeing them through her death and the funeral."

"She might have been referring to Josh taking the children to raise," Vivi said. "She might have been telling you he'll have other responsibilities now besides the Durango."

Cameron turned around, hoping his shock didn't show. "He's doing *what*?"

"He's raising the children. You mean the famous Durango gossip train hasn't made it to your station yet?"

"Apparently not," he said through stiff lips. "That's ludicrous. He can't take those kids. He's the last person who should be raising a family."

Vivi's eyebrow shot up. "Why would you say that?"

"Jesus, why wouldn't I? He's young. He's single. He's gay. He has no business sticking those children with the stigma of a gay parent. I can't imagine what any of them are thinking."

"They're probably thinking there are two little kids who have no parents and they need him, their mother's brother," she snapped.

"That's ridiculous. There's a whole other family to take them. I can't imagine why the McDonalds aren't raising all manner of hell about it."

Vivi snorted. "Oh, they won't be. I promise you."

"They'd be better than Josh. You know what Dad always said."

"I know exactly what your father always said," Miguel muttered. "Forgive me for speaking ill of the dead, especially standing here by his grave, but besides being an asshole, your father was a homophobe. He stifled it around you so you wouldn't tell him to stick it and walk away from Heiser Steel, but believe me, it was there and that's one of the ways it showed. There's not a thing in the world wrong with gay people being parents."

"Then why are Trevor's stepkids acting like turds?" he demanded.

"Because they are turds?" Vivi ventured.

"I still don't think he has any business raising them," Cameron said stubbornly. "What can he offer them that the McDonalds can't?"

"He can raise them the way his sister wanted them raised. Jewish," Vivi said.

"So what? It's church. Big damn deal."

"Shit, Cameron. Don't be an ass," Miguel said. "It's much more than church. It's *who they are.* It's their heritage. Their identity. After losing their entire family in the Holocaust, no way are those children gonna be raised not knowing that down to their bones."

"All right. Fine. I still don't get it, but whatever."

They walked in silence toward the parking lot. They were almost to the car when they came up on an older and a younger couple Cameron recognized as the McDonalds. They were talking rather loudly and the older woman sounded peeved. He started to speak but Vivi elbowed him and put her finger to her lips.

"The whole damn thing's a crock," the woman said. "Having her brother raise 'em instead of us. We need to fight it. They ought to be in Bradford with us. That's what Jimmy Joe would have wanted for them."

"Ain't no synagogues in Bradford," the younger woman said derisively. "Gotta be little kikes, according to Grandma*ma* and what it said in the will she handed us. Miriam wanted 'em Jews raised by her brother, and that's what they'll be."

"Man, did you get a load of that house? Kike Central," the younger man said. "Towels on the mirrors. Stools instead of chairs. Jackson said the little queer wouldn't get 'em a Christmas tree. Too Christian, I guess." He turned to his mother. "Gonna be honest with you, Mom. I don't want us to go to court. I'm happy leaving 'em here in San Antonio with the little queer. He can raise 'em the way their mama wanted. Unless you're willing to raise 'em up Jews."

"Oh hell no. We'd be willing to take them if you're not, but I'd have 'em singing 'Jesus Loves Me' so fast it'd make your head swim," the older man said. "The less they know about all that Jew stuff, the better."

"Doesn't matter what they do or don't know about it," the younger woman said. "They still have that Jew blood."

"I hate it," the older woman said. "That they're Jews. But they're still my grandkids. What about our heritage? Our faith? Doesn't that matter?"

"I guess not," the older man replied. "Miriam made her wishes known. And frankly, since none of us are willing to raise 'em like she wanted, I say leave things be. Let the hymies raise the kids however the hell they want to. Let them assume the responsibility. We'll come see them every so often and that will be that."

"Suits me," the younger man said. The younger woman echoed him.

"Eloisa?" the older man asked.

"Whatever. Maybe you have a point," she said slowly. "Since I'm sure as hell not driving them to a synagogue in Lubbock."

The McDonalds walked on. Miguel unlocked the car and the three of them got in. "Now do you get it?" Vivi asked Cam quietly.

"Yeah, now I get it," he admitted. "My God. Did you hear them? Kikes. Hymies. I didn't know that kind of shit was still around."

"Well, it is. Believe me, you don't need to go to Bumfuck, Texas to find it," Miguel said.

"Cameron, I know how you feel about gay parenting, and I know it's not all because of Daddy and what he thought. But Josh doesn't really have a choice," Vivi said. "He's scared to death, but he's ready to take them on. I admire the hell out of him for that."

Later as he stood at the kitchen counter and poured three fingers of whiskey, Cam thought, he admired Josh too. He sat and stared out his big picture window at the Christmas lights twinkling all over downtown. He swirled the whiskey around in the glass before swallowing a generous mouthful that burned all the way to his gut.

He admired Josh to no end for taking on the children, as unwise as it was going to prove. From what he'd heard this afternoon, Josh had no choice. The younger in-laws wouldn't have taken them at all, and the older ones detested that their grandchildren were Jewish. Josh was doing what he had to do. Admirable. Heartbreaking, but admirable.

He sighed and knocked back the rest of the whiskey before pouring himself another. This one would be the last since he had to get up in the morning. He wished he could get stinking drunk. That would dull the bone-deep disappointment, at least for a few hours.

Nothing going to happen with Josh. No hot dates. No smokin' affair. Sure as hell not the deep involvement Cameron would have been open to.

Josh was a parent. Josh was raising two children. Two school-aged children who in the blink of an eye would be teenagers who would be appalled and horrified by their gay parent and behave accordingly.

Teenagers whose lives were going to be ruined because their only parent was gay. Cameron thought of the despair on Trevor's face and shuddered. In a matter of a few years that was going to be Josh. Dealing with the disaster of a gay man trying to raise a family in twenty-first-century San Antonio.

No way was Cameron going anywhere near any of that.

Chapter Six

"Uncle Josh, I can't find my new jeans."

"Which jeans?" Josh fought back a smile at the sight of his indignant niece standing in her new bedroom with her hands on her hips.

"The pink ones with lace on the pockets."

"Oh, those jeans. They're still in the dryer. Sorry."

"Oh." Her face fell comically.

"Besides, you know you have to wear your uniform to school." Their school had a strict uniform policy, something Beth wasn't used to and did *not* like in the least.

"That uniform is ugly," Beth pouted, making a face at the plaid skirt and white polo shirt waiting for her on the dresser. "I wanna go to public school. They don't have uniforms."

Josh's lips twitched. "I know your uniform's ugly. But if you don't have it on, you get sent home. You know as well as I do that the public schools have a uniform as well, and it's even uglier than yours. Tell you what. The minute you get home, we'll dig your jeans out of the dryer. Does that work?" She nodded happily and he helped his little fashionista get dressed.

He put Pepper in the backyard with fresh food and water. Jackson was dressed and waiting in the living room with his backpack. He never argued about the uniform. The boy couldn't care less what he wore. "I like this house," Jackson stated. "I have my own bedroom."

"I like this house too," Josh said as he looked around his much-larger living room. His realtor had pulled off an absolute miracle, finding a charming 1930s yellow brick that was even closer to the theater than the other house had been. This one had almost twice the square footage, a formal dining room, a third bedroom, and a second bathroom for the kids. *Bubbe* had insisted on making the down payment and he didn't argue.

The Durango crowd had helped him pack, and he'd persuaded a local mover New Year's Day was a fine day to work a last-minute job.

Bubbe had surprised him by parting with a lovely bedroom set for Beth, and a trip to Ikea had Jackson fixed up. The McDonalds were tasked with cleaning out and selling Miriam's house and holding an estate sale, the proceeds of which would go into a college fund for the children. They sent a few treasured toys and a box of keepsakes the children might want someday, but for the most part Beth and Jackson were starting fresh, with new clothes and toys for their new life with him.

A life that was to his surprise, and *Bubbe's* visible relief, very much to his liking.

The kids amazed him. He'd been scared to death they would have no use for him, but they'd taken to him readily. He'd taken to them every bit as quickly. Of course, they missed their mother. So did he.

Beth still hadn't quite grasped the death was final concept, and more than once had asked when her mother was coming back. He'd caught them alone in their rooms crying, especially in the week after the funeral, and had assured them that it was okay to cry. He told them they could come to him when they felt sad.

They'd settled in more quickly than he'd believed possible, and to his utter amazement he loved having them around. He was busier than he'd ever been, and life was infinitely more complicated, but his days were sweet and so much richer than they were before.

He looked from Jackson to Beth. "You have everything in your backpacks? Homework? Fresh pencils? Lunch checks?" They both nodded. "Okay. Let's go."

The kids ran out the door. He followed more slowly, clicking the car door open and locking the house. He considered it a miracle the Jewish Montessori school near *Bubbe's* home had a couple of midyear openings, which made it easy for Ella to pick them up after school and get them to their Academy classes.

The early April morning was warm and the sun shone brightly, and Josh opened the sunroof of the crossover. It wasn't the same as the convertible, but he could still hear the wind and feel the air on his face. He was going too fast down a main thoroughfare with his radio on when he spotted an SAPD cruiser with its lights on behind him.

Shit. That was all he needed. A damned ticket.

He groaned and pulled into a strip center parking lot.

"Hey, wow, a cop. You got stopped by a cop," Jackson crowed.

"Be quiet, Jackson," Josh said through gritted teeth as he lowered his window.

The gray-haired police officer ambled to the window and peered inside, his eyes narrowing when he spotted the children in the back seat. "License and insurance," he said.

Josh handed them his driver's license and brand-new insurance card. The officer peered at both and then again looked in the back seat. "Your kids?" he barked.

"Niece and nephew."

"Why do you have them? Where's their mother?"

"She died and went to heaven," Jackson said quietly.

"Officer, my sister died the week before Christmas. I'm raising the children now."

"I see." He continued to stare at him suspiciously.

"If you have any questions, you can call the Durango Theatre and ask anyone who answers the phone about me and the kids," Josh said tiredly. "Or better yet, call Goldstein's Department Store and ask to speak to the manager. She'll corroborate my story."

The policeman looked again at his license and took a step back. "That won't be necessary." He looked at the children again. "Trying to get them to school on time? I'm letting you off with a warning. Remember, you have precious cargo back there."

"Yes, sir."

He wrote out a warning and Josh was soon on his way, his face burning. He didn't know if the policeman had been suspicious because he was a man, or because he'd identified them as his niece and nephew. Or if the officer had pegged him as gay. He didn't wear a label, but he didn't particularly try to hide it, either. Still, it pissed him off. The cop would never have questioned a woman.

He dropped off the children and headed to the theater. Today was Wednesday, the day Cameron frequently came by to *check in*. Josh's heart beat a little faster. His heart beat a little faster every Wednesday when Cameron walked through the door. He was looking forward to the zing he felt when Cam shook his hand or smiled at him. Or checked out his ass when he thought Josh wasn't looking.

Yep. He was more than ready to start seeing the man he'd lusted after for so long. Maybe this was the week he'd make his move. Ask Cameron out. See if the interest was one-sided.

Or maybe not. The attraction had been there on both their parts back in the fall. Josh had been ready to make his moves on Cameron and see what happened. But then… Everything changed.

Months had passed. He could finally breathe through the grief, and he and the children were settling in. They were all moving on, and he was ready to try to juggle parenting and a love life.

Recently, his interest in Cameron had come roaring to the forefront, but Cameron no longer seemed interested. He was the same gracious, polite, businesslike board chairman he'd always been. The interest in his eyes was gone. Cameron had given up on him and moved on to another man. Or maybe it had all been in his imagination in the first place.

If Cameron wasn't interested, Josh would be damned if he made the first move. Nothing like making an ass of himself in front of his boss.

He settled in behind his desk and got to work. Cameron normally came by late in the afternoon, so it was with some surprise that Josh looked up about noon and found his crush standing at the door of his office. "Wow, you're early." He cursed the way his breath caught.

"I have a meeting downtown in thirty minutes and thought I'd swing by while I was close. Anything in particular I need to look at this week?"

"Actually, yes."

"Do I need to sit down?" he asked.

"Three items, and I'll make it fast."

"In other words, sit down."

"Yeah."

Cameron sat and stretched his long legs out in front of him. Josh handed him a stack of printouts. "I thought you'd want to see these. Maggie has the gala location narrowed down to three possible venues. We need to decide by next week before they get snapped up. We're leaning toward the first one. The old Victorian house a few miles north of town. The facility is beautiful, the view is stunning, and the price is below the other bids."

Cameron slipped on a pair of reading glasses Josh didn't realize he wore, and looked down the first printout. His lips turned down and he looked at the second and the third before turning back to Josh. "How much of a concern is the cost of the venue?"

"It's always a consideration. The more reasonable the venue, the more money we make."

He looked at the printouts again. "I'm assuming Maggie did site visits."

"She did. She said all three were equally nice."

"But she didn't actually attend a function at any of them."

"No, she didn't. What are you getting at?"

"I went to a wedding at the Victorian house a few months ago. I wasn't impressed."

"Unmitigated disaster?"

"I wouldn't go that far. It was more like everything was a little off. They were still getting the last of the tables set when we arrived. One of the bartenders showed up a few minutes late. The salad bar was set out a little too early and the hors d'oeuvres were skimpy. It wasn't a disaster, and we had a good time, but our patrons are used to the best and we won't get it there."

"Then put that printout in the trash and I'll tell Maggie it's off the list. We can't embarrass ourselves in front of the Navarros. Do you know anything about either of the other two? I went to a party last year at the bank club and it was nice."

"I don't have firsthand knowledge of the other two. You and Maggie can choose between them. Next?"

"Miguel's crews are coming in next Monday to start turning the back storage into rehearsal rooms. The Academy teachers are doing a happy dance."

"God bless my brother-in-law. Next?"

He handed Cameron more printouts. "I need your signature on the paperwork here. Three more grants came through yesterday. More of Kirby Martinez's doing. For a guy I threw out on his ear, he's proving surprisingly useful."

"Trying to redeem himself?"

"Nah. Trying to impress Maggie. She's leading him on a merry chase."

"Good for her. He has it coming." He glanced at the printouts. "That's a lot of money. Okay, I'm impressed, even if she's not. Anything else?"

"Nope. That'll do it." His phone beeped and he fished it out of his pocket. "Sorry. Gotta take this."

He swiveled around in the chair and spent a couple of minutes making afternoon arrangements with Ella. As he swung back, he caught a look of undisguised lust on Cameron's face that instantly morphed into polite friendliness. *Of course.* Cameron was an actor. A good one. He was as attracted to Josh as he'd ever been. But for some reason, he didn't want Josh to know.

Which was complete and utter bullshit.

Cameron quickly rose from his chair. "I need to get to that meeting. I'll take these with me and drop them by later this afternoon." He stuffed them in his briefcase and nearly fled out the door.

Josh stared after him, baffled.

Back in the fall, they were near panting for each other, ready for one of them to make a move. Even in December when he and the children ran into Cameron and his mother, Cameron had seemed interested. Josh had been sure of it.

Now? Cameron was still attracted to him. Josh would bet his next paycheck on it, but he didn't want Josh to know. He kept their relationship strictly professional.

Josh wondered what the hell had changed.

It was still running through his mind a couple of hours later when Vivi poked her head in the door with Julie in a baby sling. "Did Miguel remember to email you?" she asked. "He said something about his crew getting started next week."

"I got something from his secretary. Monday morning, bright and early. So, what brings you and Julie over here in the middle of your workday?"

"Her pediatrician's office is close by. She was in for a well-baby check." She leaned down and gave the cooing baby a kiss. "She finally turned into a happy kid a couple of months ago, and now she never stops smiling."

Josh leaned over the desk. "I think they were telling stories all along, baby girl. I bet you never cried a night in your life."

"I should have called you at three in the morning and let you have a listen." Vivi laughed. "Speaking of kids, how are yours doing?"

Josh broke into a smile. "I like the sound of that. My kids."

"Wow. That right there tells me things are going well."

"You know, Vivi, they are. Don't get me wrong, we have our moments, but we have a lot of happy times too. Who'd have ever thought it? Me, Mr. Single-and-carefree, absolutely loving being a daddy. It surprises me."

"Doesn't surprise me in the least," Vivi said. "You've always had a soft spot for the Academy kids. You always loved Jackson and Beth. Remember back in the winter when you were so worried? Nobody else was. We knew you'd be what they need."

"Thanks. The big surprise is, they're what I need too. There's nothing in the world quite like having a little girl throw her arms around your neck and tell you she loves you. Or having a little boy tell you that being with you makes him feel safe."

"Kind of makes up for those trips to Europe you won't be taking," Vivi teased.

"Or for those dates I won't be going on."

"Seems like you could still go out on dates."

"If the guy I'm interested wanted to," he murmured under his breath.

"Huh?"

"I could if the guy I'm interested in wanted to. I don't think he does anymore."

She raised her eyebrow. "Cameron?"

His eyes widened. "How'd you know?"

She looked at him with exasperation. "I'm not blind. You two have had the hots for each other for a long damn time."

"He *was* interested in me. It wasn't my imagination."

"Not at all."

"What happened? He was blowing hot, and now he's blowing cold. I don't know what's going on with him."

Vivi's smile faded. "He has his reasons."

"What reasons?"

She smiled ruefully. "That's his story to tell. So? How have *The Music Man* performances been going?"

Josh let her change the subject with good grace and spent a few minutes filling her in on the latest *Music Man* gossip. He cooed over the baby a bit more before Vivi left, and he returned to his paperwork.

His mind was only half on his job. The other half was on Cameron and what "his reasons" might be. Josh couldn't fathom what had changed, and wondered if too much time had gone by or if Cameron was involved with someone else. Vivi hadn't given any indication those reasons were the case.

The thought struck him: it was because he was a dad. He knew a lot of men wouldn't be interested in a guy with children, but it hadn't stopped Cameron from eyeing him in December at the bagel deli.

To hell with whatever had crawled up Cameron's ass. He'd make his move when Cameron came back. The worst that could happen was they'd remain as they were. Lusting from afar.

It was about five when Cameron poked his head in Josh's office. Ella had dropped off the children for their Academy classes and he was going through a stack of applicants for the position of marketing director and lamenting the lack of qualified candidates. "Here you go." Cam thrust the stack of proposals in front of Josh. "I take it these organizations haven't yet discovered the pleasure of signing documents electronically."

"As much money's involved, I'll sharpen a goose quill if that's what they want."

"I hear that." Cameron plopped down in the chair across from him. "Why are you still here?"

"The kids are in their Academy classes and it doesn't make sense to go home only to come back later to get them." He smiled. "You get an extra hour or two of my time on Academy days."

"Oh." Cameron fell silent.

Well, shit. That wasn't the reaction he was going for. He waited for a moment, and got nothing.

Cameron looked at him with a schooled, professional expression. "Any more business before I take off?"

Josh took a deep breath, then blurted, "Let's go out to dinner this weekend." There. It was out. All Cameron could do was shoot him down. Josh wasn't going to let that happen without a fight.

Cameron's eyes widened. "Wow. That kinda came out of nowhere."

"No, it didn't." Josh ignored his pounding heart and looked Cameron in the eye. "Cam, we've been checking each other out and dancing around an attraction for a while. Why don't we do something about it?

Cameron looked at him with a mixture of want and denial. "I don't think so," he said slowly. "It would be a bad idea."

Josh looked at him in disbelief. "Why? You're unattached. I'm unattached. We have the hots for one another. Is it because I work for you? Since when has that ever stopped anybody in the theater world?"

"No, it's not that. Not really." Cameron looked troubled.

"So what is it then? Age gap? Taste in clothes? You sing baritone and I'm a tenor? You wish folks 'Merry Christmas' and I don't?"

Cameron looked at him with exasperation. "No. Of course not."

"So, what's the problem? I know you're interested. You're a good actor, but you're not that good."

A cloud passed over Cameron's face. "There are things you don't understand."

"Enlighten me when we go out."

Cameron shook his head, but said, "Okay, okay. Let's go out. You said dinner. There's a matinee Sunday afternoon of *Music Man*. I'm sitting with Mom and Aunt Katie, but they'll be in their own car. Early dinner after the show at that new place in the Pearl?"

Cameron said yes. Josh resisted to the urge to jump up and kiss him. "Let me see." He already had his weekend sitter lined up for Sunday afternoon. He fired off a text asking if she could stay through the evening and received an instant thumbs-up. "Okay. The kids are covered. Sunday evening it is." He felt his face break into a huge smile. "I'm looking forward to it."

Cameron's smile was warm and genuine. "So am I. See you then." He looked at his watch. "Gotta go. Mom and Aunt Katie made lasagna. Not about to turn down the dinner offer."

"I know the feeling. Sometimes I think the kids and I would starve if it weren't for *Bubbe* and Ella."

A bit of a shadow crossed Cameron's face but it was gone almost instantly. "Gotta love the way those little old ladies can cook."

Josh raised his eyebrow. "Next time I see her, I'm gonna tell your mom you said she was a 'little old lady.' She's the last person of her generation I'd give that label to."

"Don't you dare. She'll never feed me again. Seriously, I've gotta take off. See you Sunday."

Josh sank into his chair and hoped his grin wasn't too goofy.

Sure, it might be only lust. Once they scratched their itch, they'd move on. But Josh didn't think so. They had more in common than sex. They loved art, music, travel, and a good movie. They loved fine dining and exploring what San Antonio and other big cities had to offer. They loved the world of theater with a passion.

He smiled.

Yep. There was a solid base upon which to form a real relationship.

Chapter Seven

Cameron took the expressway exit to Southtown and fought the stop-and-go traffic clogging the streets. There were times like tonight he wondered why he hadn't kept his condo in Alamo Heights. But then he'd sprawl on the sofa in his loft and savor the view and remember why he'd moved. He carried in the generous sack of leftovers, and stashed it in the fridge. Alcohol didn't appeal tonight, so he uncapped a bottle of sparkling water and parked his ass on the sofa, a smile playing on his lips. He was either the bravest man in San Antonio or the dumbest agreeing to go out with Josh.

Dumbest, most likely.

Josh was a parent. Josh had children, who were going to throw a monkey wrench into whatever they thought they were going to have together. It hadn't escaped his notice Josh had to check with a babysitter before they could even make a date. It would be that way every time they wanted to go out.

Cameron did some quick math in his head. The boy was eight, the girl six. It would be four or five years at the minimum before they could be left alone in the evening. Even then they might not be trustworthy to stay home alone. Never mind all-night sleepovers or weekends out of town. No parent in his right mind would leave teenagers alone for an entire weekend.

It would be years before Josh could call his time his own.

None of the curtailed activities took into account his other responsibilities as a parent, and the inevitable pitfalls he would face as the gay parent of teenagers. Cameron cursed his weakness. He'd sworn not to get involved with Josh. He'd promised himself to shut down the attraction simmering between them and go back to being Josh's boss. Yet, one invitation and he'd caved, and Josh hadn't had to work all that hard to get him to say yes.

Even though he was really looking forward to their date, he knew they were doomed before they started.

He sipped the sparkling water and enjoyed the gorgeous sunset. He was about to tackle a couple of bids when the doorman buzzed. "You have a guest. Trevor Marquart. Do I send him up?"

"By all means."

He was waiting at the door. One look at his friend had him sucking in his breath. Trevor looked like hell. He'd lost weight and deep circles rode beneath his red-rimmed eyes. He looked like he was on the verge of tears. *Oh shit.* This wasn't going to be good.

Wordlessly, Cam ushered Trevor in and pointed to the sofa. "You look like you could use a stiff drink," he said quietly.

"I could." Trevor stared sightlessly out the window.

Cameron got out his best scotch and poured a generous three fingers. He got himself another sparkling water and sat down in the easy chair across from his friend. "Tell me."

"Pat and I are separating."

Big surprise. "I'm sorry, Trev."

He turned anguished eyes to Cameron. "I couldn't take it any longer. The fights. The worry. The constant chaos. The resentment. They say I ruined their lives. I don't know. Maybe they're right." He knuckled tears out of his eyes. "As much as I love Patrick, I've had enough." He tilted his head back and swallowed half the scotch, shuddering visibly as it went down.

"What did Patrick say?"

"Damn little. I think he was relieved. Maybe now the shit will stop flying and he can have a relationship with his children again."

"Don't bet on it," Cameron said quietly. "Trevor, you weren't the problem."

Trevor looked up in surprise. "I wasn't?"

"Nah. The problem with those kids is that their father's gay. They have a gay man for a parent, whether you're in the picture or not. It's more obvious being married, but mark my words, it's not gonna get any better now that you're gone. If anything, it'll be worse because Patrick will be coping with them by himself and trying to support them on a teacher's salary."

Trevor looked at Cam doubtfully. "Are you saying you think I should go back?"

"No," he said quickly. "Not if you can't take it anymore and Pat was relieved to see you go. He's going to realize you weren't the problem." He sipped his sparkling water. "Have you gone as far as using the 'D' word?"

"No. But it will come to that." He looked around the living room. "I could kick myself in the ass for selling my house. I'll never find another one like it."

"No, you won't. But Southtown's full of period bungalows and sooner or later a lovely one will come on the market. Or you could try the Deco District. There's all kinds of nice properties over there." He thought of the house the Durango crowd helped Josh vacate. Something like that would be perfect for Trevor. "Or, if you're into condo living, there's one on the third floor here that went on the market last week. In the meantime, do you need a place to crash for a few days?"

"Nah. I checked into one of those long-term residence hotels until the end of the month. That'll give me time to find something to rent and get my furniture out of Pat's house. I guess I ought to leave it with him. But right now, I'm not feeling that nice. Those kids can sit on the damned floor for all I care."

"Don't blame you."

They sat quietly while Trevor finished his drink. He promised to keep in touch and Cameron wished him the best as he walked out the door.

If that wasn't an object lesson in why gays shouldn't try to be parents, he didn't know what was.

He finished the second sparkling water. There was paperwork he should be doing, but his concentration was shot and he plopped down onto the sofa. The lights of downtown San Antonio sparkled before him. He realized with a start Fiesta was due to start next week. He'd bought the condo in July and had never seen Fiesta from this vantage point. The King William parade, which would be fun to watch, passed on the street right in front of the window. He wondered if he could see either of the downtown parades from here. It would be fun to find out.

Maybe he and Josh could go to one of the festivals together. They could eat and drink beer, and enjoy Fiesta together.

Cameron shook his head. Wishful thinking.

The nicest, sexiest, most interesting man to come his way in years, and he would have to keep it casual. It was a damn shame.

As wonderful as Josh was, he was a parent. He had years of coping with children in his future. Children who would eventually look at Uncle Josh and wonder why he couldn't be like other men. Why he couldn't give them a nice stepmother.

When they figured it out, all hell would break loose.

There was no way Cameron was going to stick around for that. He'd make sure he'd be long gone by then. Even if it did make him a first-class asshole.

He felt a pang of sorrow for Josh. The man had a hard, rough road ahead of him. Josh would do what he had to. Sadly, he had no choice.

But Cameron did.

He didn't have to get involved.

***

Josh stood at the back of the theater watching the big finale of *The Music Man*. It wasn't his favorite musical, but it had proven popular with the Durango patrons and ticket sales had been brisk. He looked out at the audience. Lots of gray hair. There were millennials scattered throughout, a reminder to him that some stories were timeless. He scanned the audience again, looking for a particular head of ash-blond hair. There he was, sitting beside his mother and his aunt. Both were enthusiastic patrons of the Durango, coming once to every show, and writing a nice check a few times a year. He would make a point to speak to them before they left.

He wondered if they knew he and Cameron had a date.

Not that he'd mention it. He had no idea if Cameron was out to his mom and aunt. Delicious anticipation wrapped its tendrils around him. He'd looked forward to this evening all week. A part of him felt a little bad for spending an evening away from the children, but *Bubbe* and Ella had both assured him it was all right. "You need a life apart from them," *Bubbe* had said firmly when he'd voiced his concern. "Otherwise, you'll never meet anyone." She'd winked and looked at him hopefully. "Is he nice? Is he Jewish?"

"*Bubbe*, it's a date, not a lifetime commitment," he'd protested with a laugh. "Besides, do you know any other gay Jewish men in San Antonio?"

"Well, no. But one can hope," she'd replied dryly.

The curtain lowered and then rose again for the actors to take their bows, and the cast lined up in the lobby to shake hands and greet the audience. Josh spotted Mrs. Heiser and her sister-in-law leaving the auditorium, and made a beeline for them. "Thank you so much for coming," he said as he hugged Mrs. Heiser and shook the other woman's hand. "Did you enjoy the show?"

"Oh, definitely," Mrs. Heiser replied.

"It was very well done," Katie added. "They always are."

"Coming from you, that's high praise indeed. Tell me. When are you going to grace our stage?" Katie Heiser had been a music teacher and had done musical theater as a young woman. Her niece and nephew had been after her for years to audition for a role at the Durango. She had yet to take them up on it, but Josh hoped someday she would change her mind.

They exchanged a few more pleasantries. He tried to keep his eyes on the ladies but found himself sneaking glances at Cameron he hoped nobody else noticed.

Josh had to stay until the actors were gone and the crew had cleaned up backstage. By then he'd be free to lock up and leave. He and Cameron would have time for a leisurely dinner before he had to get home. There wouldn't be time for any more than that. Which was all right. He didn't hit the sheets on a first date and he doubted that Cameron did either. When the time was right, he'd figure out the logistics.

Josh took his place with the actors, greeting their guests and thanking them for their attendance and support. The actors left and the crew busied themselves with cleaning up. Josh left them to their work and went to his office, where he sat behind his desk and tried to do paperwork. He couldn't keep his mind on what he was supposed to be doing and was about to throw in the towel when crew chief Jeannie Cruz stuck her head in the door. "We're done," she said cheerfully.

Not a moment too soon. He thanked her and locked the front doors.

Cameron was nowhere in the building, so Josh exited through the back and crossed the parking lot, where he found Cameron leaning against his Mustang with his legs crossed in front of him. He looked up with a smile that was wickedly flirtatious. "Arthur's still good?" Cameron asked.

Josh nodded. They climbed in their vehicles and Cameron put down his cartop. Josh opened his sun roof.

The air was warm, teasing Josh's hair as they made their way across town to Pearl. Once a brewery, The Pearl was now a repurposed mixed-use destination with apartments, hotels, restaurants, shops, and other attractions inviting San Antonio to enjoy. He parked his crossover in a space next to Cameron on the top floor. "The Pearl is busy tonight," Cameron observed as they drifted to the rail and peered down at the grassy commons.

"The Pearl is always busy. That's part of the fun." Josh grinned. He gestured in front of him. "Shall we?"

The elevator whisked them down to street level. Together they ambled slowly toward a popular new restaurant, stopping occasionally to do a bit of window shopping. "Nice outfit," Cameron said, gesturing to a jeans-and-shirt combo in the window of a men's boutique. "Looks like something I'd see at Goldstein's."

"It does," Josh agreed. "I'll mention it to *Bubbe*. She's thinking about opening up another store and The Pearl might be the place to do it."

"It might. I shop at the one out close to the loop."

"I thought I spotted you in Goldstein's merchandise. You shop there often?"

"The only stuff I don't buy there are my factory floor work clothes. You get most of your clothes from your grandmother's?"

"Pretty much. She's managed to go after the younger crowd while holding on to her older, more establishment customers. She's a seriously savvy businesswoman. Even though her managers make most of the buying trips these days, she still goes every so often. She misses the trips to New York. She and *Zayde* used to love to make those treks."

"Was *Zayde* your grandfather?"

"He was. Saul Goldstein. He was a lot older than *Bubbe*. He came over from Germany in 1935 to work as a tailor. He'd planned on getting his business going, make a little money and send for his family. Like a lot of families who couldn't believe what was happening, they waited too late. He lost everyone in the Holocaust."

Cameron winced. "Shit. That sucks. What about your grandmother?"

"She did too. It's a stroke of luck that she didn't die along with them."

Cameron's eyebrow flew up. "How?"

"*Bubbe*'s mother was close to Katherine Kirby, an English girl she'd gone to boarding school with. Katherine invited then nine-year-old Clara Ehrman to go to England to attend school with Katherine's daughter Jennie for a few months in the fall of 1938. Timing is everything in life."

"*Kristallnacht*."

Josh nodded. "My great-grandparents got word to the Kirbys, and *Bubbe* stayed with them in England. After the war they tried to find the Ehrmans, but learned the entire family had been wiped out."

"She had no family left at all?"

"Not of the Ehrmans, no. The Kirbys became sorta like family. *Bubbe* and Jennie Kirby were close. When Jennie married an American serviceman and moved to San Antonio, *Bubbe* followed her here, met and married *Zayde*. You know Jennie Kirby's grandson and namesake."

Cameron's eyes widened. "Kirby Martinez? Maggie's asshole boyfriend?"

Josh laughed out loud. "Yep. That Kirby."

"She didn't give up her Jewish faith, living with a Christian family in England?"

"No. If anything, her faith became stronger after her family was killed. She remained part of the Jewish community. I give the Kirbys a lot of credit. At first they kept her identity a secret in case England was invaded, and were ready to pass her off as their niece. When they felt like it was safe, they contacted the local synagogue, who took her into their community."

"Says a lot about them that they went to the trouble. A lot of people wouldn't have."

"They knew she felt alone, what with her family gone and living in a Christian home away from the Jewish community. Marrying *Zayde* and having a family helped, but on some level she never got over the loss. *Zayde* didn't, either."

"A lot of Holocaust survivors feel that way?"

"They do."

Arthur's was busy, but they were seated quickly. The menu featured unfussy, locally sourced dishes cooked with fresh ingredients. Josh zeroed in on a roasted chicken dish with sautéed squash while Cameron opted for grilled pork chops and smoked peppers. The waiter brought them a big basket of warm rolls with whipped butter. "Umm, delicious," Josh said as he bit in. "This was a good idea."

"It was." Cameron met his gaze with heat in his eyes.

Josh swallowed as his cock twitched. *Wow.* Serious smolder. He gave Cameron his best *fuck me* expression, which had landed him in more than one bed over the years.

Cameron's brows went up as he smirked.

Their server brought their salads and drinks, breaking the spell. Josh dug in, not realizing until now how hungry he was. Cameron appeared equally ravenous and the table was quiet for a few minutes.

"What about your family?" Josh asked. "Aunts? Uncles? Cousins?"

"Not a cousin to be had." Cameron wiped his mouth. "Mom's only brother was killed in Vietnam, and my Aunt Katie never married. You knew Dad, of course. He used to come to all Vivi's shows."

"Tall dude that looked a lot like you. Sure, I remember him. Nice guy. I felt for you when you lost him. I lost my dad when I was a sophomore in college."

"He must've been young."

"Not that young. He was over forty when I was born. He'd been a man-whore for years. He was *Bubbe* and *Zayde*'s one and only and they had about given up on grandkids when he finally married my mother. She ran off to Israel with her boyfriend when I was a baby. *Bubbe* and *Zayde* raised Miriam and me since Dad went back to screwing around."

Cameron grimaced. "My parents had their faults, but their marriage wasn't one of them. They were good parents. I'm sorry you didn't have that."

Josh shrugged. "Yeah, I resent 'em, but it's a dull ache now. You don't have to feel sorry for me. I had *Bubbe* and *Zayde*, and they were the best."

"Sounds like."

Their food arrived and tasted as good as it looked. As they ate, Cameron continued to gaze across the table. He was hot for Josh and he let it show. Shivers ran down Josh's back at the unbridled desire in Cameron's eyes.

Inwardly he cursed the time constraints he was under. It wasn't like him to jump into bed on a first date. But tonight he would've done it in a heartbeat. He'd lusted after Cameron for so long, and Cameron returned the favor.

It dawned on him how much harder dating was going to be with the children in his life.

They cleaned their plates and the waiter brought dessert menus. "Anything appeal?" Cameron asked as they perused the menu.

"The cheesecake, but after a half chicken no way I can do it justice."

"Same. Why don't we split it?" Cameron made the suggestion sound sexy.

Josh nodded. They could eat it off the same fork.

Cameron looked at him thoughtfully. "So it was you and your sister, and your grandparents. Now it's you, your grandmother, and your children. That's so sad."

"Yeah. But we have each other."

"It's sad you're the only one to raise the children."

Josh felt himself stiffen. "I agree it's sad their mother's gone, but I don't get why you think it's sad I'm raising them."

Cameron looked at him with puzzlement. "Of course it's sad they have to be raised by a gay man. That right there's heartbreaking."

"A gay man? You think it's sad because I'm gay?"

"Well, yeah. It's bad news for them, and it's bad news for you."

Josh shoved down his disbelief. Surely he didn't hear what he thought he heard. "I'm not following you. Why is it such bad news for everyone I'm raising the children?"

Cameron looked at him patiently. "Because you're gay. Gay men shouldn't ever raise children. It not only wrecks the man's life, but it wrecks the children's as well."

"You think I'm gonna wreck the kids' lives?" Josh fought to keep his voice even. "Please explain to me how. I thought I was doing a pretty damn good job of parenting them."

Cameron looked a little uncomfortable. "I didn't say you weren't. I have no doubt you're doing the best you know how. But as they get older, that's not gonna cut it. Simply the fact that you're gay is going be a problem."

"You lost me. Why is who I sleep with going to be such a big problem for them?"

"Because they, and all their friends, are gonna know it. They're going to be the ones with *that* father. Or *those* fathers. Which leads me to the other big drawback. Men aren't interested in anything long-term with a single father. Most of us realize kids are a bad deal all the way around."

Josh felt his eyes narrow. "I see."

"No, I don't think you do. One of my good friends and his husband separated last week because of his husband's children. The kids are acting out, big time. They resent the hell out of being raised by a gay couple." He took a breath. "I get that you have to raise the children. I overheard Miriam's asshole in-laws at the funeral. You had no choice. You took the kids and I respect you for doing it. But you need to prepare yourself. In a few years it's gonna get bad and you need to be ready."

"Why are you sitting here telling me this shit? This your way of telling me you're not interested?"

Cameron looked embarrassed. "I guess that's how it sounds."

"Tell you what. I can take a hint. You think things are going to go south in the Goldstein household, and you don't want to be part of it. That's certainly your prerogative, and I guess it's better to find it out now before I invest time and interest in you."

"Josh, I'm sorry."

He shrugged. "So am I. The sex would have been phenomenal."

Cameron nodded. "The whole situation's sad."

"It's not the situation that's sad. It's you who's sad."

The waiter brought the piece of cheesecake. "Here, you take it." Josh pushed the slice toward Cameron. He fished out his wallet and counted out enough to cover his meal and a generous tip. "I'm going to run." He slapped the money on the table and stood. He took a step but turned around and leaned over the chair. "I'm going to say this for the record. I have no idea what's coming down the pike in the years to come. You may be right. What I do know is I *love* being their father. I love fixing their breakfast and taking them to school, and cooking their dinner. I love supervising homework and getting them to bed. I don't even mind the damned laundry. But you wanna know the best part? It's when Beth throws her arms around my neck and tells me how much she loves me. Or when Jackson says I'm the best uncle in the whole world. That and more makes me think you're full of shit."

Cameron's expression froze in neutral. "I hope you're right and I'm wrong. See you at the theater."

Josh strode out of the restaurant and made his way to his car. The sun had gone down and the air had cooled considerably. He opened the sunroof anyway, the blowing wind ruffling his hair as he whipped the car onto the street.

His cheeks burned as he replayed their exchange. Cameron didn't think he had any business raising Jackson and Beth. He thought it would ruin Josh's life. He thought it would ruin their lives. Josh couldn't stomach the idea of not having those children under his roof. No one but him could be their father.

Fuck you, Cameron Heiser.

The television in the living room was tuned to a Disney movie when he let himself in. Jackson and Beth sprinted toward the door. "Uncle Joshie, I missed you." Beth threw herself into his arms. "Did you have a nice day?"

"Yes, I had a nice day." Evening? Maybe not so much. "Did you have a nice day?"

"Miss Carmela took us down to Woodlawn Lake and we played on the swing and monkey bars with a bunch of other kids. That was fun."

He turned to Jackson, who wrapped his arms around Josh's waist. "I had fun too. Even if the kids were all little, like Beth."

"I'm not little," Beth sputtered.

"Are too."

"Am not."

"That's enough," Josh said firmly, hiding his grin. "Are we ready for tomorrow?"

The kids assured him their clothes were laid out and their homework was ready to go, so he let them return to their movie. He spent a few minutes consulting with Carmela before paying her fee and adding a bonus for staying into the evening.

He refrained from drinking alcohol in front of the children, and fished a soda out of the fridge and sank down in the easy chair in the alcove off the kitchen where he could see into the living room where the kids were sprawled in front of the TV.

His heart bubbled over with love. He'd loved them from the time they were born, but while Miriam was alive it was the love he had for his sister's kids. Now he loved like a father. He hadn't blown smoke up Cameron's ass. He loved being their father. He loved it with all his heart.

Sure, he had enough sense to be concerned about the future. He didn't know the first thing about bringing up teenagers. There were bound to be pitfalls, but he never dreamed it would be as bad as Cameron said.

Maybe Cameron was right about what it would do to his life. Damn few men were interested in a relationship involving a ready-made family. Cameron sure as hell wasn't. Josh would be damned if he subjected the kids to a parade of men in and out the front door. Which was going to make dating harder than he'd even imagined. It might even cost him the happily-ever-after he'd expected would be his one day.

He looked over at Jackson and Beth. Jackson was still absorbed in the movie. Beth was yawning and fighting sleep, and it wouldn't be long before he swooped her up and put her to bed. He loved them so much.

If he had to put his love life on hold for them, it was a sacrifice he was willing to make. They'd lost their parents, and though Josh hated to acknowledge it, in the near future, they'd lose *Bubbe* too.

He *had* to give them all the love they needed to thrive.

Chapter Eight

Son of a bitch. There went any chance he was going to have with Josh Goldstein.

It had been going so well.

Cameron watched with a stone in his gut as Josh strode across the crowded restaurant and disappeared into the night. He cursed himself for not keeping his mouth shut. Josh's decision to take the children hadn't been any of his business. He knew damned well the man hadn't had much of a choice, but he'd mouthed off anyway, spewing shit right and left, making Josh angry enough to walk out on their date. For the life of him, he didn't know what had possessed him to say the things he had.

Yeah, he did. There was going to be all kinds of hell to pay in the future, and Josh needed to know it.

With all the diplomacy of a sledgehammer, he'd put Josh's back up and most likely fucked up any possibility of ever getting Josh into his bed. Which was a damned shame, considering the sparks between them. Cameron shook his head and got out his wallet. Now he'd consider himself fortunate if their professional relationship went undamaged.

***

Cameron leaned back and ran his hand across his middle. "I wish I could eat like this every day. Mom's pot roast and the best tamales ever. Thank you so much for making them, Mrs. Abonce." Miguel's mother beamed at the praise.

Miguel eyed his own empty plate. "I wish we could too. Only then we'd all weigh three hundred pounds. It's good that Sunday comes only once a week." Since Julie's birth, the Heisers and Miguel's mother and grandmother had been getting together Sundays for family dinner. Cameron thoroughly enjoyed the food and the company, even if he wasn't all that into the baby they'd all come to visit.

"So, little one, wanna come to Daddy?" Miguel asked as Julie banged her spoon on the high chair. "Has she eaten enough, ladies?"

"She's fine," Mrs. Abonce and his mother said in unison. Vivi nodded her agreement and Miguel lifted her from the high chair. He cuddled the adorable little girl close. "You're the most spoilable baby in San Antonio, aren't you?" he crooned.

"Love spoilin' my granddaughter," Betsy cooed. She wiggled her outstretched fingers. "My turn."

She held out her arms and Julie lunged toward her grandmother. His mother cuddled her for a minute, then she turned to Cameron's Aunt Katie. "Isn't she the prettiest baby you've ever seen?"

Aunt Katie made kissing noises at Julie. "Getting prettier by the day. Miguel, who ever thought your face would be so perfect on a little girl?"

"I hope that's still true when she's fifteen," Miguel said dryly.

Betsy kissed Julie's forehead. "Cameron, would you like to hold Julie for a few minutes while Vivi and I cut everyone a piece of pie?"

"I...uh—" Betsy rose and deposited the squirming baby in his lap before he could stop her.

Julie looked up with a drooly grin and promptly burped a glob of pureed peas and turkey on his shirt. He looked down at his shirtsleeve in dismay and over at Miguel, who was snickering. "She knows right where to aim. I hope that shirt isn't dry clean."

It was, but Cameron shrugged. "No big deal." He wasn't going to admit not having enough sense to wear a washable shirt.

To his immense relief, no more turkey and peas came up. He managed to hold the squirming baby for a few minutes until Miguel took pity on him and handed Julie to her great-grandmother. The octogenarian had raised a big family and was in her element, cooing and playing peekaboo. Cameron watched as the old lady kept the baby entertained.

He wished he felt that comfortable with the child.

His mother and sister brought big slices of pie to the table, and between them, they managed to eat an entire pecan pie. Miguel gave Julie a bottle. Cameron and the women cleared the table while Betsy and Katie made plates of leftovers to enjoy the next day.

"No, you keep the rest," Betsy said when Vivi wanted to send her mother and aunt home with more. "You and Miguel won't have to cook 'til Thursday." Miguel's mother and grandmother said they already had a fridge full of leftovers from Miguel's sisters.

Vivi looked at Cameron. "You want to take some with you?"

"Uh, yeah."

The ladies all said their good-byes not long after, leaving Vivi and Cameron to finish cleaning up and putting things away. "One more Sunday come and gone," she said as she sliced the roast. "It's nice having both grandmothers so close to her. Lots of cousins on Miguel's side. His sisters' children love her."

"That's something we missed out on," Cameron said thoughtfully. "No cousins."

Miguel came in carrying the bottle, sporting a towel on his shoulder. "She's down for the count. What's this about cousins?"

"We don't have any," Vivi answered. "That's all right. Miguel's family makes up for it."

"How many does she have?" Cameron asked.

Miguel thought a minute. "Nine."

"Whoa. That's a lot."

"Not really. Miguel has seventeen," Vivi observed.

"Big families." Miguel shrugged. "The Heiser family is miniscule by comparison."

"Yeah. You think about it, our family's not that big. It's not like the Goldsteins, though," Vivi said thoughtfully. "Unless Josh has aunts and cousins out there we don't know about."

"There aren't," Cameron said. "Just Mrs. Goldstein, Josh, and the kids."

Miguel raised an eyebrow. "You know this because?"

"Josh told me."

"And when would Josh have told you this?" Vivi's eyes danced with amusement.

"We went out to dinner one night." Cameron hoped he sounded casual.

Vivi turned to Miguel and held out her hand. "I won that bet. Pay up, buddy." She turned to Cameron. "I bet Miguel twenty bucks you and Josh were on your way to becoming an item."

"Miguel, put your wallet away. Vivi lost that one."

Vivi's eyes narrowed. "But you said you went out to dinner. You're not trying to pass it off as a business meeting, are you?"

Cameron looked at her with irritation. "No. It started out a genuine, bona fide date. It ended in a complete and total clusterfuck and will not be repeated. That's all I have to say about it."

"No, it's not," Vivi stated firmly. "If you don't tell me what happened, Josh will."

"Fine. It's not that big a deal. I made the mistake of voicing my opinion about him raising the children, and tried to warn him there'd be pitfalls ahead. He didn't take kindly to it."

Vivi froze. "You did what?"

"I told him how it's gonna be in a few years. When they're teenagers and resent the hell out of having *that* father. I told him he better get ready for it. He got bent out of shape and said I was full of shit."

Vivi slammed a plastic carton on the counter. "I don't blame him. That's a crap-ass thing to say and a crap-ass way to feel."

"It's the truth. I'm not blowing it out my ass for the hell of it. Trevor moved out of Pat's house last week. The kids have been absolute asswipes about the marriage, and Trev couldn't stand it anymore."

"That's because their father lets them get away with shit. Do you think Letti and Owen would put up with that out of Sophie and Marco for half a minute?" Vivi asked.

"Don't throw those kids up to me. Letti and Kevin are raising them. They don't live with Owen and Wade. You know, the Aldrete kids are the exception, not the rule. I'm as sorry as I can be I hurt Josh's feelings. I sure as hell didn't mean to. But gay men have no business trying to raise a family. I know for a fact I don't."

"Is that why you'll barely hold my little girl?" Vivi demanded.

"Babies have always made me nervous. You know that," Cameron said defensively.

"It's one thing if babies make you nervous. It's another entirely to declare an entire group of people has no business raising children because of something that might happen."

"In their defense, they didn't have a choice," Cameron said.

"But you do," Miguel replied. "You made that choice the night you went out with Josh. Then you did the thing to screw it up with him. You hurt his feelings, you walk away feeling righteous about your version of the truth, and you're out of a situation you didn't want to get involved with in the first place." Miguel shook his head. "Way to go, slugger."

"No…but…I—"

"Jesus. That's exactly what you did," Vivi jeered. "You sabotaged things from the get-go. You put the brakes on it so you won't have to get involved with children. Damn, Cam, are children that terrible? Do you dislike them that much?"

"I like children fine and I care about what's good for them. Why do you think I avoid them like I do? It's not that I dislike them. It's that I'm bad for them."

Miguel and Vivi looked at him as though he'd sprouted a second head. "Why do you think you're bad for them?" Miguel asked.

"Don't you remember? Dad always said so."

"Please. Your father spouted a lot of bullshit," Miguel said. "Tons of it. God knows, I had to listen to him spout it often enough."

"You lost me," Vivi admitted. "I don't remember Daddy ever saying any such thing."

"He always said gays had no business trying to raise a family. It was almost a mantra with him," Cameron reminded her.

"That wasn't about you in particular. Daddy didn't know you were gay," she protested.

"Yes, he did," Cameron and Miguel said in unison.

"Oh. And you took it personally?" she asked.

"He meant it personally."

"So, because of something your homophobic father said, you've decided that you have no business around children. Really?" Miguel asked. "I gave you credit for more sense than that."

"What makes you think it's only Dad's opinion I'm basing it on? Yeah, maybe he started me thinking like that, but I've seen damned little evidence over the years to prove me wrong. Besides, having kids around plays hell with your freedom. I don't want that."

"Josh is a no-go because of Beth and Jackson. Cold, Cameron." Vivi looked at him disapprovingly.

"Cold, but honest. No way in hell I'm getting involved with a man who has children. I'm bad with kids, I have no interest in kids. Kids are better off a mile away from me. I'm sorry, but the children put him completely off limits as relationship material."

"What's wrong with some smokin' hot sex and then you go home?" Miguel asked. "Having a little fun after the sun goes down?"

Because that's how it would be with Josh. A relationship.

Maybe they could pull it off. Enjoy some hot sex and nothing more. With Josh knowing the way he felt about the kids, there was no way Josh would want anything to do with him but as a hot lay. They could have their fun and go their separate ways. No harm. No foul.

It was sure as hell worth a try.

Chapter Nine

Josh scooted the last bite of Ella's pancakes around in the warm maple syrup and popped them into his mouth. "Umm, those are so good. Ella, nobody makes pancakes as well as you do. Except maybe you, *Bubbe*."

Both ladies beamed. Jackson looked at *Bubbe* curiously. "You make pancakes? I thought you looked at catalogues and picked out shirts."

The adults bit their lips to keep from laughing. "I do look at catalogues, but before I got this old I used to make pancakes for your mother and Uncle Josh all the time."

"Did Mom like them?"

A shadow crossed *Bubbe*'s face before her gentle smile returned. "She did, *boykin*. So did Joshie."

Josh swallowed the lump in his throat. As painful as it was sometimes, he and *Bubbe* both felt it was important to keep Miriam's memory alive. They mentioned her every chance they got, and readily answered all the children's questions about her. So far neither child appeared particularly curious about their father. Josh wondered if the McDonalds ever talked about him the way they reminisced about Miriam. Perhaps not. It'd be hard to have anything positive to say.

Bubbe answered a few more questions while the children finished their breakfasts. Ella whisked the dishes to the kitchen, and Josh followed her in and started loading the dishwasher. "Ella, I can do this. Why don't you go pack up the scooter and get *Bubbe* ready? If you don't get to the zoo early, parking will be a problem."

"It'll be a problem anyway. If Mrs. Goldstein's on the scooter, it won't matter if the rest of us walk a little."

Ella disappeared and Josh finished up in the kitchen. He'd started the dishwasher when *Bubbe* came in. "The *kindelah* are helping Ella load the scooter pieces in the trunk."

"Will it all fit?" *Bubbe* owned an ancient Lincoln with a huge trunk, but he still wasn't sure the disassembled scooter could be placed inside.

"It's a tight fit, but we manage. I may break down and get a crossover like yours, but bigger."

"You and Ella would enjoy it." He looked at his grandmother. "You're dying to ask me something. Go on?"

Her face was all innocence. "Did you have fun on your date? The one you went on a couple of weeks ago?"

Josh sighed. He knew this was coming. "No. I didn't. In fact, I got up and walked out of the restaurant."

"Ouch." She looked at him curiously. "What happened?"

"Cam has a burr up his uh…backside about gay men raising children. He started in on how sad it is, how they're going to resent me when they're teenagers. How it's going to ruin my life and theirs. It made me mad, I left."

"Good. You don't need to listen to that kind of thing." She tilted her head. "Did you say Cam, as in Cameron Heiser, your boss?"

"Yeah, that Cam. It was a mistake to ever go out with him. We should've kept our relationship strictly professional."

"You probably should have," *Bubbe* agreed. "Did he give you any reasons for his strong opinion on the subject?"

"A friend of his recently left his husband because of the husband's children." He looked at his grandmother. "I told him he was full of it, but now it has me worried. What if he's right? What if the kids and I are facing a disaster in a few years' time?"

"What I know about gay men being parents you could put on the head of a pin and still have room to go dancing. I've never known any gay parents. Lots of acquaintances and business colleagues. If they're parents, they didn't talk about it." She pointed her finger. "Don't you have friends who are gay parents? Your actor friends at the theater who got married a few months ago. Doesn't one of them have children?"

"Owen and Wade. Yeah. Owen's ex and her husband are raising them. Not Owen."

"They still have a gay father. It might be worth talking to them. I remind you, there's no reason to start borrowing trouble. Take each day as it comes. Besides, you're absolutely wonderful with the children. There's no reason that won't continue." She patted his hand. "I'm sorry your date didn't go well. I know you're disappointed, but if he feels that way about your children, you don't need him for your boyfriend. There are other men out there who'll feel differently." When he looked at her doubtfully, she added, "Trust me."

"I hope you're right. As much as I love the kids, I don't want to go through this life alone."

"You won't."

Ella and the children came in, which gave Josh a chance to remind the children to behave with *Bubbe* and Ella.

The sun was bright and the breeze was warm as he drove toward the theater. Fiesta was in full swing and many of San Antonio's storefronts and front porches were festooned with paper flowers, garlands, and *piñatas* in bright colors. He made a mental note to rescue their *piñatas* from *Bubbe*'s shelf where they still sat, or take the kids back to the *piñata* store and get each of them another. He had plenty of room to hang them on the front porch or display them in the house. He and the kids would love them.

He swung into the parking lot and breathed a sigh of relief when the familiar Mustang was nowhere to be seen. Even after nearly a week, he was in no mood to face Cameron. No one could predict the future, but Josh was going to do everything he could to ensure his kids were well adjusted and kept open minds about a whole host of topics.

As he picked his way through the cluttered construction site, he sent up a silent *Thank you, Miguel*. Soon there'd be another much-needed rehearsal studio.

He was later than usual. The Academy Saturday program was in full swing. Production manager Miranda Jenks, who doubled as their hair stylist, was working at her desk on a wig for the upcoming production of *Shrek* and Rachel was sitting in front of her computer talking animatedly with someone on the telephone. He was deep into reading resumes for the still-unfilled position of marketing director when his phone rang. A panicky Jessica was on the line. "Josh, bring everyone you have in the office and get over here. We have a situation."

Josh leapt from his chair. "Rachel, Miranda, Jessica's got a situation and needs some help."

The three of them ran for the Academy, where they could hear a commotion the moment they opened the door. They raced through the waiting room and the labyrinth of studios to the smaller practice room in the back, where Jessica stood in front of a cluster of high-school-aged girls dressed in leotards and leg warmers. They cowered in the corner, horrified, as a big man waved a chair and shouted at Academy student Emma Ellis at the top of his lungs.

Oh shit. Josh ran up to the man and yanked the chair out of his hands. "What's going on?" he demanded, quickly passing the chair to Miranda.

The big man turned and Josh gagged at the smell of cheap whiskey. "Gimme that back," the guy said as he lunged for the chair.

"No, you don't," Miranda said as she handed the chair over to Rachel, who ran out the door with it. "Why the hell are you here and what do you want?"

The man eyed Miranda angrily. "You know what I want, Miranda. I want my little girl to stop this bullshit and come home." He belched and lurched drunkenly toward Emma. "This fucking theater cost me her mother. Now she's moved in with her fancy-assed grandparents so she can come here. You come home, girl, where you belong and stop this shit."

Ross Ellis. The Summersets' alcoholic son-in-law. Wonderful. Emma's grandparents, Byron and Barbara Summerset, were some of the biggest Durango supporters, and her uncle was married to Letti Aldrete. "Mr. Ellis, you can't come back here while classes are in session," Josh said firmly. "You'll have to take this up with Emma somewhere else."

"Where? You think my in-laws will let me within a mile of their million-dollar mansion?" He took another step toward his daughter. "Emma," he bellowed. "Get in my truck."

"Like hell," the girl snarled, advancing on her father. "I wouldn't go home with you if you were the last man alive. You're a worthless prick, and I hate you." Her hand snaked up and she slapped the fire out of him.

Josh froze in astonishment. This furious girl wasn't the shy and retiring Emma they all knew and loved.

Ellis stumbled backward, holding his hand to the side of his face. "You little bitch. You're worthless. Just like your mother."

"Shut the hell up, Ross," Miranda snapped, stepping between them. "Get outta here. She's right. You are a worthless prick."

Ross waved a fist at Miranda. "This is all your fault. You brought Renee here in the first place. Get out of my way, bitch. I'm taking my girl home."

Emma's face paled. This was going south fast. Josh looked around. Jake Pierce, one of the Academy fathers, had followed them into the room. He nodded to Pierce and motioned with his head toward Ellis. The retired Army officer took Ellis by one arm and Josh took him by the other. "Time to go, asshole," they said in unison as they frog-marched Ross to the door and sent him sprawling onto the sidewalk. Josh stepped out and got up in his face. "Stay the hell away from my theater. You come near here again and I'll call the cops. Got it, asshole?"

Ellis stumbled to his feet. "Fuck you, Jew boy." He staggered toward a dirty pickup parked halfway down the street.

Josh turned to Jake. "Thanks. I'm not sure I could have handled him on my own."

"No big deal."

Marci Lark, another Academy parent and Jake's girlfriend, shook her head. "Chronic alcoholic. You don't give off those kinds of fumes from a weekend bender."

Josh hurried back to where Emma was sobbing quietly in Jessica's arms. "I've already put in a call to Barbara Summerset," Miranda said quietly.

"Poor kid. The bastard had to embarrass her in front of her entire dance class," Josh said.

Miranda's face darkened. "The SOB's guilty of a whole lot more than that."

"You know him?" he asked, surprised.

"His late wife was my best friend. I got her involved here. That's what he meant by it being my fault."

"Which it isn't, of course."

Miranda nodded and turned to Emma and Jessica. The women appeared to have things in hand. He stopped to again thank Jake, then wandered back to his office. Josh put his head in his hands for a moment. Another fucked-up family. A nice kid with a drunk for a father. At least Emma had her grandparents to turn to. Josh sighed. He supposed no parent-child relationship was easy. He ran his fingers through his hair and looked up to see Rachel standing in the door. "Mrs. Summerset came and got Emma. Jessica got the other kids settled down and are back to dancing."

"We'll get a half-dozen calls from the helicopter crowd demanding to know if their little darlings will be safe in our theater from now on," Josh said tiredly.

"Jessica knows how to soothe ruffled feathers." She sat across from him. "So? How'd your date go with Cameron?"

"You know about it?"

"Josh, everyone knows about it. We know you went. We don't know how it went, or if there'll be a repeat. Neither of you has said a word. It's been almost two weeks and we're all dying to know. So spill."

"You want to know how it went. Okay. It didn't go at all. I got up and left. There won't be a repeat. Not the best date I've ever been on, and that's probably true for him as well."

Rachel's mouth dropped open. "Whoa. That's not what I expected to hear. What happened?"

"Difference of opinion."

"About what?"

"Beth and Jackson and my suitability as a parent."

"Okay. Now you lost me. Why wouldn't you be a good parent for them?"

"Because in the World of Heiser, gay men can't raise children and shouldn't even try. They'll resent me when they're older and have *that* father. He felt this burning need to *warn* me of the perils to come. I got pissed off, and told him he was full of shit."

"Which he is."

"Maybe. Listen, nobody's kids are perfect, and no parent-child relationship is without its ups and downs. What I take offense to is that being gay will make a difference. I'm raising those kids to be loving and open-minded. Do I think there'll be assholes who'll say things about their gay dad? Sure. The same as there'll be assholes who'll say things about them being Jewish. We're not going to stop being Jewish because there are anti-Semites in the world, and I'm not going to stop being gay. Period."

"Exactly." Rachel crossed her arms in front of her. "Cameron has some self-hating issues, and he's laying them off on you. His problem, not yours."

"*Bubbe* suggested I talk to Wade and Owen."

"Good idea. You can catch them after they teach the boys' singing class. Brian got called into work. They're on their way over to fill in for him."

He looked at his email. "I've got at least a half dozen more resumes to go through, and I'll go looking for them."

She nodded. "Good." She slapped his desk and stood. "Now, I've gotta go back to looking at shows for next year."

"What are you going to shock us with?"

"I'm looking at *Cabin in the Sky*. It shouldn't shock anybody."

"All black cast?"

"We can do it."

"Works for me. You gonna play the lead?"

"I'd rather cast my sister Amy. She'd be fantastic. But that's far in the future. Now, I'm getting out of your hair so you can get finished in time to pick Owen's and Wade's brains this afternoon."

He went back to the resumes and by the time the singing class was almost over he had narrowed the applicants down to three for interviews in the next few days. He returned to the Academy and found Owen and Wade finishing up the class of teenage boys trying to learn to sing in their new, often wobbly, voices. Owen's velvety baritone was an interesting contrast to Wade's high, sweet tenor. Josh thought they were a perfect lesson in how there was a place in the theater for a voice in nearly any range.

He slipped inside the room and plopped down on a stool in the back. Wade and Owen finished up a few minutes later, smiling at each other like grinning idiots. They'd gotten married a few months ago on the beach in the small lake community where Wade had grown up.

When they saw him in the corner, they came over and greeted him with smiles and hugs. "Checking out our class? Making sure the parents are getting their money's worth?" Wade teased.

"No. I'm here to ask a favor." Suddenly shy, Josh hesitated.

"Spit it out," Owen prompted.

"I want to ask you about parenting," he blurted. "I've been told being gay is going to ruin my kids' lives."

"Whoever told you that is an asshole. Follow us to this coffee shop we've fallen in love with."

He followed Wade's pickup truck up the street and out of the Deco District into a fifties-era neighborhood with strip malls and eateries lining the avenue. They pulled into the parking lot of the coffee shop. It wasn't new, but an investor had bought and refurbished it after ten years of the store sitting vacant. Josh followed them into the café, decked out in full fifties retro, and froze when he spotted Owen's two children sitting in a large booth in the back. "I didn't mean to intrude on a family lunch," he said quickly. "We can talk later."

"Nonsense," Wade said. "If we hadn't wanted you to join us, we wouldn't have invited you."

"Besides, you wanted to ask about having gay parents. There are two experts." Owen gestured toward the teenagers.

"I guess so, huh?"

The hostess escorted them to the booth and set three more places. Owen slipped in beside Sophie and gave her a kiss. Wade slipped in beside Marco, who gave him an enthusiastic fist bump. Sophie looked at Josh warily. "I hope Mom didn't send you to try to change my mind about majoring in engineering."

Josh held up his hands in surrender. "Nope. That ship has sailed, and she knows it."

Marco looked across the table. "She wouldn't do that. She's too busy with Everly. Speakin' of. You wanna see a picture of my little sister?" he asked, beaming.

"You bet."

Josh slid in beside Owen. Marco and Sophie whipped out their phones and showed off pictures of their tiny sister, born last month. The men all oohed and aahed over the baby. They made small talk until the waitress took their orders. Then Owen turned to the kids. "Josh wanted to ask you something you know a lot about."

Sophie and Marco looked at one another.

"My sister died last December, and I'm raising her kids," Josh began tentatively.

Marco shook his head. "Sorry about your sister."

"Yeah. So, so sorry," Sophie said.

"Thanks." Josh paused, trying to find the right way to broach the subject with teenagers. "Recently, someone told me it wasn't a good thing for me to raise Beth and Jackson. That a gay man has no business raising a family, and it's bad for the kids. Apparently, all hell is going to break loose when they're teenagers. One of this person's friends has stepkids about your age and it was messing them up. I asked your dad and Wade about it and they brought me here to talk to you."

Sophie and Marco looked at one another and shook their heads. "Hasn't ruined mine," Marco said.

"Mine either. Why would it?" Sophie looked confused.

"You don't feel self-conscious about your friends knowing? They don't give you a hard time about it?"

"Mine don't," Sophie said. "But then mine are mostly from the theater or the engineering club. My theater friends all know Daddy and Wade, and my engineering friends like that Wade's an engineer."

"A couple of my friends have," Marco admitted. "Soccer team. Different from theater people."

"What did you say?" Josh asked.

"I said I'd rather have a gay dad who was faithful than a straight dad who cheated. Shut them up real fast." He grinned. "I'd heard a little gossip myself."

Josh bit down on his lip to keep from laughing. Owen winced. "Marco, you didn't."

"Why not? Marco has a point," Wade snickered.

"Well, I guess he does."

Sophie leaned forward. "I've heard the gossip, Josh. *All* the gossip. I can imagine who told you all this. I like Mr. Heiser, but he's old. He's into the way things were twenty years ago. It's not like it was then. It's great Daddy and Wade love each other. It's great Mom and Kevin got married and have a baby together. My parents are *happy*. That's all I care about."

"Sounds like his friend's kids are using it as an excuse to be shits," Marco stated. "Hey, Soph, you think we oughta try it?"

"Are you kidding? Mom would kick our asses 'til our noses bled."

"Maybe Cameron's friend ought to try that," Owen murmured under his breath.

Josh smiled, relief coursing through him. "Thanks, y'all. I feel a whole lot better."

"For what it's worth, I think you'll be a great dad to a couple of teenagers," Sophie added. "From what everyone says, you're already a great dad."

Their meals arrived and Josh bit into his fat, fifties-style burger. Once again, *Bubbe* was right. Owen and his family knew a helluva lot more about gay parenting than Cameron did. Of all people, they should know.

Chapter Ten

Josh looked over the notes he'd made during the three interviews for marketing director and shook his head. What a disappointment. They'd all seemed so good on paper. After he'd met them face-to-face, red flags had flown by the end of the interviews. He wouldn't hire any of them. He was in the middle of writing the board a brief memo to that effect when he looked up to find Cameron poking his head in the door. Wednesday. Cameron's usual day to come by the theater. Much to Josh's relief, Cameron hadn't shown up last Wednesday. But he was board chairman, and disastrous date aside, he wasn't going to stay away forever. Josh looked him in the eye, hoping his wariness wasn't too obvious. He dipped his head and forced himself to smile. "How's it goin'?"

"It's goin'." Cameron smiled crookedly.

Josh sucked in his breath, again feeling the magic that sparked when Cameron was near, and cursing himself for feeling that way. Cameron looked at him uncertainly. Josh looked back with equal trepidation.

Josh finally spoke. "I'm in the process of writing an email to the board about the marketing position. If you have a minute, I can fill you in now."

Cameron hesitated before stepping into the office and closing the door behind him. He sat across from Josh. "Which of them are you hiring?"

"None of them."

"They bombed?"

"Let's say, red flags were gusting in the wind."

"Tell me about it."

He did, and Cameron agreed with his assessments. "Any other business I need to know about?"

"That was it."

Cameron started to get up but appeared to change his mind. He sat back down and looked Josh in the eye. "I'm sorry about the other night at the restaurant. I said some things that were blunt and tactless, and I hurt your feelings."

Josh raised one shoulder. "You have an opinion and you expressed it. No harm done."

"There was plenty of harm done. I as much as told you that you were going to be a shitty parent. That's not true."

Thank you for that. He sat quietly, waiting to hear what else Cameron had to say.

"Anyway, I'm sorry my remarks were so hurtful. I do have concerns about you raising the children. It's just that—"

"No." Josh threw up his hand, palm out. "Don't say another word."

"Huh? You don't want to hear what I have to say?"

"Ah, no. You've made your position perfectly clear."

"I see."

"I don't think you do." Josh's voice softened. "I've talked to several people since I talked to you. All of them pointed out that your opinion is an opinion. There are other thoughts on the topic besides yours, and other people with more insight into the situation than you have."

Cameron's eyebrow shot up. "Mind telling me who?"

"Owen. Wade. Sophie and Marco."

Cameron nodded. "You're right. They would know."

"They do. They shot down every one of your arguments. Sophie said her parents were happy and that was all that mattered. Marco said your buddy's stepkids are using him as an excuse to act like shits. Sophie said you meant well but were twenty years behind the times. If anybody would know about having a gay parent, it's those two."

"Except their mother raised them. Not Owen."

"Not true. Owen might've checked out when he got injured, but he's been as much of a parent as our fathers were." Cameron opened his mouth, but Josh kept talking. "Everyone in those kids' lives knows their father is gay. Owen wears a big gold ring Wade put there and they go to all the kids' stuff as a couple. Marco and Sophie are as likely to catch shit as your friend's brats, but they don't use it as an excuse to be shitty at home."

"Good for them. It worked out for the Aldrete family, and I'm the local dinosaur. I hope it works out with Beth and Jackson, for the kids' sake as well as yours."

Josh leaned forward. "Not that it's any of your business, but I'm committed to being the best parent I can be. Those kids deserve nothing less. There's a lot you don't have any perspective on, such as being Jewish and raising your children to be. Do you think, in this town where most of the population is not Jewish, the kids won't hear shit? They will. We won't stop being Jewish, and I won't stop being gay. We can't change how other people behave, but I'm going to make sure my kids know how to handle how other people behave. Got it?"

"Got it." He paused a moment. "I have a condition."

"Which is?"

"We give it another shot. We go out again. There was some real magic going on until the children came up. I'd like to experience that with you."

Josh wondered if he could put aside how he felt about Cameron's tunnel vision. The man was hot as sin, and Josh hadn't been with anyone in a long time. No relationship, but he could use a few good workouts between the sheets. "I wouldn't mind giving it a try." He held Cameron's gaze. "No more about how I raise my children."

Cameron nodded solemnly. "No more talk about the kids."

Josh felt a small smile steal across his face.

"I'm free this evening," Cameron said. "I finished writing up bids long before I thought I was going to. You?"

"I can be done for the day as soon as I save a file and shut this thing down." He checked his watch. "The kids have Academy until eight. That would give us nearly three hours. Does that work for you?"

"It does. Shut down your computer and let's go."

Cameron suggested a hole-in-the-wall Mexican place he'd been going to since high school on the edge of downtown. Josh knew the place well and soon their cars were parked side by side in the strip mall parking lot backing up to a small urban park. They were seated in the rundown but spotless old café, with a worn linoleum tile floor and fifties-style Naugahyde booths. The waitress brought them water and menus. Canned mariachi music played softly in the background and conversations carried on mostly in Spanish surrounded them with the ambiance well known to many San Antonians. "This place reminds me of a café in Mexico City when I went down there as a freshman in college," Cameron said. "You ever been?"

"To Mexico? Not the interior. I've seen all the cruise ship stops on both Mexican coasts."

"Avid cruiser?"

"Sort of. After I got out of college, I spent a year entertaining on cruise ships. Fun for the first six months and then it got old. When a job became available at the Marquee Theater, I jumped ship so fast it would make your head swim. Puns intended."

They took a look at the menu, most of which was in Spanish. Josh didn't speak Spanish, but he understood enough to choose his favorite *carne guisada* tacos. He was surprised when Cameron ordered his *chile relleno* in decent Spanish. "Where'd you learn to speak Spanish?" he asked after the waitress left.

"Basics in high school. The language of steel fabrication and construction from Dad. My father insisted I learn it passably well so I could communicate directly with the guys on the factory floor, many of whom speak limited English. Vivi didn't have to since she wouldn't work in manufacturing, but she was expected to nail down office skills."

"You both have MBAs?"

"We do."

"I've heard you're something of an artist. Vivi and Miguel rave about your wrought-iron designs."

The side of Cameron's mouth turned up. "My little sideline."

"A businessman with the soul of an artist."

"The opposite could be said of you. The trained artist running a business."

"It fits me. It fits us both, really. We get to use both sides of our brain and are happier for it. How'd you get started with the wrought-iron work?"

Cameron broke into a smile. "Felipe Medrano. One of Dad's most talented fabricators. He took the boss's son under his wing when I expressed an interest. He taught me everything he could during the summers I was in high school. Dad never said, but Felipe and I could tell it pleased him no end to have him teach me. It kind of made up for some of the hell I raised."

"You raised hell?"

"Are you kidding? Entitled rich boy with money and a car? Okay, I never did drugs, except smoking a little reefer, and obviously, I never screwed around. With girls, that is. But I never met a can of beer I didn't like, or a speed limit sign I obeyed. Alamo Heights PD had to bring my drunk ass home more than once. How about you?"

"Actually, no. I was a good kid in high school and college. *Bubbe* and *Zayde* had already begun to suspect I was gay, and I didn't want to do anything else to disappoint them. I made up for it on the cruise ship. The parties in the crew's quarters rivaled anything that went on with the passengers, and I was right in the middle of it as often as I could be. It's a wonder we didn't all get kicked off the ship. I was known to really cut loose during the shore stops."

"Really?" Cam grinned.

"I'm in the Caribbean. Land of rum runners and margaritas. Combine the island vibe with a gay boy who finally feels free to be who he is, and, well, let's say I flew my freak flag."

Cam's brow went up as his grin widened.

"A particular one-afternoon stand in Jamaica was with a tour guide, whose name I can't remember. He was hotter than a two-dollar pistol. Between the booze and the hot sex, I got back to the ship just as they were closing down the tendering entrance. I damn near missed the boat. Literally."

Cameron laughed. "Get into any trouble?"

"Nah. I sneaked back to the cabin and managed to sleep it off before my first performance. That wasn't the only time I went a little wild on shore, but it was the most memorable."

Conversation was nonstop, even after their meals arrived. They agreed that the food was every bit as wonderful as they remembered from their last visits. "We'll have to come here again sometime," Cameron said as he forked up the last of his *chile relleno*.

A shiver ran down Josh's back. *There'd be a next time?*

If they didn't mess things up again.

Josh nodded. "We will." He caught and held Cameron's gaze.

Lust, longing, desire. It was all there in Cameron's expression. He hoped Cam saw what he felt. He certainly wasn't trying to hide it. He wanted, no needed, Cameron to know how much he wanted him.

Cameron grabbed the check. "You can get the next one," he said quickly before Josh could object.

The sky was clear and despite the downtown street lights, Josh could see the stars twinkling overhead. Cameron grasped Josh's hand and gestured to the small park next to the parking lot. "Shall we?"

Josh nodded. At this hour, they had the park to themselves. The air was warm and the wind was breezy. Cameron's hand enveloped his. Warm, calloused fingers wrapped around Josh's hand, and Cameron moved his thumb over the pulse point on Josh's wrist.

He was acutely aware of the man walking beside him. His height. His stride. The warmth of his body, and the sound of his breathing in the dark night. His own breath caught in his throat and his cock hardened with each step they took.

It was time to do something about it.

Josh stopped beside a park bench and turned. "I've wanted to kiss you ever since I laid eyes on you three years ago," he stated.

Cameron's lips twitched up into a smile. "So why haven't you?"

"The time wasn't right." He reached up and hooked his arm around Cameron's neck, rising on his tiptoes as Cameron lowered his face. Their lips met in a collision of pent-up desire, three years' worth of daydreams and lust exploding as they wrapped their arms around one another.

There was nothing tentative about Cameron's touch. Josh opened his mouth and Cameron's insistent tongue initiated a duel for dominance Josh could've played for hours.

They stepped into the embrace, plastering themselves together from head to almost all the way to their feet. Josh lowered his hands to explore Cameron's hot body, which had turned him on every time he was around this sexy man.

Cameron's shoulders were broad and hard, his chest muscular from handling steel and iron, his abs rock-hard and his ass tight. His thighs were strong as they pressed into Josh's and he felt Cameron's long, hard cock poke him in the stomach

Josh's heart pounded in his chest, his breathing hitched, and blood rushed into his groin as he relished the sensation of finally, *finally* having this delicious, wonderful, desirable man in his arms.

It was better than the best fantasy he'd ever had.

They held on to one another for long moments, and Josh moaned in protest when Cameron finally lifted his head. His breathing was ragged and his eyes were glazed. "Damn. You're addicting."

"So are you."

Cameron rested his hands on Josh's shoulders. "Don't usually jump into bed with a man on a first date. Even if I really want to."

"Me neither, but I'd do it with you." He grinned. Josh reached up and pulled Cameron's head down as he captured his mouth.

This time their tongues touched lightly. Their exploration almost tender. This was the other side of their passion, which would be as delightful to explore as the demanding side.

Josh could hardly wait.

They kissed for long moments before Cameron raised his head and gently pushed Josh a few inches away from him. "If we don't stop now, we won't stop at all."

Josh nodded.

They held hands as they walked toward their cars. "When can we go out again?" Josh asked as he unlocked the crossover.

Cameron cocked his head. "Friday, and it'll be a real date."

A real date didn't need code decryption. Cameron wanted Josh in his bed.

"Let's plan for Friday. We can decide what and where then."

"Works for me." Cameron squeezed his hand. "I'd kiss you again but we're kind of public here."

Josh looked around. There were other people in the parking lot who wouldn't appreciate the PDA, but he was tempted to kiss Cameron anyway.

***

Josh sang on top of his voice as he headed to the theater. He and Cameron were back on track. Their evening out had been a success. Friday would be a *real* date. Cam wouldn't have said those words if all he wanted was a booty call. Nope. He wanted them to become lovers.

He wanted them to have a real relationship.

Apparently, he'd changed his mind about getting involved with a dad. He was willing to set aside his reservations and wanted to see if they could forge something between them.

Josh couldn't barely contain himself.

Chapter Eleven

Cameron whistled as he stepped out of the shower. Tonight was the night. He and Josh were taking the next step. They were going to become lovers. A delicious shiver ran down his back as he pictured Josh naked in his arms, moaning in ecstasy as they moved together. Josh was one hot piece in his sexy but elegant duds. Cameron's dick hardened as he pictured Josh's tight butt out of those expensive jeans he liked so much. If the man was sex on a stick in his clothes, he was bound to be even hotter out of them.

Cameron's dick sprang to life in front of him, waving in the steamy bathroom. "Down, Johnson," he laughed. He toweled off and stared at his face and his body in the mirror.

He'd never been accused of being handsome; he looked too much like Tripp Heiser. His lovers had never seemed to mind, using words like *arresting* and *interesting* to describe his face.

These days, his body concerned him. He rubbed the steam off the mirror and stared at himself for a moment. Not the body he'd had at twenty-five, or thirty, for sure. But he'd developed a set of muscles over the years wrestling with heavy steel and wrought iron, along with occasional trips to the gym. He looked at himself critically. Fit enough, but not the build of a young man. A niggle of insecurity tickled in his mind. Josh was probably used to lovers his own age. Not someone staring forty in the face, with the body to prove it.

He needed to quit thinking like this. Josh wasn't naïve. He probably had a damned good idea what Cameron looked like naked and was planning to have sex with him anyway. He was being ridiculous to get all worked up about sex, which would lead to nothing more. Only he hadn't cared this much about pleasing a man in a long time.

He pulled on the boxer briefs and tee he'd laid out on the freshly made bed. A quick shave dealt with the five o'clock shadow. He'd considered wearing jeans but instead opted for charcoal slim-fit dress slacks and a wine-red button-down that he left open at the neck. Dress boots and a leather bomber jacket completed the ensemble.

He looked down at himself. Great for this evening. Not so great if they went out for breakfast in the morning. Grinning, he got out a small duffel and threw in jeans and a concert tee and a change of underwear. He always liked to be prepared.

Maybe he *had* learned something more than making fires in Boy Scouts all those years ago.

He tossed the duffel in the trunk of the Mustang. The GPS took him to the charming Art Deco neighborhood where the Durango was located and directed him to the classic medium-size craftsman they'd helped Josh move into back in the winter.

The houses on the street were a mixture of small and large, all built during the Art Deco craze of the twenties and thirties. A delightful neighborhood. Cameron could see Josh enjoying it. Not a great neighborhood for schools, however. Josh must be using a private school for the kids.

Cameron blinked. He didn't know what made him think of that.

Actually, he did. He and Josh might not have talked about his children, but it had been on Cameron's mind ever since they'd agreed on tonight's date. He reminded himself as he turned onto Josh's street, regardless of how compatible he and Josh might be, how spectacular the sex or how charming the company, this was a casual relationship. Nothing but fun and games with a definite expiration date. He understood this, and so did Josh.

At least he thought Josh understood. *But you don't know that for sure.*

He wasn't going to go out of his way to point it out. The last thing he wanted was for Josh to have second thoughts about getting in bed with him.

He felt a smile steal across his face as he pulled in behind Josh's crossover. A lop-eared mutt had his nose to the window and greeted Cameron with enthusiastic barking Cameron wasn't sure was totally friendly.

He rang the old-fashioned door chime and in a moment Josh appeared with the dog under his arm. "Come on in. I'll put him away." His hair was wet and he wore a damp tee and a pair of skinny-fit black jeans. Cameron's mouth watered at the sight of Josh's hard chest and washboard abs through the fabric of the tee.

Josh Goldstein was ripped.

Josh disappeared for a moment before sticking his head out from a doorway. "I'm sorry I'm not ready. I had to run the kids by *Bubbe*'s on the way home. I won't be but a sec. Have a seat. Or better yet, I have all kinds of things to drink in the fridge. Help yourself to something."

Cameron opened his mouth to ask after Mrs. Goldstein, but Josh disappeared too quickly. He wandered through the living room, charmingly furnished like the set of a nineteen forties movie, past an unfurnished dining room, and into the kitchen, which was dominated by a black-and-white chrome table and chair set that was either a retro piece or incredibly well preserved.

He peeked in the fridge and snagged a craft beer from a Hill Country brewery. He sat down on the surprisingly comfortable Danish Modern sofa and sipped his beer while he looked around the room. It had the requisite sofa, chairs, and glass coffee table. An Art Deco curved walnut cabinet held a big-screen TV on a pedestal. All stylish, but for the laundry basket of toys next to the cabinet and the stack of children's books on the coffee table. The toys and the books didn't spoil the ambiance of the room, but they were a potent reminder that children were a permanent part of this household.

Which shouldn't have bothered him, but somehow did.

He tore his eyes from the toy basket and continued his perusal of Josh's living room. A bookcase in the same style as the cabinet held books, exquisite blown-glass figurines, and a collection of framed photos, many of which featured a younger Josh with his sister and grandparents.

Others were of Beth and Jackson at various ages, including some with Josh that had been taken in the last few months. There were photos of Josh at the theater, posing with the casts of the various productions. There were no pictures of Josh with a man, but there were enough of him wearing gay pride tee shirts and carrying a rainbow flag. Obviously, he was comfortable with who he was.

Cameron already knew that, but there was a lot he didn't know about Josh. Things he might learn in the next weeks or months, and things he would never learn if their relationship remained superficial. Which was sad. Cameron would have loved getting to know Josh well. His likes and dislikes. His quirks. His foibles. What made him tick.

It was a damned shame they couldn't do that.

Josh appeared a couple of minutes later. He'd added a pink dress shirt and a black jersey blazer and dressy ankle boots and looked like a million dollars. "Damn. You clean up nice," Cameron breathed.

"So do you."

They took in one another for a moment. Then Cameron gestured to the living room and kitchen beyond. "I love what you've done in here. I especially love that wonderful kitchen table set. Wherever did you find it?"

"In an antiques store in Comfort. It had been in a seldom-used lake house. I brought it home and cleaned it up. It's not strictly Art Deco but it works in here. At some point I'll have to replace the vinyl on the chairs but it's fine for now." He smiled ruefully. "Maybe I can take the time to find a dining room set."

"It's more than fine. I love it. With such a nice kitchen set, you can take your sweet time on the dining room." He gestured toward the front door. "Shall we go?"

Josh smiled. "You bet."

"Hey, would you like me to drive? Or would you rather drive?" Cameron paused a minute. "I changed the sheets."

"So did I."

They both burst out laughing. "You drive and we can spend the night here," Josh said.

"Works for me. Are you okay with one of the restaurants in Market Square?"

"*Yes*. Mexican food or Mexican food. The nectar of the San Antonio gods."

"It sure is."

They got in the Mustang and while Cameron headed downtown, Josh spent a good ten minutes oohing and aahing over the vintage interior. "Who did your restoration for you?" Josh breathed as he fingered the leather seats.

"Restoration, my ass. My dad was the original owner. We just took care of it."

"Wow. No upholstery work, no detailing, no nothing?"

"I have it detailed every so often. But that's it. Miguel's told me more than once he'll pay me six figures for it if I ever want to sell. I told him the backseat's too small for a car seat." Cameron snickered. "Her Beamer and his Lexus are long gone and now they're in a couple of crossovers. Nice crossovers, but still."

An odd expression crossed Josh's face. "They're not so bad."

"Oops. Sorry."

They got one of the last spots in the parking garage. San Antonio's landmark El Mercado was teeming with locals and tourists. Fiesta was over, but the special vibe of San Antonio hadn't gone away and down here never faded entirely.

The two big buildings housing the market were closed, but the plaza was filled with carts loaded with everything from leather wallets and checkbook covers to artisans making jewelry out of beads and wire. The food vendors hawked mouthwatering offerings of *gorditas* and sausage on a stick.

They bypassed the vendors and instead put their names on the waiting list for the newer of the two restaurants, the one that featured heaping plates of sizzling fajitas as their signature dish. Waiters circulated on the patio waiting area taking drink orders and they opted for the restaurant's other specialty, frozen margaritas that were to die for.

There wasn't much room left on the long bench underneath the narrow patio, giving them the perfect excuse to sit shoulder to shoulder and thigh to thigh.

Josh's body was warm, and the muscles in his legs hard next to Cameron's. He was tempted to cut to the chase and take Josh in his arms right then and there, but he'd learned over the years to savor the buildup and could've sat like this for hours, with Josh's smokin' hot body next to his. He glanced over and saw the same contentment on Josh's face that was on his own.

It wasn't all physical, and Cam wasn't sure that was a good thing.

They were finishing up their margaritas when their name was called and they were shown to a table upstairs in an area that was secluded and much quieter than downstairs. They chose to sit at right angles to one another and Cameron reached out and gave Josh's hand a squeeze. "Did you arrange for this when you made the reservation?" Josh asked quietly.

"I might have," Cameron admitted with a smile.

"Thanks. This is nice."

They ordered fajitas and another round of margaritas. Cam made no attempt to hide the longing in his eyes as he gazed across the table at Josh. He was at half-mast already thinking about the delightful things they would be doing to one another before the night was out. Josh returned Cameron's gaze with an expression that smoldered. There was no flirtation whatsoever. He'd never seen Josh this intense or focused, or with such blatant desire in his eyes.

It would be interesting to find out if Josh was this intense in bed.

Or if he was a playful lover.

Maybe he was both.

They stuffed themselves with fajita tacos and split a piece of *tres leches*, feeding it to one another a bite at a time. Cameron laid claim to the bill before Josh could object. "You can pay for the drinks at the nightclub. *El Rio Rojo* work for you?" The upscale club was owned by the Navarro Corporation. They'd been one of the theater's biggest donors and supporters.

"I'd rather go someplace where we can dance," Josh said. "Dance and hold one another. We can't do that at *Rio Rojo*."

"No, we can't." Cameron thought a minute. "How about the Minotaur?"

"Sure."

They held hands on the way to the car. It had been a while since Cameron had been to the upscale gay bar in the cluster of LGBT-friendly bars and grilles along a short stretch of North Main. The parking lot was full and the sound of a live band spilled out the open door. Cameron put his hand on the small of Josh's back and they went inside.

Josh paid the cover charge and a smiling host ushered them to a small table close to the dance floor. The band was starting a fast, danceable tune from the nineties Cameron vaguely remembered from high school. Single dancers and couples gyrated with varying degrees of coordination, but with universal enthusiasm. Josh was practically bouncing in his chair. "A favorite of yours?" Cameron asked over the music.

"We did a routine to it on the ship. Now I want to dance every time I hear the song."

Cameron gestured to the dance floor. "By all means, go for it."

Josh was out of his chair like a shot. He hit the dance floor and immediately went into a routine that soon had the space cleared around him. He bounced, wiggled, and shimmied in a dance that was full of energy and as sensual as hell.

His body was one with the music, dipping and swaying. His hips swiveled and his arms swayed above his head and his feet moved in perfect synchrony. Cameron stared, mesmerized, as Josh took command of the dance floor. He'd seen a lot of dancing at the Durango and a lot more in the gay clubs over the years, but never had he seen a man with Josh's moves. Never had he seen a man turn dancing into a feast for the senses.

It was practically foreplay.

The song came to an end and the club erupted in applause. Josh blinked and then took a bow. He was smiling sheepishly as he sat back down at the table. "I kind of forget myself when I'm dancing."

"I could tell." Cameron looked at him curiously. "How did you get away with dancing like that in a cruise ship show?"

"It wasn't in the main show. It was part of a late-night lounge act that was strictly eighteen and above. We went on right after the raunchy comedian. The audience loved it."

"Gay or straight?"

"Mixed crowd. Half the dancers were girls and the straight guys *loved* them. I autographed chests and boobs alike."

"Fended off passes right and left, I'll bet."

Josh shrugged. "Part of the job. I sure as hell never fooled around with the passengers." He gave a mock shudder before grinning. "I got enough action down in the crew's quarters."

Cameron laughed. "So you said."

The waiter took their order and reappeared a moment later with their drinks. They sipped and held hands while they listened to the band. The talented combo played a couple of moderately fast dance tunes and then came on with Eric Clapton's "Wonderful Tonight." Cameron gestured to Josh. "Would you like to dance?"

Josh nodded, a half-smile on his face as they stood. They moved into one another's arms, clinging tightly on the dance floor as Clapton's sweet lyrics and melody filled the room. The dance floor filled quickly with swaying couples. As far as Cameron was concerned, it was only him and Josh, holding on to one another and moving together in graceful and sensual tandem.

He buried his nose in Josh's hair and breathed in a combination of sandalwood soap and Josh. His body was hard, warm, and slightly damp from his earlier exertion on the dance floor. He could feel Josh's heart beating as well as his own. His swelling cock brushed up against Josh's six-pack and Josh's poked into his upper thigh. The music pounded in his ears as Cameron gave himself over to the sensual spell Josh cast. He couldn't remember wanting a man the way he wanted Josh. He'd never lusted after a man so hard in his life.

From the way Josh was clinging to him, Josh wanted him every bit as much.

The song ended and another slow number began. They held one another through three more songs, getting hotter and hotter with each dance. Cameron led Josh by the hand back to their table. "Do you want another drink?" he asked as they sat down.

"Frankly, I'd rather go back to my place and fuck your brains out." Josh's smile held a treasure chest of sensual promise.

"Well, that was plain enough." Cameron smiled to himself. He was going to love sex with Josh.

Josh left enough money to pay for the drinks and a generous tip. They held hands as they walked out to the car. The air was warm and a silvery half-moon shone low in the sky. They got in the car and Josh leaned over the console. "Kiss me. I need something to hold me until we get back to the house."

Cameron leaned forward. Their lips met, and Josh's fingers fisted in Cameron's hair as their tongues fought a sensuous duel. Cameron grabbed on to Josh's muscular biceps. Already turned on by their dancing, Cameron's cock swelled in his pants and his breathing became ragged. He was on fire. He could hardly wait to get into Josh's bed.

Josh broke the kiss and abruptly pulled away. "Let's go. Before I take you in the backseat." He grinned wolfishly. "Or would it be an old Heiser family tradition to do that?"

"It's been known to happen." Cameron's lips twitched. "Mom even mentioned it a time or two."

"Ewwww. I know your mother. Not a mental image I really wanted, thank you very much."

Cameron snickered. "Me neither."

The streets were mostly empty this late in the evening. Cameron set the GPS but wouldn't have needed it as he sped through the streets toward Josh's home. He pulled up beside the crossover, and then they were in the living room, plastered from head to toe in a tight embrace.

Cameron ran his hands down Josh's hard body and cupped his butt, bringing him closer and relishing the feel of his cock poking into him. He breathed in Josh's unique aroma. Damn. The man really did it for him. He'd never wanted to fuck a man so badly in his life.

Without being asked, Josh led Cameron to a beautifully appointed bedroom with an Art Deco Waterfall bedroom set, complete with a curved wood king-size bed, a high chest, and a vanity complete with a round mirror and a stool. The room was gorgeous and totally Josh. Any other time, Cameron would've commented on it. Right now, the only thing on his mind was getting Josh in that great big bed and working him out 'til he couldn't breathe.

He laid another kiss on him, this one hot and sweet and full of promise, and shucked his jacket and his shirt. Josh removed his jacket and shirt before kicking off his boots. He reached out and jerked Cameron's tee shirt out of his pants. "Slick or hairy?" he asked as he whipped the shirt over Cameron's head.

"Definitely hairy. And it's gonna stay that way."

"Works for me." Josh ran his fingers through the hair on Cameron's chest. "Really, really works for me."

"How about you?" Cameron asked as he tugged on Josh's tee shirt.

"Hairy enough. I had to wax on the ship for the costumes. Hated it. Haven't gone near a waxing salon since."

"I don't blame you. If a lover doesn't like the real you, then bye-bye." Cameron eased the shirt up and over Josh's head. He sucked in his breath and stared a minute at Josh's naked torso. "Perfection. Absolute perfection." He reached out and reverently ran his hand down Josh's chest. "The hair works on you. Stay out of the salon."

"Perfection my ass. I'm far from that," Josh said. He undid his belt and wiggled out of his skinny jeans. Cameron sat down on the side of the bed and tugged off his boots and socks, and then removed his pants and his boxer briefs in one motion, leaving him naked. He looked down at his nearly forty-year-old body, and then over at Josh's, and winced.

They were over ten years apart, and every one of those ten years showed.

Josh stepped over to where Cameron sat on the edge of the bed. "Why are you looking at me like that?"

"Because I forget how glorious a twenty-something body is compared to what I'm walking around in. You're gorgeous. Your face and your body."

Josh shrugged and let his gaze travel down Cameron's naked body. "Accident of youth and nature. So happens I find tall guys with great shoulders, interesting faces, and even more interesting brains," he paused a moment and grinned, "and really long, thick cocks sexy as fuck." He reached down and caressed Cameron's jutting cock. "Yep. Really love those cocks. So how about you make like the stud I know you've gotta be."

Cameron's heart swelled. Josh was right. He had nothing to feel bad about. Josh was here, clearly into him, and wanted Cameron as much as Cameron wanted him.

This was going to be good.

They shared another sheet-scorching kiss. Josh went into the nightstand and pulled out lube and a strip of condoms. "Come here." He slid across the bed and motioned for Cameron to follow.

Cameron didn't have to be asked twice. He scooted onto the bed beside Josh. "Are we gonna lick ice cream cones first or dive right in?" Josh teased.

Cameron choked on his laughter. "Is that what we're calling it these days?"

"Beats those terms they taught us in that college sexuality course."

"You mean like fellatio and anal intercourse?"

"You took the course, too?"

"I did." Cameron's face sobered. "I made sure homosexuality was covered before I signed up. I knew by then that I was living my life as a gay man and I wanted to find out everything I could about it."

"I kinda did the same. I was also thinking I could draw on what I learned to make my characters come alive on the stage. Gay and straight. You know the most important thing I learned? The sexiest organ in the human body is our brain. The prof was right. Because my brain is looking at you and thinking up all kinds of things we can do. What'll it be?"

"Aw, hell, let's dive right in."

"Gotcha."

They shared a hard, sweet kiss as their hands roamed each other's bodies. Cameron relished touching Josh's hard, fit, chiseled-to-perfection naked body. The hair dusting his chest and flaring around his cock was a couple of shades darker than the ash blond curling on his head. His cock jutted up, and Cameron leaned down and took it in his mouth, sucking powerfully and bringing Josh up off the bed. "What was that about? I thought we were diving in."

"We are." Cameron grinned. "I just wanted a taste."

"You keep that up, that's all that's gonna happen. At least on my end," Josh warned.

"Ah, yes. The hair-trigger cock of youth. Hand me a condom, Josh. Time to get busy."

They both suited up, but they were in no hurry. Which was weird given how hot they were for each other. Instead, they shared more kisses and caresses, their hands wandering thighs, abs, and asses. Finally Josh rolled over on his stomach. "I'm ready."

Cameron rose over him. He caressed Josh's butt and lubed him up, testing him with two fingers, stretching him, before easing in an inch at a time, careful to give Josh time to stretch some more.

When he was confident Josh was ready, he moved, slow at first, finding his rhythm as he held on to Josh's hips and plunged into his tight depths. He began to move faster until he was breathless, and felt himself racing toward a climax that was way, way too soon.

He couldn't stop himself. He'd wanted Josh for too long, and he'd wanted him too badly to slow the plunge into ecstasy. Shuddering, he pushed into Josh as his body erupted, his cock pulsing as the orgasm of a lifetime overtook him. He shuddered for long moments as he emptied into the condom. "God, Josh, I—"

Josh looked over his shoulder with a Cheshire cat grin. "Awesome, big boy. Get that thing off you and turn over. My turn."

Cameron shed the condom and obediently turned over. His body quivered at Josh's claiming. Showing the same consideration Cameron had, Josh made sure Cameron was ready before he eased himself into Cameron's willing body.

Most of the time, Cam topped, but he wanted Josh inside him and relished the feel of Josh's body riding his. His cock began to harden as Josh moved faster. He could hear the air sawing in and out of his lungs as his orgasm neared.

Josh came with a shout and a jerk as he slammed into Cameron's body with a cry of triumph. Cameron felt his own cock tremble as he fired off like a rocket.

He'd never in his life had two orgasms less than ten minutes apart.

He'd never had a lover as hot as Josh Goldstein.

Josh rolled off and lay sprawled up against him, and shut his eyes. "I'll tell you how wonderful that was in a minute. Gotta get my strength back first."

Cameron turned over and threw his arm across Josh. "It was pretty damn wonderful."

Josh looked at him curiously. "You always have a doubleheader like that?"

Cameron felt a blush steal across his face. "Nope. That was a first. It seems you bring out the teenager in me."

"Hell, I couldn't do that when *I* was a teenager." Josh sat up and pulled the condom off his shrinking cock. "You want something to eat?"

Cameron's lips twitched. "I guess I'm not the only one who gets the postcoital munchies."

"Ooh, more of them fancy words. Let's go see what's in the fridge and I'll let Pepper out in the backyard for a minute."

Buck naked and clearly comfortable with his nudity, Josh leapt out of bed and took Pepper out of the bathroom. He let the little dog out in the back while Cameron looked through the well-stocked refrigerator. "Wow, you eat good for a bachelor."

"Remember, I'm feeding kids and have to cook for them. *Bubbe*'s always sending something home for us. Under that foil is some of her roast. There's enough for two sandwiches."

"Sounds good. Where's the bread?"

Josh pointed out a bread box on the counter. Together they assembled thick, tasty sandwiches of roast beef, sliced cheese, and romaine lettuce. "The chair's going to stick to your bare ass," Josh warned as Cameron pulled out a kitchen chair. "Come on. We'll be more comfortable in the bedroom."

Josh let the dog in, and he curled up on a little dog bed in the corner of the living room. Cameron followed Josh into the bedroom, where they leaned back on pillows piled against the headboard and munched their sandwiches. Now that they'd had sex, the euphoria was fading and reality was rushing in to take its place. It had been good. A little too good. It was the kind of good that led to caring. Relationships. A future together. All the things that Cameron had promised himself wasn't happening.

Keep it light, he reminded himself. *Keep it casual. It's a good time and nothing more.*

Josh turned to Cameron. "That was the best sex I've had in my entire life. Hands-down. I'm no virgin. Far from it."

"Me too," Cameron admitted. "I hope it's not going to be a one-time thing," he blurted before he could stop himself.

"It's not. I promise you." Josh ran his hand down Cameron's arm. "It'll happen again. Soon, and often."

"Let's spend tomorrow together," Cameron said impulsively. "I have a function in the evening but I'm free until then."

Wait. What? It was supposed to stay casual.

At this rate it wasn't going to. And Cameron couldn't bring himself to care.

"I can check with *Bubbe* when we get up. If time's limited, we can do something in the morning. Wild sex, or do you want to go out?"

"How about wild sex and then we go out? There's a traveling Picasso exhibit at the McNay Museum. Have you seen it?"

"No, but I'd love to." Josh looked down at Cameron. "I promised you we would have sex soon. I didn't realize it would be this soon."

Cameron looked at his swelling cock. "I'm all for soon. As in right now."

"Works for me."

They put their empty plates on the floor. Cameron took Josh in his arms. This time they went slower, with drawn-out, drugging kisses and caresses that lasted endless minutes before they moved to the main event. No less passionate than earlier, but after they came together in one another's arms, they touched and stroked one another for long minutes before Josh stuffed a pillow under his head and curled up next to Cameron with his arm across Cameron's waist. Soon he was snoring softly by Cameron's side.

Cameron stared into the darkness. Every inch of his body was limp with bone-deep satisfaction. He hadn't lied to Josh. It had been the best sex of his life.

Until one or both of them called a halt to their lighthearted dalliance.

He'd be damned if he let it go any further.

Even if Josh was the man of his dreams.

Chapter Twelve

Josh lay beside Cameron as the soft rays of early morning filtered through the translucent shades covering the bedroom windows. He stared across the bed at Cameron's sleeping form. His lover was sprawled on his back, arms and legs spread out as his chest rose and fell under the satin sheet. His breathing was even, quiet huffs interspersed with the occasional soft snore as he slept deeply. His face was relaxed and appeared younger. It made Josh wonder what kind of stress Cameron lived under. Between managing Heiser Steel, which had been recently rescued from bankruptcy, and his responsibilities at the Durango, most likely the stress level was pretty high.

Raising children had its stressors. Which gave Josh pause. If what they shared developed into a relationship, inevitably Cameron would, at least peripherally, be involved with Beth and Jackson. More responsibility. More commitments. More time.

But more joy. At least he hoped Cameron would see it that way.

He felt Cameron stir beside him. He turned over. Cameron blinked and looked around curiously for a minute. Then his face cleared and he turned over on his side. "It took me a minute to remember where I was."

"What? You forgot about last night?" Josh asked in mock indignation.

"Hell no, I didn't forget last night." He smiled sheepishly. "I don't usually spend the night with my lovers. I usually go home afterward."

"I feel honored."

Cameron held out his arms and Josh slid into them. He snuggled next to Cameron's hard, warm body. His shoulders were broad and his arms were ropy with muscles. Josh ran his fingers through the thick pelt of dark blond hair on his chest and placed a tender kiss on his shoulder. "I'm glad you stayed," he murmured into Cameron's bare skin.

"After the kind of sex we had last night? You're damn right I stayed. I meant it, Josh. I have never in my life had sex like that."

"It was a whole 'nother ball game."

Cameron kissed Josh's forehead. "Up to playing a little more ball?" He rose up and met Josh's lips in a hot, sensuous kiss.

Josh slid his arms around Cameron's narrow waist. "Which of us is up to bat?"

"Either. Or we can go for ice cream this morning." He grinned wickedly.

Josh laughed. "You know, I may be sorry I ever said that."

"You may. I don't intend to let you forget it." Cameron ran his hand lightly over Josh's cock. "Ice cream it is."

They kissed some more and then began nibbling a leisurely trail down one another's bodies. The sharp edge of their passion having been slaked the night before, their progress was slow and languid, their kisses and caresses leisurely, but no less sensual.

Josh trembled as Cameron kissed and licked his way down his chest and stomach, his lips hot and moist, his tongue warm and rough against Josh's bare flesh. He loved touching Cameron, his lover's skin warm and velvety where Josh's lips roamed.

Slowly, slowly they made their way down one another's bodies. Waists. Stomachs. And then lower.

Josh took Cameron's throbbing cock into his mouth, hard as a rock, yet velvety to the touch. He gasped as he felt Cameron take his cock deep into his mouth and suck, at first gently and then with increased pressure as Josh swelled. Slow, fast, hard, soft. Josh found himself mimicking Cameron's touch. Harder and harder, higher and higher, until they exploded in shudders of mutual climaxes. Josh's orgasm seemed to go on, as Cameron jerked violently in his mouth.

Damn.

Josh waited until the last of Cameron's tremors faded, then slowly pulled back, releasing Cameron's softening cock as Cameron released his. They scooted back and stared at one another with satisfaction. "We didn't even need chocolate sprinkles," Cameron teased.

Josh smiled wickedly. "No. I'd rather taste myself on your mouth."

"I could oblige." He leaned forward and they kissed long and lingeringly, savoring the taste of one another as they licked, nipped, and nibbled. "Better?" Cameron asked.

"You bet."

They scooted up and propped pillows against the headboard. "So are we still on for the museum?" Cameron asked.

"Picasso, for sure. We can make breakfast here or hit this little bagel place over in Alamo Heights. Let me double-check with *Bubbe* about the kids and we can shower and get ready." He punched in *Bubbe*'s number and Ella answered. "Checking on the children."

"They're good. I'm glad you called. How soon are you going to be here to get them?"

"If it's not a problem, I was hoping to leave them a few more hours so Cameron and I could see the Picasso exhibit at the McNay."

"Actually, there is a problem."

"Is *Bubbe* all right?" he demanded.

Ella laughed. "Madder than a wet hornet, but otherwise fine. Her manager and assistant manager at the downtown store got into it this morning and the manager fired half the sales force, most of which were the assistant manager's hires. Both men are threatening to walk out and there's barely a skeleton staff to cover sales this morning. On a Saturday, no less."

"She has to go down and straighten out the mess." Josh felt his face fall. "I'll shower and come straight over."

"Thanks."

He clicked off and turned to Cameron. "*Bubbe* has a crisis at the downtown store and has to go and straighten it out. They need me to pick up the children ASAP."

Cameron's eager expression cooled. "I thought you said they could keep the children. I thought we were good for at least the morning."

Cameron was put out.

Tough shit. "No, I assumed they could, based on *Bubbe*'s usual leisurely Saturday. But she has to go in and I have to get the children."

"Can you get another sitter?"

"At this late date, I don't see how. Carmela needs at least three days' lead time." Josh hoped his exasperation didn't show. He crawled out of bed and gathered clean underwear from his dresser.

"It wouldn't be the same, but I'll probably take them to the Dozeum or the park. You're more than welcome to come with us."

"No, thanks. I'll pass," Cameron muttered.

"I'm sorry. I was looking forward to it."

Cameron was quiet for a minute. "It doesn't matter." He got out of bed and reached for his duffel. "It's no big deal."

Then why are you being such an asshole about it? Josh forced himself to smile. "You want to take a shower before you go?"

"Nah. I'll shower at home." He threw on his jeans and a concert tee shirt before taking Josh into his arms. "It was really great. We need to do it again. Soon."

"We do. I'll check my calendar and we can make a date for next weekend." He slid his arms around Cameron's shoulders. "I need one for the road before you walk out of here."

Cameron tightened his hold and lowered his head. Their kiss was hard and sweet.

Josh walked Cameron to the door and stood at the window as Cameron drove away. He knew Cam was pissed off by their change in plans, but he was going to have to learn. As much as Josh liked him, as much as he wanted a relationship, the children came first.

Cam was going to have to get used to it.

Josh swallowed as he went back in the house.

At least he hoped Cameron would get used to it. Some lovers never did.

***

Hot air shimmered up off the sidewalk as Cameron pulled into one of the angled parking places in front of the Durango. He normally parked in the back lot, but he was only going to be here long enough to sign some paperwork, and he didn't want to disturb whatever rehearsal was going on in the storeroom-turned-rehearsal studio. Jessica and Rachel loved having the additional space. Everyone else was griping good-naturedly about the inconvenience of either disturbing rehearsals or having to walk all the way around the block to the front door. Cameron considered it a toss-up. It was a minor adjustment in the overall scheme of things, and he wasn't going to waste time worrying about it.

The blast of air conditioning was a welcome relief. It was only June, but summer in San Antonio was already in full swing and a lot of San Antonians were already hiding behind air conditioning, or burying themselves neck-deep in the swimming pool. Others, particularly those with children, were braving the heat. Last week Josh had come to the door for their date red-faced and sweaty, having just gotten home from an afternoon at the zoo with the children. He'd taken a few minutes to shower and change, which had earned them a glare for being late from the maître d' at the new restaurant. Cameron had bitten his lip rather than comment on it. Josh was trying. He really was, but sometimes Cameron felt like an afterthought.

Josh wasn't in his office, but he heard his lover's voice down the corridor along with feminine voices and giggles. Mystified, he followed the sound down the hall and stopped in his tracks in front of Miranda's cubby, where Josh, Jessica, Rachel, and Miranda were clustered around Princess Fiona. Cameron blinked. The makeup, hair, and costume were spot on, to the point that there was no way he could tell who was under the makeup and wig. He whistled under his breath. "Miranda, you've outdone yourself." He peered at Princess Fiona. "Who's under there?"

Miranda looked at the girl proudly. "It's Emma. Barbara and Byron's granddaughter."

The girl whose father Josh had thrown out of the theater.

Thank goodness she'd come back. There had been some talk the child was too embarrassed to return.

Emma grinned as much as she could under the Fiona face. "I guess that means the makeup works."

"It really does. I'm looking forward to opening night."

"Thanks, Mr. Heiser." The girl beamed under the green.

Josh turned to Cameron. "Did you find those papers I need you to sign?"

"Nope. Just got here. You want to show me what and where?"

"Will do. Ladies, will you excuse us?"

The two of them ducked out and went down to Josh's office. Cameron shut the door with a decisive click and held out his arms. "Come here. I need my Josh fix."

"I need my Cameron fix."

They moved into one another's arms for a long, hot, sexy kiss. Cameron felt his cock start to swell. Damn, he was horny. Holding Josh in his arms only made it worse. Josh had not been able to get a babysitter last weekend and it had been nearly two weeks since they'd been able to be together. Which was too damned long.

They held one another for long minutes. When they loosened their hold and took a step back, he said, "I've missed you in my arms."

"I've missed you too." He grinned. "But we're good for Saturday night. Carmela's covering me for the show and said she could stay as late as I needed her to." It was the first weekend of *Shrek* and typically Josh made all three performances on opening weekend.

"Does that include until morning?"

"It does. We can spend the night together gazing out your picture window and doing all kinds of things that don't involve sleeping."

"What about Sunday? Any possibility there?"

Josh's smile dimmed. "Not really. I'm taking the kids to the show, and then to *Bubbe*'s for dinner." He paused for a beat. "Would you like to come with us Sunday? *Bubbe* would love to have you."

"No," he said a little too quickly. "I don't want to impose."

Josh opened his mouth and closed it. "Okay then. We'll go out Saturday night after the show and spend the night at your place." He handed Cameron a stack of papers. "I put sticky notes on all the places you need to sign."

Cameron sat down at Josh's desk and started going through the papers. Josh sank into his chair. "Come on, weekend," he murmured.

Cameron looked up. Josh looked tired. Really tired. He had deep circles under his eyes and his face was drawn. "Are you all right?"

Josh smiled weakly. "Sure. It's fatigue. Same as the rest of the world."

Cameron wasn't so sure of that. But for now, he'd take Josh's word for it.

***

Josh leaned against Cameron's sofa and stared out the window at the downtown San Antonio skyline, his nude body dimly illuminated by the glow coming through the window. "I never get tired of this view," he said as he rubbed his hand up and down Cameron's side.

Cam was sprawled out in front of him on the fluffy duvet they'd thrown down on top of the thick area rug in the sitting area in front of the windows. Together, the rug and the duvet were comfortable, and Cameron had gone to sleep more than once while enjoying the spectacular view.

They had not been back to Josh's since their first night together, and the floor in front of the window had sort of become their spot for talking and gazing at the view and having sex. After the show tonight, they'd left Miranda to lock up and had broken every speed law to get here. Their sex had been a frenzy of want and need, touching and tasting and stroking one another. The room smelled of sex, and the floor was littered with empty condom wrappers. An almost-empty tube of lube sat on the end table beside two empty wineglasses and a seriously depleted cheese tray. Cameron stretched and glanced over his shoulder at the sweating bottle of wine on the kitchen bar. "You want a little more wine?"

"Don't mind if I do," Josh murmured. Cameron reached for the wine and poured them each another glass. "Mmm, this is delicious," Josh hummed as he sipped the Cabernet. "I've about forgotten what a good bottle of wine tastes like."

Cameron tried and failed to hide his wince. "Too pricy?"

"No occasion to drink it. It doesn't exactly go with peanut butter sandwiches and Cheetos." He looked over at the cheese tray. "You mind if I kill the rest of the cheese? Not much opportunity to nibble this anymore either."

"I'm sorry," Cameron murmured.

"It is what it is," Josh said. "Part and parcel of being a parent." He yawned. "Sorry." He looked embarrassed. "Long day."

"What time did you get up?" Cameron sipped his wine.

"Beth and Pepper were up by seven. Since then, I guess."

"You couldn't have parked her in front of cartoons for a couple of hours?"

"She's still young enough to need supervision. Plus, she was hungry. It's okay. I don't mind."

He was wearing himself out. The bags under his eyes were even deeper tonight. Josh might not be all that old, but he was juggling a lot of responsibility, between the Durango and the children, and he was doing his best to make time to see Cameron. Maybe that wasn't such a good idea, Cameron thought as guilt washed over him. Maybe

Josh was doing too much, trying to fit in dates along with everything else he had going on. "You should've told me how long you've been up. We could have postponed."

"Until when?" Josh asked. "As it is, it's been two weeks. It was tonight or God knows when."

Cameron bit his lip. Was a casual thing like they had going worth Josh's exhaustion? A relationship would be one thing. But this wasn't a relationship. For want of a better word, it was a fling. High-class booty calls. A few nights of fun.

Even if sometimes it felt like a whole lot more.

He drew in a deep breath. "If it's too much for you, maybe it'd be better if we stopped seeing each other."

Josh sat straight up and looked at him in horror. "Too much for me. Stop seeing each other. Whatever makes you think that?"

"Trying to fit us in with everything else you have going on. Is it too much?"

"*No,* it's not too much. It's not like I get to spend hours and hours with you. Hell, it's been two weeks since I saw you last. It may be another two before we can get together again. I would hardly call that too much." He leaned down and gave Cameron a hard, swift kiss.

Cameron's arms tightened around him and they held on to one another in a kiss that was more reassurance than passion. They rolled onto the soft duvet, not letting go of one another, and it wasn't long before Josh had fallen asleep in Cameron's arms.

Cameron found sleep elusive. Despite Josh's reassurance, the nature of what was happening between them was beginning to worry him. This was supposed to be casual, fun, nothing serious. But there was nothing lighthearted or casual about the way they came alive in one another's arms. There was real caring there. Josh's eagerness to go out with him despite being exhausted was going a lot further than a booty call warranted. They were getting into dangerous territory. They were starting to care too much.

Damn it. They needed some distance. They needed not to try so hard. If they went a few weeks without seeing one another, that was okay. They needed to keep it casual. They needed to not care so much.

Anything else was a disaster waiting to happen.

Chapter Thirteen

Josh clipped Pepper's leash onto his collar and called down the hall. "Get a move on or there's not gonna be any food left in the stalls."

Jackson came running down the hall, dressed in a red shirt and orange shorts. Josh took one look at him and shook his head. "No. Just no. Jackson. We've talked about this."

Jackson looked down at his clothes. "What's wrong?"

"Red and orange together? You know it doesn't go. Switch out the shorts to gray or black."

"Uncle Josh, it doesn't matter. Not really."

"It does to me."

"Awww."

"Humor me. I'm old and cranky."

"Awwright."

Jackson disappeared and Beth appeared a moment later, perfectly coordinated in pink shorts and a matching tee with lace around the neck. "Do I look okay?" she asked.

"Perfectly beautiful. Jackson, the black shorts are much better. Thanks for indulging me."

"S'kay."

"Are we ready?"

The kids nodded. Josh locked up behind them and they started on foot toward Woodlawn Lake and the Fourth of July festival, complete with live music and dancing, a carnival with games and rides, a mechanical bull, children's activities, a 5K run, food and drink, and a fireworks show at dusk.

Last year he'd done the run, but this year he had the children in tow and they would spend their time doing things Beth and Jackson enjoyed. American flags flew from nearly every front porch in the neighborhood, and red, white, and blue bunting decorated windows and railings.

The kids had plenty to talk about as they walked the blocks to the park adjoining the small lake. They were both enrolled in the Academy summer camp and appeared to be having a ball.

Josh listened with half an ear, the other half of him thinking about his last date with Cameron. It had been harder to arrange dates than he'd thought it would be. Both Carmela and the teenage girl he used on occasion were popular sitters and often booked far in advance, and he'd be damned if he imposed on *Bubbe* and Ella too often.

He and Cameron still managed to see one another, slipping away last week for a night together in a Fredericksburg bed-and-breakfast. They'd dined on exquisite schnitzel with all the trimmings at a German bistro before enjoying live music and wine at a couple of the wineries also offering evening entertainment. Their luxurious room overlooked the beautiful creek meandering through town, and they'd enjoyed the view while indulging in more wine and each other until they'd fallen asleep in one another's arms.

He was getting hard thinking about it.

The sex was spectacular, but they were building a real relationship, with affection and all the things a good relationship had. It was why he was trying so hard. He and Cameron had something special, and as far as he was concerned, it was worth all the hassle, the juggling, and the sleepless nights to see where it would take them. Even if they didn't eventually end up under the canopy, their now was real.

It was glorious.

They could hear the live band from a block away. Pepper barked and pulled on the leash. The children started to run ahead and Josh grabbed for their hands, nearly dropping the leash in the process. "Stay with me," he said firmly. "You don't want to get lost in the crowd."

It was hot, crowded, and noisy, and they enjoyed every minute of it. They stuffed themselves on fajita tacos, sausage on a stick, and *gorditas*, washed down with sodas.

He introduced the kids to the pleasures of *bunuelos,* and after a session in the children's section, treated themselves to a second round of the sugary, cinnamon-flavored treats. They rode a couple of the rides and Josh tried and failed to win a stuffed monkey at the carnival.

Come sunset they settled down in the grass, and the three of them watched with childlike delight as a dazzling display of fireworks lit up the sky. Afterward, he shepherded the tired children down the sidewalk to the house. The day had been almost perfect.

It would have been perfect if Cameron had been with them.

His smile dimmed. He'd asked Cameron to come. He'd asked Cameron to do a lot of things with them since they'd begun dating. But his lover had yet to take him up on any of his invitations. There was always a reason. He didn't want to impose on *Bubbe*. He had a custom job that had to be finished. He was taking his mother someplace. If Josh didn't know better, he'd think Cameron was doing his best to avoid being around the children. Which was strange.

He'd jumped into this relationship wholeheartedly. A relationship that was inevitably going to involve Jackson and Beth. It would have to involve the children if it was going to survive.

The children weren't going anywhere.

They all tumbled into the house. With the grime and all the sweating the children had done, Josh insisted on showers. Beth was so tired she fell into bed and was asleep by the time he kissed her good night. Jackson was propped up on a pillow reading a story on his iPad. "I had fun today," he said when Josh came in to tell him good night.

"So did I."

"You know what else the Fourth is? Mom always said it was her signal to start planning my birthday party. It's coming up in two weeks. Is it a signal for you, too?"

Birthday? Oh my God. He'd completely forgotten about it.

And here he thought he had the parenting gig all figured out.

"Uh, yes, it sure is," Josh said quickly. "What do nine-year-olds do for a birthday party these days?"

"There was a swimming pool at the lake. Why don't we have a swimming party? I love to swim, and so do my friends."

He didn't know the first thing about putting together a swim party, but there were plenty of Durango parents who did. He would talk to some of them tomorrow and put together a plan. "That sounds like fun. Let me make a few phone calls and see if the pool will let us do that. If they say yes, a swimming party it is."

Jackson threw his arms around Josh's neck. "Thanks, Uncle Josh. You're the best uncle in the whole world."

That right there made all the sleep deprivation worth it.

He kissed Jackson good night and sat down at the kitchen table with his iPad. A satisfied smile graced his lips a few minutes later. He would find out for sure tomorrow, but a swim party seemed doable.

He loaded up the notepad function and started making a guest list. They would invite all the kids in Jackson's Academy class. He would see if Jackson wanted to invite any of the children in his class at school. There were some little ones they could include as well. Letti and Jessica's little girls were too small, but Julie Abonce could certainly splash a bit in the water, and Vivi would enjoy the cake and the company. As would *Bubbe* and Ella.

Of course he'd include Cameron. Despite his ongoing resistance, Cameron wasn't going to skip something as important as Jackson's birthday. His nephew was celebrating a milestone, and Cameron would be there to celebrate with them.

Because that's what people in relationships did.

***

Josh kept one eye on the pool as he unloaded paper napkins and cups from the grocery sacks. The shallow end was filled to the brim with Jackson's classmates both from school and from the Academy. As one of the Academy mothers had suggested, he hired four off-duty lifeguards to supervise the party and organize some water games. Currently, the kids were engaged in an energetic game of keep-away. They were shrieking and laughing, and seemed to be having a wonderful time. He scanned the crowd and spotted Jackson, who sported a happy smile as he bounced the ball toward one of his teammates. Josh smiled with satisfaction. The guest of honor was having a great time.

Looking at him, Josh found it hard to believe the child had lost his only remaining parent less than a year ago.

Maybe that meant Josh was doing a good job as a parent. He sure hoped so.

Academy dad Jake carried in the cooler with the sodas and ice cream. "Where do you want me to put this?" he asked.

"There's room on the second table for now. Once the ice cream and sodas are unloaded, we can put it over by the loungers."

Jake set the cooler on the table. Josh snickered as Jake copped a feel of his girlfriend Marci's butt as he walked past her. Marci and Vivi were setting up the main table where Jackson would blow out his birthday candles and the children would enjoy cake and ice cream. Jake had already brought in a smaller cooler that contained adult beverages and snacks. "You need to have something for the grown-ups as well," *Bubbe* had instructed him. "Some of us have outgrown cake and ice cream. Even if you haven't."

He'd laughed and bought the same cheese tray Cameron treated him to on their evenings together. He added an assortment of crackers and a fruit tray.

Speaking of. Where was Cameron? He'd sent Cam the same emailed invitation everyone else had gotten. He hadn't heard from his lover but assumed Cameron would be here. Not to worry, he told himself. It was early yet. *Bubbe* hadn't arrived as well. Cameron would be here sooner or later. Josh was sure of it.

Jake and the women helped Josh get the tables set up. *Bubbe* and Ella arrived and Ella helped his grandmother get settled in a folding lounge chair with an attached umbrella. *Bubbe* sported a fashionable pair of capris with a flowy top that would do a world-class resort proud. "You look so pretty, Mrs. Goldstein," Vivi said as she gave her a quick hug. "You make the rest of us look bad." Vivi wore a modest bikini and Marci a skimpy-cut one-piece, and both were wet from the pool.

"Girls, if I had a body like yours I'd have less on than you do," *Bubbe* said dryly.

Bubbe and Ella entertained Julie, who was parked in her stroller watching everything going on around her. The adults got the table set and the food put out. The lifeguards finished the games, and Josh called the children to the picnic table. He glanced toward the entrance and then toward the parking lot. No Mustang. No Cameron. Josh was beginning to get worried. Since he hadn't gotten a *failure to deliver* notice, the email had to've gone through. Cameron had known about the party. Maybe he'd been held up. Josh pulled out his phone. No message, no text, no email. Perhaps Cameron hadn't texted because he was on his way. Josh would give it a few more minutes before he became concerned.

The minutes ticked by, and Josh forced his attention back to Jackson's party. They all sang "Happy Birthday," and the adults passed out sodas and plates of cake and ice cream. It took a bit of doing, but he'd persuaded Jackson his guests would rather return to the pool than watch him open gifts. While the lifeguards resumed water games, the adults carted the gifts to Josh's car and then sat down at the table by themselves to enjoy the adult snacks, laughing when Jake cut a huge piece of cake to go with his other food. "What can I say? I'll never outgrow chocolate cake," the man laughed.

Josh choked down his disappointment at Cameron's continued absence, and tried to enjoy the company of his guests. Vivi sat Julie on her lap and fed the baby small globs of cake and icing. Julie took one bite and batted her hands up and down for more. "Look at that. She loves it," Vivi crowed.

"You didn't know that?" Josh asked.

"This is her first cake."

"Man, babies always love cake," Jake said. "My daughter Angela loved it."

"Not always," Marci said. "Monique didn't and still isn't all that fond of it. I cut her a teeny piece today and doubled the ice cream."

"Every baby in our family loved it," *Bubbe* said. She pointed to Josh. "This one climbed up on the table and got into his sister's birthday cake one year." Josh groaned and shook his head.

Vivi's eyes danced wickedly. "Tell us more, Mrs. Goldstein."

Bubbe was happy to oblige and filled them in on every embarrassing story she could think of. The parents started to arrive and one by one the young guests were spirited away. When they were down to *Bubbe*, Ella, Vivi, the children, and him, he told Beth and Jackson they could have a couple more minutes in the pool and sat down. "You ladies want another soda?" he asked. "Or do you all need to get home?"

Bubbe and Ella nodded. "I'd love a soda," Vivi said. "Miguel's on a job site and won't be home for a while."

Josh fished out another soda for each of them. "You had a good turnout," Vivi said as she plunked Julie into her stroller and took the soda.

"You certainly did," *Bubbe* said. "It reminded me of some of your birthday parties."

He glanced toward the parking lot. "The only no-show was Cameron."

"Cameron?" Vivi looked surprised. "Why would you have invited him?"

It was Josh's turn to be surprised. "I thought he'd want to come," he said, blushing a little. "That's kind of what you do when you're in a relationship with someone. You come to events important to them."

Vivi got a strange look on her face. "I didn't realize you and Cameron were in a relationship."

"I don't know what else you'd call it," he said slowly, not sure how much he wanted to say in front of his grandmother.

"He said... I thought you were dating. Mostly casual. Nothing heavy." Vivi looked uneasy.

"He said"? What the hell had Cameron said to her?

Bubbe's eyes narrowed. She looked from Josh to Vivi, but said nothing. "Semantics," he said quickly. "That's all."

"I...I'm sure that's it," Vivi stammered. "Have you been pleased with the way the *Shrek* performances have gone?" she added in a rush.

Something was wrong. Something was seriously off if an actress of Vivi's talent couldn't hide it. *I thought you were just dating. Mostly casual. Nothing heavy.*

Cameron must have told her that.

Why would Cameron lie about their relationship? Why wouldn't he be willing to tell his own sister how close they were? What they meant to one another?

Unless it didn't mean to Cameron what it meant to him.

Despite the July heat, a shard of ice pierced through Josh's heart. Maybe what they had meant nothing more to Cameron than great sex and a few laughs. Why had he told Josh he wanted to go out on a "real date" if he didn't want the real relationship that went with it?

Damned if he knew. But he'd sure as hell be finding out.

Vivi was on her way a few minutes later. *Bubbe* stood with her walker so Ella could pack up the folding chair. She reached out her hand to Josh. "Are you in what you young folks call a relationship?" she asked quietly.

"It feels like a relationship to me," he said tightly. "There's a whole lot more going on than...than...you know." He felt his face turn bright red. "At least there is on my part."

She looked troubled. "He's not Jewish."

"*Bubbe*, this is San Antonio. I don't know which is smaller, the gay community or the Jewish community. What are the chances of me finding a Jewish man to fall in love with? Besides, now I'm wondering how serious he is about us. You heard his sister."

"It might behoove you to have a talk with him," she said. "Find out how he feels. How serious he is." She patted his arm. "Your generation, God love you, but you put the cart before the horse. You jump into bed, and then try to work things out. We talked first."

"And then you jumped into bed?" he asked.

Ella choked back a laugh. *Bubbe* snorted and swatted his arm. "Talk to him. It's not only you that's involved." She tilted her head toward the pool. "You have to take them into consideration as well."

Josh nodded. "I know that. Believe me. I know that."

"I know you do, Joshie." *Bubbe* and Ella said their good-byes.

He gathered up the kids and drove home, where he and Beth spent a good hour watching Jackson open his gifts. Miracle of miracles, his teenaged sitter was free, so as soon as the kids were in bed he hopped in the car and headed toward Southtown, hoping Cameron was home and not, dread the thought, out with another man. The Mustang was in Cameron's designated parking slot and light shone from his big window.

Josh fought down the urge to drive right by the building and go home. His heart was sledgehammering in his chest, and his palms were sweaty. He didn't know what he was going to find out when he confronted Cameron, and a part of him didn't want to know. If what he feared was correct, his lover had been playing him for a fool.

But he needed to know one way or the other. He parked in one of the guest spaces. The doorman recognized him from previous visits and waved him through. He almost chickened out at the elevator, but took a deep breath and rode up to Cameron's floor. He knocked on the door, quietly at first and then with more volume. It seemed like forever but it was probably less than a minute before Cameron answered the door. "Josh?" He looked surprised. "Did we have a date tonight? I thought you had the birthday party."

"I did. It's over," he said tightly.

"Come on in."

Cameron's smile didn't quite reach his eyes. He wasn't happy to see Josh.

Josh stepped inside. A man about Cameron's age sat on the sofa. Neither of them was dressed to go out and the condo smelled of Chinese takeout. Jealousy stabbed Josh in the gut as he looked across the room at the good-looking man and his hands clenched into fists that longed to poke a hole in the wall.

His worst fears had been confirmed. Cameron was seeing another man.

He looked from Cameron to the man and he felt his face tighten. "I'm sorry I interrupted," he said, taking a step backward. "We can talk later."

The man looked at Josh and rose from the sofa. "Not necessary. I need to be on my way." He wasn't quite smiling as he crossed the room and offered his hand. "I don't believe we've ever met. Trevor Marquart. Cam and I go back a long way."

"Oh. Sorry. Trevor, this is Josh Goldstein. The executive director at the Durango. Josh, this is Trevor. He moved into the condo below mine."

Josh gritted his teeth. "Nice to meet you." He shook Trevor's hand, hoping his antipathy toward Cameron's friend didn't show. Cameron gestured to the cartons on the kitchen counter. "There's plenty if you want to make a plate."

"I'll pass."

"I'm outta here," Trevor said. He looked at his watch. "Pat should be here in a few minutes."

Josh felt another stab of jealousy when Cam gave Trevor a bro hug. "Good luck tonight."

"Thanks. I need it."

Trevor left and Cam shook his head. "I don't know why they don't go ahead and end it and put everyone out of their misery."

"End what?"

"Their marriage. Trevor moved out because of the kids, but he and Pat still get together all the time. I don't know why they both insist on hanging on."

"Maybe they love each other," Josh said tightly.

"I'm sure they do. Sometimes that's not enough. Anyway, come on in and sit down. Or did you want me to throw on some clothes so we can go out?"

Josh gestured to his jeans and tee. "I didn't come over for that. I want to talk to you."

"Okay." Cam took his usual easy chair and left Josh the sofa. "What's on your mind?"

Josh hesitated for a moment then plunged in. "Today was Jackson's birthday party."

"I know. You sent me the notice so I would know we couldn't go out tonight. Although I guess we could've."

"That's not why I sent you the invitation. I sent it to invite you to the party."

"Oh." He laced his fingers in front of him. "Was it a nice party?"

"It was a great party," Josh said tightly. "I thought you'd want to be there." He paused but Cameron said nothing. "It's the kind of thing someone in a relationship would do."

Cameron sat up straight and looked at him. "It is. If we were in a relationship, I would have gritted my teeth and gone. But we're not in a relationship," he said more gently.

"Then what in the hell would you call it?" Josh said tightly. "No. Wait. Just dating. Mostly casual. Nothing heavy. How'm I doing?"

Cameron's eyes narrowed. "Actually, you couldn't have described it any more perfectly. Because that's all it is, Josh. A hot and heavy affair with an expiration date. You know that."

"That's not the impression you gave me."

Cameron raised his eyebrow and looked at him coolly. "When did I give you the impression it was anything but casual?"

"That night at the Mexican food place. When we talked about going out. You said you wanted to go on a 'real' date." Josh held up his fingers in quote signs. "You said a 'real' date and that means a real relationship."

"In what world?" Cameron asked shortly. "It doesn't mean a relationship. It means sex. Hot, sweaty sex like we've had on the rug here. That's all."

Josh took a jagged breath and willed the tears not to fall. "None of it meant anything to you. The lengths I went to so we could get together. The nights I gave to you instead of spending them with the kids. I turned myself inside out to have a relationship with you, and to you it's *casual*?"

"Yes, that's all it is to me. It's all there's ever gonna be for you and me. You've been deluding yourself if you think otherwise."

Josh sucked in his breath and cursed the tears that threatened to overflow. "You deliberately left me with the wrong impression. You said a 'real' date. I thought you meant a real relationship and you knew it."

"The hell I did. Damn it, Josh, you're the one who came up with the real relationship in your mind. You should've known from the outset I'm not and never will be willing to get involved with you for real."

Josh jerked back as though he'd been slapped. "The kids," he said dully.

"Yes, the kids." Cameron ran his fingers through his hair. "You know how I feel about that. Gay men and families don't mix, I don't care how sweet-smelling the unicorn farts are at the Aldrete households. Trevor and Pat—"

"Maybe Pat oughta slap shit out of the brats and be done with it," Josh snapped. "If the kids are being assholes, it's the parents' fault. You think a Jewish father would put up with that?"

"I have no idea. That's the other thing. Even if I was completely on board with gay families in general, which I'm not, you're raising Jackson and Beth in the Jewish faith. If you do end up with somebody someday, he has to be willing and able to teach them about their heritage. I couldn't do that. Hell, Josh, I can't be anything those kids need if I wanted to. Which I don't. I want *no part* of kids in any way, shape, or form. You knew that and chose to ignore it."

"No, I thought you'd had a change of heart. My bad." Josh sniffed. "At least about a relationship, if not about them. Thank you for clarifying things for me."

They stared at one another for a minute. "Are we good?" Cameron asked.

Josh stood. "What you want is a booty call every so often. You don't want my love. You don't want all the good things I could offer you because I'm raising a couple of children who lost their parents, and you don't want to be bothered with them."

Cameron looked at him with exasperation. "Shitty way to put it, but that's pretty much it. I *don't* want any part of children, yours or anybody else's. It's casual or nothing."

"Then it's nothing. You can take your booty calls and shove them up your ass. I won't be the boy toy of a middle-aged Peter Pan who wants the good sex and nothing more. I want a *real* man who wants to be part of all of my life, including the part with the kids."

"Good luck finding him," Cameron snarled.

Josh curled his lip. "He's out there somewhere. If he's not, so be it. The kids come first." He looked at Cameron, anger and sadness warring within him. "It's a shame you're such an ass. We could have had something really wonderful."

Cameron sat frozen. Josh spared him a look of disgust before throwing his shoulders back and marching out.

He made it as far as his car before dissolving into tears.

He'd been stupid. Plain stupid. He'd known damned well Cameron didn't want any part of his children or the life he led with them, and he'd gotten involved with him anyway. He'd made the mistake of starting to really care about a man who wanted nothing more from him than hot sex.

He'd be damned if he invested one more minute with a man who felt that way.

They might be few and far between, but there were men out there who'd be good with him having children. Who would want to be part of their lives.

That was the kind of man Josh needed.

If and when he could get Cameron Heiser out of his system.

Chapter Fourteen

Cameron leaned against the side of the pool and sipped his Corona. The hot August sun beat down on his hat and shoulders, and heat shimmered up from the concrete surrounding the pool in Vivi and Miguel's backyard. His mother, aunt, and the Abonce ladies had taken a few pictures of Julie in the water and retreated to the air conditioning for some lively rounds of Trivial Pursuit, leaving only him, Vivi, Miguel, and Julie in the pool. Vivi held Julie as the little girl kicked and splashed in the water, water wings on her arms providing a second layer of safety. "She does love it in here," he commented to Miguel as Julie enthusiastically kicked her legs in an attempt to get away from her mother.

"Yep." Miguel looked at Julie and held out his arms. "Come to Daddy, princess. Let go of her, Vivi, and see if she can kick her way over to me."

"You're a little far," Vivi said. She moved until she and Julie were only about five feet from where he and Miguel stood in the water. "Okay, Julie. Go to Daddy." She turned Julie toward Miguel and gave her a little push.

The three adults held their breath. Julie bobbed in the water for a minute before kicking her feet. Unfortunately, she remained stationary with her legs pointing straight down. Vivi tried to turn her so that her legs would propel her, but the minute she let go Julie was again bobbing aimlessly and getting more frustrated by the minute. The child set up a howl and reached out her arms to her mother. "Okay, okay," Vivi said as she scooped the baby up and held her close. "We're not dog-paddling to Daddy this afternoon."

"Daddee! Daddee! Daddee!" She held out her arms toward Miguel.

"Come here, Princess. Daddy has you," Miguel crooned. He looked over Julie's head to Vivi. "We'll try again in a couple of weeks." He turned to Cameron with a huge grin. "Being a dad. There's nothing better in this world. Ya know?"

"If you say so," Cameron murmured.

"Actually, he doesn't," Vivi said tartly, kicking over to them and leaning against the side of the pool. "Not one bit interested, are you, Cam?" There was a bite in her tone.

"No, I'm not." Cameron's eyes narrowed. "Everyone in my life knows it."

"If they didn't, they certainly do now." She picked up his bottle and took a huge drink.

"That's my damned beer. Get your own."

"Tough. It's hot and I don't feel like getting out of the water."

Miguel looked from Vivi to Cameron. "Is there something I'm missing?"

"No," they said in unison.

"Whatever. Princess, want to play with your rubber duckie and leave the two grouches over here?" Miguel treated them to a knowing smirk and waded Julie over to her basket of toys on the other side of the pool.

Cameron waited until Miguel had Julie out of earshot. "You've had a cobb up your butt ever since I walked in your door today. Care to tell me what it's about?"

"You know damned well what it's about. You were an ass to Josh, dumping him because of the kids."

Cameron gritted his teeth. "Actually, he's the one who told me I could take my booty calls and shove them up my ass as he walked out my door."

"Was that before or after you told him he couldn't ever be anything to you because of the kids?"

"It was after I reminded him that he's known all along how I felt about children and I'd never get serious about a man who had them. Damn it, Vivi, he should've known from the outset how I felt. If he chose to ignore it, I'm sorry." He took a breath. "For what it's worth, I miss him like a son of a bitch."

"I think he misses you, though I can't imagine why."

Cameron's temper flared. "Do you think I liked hurting him? You think I'm not hurting as badly if not worse than he is? You think I like having to turn my back on the best man to come my way in years?"

Vivi shook her head. "What I don't understand is why."

"Why what?"

"Why any of it. Why you didn't make damned sure he understood where you stood from the outset instead of assuming he understood. Why you insist on keeping it light and casual if he's the man of your dreams. Why you are so damned determined you want nothing to do with children. Gotta admit," she shrugged, "I don't get it."

Cameron drained what little beer Vivi had left him. "I didn't spell it out because I was afraid Josh would do exactly what he did. Tell me to take my casual hookups and shove them. Selfish, I know, but I wanted to be with him too much to risk it."

"So you lied by omission and now you're both hurting like a son of a bitch. Smooth, Cameron. Real smooth."

"I blew it. I get it."

"You need to make it right."

"I'm not sure I can," he admitted softly. "I don't know what to say that's not gonna hurt him more."

"How about 'I was wrong about the kids and I'm cool with you being a father'?"

Cameron stood up straighter. "Because *I'm not wrong,* and I'm sure as hell not cool with the children."

"Which I can't understand. This business about gay parents is complete and total BS. It's like you don't want to give that up because it's a good excuse. It gets you off the hook. Hey, I'm gay, therefore I won't be any good with kids. Why don't you admit it's not gay parenting in general that gives you hives, it's the thought of being one yourself that makes you itch."

"Vivi, dearest, I'm way ahead of you there. You're right, the thought gives me hives. I'd make a shitty parent, and I know it. No, it's not about what Dad used to say, so don't bother to trot that out. It's what I know about myself. I don't want to do all the things a good parent does. I have no interest in Dr. Seuss and PTA, and rushing to pick kids up from school. I don't want toys all over the floor, or to go shopping for Santa. I want the freedom to stay late at work if I need to, and work all day Sunday on a custom chandelier if the spirit moves me. I want the time to serve on the Durango board and do the occasional show. I want to take my vacations in Europe or Fiji, not Disneyworld. Bottom line, I like my freedom and I don't want to give it up."

Vivi was silent for a minute. "You're right. Selfish. But if that's really how you feel, okay. It's not the Cameron I grew up with. You weren't that self-centered."

"That's not fair. Selfish and self-centered? I busted my balls getting Heiser Steel back on track so the Heiser family and nearly a hundred employees wouldn't starve to death. Am I such an SOB for wanting the rest of my time for myself?"

"The company's back on track. It doesn't have to swallow either of us the way it did two years ago. You could make time for yourself, Josh, and his children if you wanted to."

"I'm no good with kids and never have been. I don't know what to say or what to do."

Vivi was quiet for a minute. "Now we're getting somewhere. All the rest of this 'gays are bad dads, you want your freedom.' It's all bullshit, and we both know it. What it amounts to is that you're scared shitless at the thought of being responsible for children."

"I'm scared to death of it because it's inevitable I'm gonna fuck it up. Those kids deserve better than me."

"So you won't get involved with Josh because you think if you do, you'll mess up the kids. Isn't that a bit of a stretch?"

"No, it's common sense. Let's play what if. What if I got involved with Josh? Inevitably it would involve the kids. What if I messed them up and they ended up like Trevor's stepkids? Vivi, you wouldn't believe the shit show that's turned into."

Vivi rolled her eyes. "Are we going there again? How bad can it be?"

"Denise is pregnant and Paul was arrested for drug possession."

"That's because their father spoiled them rotten and never set limits. Josh isn't like that. I see him with them all the time. He may be young and fun, but he sets limits and has expectations. He's good with them. There's no reason why you couldn't be as well. If you tried."

"He's gay. So am I."

"His sexuality doesn't enter into it. Neither would yours."

He reached over and patted her hand. "Vivi, I wish I believed you. I appreciate the vote of confidence more than you know. You're probably right. I doubt Josh's sexuality matters one bit, and mine probably wouldn't either. The problem is that Cameron Heiser doesn't know the first thing about kids and would be a crap-ass parent. I'm not built to be a good father. End of story."

"I hate you feel that way about yourself because you're wrong. You'd be a fine parent. I wish you weren't so down on yourself. Maybe one of these days you'll change your mind."

Cameron shrugged. "Maybe. But don't hold your breath. If I ever do, which is damned unlikely, it won't be any time soon."

***

Josh pulled in under the portico and pulled over to the curb. Beth and Jackson scrambled from their car seats and ran for the door, Beth squealing in delight as she spotted some of her little classmates. The traffic monitor stepped to the passenger window and Josh handed her a pile of paperwork. "When is the school gonna go online?" he teased as the monitor went through the pile checking off each item.

She grimaced. "Can't be soon enough." She checked off the last of the items. "You and an Ella Berger are the only people authorized to pick up the children?"

"Same as last year."

She wished him a nice day and he headed to the Durango. It was hot already. But that was August in San Antonio for you. This early in the morning, the theater was deserted. He had paperwork to do, mounds of it, but his mind kept wandering from the task. Today was Wednesday, the day Cameron frequently came by the theater to check in. Josh's stomach clenched. He'd only seen Cameron once since he left him. He and his stone-faced ex-lover had taken care of theater business in record time. Cameron left immediately after.

He'd considered trying to talk to Cameron, but from the tightness in his jaw and the polite coolness in his eyes, he figured it would do no good. He missed him badly, both in and out of bed. For the life of him, he couldn't understand why Cameron felt the way he did. Why he was so down on children he would refuse to get serious about a man with them.

He finally got into the groove and was deep in the pile of paperwork when Vivi knocked on his door with Julie in her stroller. "Well, hel-lo, Princess Julie," he said as the baby's face split into a toothy grin.

Vivi rolled her eyes. "Don't you start that too. She'll be wanting tutus and a tiara for her third birthday."

"That's okay. Tell her being a princess is a political position and it's her job to take care of her subjects."

"I'll have to remember that."

"Social visit, or are you here to audition for *Ragtime*?"

"Like I have time to do a show? Julie had a well-baby check and her pediatrician's a few blocks from here. How's it going at your house?" she asked a little too casually.

He looked at her knowingly. "You mean am I still pissed as hell at your brother and hurt beyond belief? Yep. If you're asking about the kids, they're fine and were happy to be back to school this morning."

"Glad to hear the kids are doing well, but yes, I was asking about you. When I talked to you last, you were upset."

"Still am, for all the good it will do me. Normally I would never go behind someone's back and talk about them, but I'm going to break my own rule and ask you something. Do you have any idea why Cameron's so opposed to children in his life? I don't get it. Kids are a handful. Now that I have two, I can see how much. But there's so much joy along with it. They've become the best part of my day. Except for his attitude toward children, Cameron's a nice man. Why is he so convinced he's bad for kids? Or does he think every gay man's bad for kids?"

"It's not the gay thing. I finally got him to admit it. It's *him*. He's believes he isn't good for children."

"Is it your dad talking?"

"Daddy might have started the ball rolling in that direction, but Cam's taken it well beyond anything Daddy ever said. It's a damned shame. Cameron would be fine with children if he could get past the mental roadblock. Which is a big if."

"In other words, don't get my hopes up."

"You got it."

Vivi left with a promise to have him and the children over to dinner soon. He sat down and went back through the resumes and called his most promising candidate. He was getting off that phone call when Ella came through the door with Beth and Jackson. "Miss Ella said we're going to Academy," Beth said excitedly. "She said the new classes are starting today."

"They are," he said. Beth was practically dancing on air and Jackson looked excited too.

He smiled to himself. They'd be up on the Durango stage in no time.

Jessica was her usual warm and welcoming self. "They'll be at least two hours this evening, with two classes each. As early as you got here this morning, you have time to go home and come back if you want to."

Josh thought of the pile of dirty laundry in the utility room and nodded. He went to his office and was shutting down his computer when Cameron strode in and shut the door firmly behind him. His eyes burned with lust and longing. "To hell with it," he said as he reached for Josh. "Come here. I need to kiss you."

"Why the fuck should I?"

"Because you want me as bad as I want you. Now get over here before I crawl across your desk."

Fuck it, he'd think about it later. Josh moved across the office and melted into Cameron's waiting arms. Their kiss was neither kind nor gentle as they ravaged one another. Weeks of pent-up longing exploded in a bonfire of want and need, their lips fused and their bodies plastered together.

Josh's body knew what it wanted as he pushed his groin against Cameron's thigh. Cameron's arms were wrapped around him and cupping his ass, pulling him up so their pelvises were touching. They held on to one another for long moments before Cameron loosened his hold and stepped back. "I want you," he rasped.

"I want you too," Josh said. "What about the kids?"

"Just for this afternoon, it doesn't matter." He looked at Josh's office door. "Damn. No lock."

"I live five minutes away, and the kids are in Academy for the next two hours," Josh said breathlessly.

"Lead the way."

Chapter Fifteen

Cameron pulled into Josh's driveway behind the red crossover. His hands shook on the steering wheel. For the first time in what felt like forever, he and his lover were going to be together. He leapt out of the Mustang and met Josh on the front porch. Josh's fingers trembled as he unlocked the front door. The door was barely shut when Josh slammed him up against the door and covered his lips in another scorching kiss. Cameron wrapped his arms around Josh and pressed his ass into his crotch. Josh's cock was as hard and ready as his own. His lover's chest pressed into Cameron's and Josh's arms were wound around his neck. "It's been too long," he murmured against Josh's lips.

"Too damn long and if we don't get to the bed I'm going to fuck you against the damned door," Josh replied. He took his hand and they ran through the house and didn't stop until they were standing by the bed.

Their clothes went flying, and they collapsed together in one another's arms, their hands moving all over one another's bodies. Their bodies were entwined from head to foot, with nothing between them. Late afternoon sun filtered in the closed blinds and dappled them in a hot yellow glow.

Their kisses grew more feverish, their embrace more urgent, until Josh reached into the nightstand and withdrew a strip of condoms and the lube. "Hurry," he urged. "I'm not going to last. I want you too badly."

Cameron rolled the condom over his cock. He flipped onto his stomach and Josh straddled him, easing into his body. Cameron trembled as pleasure washed over him. His body was joined to Josh's in the most intimate way possible. They were where they needed to be. They were where they were supposed to be.

Together.

They moved in tandem, slowly at first but then faster and faster until Josh exploded above him, shouting out his name as he came. Then it was Cameron's turn. He bore Josh into the comforter, covering his body and again joining them, and soon he too was crying out with pleasure as he let go. Cameron's body shivered and shook with the force of his orgasm, trembling from head to foot as powerful contractions engulfed him.

He waited until the last of the tremors died down, then withdrew from Josh's body and lay on his back with his forearm thrown over his chest. He turned his head and peered at Josh, who was staring at him. "Now that the lust is behind us, maybe we ought to try to figure out what the fuck just happened," Josh said dryly.

Cameron barked out a laugh. "If I have to explain it to you, then I must have done a shitty job of it."

Josh looked at him with exasperation. "That's not what I meant and you know it. Three weeks ago, you said you weren't interested in a relationship, and I made it clear I'm unwilling to settle for less. What we just shared was far from a booty call, and we both know it."

"I couldn't stay away. I tried. But you...me—" He gestured helplessly.

"What are we going to do?"

Cameron leaned forward. "I'm going to kiss you again. That's what we're going to do. We're going to kiss and hold on to one another until we're spent."

"But—"

"We'll talk afterward. I promise. Please, I need you again."

Josh handed over another condom. They spent long moments touching and stroking, taking their time as the excitement between them slowly grew. Their kisses were long and drugging, their caresses tender. Cameron was overcome. His heart beat harder, his skin felt tighter, his breath more jagged. His loneliness had been painful. In his empty bed with only memories to cling to in his dark bedroom, he ached for Josh.

He hadn't come to the Durango this afternoon planning to rekindle anything. But he'd taken one look at the man he missed so much and something inside of him snapped. Here they were, in bed going at each other like teenagers. They touched, stroked, and kissed and when their bodies joined, Cameron felt something he'd never experienced before. He was where he belonged.

When they were limp and spent in one another's arms, Cameron reached over and pulled Josh close to him. "I've missed you."

"I've missed you too."

Josh cuddled for a few minutes before easing out of Cameron's arms and sat up. "Where are you going?" Cameron asked as he brushed his hair out of his eyes.

"The kids' Academy classes are almost over. I need to get dressed and go get 'em."

Cameron sighed. "Now for the reality check."

"You could say that." Josh hopped up and found his boxer briefs on the floor. "Does your car have mine trapped?"

"It does." Cameron got out of bed and found his briefs. He bit his lip and looked over at Josh, who was shimmying into his jeans. "What do you think? Do we try this again?"

Josh zipped his jeans and handed Cameron his tee shirt. "I haven't changed my mind. I want a relationship. I'm not willing to settle for less." He gestured at a doll on his dresser. "I'm a parent. They may call me Uncle, but in all but name, I'm their father. That's never going to change."

"I know that. I was a selfish ass and said I didn't want a relationship. I miss you too much not to try, even if we don't get to have much time together."

"Which we won't if you expect me to keep my relationship with you separate from my life with my kids."

"That's what I want. It's already limited our time together. I understand that."

Josh said slowly, "Would you really be willing to do that? Spend what time together we can manage?"

"It beats no time at all." Cameron put his hands on Josh's shoulders and kissed him gently on the lips. "Let's give it a try."

Josh looked at him and tilted his head.

"We'll give it our best shot," Cam stated. He picked up Josh's shirt from the floor and handed it to him. "Here. We need to hurry."

Josh looked at the clock and gave a little yelp. They dressed quickly and headed for the front door. "When can we get together?" he asked as Cameron followed him out the door.

"That's up to your schedule, not mine." Cameron felt himself smile crookedly.

"I'll call my sitters and see what Saturday night looks like. That work for you?"

"It does." Cameron reached out and gave him a one-armed hug. "I'm looking forward to Saturday already."

He hopped in the Mustang and backed out. Josh hit the gas and took off for the theater. Cameron followed him more slowly down the street. He was certifiably crazy. He had to be. After years of staying as far away from children as he could, he'd just committed to a relationship with a man with a family.

He'd missed Josh too much to ignore. He could do this. Single parents had love lives separate from their families. A lot of them insisted on it. Josh could do the same. It would limit their time together, but Cameron could live with that.

Josh could have him, and Josh could have the children. Just not together.

Cameron and the kids would never work.

He knew that even if Josh didn't.

***

Cameron whistled under his breath as he locked the doors of Heiser Steel and climbed into the Mustang. The factory had been quiet on this rainy September Saturday, with only him and a pair of tacky lion gates he was finishing up. If the rain stopped, installation was scheduled for Tuesday afternoon and he would take an afternoon away from the office to supervise the project. Vivi had found an excellent office manager, much to Cameron's relief. His sister and the new manager handled the parts of running Heiser Steel he hated the most, leaving him more time for his custom projects, which were becoming a bigger part of their business by the month.

Traffic was light and he made it to his condo in record time. His cock twitched as he shucked his sweaty work clothes and took a long, hot shower. He'd been walking around with sex on his brain since he and Josh had made the date for tonight. Despite the workout in bed on Wednesday, or maybe because of it, his cock had been at half-mast for most of the week. The babysitter Josh secured was willing to put the children to bed and stay late into the night, which would give them hours to do all sorts of wonderful things to each other.

Cameron donned his best underwear and went through his checklist one more time. Condoms and lube on the coffee table. A cheese tray and a good merlot to pair with it. Reservations at an elegant downtown steak house. It was going to be as lovely an evening as he could make it.

They were officially in a relationship now, and Cameron wanted it to be a good one.

He was buttoning his shirt when his phone rang with Josh's ringtone. "Are you ready?" he asked, not bothering to hide his eagerness.

"Uh, about that. I've run into a snag. A major one."

Uh-oh. "What happened?" he asked, hoping his irritation didn't show.

"The babysitter called and canceled. She's running a hundred and two fever and sick as a dog with the flu bug. I tried a couple of her friends and they're sick too. I'm sorry, Cameron. I don't have anyone else I can call."

Cameron thought about the cheese and wine in the refrigerator and his mood took a nosedive. "What about your grandmother? Could she pinch-hit tonight?"

"She's with Ella and the Goldstein buyer at the Dallas Market or I would have called her."

"Oh." Cameron felt his spirits sink even further. "I guess everything's off for tonight."

Josh hesitated on the other end of the line. "Not necessarily. You could come over and have dinner with me and the kids. I could put them in the car and run to the grocery store for some decent steaks."

"I don't think so," Cameron said slowly.

He could feel Josh deflate over the phone. "We'd love to have you," he told Cameron quietly.

Cameron stifled a sigh. "You know how I feel about that. I told you I don't want any involvement with the children. I'm not good for them or with them."

Josh sighed audibly. "Cameron, you're wrong. I don't have time to argue the point with you right now, but I wish you would think about one thing. I'm not just a single parent. I'm their only parent. I don't have an ex-husband or wife to hand them to every other weekend and I'm totally dependent on hired help who can and will let me down on occasion."

"I know that," he said irritably.

Josh was quiet for a minute. "I'm truly sorry. I hate missing tonight as much as you do. But the kids…" He trailed off helplessly.

"I get it, Josh. Honestly."

"Thanks. I'm really sorry. Are you absolutely sure about dinner?"

Cameron hesitated. "Not tonight. Maybe later." Much later if he had his way about it.

"Stay in touch."

They said their good-byes. Cameron canceled the dinner reservation and got out the cheese tray and the gourmet crackers he'd bought to go with them. He sat down at the kitchen table and started in on the tray. Bone-chilling dread snaked down his back.

Now that they were back together, he was starting to fall for Josh in a big way. As in, falling in love with him. He wasn't sure Josh felt the same way. Josh cared about him and wanted a relationship with him, but he loved the kids more.

Josh loved being a parent. He said so on more than one occasion.

Cameron tried to swallow the cracker that'd gotten stuck in his throat. He tried and failed to shake off the icy tendrils threatening to envelop him. He wasn't stupid. If it came down to him or the kids, Josh was going to choose the children. They came first.

As they should.

Cameron got up and found a beer to wash down the crumbling cracker. It was a hard pill to swallow knowing the relationship, which was becoming so important to him, didn't come first, and with the children in the picture, probably never would. Children who deserved the best that Josh could offer them.

Children who would be better off without him in their lives.

His appetite gone, he sighed and covered the cheese plate. The onus was on him. Josh had tried to spend time with him tonight. It wasn't his fault their evening together had fallen through.

Josh was doing his best to juggle their relationship with his responsibilities as a father. Cameron was going to have to meet Josh halfway if they were going to have a snowball's chance in hell of making it work.

He picked up the phone and stared at the screen for a minute before putting it back down. It was too late to accept the invitation for tonight. Josh had probably already started cooking for him and the kids and he'd demolished half a plate of cheese slices. The next time Josh asked him to have dinner with him and the kids, he was going to accept. He was going to grit his teeth and go sit down with them and have a meal.

And hope the evening wasn't a disaster.

Chapter Sixteen

Josh put the finishing touches on a simple salad. The potatoes were boiling and almost soft enough to mash and the aroma of Ella's fried chicken wafted from the pan warming in the oven. Iced tea was chilling in the refrigerator and a pot of green beans bubbled gently on the stove. A bowl of Ella's cream gravy sat in the microwave to be heated at the last minute. He took a step back and surveyed the scene. The cooking was under control and, with the chicken already fried and the gravy already made, the quintessential Southern dinner would come together perfectly.

He hoped Cameron and the children would come together as well. What would happen at his dinner table worried him a whole lot more than the menu.

He turned to the table, shaking his head at his own foolishness. He'd angsted over the meal for three days, veering between serving something simple he knew for sure the children liked, or something more sophisticated for Cameron. He'd decided to split the difference and serve old-fashioned comfort food on everyone's list of favorites.

But he was still worried about how Cameron and the children were going to do together. He was surprised that Cameron had relented and agreed to come over for dinner. When he'd called two days ago to break another date —the sitter was still sick and *Bubbe* had come down with something as well—he'd expected his tentative invitation to be turned down. Hesitantly, Cameron had agreed to come and was due in about ten minutes.

The only thing left was to set the table. Josh stuck his head in the living room, where the kids were building an elaborate Lego structure on the floor in front of the television. "Hey, munchkins. You want to come set the table for Uncle Josh?"

Beth hopped up and headed for the table. Jackson followed more slowly. "Do I hafta?" he whined.

"You eat at this table?" Josh asked, fighting back a smile.

"Yeah. All right. I guess we have to carry our plates to the sink afterward too."

"You guessed right." He fought not to laugh. "Wash your hands before you handle the knives and forks," he reminded them as he steered them toward the sink. "Remember, we're setting it for four tonight."

Jackson went to the drawer and counted out four knives and forks and handed them to Beth. She set a knife and fork in front of each chair. "Who's coming over?" she asked as Jackson handed her the spoons.

"A good friend of mine," he said, struggling to sound casual. "His name is Cameron and we work together at the theater." He lifted the lid to check on the potatoes.

"Is he the big tall man I saw hugging you in your office when you didn't think anybody saw?" Jackson asked. "Is he your boyfriend?"

Josh dropped the lid on the counter next to the stove. *Oh hell.* "Well—"

"No, silly," Beth piped up. "They're friends. Uncle Josh can't have a boyfriend. He's a *boy*."

"Oh. All right."

Okay. They didn't teach kids about homosexuality in third grade.

"Uncle Josh could have a girlfriend," she went on. "Do you have a girlfriend, Uncle Josh?"

"No, sweetie, I don't."

Never have, never will.

He wondered how soon they would have to have the *Uncle Josh is gay* talk. Probably sooner than later. The kids weren't going to stay this uninformed for much longer.

He and Cameron really needed to put a lid on the PDA at the theater.

The doorbell rang and the kids raced to answer it. Josh followed more slowly, curious as to how Cameron and the children were going to react to one another. He found Cameron frozen in the door clutching a bottle of wine and the children chattering endlessly. "Hey, guys. How about you stop talking for a minute and invite Mr. Cameron inside?" he asked gently.

"Oh, sorry. Come on in." Beth reached out and took Cameron by the hand.

Cameron let her guide him in the house and then slipped his hand out of hers. His eyes darted from one child to the other. "Cameron, this is my niece Beth and my nephew Jackson. Kids, this is Cameron Heiser."

"Hi, glad to meet you," Jackson said, offering his hand.

"You too." Cameron took the boy's hand and shook it.

He shook Beth's hand as well and then looked at the children uncertainly. "Glad you could join us tonight," Josh said quickly. "We're set up in the kitchen. I haven't gotten around to finding a dining room table. Come on back."

The kids went back to their Lego project and Cameron followed him into the kitchen. "Smells good." He handed over a dry Riesling. "This is supposed to taste good with chicken."

"It will. Ooo. It's still cool. A couple minutes in the freezer while I mash the potatoes and it'll be ready to go." He turned to Cameron. "Thank you for coming tonight. I hope to have the sitter issue solved by next weekend." He lowered his voice. "I'm horny as hell."

"Me too. Next weekend can't come soon enough."

"Or we could—" He gestured toward the bedroom. "They go to bed early."

"You really think you can take me to bed with them right next door?" Cameron asked dryly.

"I guess not."

Although married couples seem to manage with no problem.

Maybe it was different for single parents.

He and Cameron chatted while he mashed the potatoes. He nuked the gravy and shepherded the kids through washing their hands again while Cameron poured wine for the grown-ups and milk for the children. Josh opted to serve buffet style off the counter and took a few minutes to make the children's plates, and he cut their meat while Cameron served himself. "Go ahead and start," he told the three of them. "Don't wait on me."

The children dug in. Josh served up his plate and sat in his usual spot between the children. "Referee?" Cameron asked dryly from the chair on the end.

"Sometimes. Mostly they need a bit of help now and then."

Jackson looked up indignantly. "I do not need help. She does, but I don't."

"Yes, you do." Beth glared across the table at them.

"No, I don't," Jackson shot back.

"Enough," Josh said firmly.

"But—"

"One more word and you don't eat," Josh told Jackson.

"Awright." He stuck his fork in his gravy-covered potatoes.

Josh bit back a smile. He looked across the table, expecting to see Cameron doing the same. But Cameron's expression was blank, but for faint disapproval.

Josh stifled a sigh. They were just being kids.

The table was quiet for a few minutes while they all ate their dinner. Then Josh turned to the children. "Why don't you kids tell Cameron about your Academy classes? He's part of the theater too, and I'm sure he'd be interested."

Jackson didn't have much to say, but Beth treated them all to a blow-by-blow description of her dancing class with Jessica. Josh sneaked a few peeks at Cameron, hoping he would take the hint and ask her a question or two. Cameron listened politely, but didn't ask the eager child anything, leaving Josh to prompt her with a couple more questions, and then let her wind down on her own.

Then he tried to get Cameron to tell the children about making custom gates, thinking Jackson might find it interesting. But Cameron's answers to Josh's questions were brief and awkward, and he made no attempts to talk to the children about anything else. Josh tried again with the children's school, but by then Jackson and Beth had mostly cleared their plates and were getting restless. Inwardly he threw up his hands. Cameron wasn't going to talk to the kids.

He gave up and excused the children, reminding them to take their plates to the sink. Jackson stacked his empty glass on his plate and started for the counter. Beth watched her brother and then picked up her half-filled glass of milk to do the same. But she set it on a chicken bone in the middle of her plate and it promptly overturned, splattering across the table and into Cameron's half-empty plate. Cameron jumped out of his chair and snatched up his napkin, murmuring something under his breath as a stream of milk ran off the table onto his pants.

Josh leapt up and grabbed the glass off the table. "Jackson, hand me a dish towel," he said sharply.

Jackson shoved a towel into his hand and Josh frantically wiped up the running milk. Beth put her face in her hands and burst into tears. "I'm sorry, I'm so sorry, I didn't mean to spill it."

Josh put the towel onto the table and gathered her into his arms. "It's okay, sweetie. We know you didn't. It was an accident." He glanced up at Cameron, who was watching with hooded eyes. "Everything can be wiped or washed." At least he hoped so. Cameron loved to wear clothes that had to be dry-cleaned.

He took Beth onto his lap and glanced over at Cameron's milk-covered food. "You might want to make another plate," he told Cameron. "There's plenty of food and clean plates in the cabinet."

Cameron stared down at his half-eaten dinner for a minute before making himself another. Josh got Beth settled down and helped her wash her hands before sending her into the living room to join her brother. He removed the milky towel from the table and sat down to his own lukewarm plate. "Why don't you nuke it?" Cameron asked when he took a bite and made a face.

He warmed the plate and sat down tiredly. "Is it always this exciting at dinnertime?" Cameron asked.

Josh shrugged. "Beth doesn't pour her milk all over everything at every meal. But accidents happen. It's part and parcel of raising children."

"I'm sure it is. Eat your dinner. You look exhausted."

Cameron looked like he'd rather be anyplace else.

They finished their dinner mostly in silence. They could hear the children's faint chatter coming from the living room. Under other circumstances their silence would have been comfortable, but tonight it was anything but.

While he wouldn't rate the evening a complete and total bust, it hadn't been a whopping success either. They carried their plates to the dishwasher and together they started putting away the leftovers. "The food was delicious," Cameron said finally. "Did you fry the chicken?"

"Me? Hardly. It's Ella's. Her gravy too. I did the rest." He pointed to a plate covered with aluminum foil. "Ella made a cake for *Bubbe*, and she sent half of it home with me."

"How's your grandmother feeling?"

"Better, but not great. The doctor said it's a good thing she didn't get the nasty version of the flu that's going around. It could have landed her in the hospital."

They packed away the leftovers and cut big pieces of cake. The silence between them had become almost companionable and Josh felt himself start to relax. They heard a yowl come from the living room. "That's not where it goes," Jackson said indignantly. "The houses all go on this side."

"I want some on my side too," Beth protested.

"Do you need to go intervene?" Cameron asked.

"Let's give it a minute and see if they settle it."

There was a little more give and take and things appeared to have settled down. Then they heard Jackson again. "I don't think he likes us."

"You don't think who likes us?" Beth asked.

"Mr. Cameron. He didn't want to talk to us. Just like Uncle A.J."

"Oh. But Uncle A.J. doesn't like us because we're Jews. Does Mr. Cameron not like Jews, either?"

"He likes Uncle Josh and Uncle Josh is Jewish. I don't know why he doesn't like us."

Josh felt his face start to burn. "I...you...uh—"

Cameron looked at him solemnly. "I'm sorry I gave them the impression I don't like them."

"But you don't."

"It's not that I don't like them. I have no reason not to like them. They're well-behaved and charming. It's me. I don't have a clue what to say or how to act. I've been like this my entire adult life. I'm sorry." He stood up and got out his keys. "I'm off then. Thanks for a delicious meal."

He left before Josh could answer him.

Josh had been mistaken earlier. The evening had been a complete and total bust.

Josh pushed away his piece of half-eaten cake. He sat by himself in the kitchen and gave in to his deep disappointment.

Cameron had that look about him. He was getting ready to bail. Despite the relationship they both wanted so badly. Despite their need for one another and the loneliness when they weren't together. Despite everything good they had going for them, Cameron had one foot out the door.

The children were a big a stumbling block. Cameron had tried to tell him.

He hadn't believed him then.

But he believed him now.

Chapter Seventeen

A warm October rain blew in Josh's face as he ran from the car to the backdoor of the Durango. He was probably the first one to arrive for what promised to be a long day. He had a pile of paperwork to slog through this morning, and an email full of resumes to go through, and interviews to schedule. The marketing director he'd hired last month lasted exactly three weeks before she decided that Tampa was calling her name in a way San Antonio wasn't. The Academy had classes until ten p.m., and *West Side Story* rehearsals were in full swing. The Durango at its busiest and best.

He shook the water off his face and out of his hair and made his way through the rabbit warren of hallways to his office. The picture of him with Jackson and Beth he'd put on the wall caught his eye and he smiled. He wasn't going to see too much of them today. He would pick them up from school and take a couple of hours late in the afternoon to hang out with them before returning to the theater. He'd hired a lovely new sitter he used in the evening, a retired nanny who worked for the same agency where Vivi had found her sitter. She came at a steep price, but she was worth every penny *Bubbe* paid her.

"Let me do this much for you," his grandmother insisted when he'd objected to her picking up the tab. "You have a demanding full-time job you need to keep." He'd swallowed his pride and thanked her from the bottom of his heart. He didn't know what he would do without her and Ella.

He sighed and turned on his desktop. Even with their considerable help, being a dad wasn't easy. He was tired. Bone tired. Having the children in his life continued to be an indescribable joy. At the same time, the newness of parenthood had worn off and it hit home exactly what an enormous commitment of time and energy parenting was, if it was done right. The Durango was hopping, necessitating long hours. He tried to maintain a constant juggling act, trying to do justice to the theater and the children. There were days he felt he was giving everybody and everything the short shrift.

Then there was Cameron.

Josh rubbed the space between his eyes. Between his job and the children, his lover had gotten screwed over. They had finally gotten away for an evening together a week after the disastrous dinner. They had dined, danced, had phenomenal sex, and carefully avoided the elephant sitting on the sofa.

Josh had left Cameron's apartment in the wee hours of the morning, refreshed and convinced they could make it work, but the relationship had gone downhill after that. Due to the demands of his job, he'd missed so many evenings with the children, he didn't want to miss any more.

"You need a social life," Cameron had argued impatiently.

"They need a little time with me more," Josh had protested. "If you'd only—"

"I told you up front, no involvement with the children," Cameron snapped before he could finish his sentence. "We tried. It didn't go so well."

Yes, and whose fault was that?

Josh had bitten his tongue. Cameron had tried with the children. Sort of.

He and Cameron had been naïve thinking he could carve out the time for a real relationship that didn't involve the children on some level. Having never been a dad before, he hadn't known.

He didn't hire a sitter for a few more nights, even though Cameron had wanted him to. The children barely saw him as it was. They deserved as much time with him as he could give them.

Which pretty much left Cameron sucking wind. He wasn't going to put up with it for much longer, but there was no middle ground. The kids came first, and Cameron wouldn't spend any time with Josh if the kids were around.

Josh willed back tears. He sublimated his "issues" as best he could and plodded through the paperwork. He spent the rest of the morning going through the emailed resumes, each one more discouraging than the last. It was close to noon when Rachel popped her head in the door. "I'm making a take-out run to the hamburger place up the way. You want anything?"

"Thanks, but no. Ella brought over a pot roast last night and I'm having leftovers and doing a little laundry on my lunch hour."

"Bet you enjoy the peace and quiet."

Josh smiled. "That too."

It was another hour before he shook loose. He made the short drive to his place, let the dog out, started a load of laundry, and was eating a thick, tasty sandwich when the doorbell rang. He made a face and went to the door. Cameron on the front porch with his hands in the pockets of his overcoat, sad written all over his face.

Josh's heart plummeted. He knew what was coming before Cameron even opened his mouth. He swallowed the lump in his throat. "Come on in. How did you know I was home?"

"Rachel told me."

Cameron followed him into the kitchen. "Want a sandwich?"

"Nah. I've already eaten."

They stared at each other. Josh felt his eyes start to fill. "I can guess why you're here."

"I'm sorry, Josh."

"So am I. Sit." He gestured at the kitchen table and sank down in his chair. "I tried. I honestly did. I thought I could do it. I thought I could juggle it all, but I can't. I can't be the executive director of the theater, be any kind of dad to the children, and be the lover you deserve." He looked at Cameron through a veil of tears. "I didn't realize how hard it would be to carve out some us time."

"I know," Cameron said. "I thought we would have at least some time together."

Josh bit off the comeback he was dying to say. He had gone into this relationship knowing exactly how Cameron felt. Instead he shook his head. "I thought we would too."

Cameron looked at Josh wistfully. "For what it's worth, I think you have to be one of the most fantastic parents I've ever seen. I take back everything I ever said about gay parents and gay parenting. Those kids are lucky to have you." He knuckled the moisture off his face. "I wish to hell I could be."

"Why can't you?" Josh asked.

"You saw me with the kids. I was terrible with them that night. Hell, I left them thinking I don't even like them. The sad thing is, I'm no better with Julie, and she's my flesh and blood. Those children don't need somebody like me in their lives. Besides, they're Jewish kids."

"What the hell difference does that make?"

"They need to be instructed in their faith. They need to grow up with a soul-deep understanding of their heritage. Of who they are. I can't do that for them. I'm a sixth-generation Methodist." He stopped and took a breath. "Raising children. That script wasn't written with me in mind. It's not a role I can play."

"What now?"

"You go on with your life. You go out, date, meet people. Look for that special someone. He's out there, and he'll be as good with the kids as you are. He won't be the fucking failure I am."

Josh opened his mouth and closed it. He didn't know what to say to that. Maybe Cameron was right. Maybe he *was* hopeless with children, and the children were better off if he and Cameron called things off.

Even if it killed him to do it.

"I'm not going to argue with you." Josh reached across the table and ran his hand down the side of Cameron's face. "I'm going to miss you."

"You'll still see me. You work for me."

Which was going to hurt like a son of a bitch.

They looked at one another longingly. "Can we be together one more time?" Cameron asked.

"It's going to make things that much harder, but yeah. One more time."

They stood, and slowly, painfully, they came together in an embrace that was tender and desperate. Their lips met, the tears on their cheeks mingling as they kissed. Then Josh took Cameron by the hand and led him to the bedroom. Cameron looked around the room wistfully. "Under different circumstances, we might have shared this room," he said softly.

"Let's not torture ourselves with thoughts of what might have been. Let's enjoy what we have right now."

Cameron nodded. Knowing it was their last time, they watched one another strip. A piece at a time, slowly their clothing came off until they were naked. As Josh moved into Cam's arms, he swore he felt something in his heart break. Holding one another in a head-to-toe embrace shook Josh to his core. His cock swelled and he could feel Cameron's doing the same. His hands roamed Cameron's strong shoulders, powerful back, and tight, muscular butt as he tried to memorize every nuance of his lover's body for when memory was all he had left. They stood together for long moments before toppling onto the bed together.

Their lips and tongues tangled until Josh pushed Cameron down into the comforter and began to kiss his way down his lover's body. His lips caressed Cameron's neck, then he worked his way down Cameron's powerful chest, stopping to lave attention on his flat nipple before his lips drifted lower, following the happy trail first to his belly button and then down his body to the treasure trove below. His lips engulfed Cameron's thick cock and he tongued it lovingly before taking him in his mouth and sucking him deep. "You need to stop, unless you want me to come in your mouth," Cameron cautioned.

Josh raised his head. "You can come twice today," he said quietly. "Like this and inside me."

He put his mouth around Cameron's cock and massaged the area below his balls until Cameron bucked and came, shooting jets down his throat. Josh had barely taken a breath when Cameron flipped over and pushed him into the covers. "Your turn." He looked at Josh with eyes that shimmered. "Let me make this good for you. Let me make this the best."

Cam was passionate and tender as he kissed Josh from head to toe, stopping and lingering on places he knew Josh loved to be touched. When he wrapped his lips around Josh's cock, Josh let Cameron carry him away to a place where he didn't have to think about this being their last time. Good to his word, Cam made it the best, and brought him to a swift, bone-shaking climax.

Another precious memory he would treasure.

They lay tangled up as they caught their breath. Josh didn't want to move, talk, or think. But as he began to stroke Cam's chest, he asked, "Are you ready for round two yet?"

Plenty of times before, they'd gone slow, teasing and tantalizing for maximum effect. They'd had fun in bed. Experimented, laughed, and played. Sex with Cam was monumental. Right now, for the first time ever, they made love.

When they were spent, Cameron pulled away, heartbreak written on his face as he looked down at Josh. "I have to kiss you one more time," he said. He captured Josh's lips tenderly in a kiss that was full of love, sorrow, and the most painful of regrets.

Josh poured all the love he had in him into the kiss, wanting to send Cameron out the door knowing despite this heartbreaking finale, Josh loved him with all his heart.

Cameron left the bed and dressed quickly. Josh watched, his heart shattering into tiny pieces. Cameron turned and looked at Josh for the last time, his eyes glassy but his face otherwise expressionless. Then he left the bedroom and a few moments later Josh heard the front door open and close.

Josh dragged himself from the bed. He let Pepper back in the house and took a quick shower, climbing into a fresh set of clothes. He would have to double his efforts this afternoon. He had a ton of work to plow through. He would have to cut short his time with the kids.

The thought stopped him cold.

If he'd been willing to cut a little more of his time with the kids, maybe he wouldn't have lost Cameron. What kind of an asshat parent did that?

Climbing into the crossover, he shivered and coughed. Damned allergies on top of everything else. He felt down physically and mentally. Depression and grief. He'd lost the man he'd fallen so deeply in love with that he doubted he would ever get over it. He wished things had been different. That Cameron was the kind of man who was into family and kids.

They had become Josh's reason for getting up in the morning. They were the sunshine in his day. He'd never before understood the phrase "the light of my life," but he did now.

He coughed again and cursed. He had to get his head out of his ass before he walked in the theater. Losing Cameron felt like someone had taken a plunger and sucked the happy out of him.

Chapter Eighteen

Cameron cursed and put down his anvil, scowling at the shitty curve he'd formed on one of the outer ribs of a wrought-iron chandelier. The elaborate construction was one of a multi-chandelier order he was fabricating to light the main dining room of a rustic high-end steak house being built on the far north side of town. The chandelier was Western in design, but ornate.

Typically, Cameron would've spent the afternoon happily in his element, heating and bending the rods of iron into the shapes he would weld. But this was the third rod he'd screwed up today. He looked down at the piece in disgust. He would have to let it cool and have another go at it tomorrow. He couldn't afford to scrap it, or any of the pieces he'd already botched, and still make a profit. At the same time, his pride and the reputation of Heiser Steel wouldn't permit him to deliver anything that wasn't the absolute best. If he got in tomorrow and the rods couldn't be reshaped to his satisfaction, he'd have to scrap them, profit or not.

Sighing, he left the poorly curved rods to cool and switched off the electric forge. He took off his welder's mask and went in his office, wiping the sweat from his arms and forehead before plunking down in his desk chair to tackle the higher-than-usual pile of paperwork on his desk.

Three days ago, Miguel had called and told him Vivi was sick with the flu. She was flat on her back and would be for the next week. Cam was back to doing her job along with his. Somewhat. At least he had support staff to do the ministerial work.

He had to go by the theater this afternoon. Rachel had called and told him there were some items that needed his okay. He hoped Josh wasn't going to avoid him. As painful as breaking up with him had been, as badly as they both hurt, they still had to work together. Cameron believed they could find a way. Otherwise, one of them would have to leave. Cameron didn't want to, and he certainly didn't want Josh to leave. He was the best executive director the Durango ever had. As board chair, Cameron wasn't willing to lose him.

After plowing through some work, he checked the time. Four p.m., but he'd come in before the sun was up, and if he was going to have time for a quick shower, he had to leave now. He made it to his condo quickly, left his sweat-stained work clothes in a heap and let the hot water pound on his back. He rolled his shoulders under the hot spray, willing away the tension plaguing him since he'd walked out of Josh's house four days ago. He shook his head. Other people got depressed after a breakup. They got drunk and swore, or cried and ate a carton of ice cream.

He got tense.

Which made his back hurt, and gave him a banger of a headache.

Maybe he should try ice cream.

All the second-guessing he'd done since that heartbreaking afternoon wondering if he should've done something differently when there was nothing different he could've done. He and Josh had tried. It hadn't worked.

Playing the maudlin story on repeat fed the tension. He knew it, but he couldn't stop himself.

He was fucked.

He'd fallen in love with Josh hard, and he was going to stay in love with him, even after Josh moved on and found his *One*.

Cam had already found his *One*. And, failure that he was, he'd walked away from him.

He swore as he pulled on a shirt and a pair of jeans. He knew he was the problem. *He* was the one who wasn't good with kids. *He* was the one who couldn't be a decent parent even if he tried.

By the time he got to the theater, he was cursing out loud. He sat in his car for a minute, working up the courage to walk in and face Josh. Gritting his teeth, he went in the back door. He could hear the girls' singing class in the Academy practicing "The Crime of the Century" from *Ragtime*. A few steps on he heard the sound of a set being nailed together on the stage.

He made his way through the auditorium and into the maze of offices. Taking a deep breath, he knocked on Josh's door and stuck his head inside. The light was off, the computer was shut down, and Cam could see a couple of days' worth of unopened mail. He blinked and stared at the pile of mail on the desk. Josh never left his emails unanswered or unopened.

Something was wrong.

He shut Josh's door and knocked on Maggie's. Her office door was locked. The room behind the door was silent and there was no light coming from under the door. Cameron checked his watch. It wasn't that late. Josh and Maggie were the two who stayed the latest.

Which left Rachel.

He knocked on her door and was treated to a strangled "Come in." Rachel was coughing into a handkerchief and looked like warmed-over roadkill. "Let me guess. The flu?"

Rachel smiled weakly. "I probably should be home, but with both Josh and Maggie flat on their asses, somebody needed to be here."

Josh is sick.

"You don't need to be here if you're sick," Cameron told her. "We can close the offices for a day or two. How sick are they?"

"According to Kirby, Maggie's sick as a dog. He's staying with her and hoping not to catch it himself. I don't know about Josh. All he said when he called was that the doctor told him to stay home and to tell his grandmother and her caregiver to stay a mile away."

"Who's taking care of him? Who's taking care of the kids?"

"Nobody, I guess."

"Somebody needs to be taking care of those kids."

Rachel laid her hand on his arm. "Cameron, sick parents have been taking care of their children since the beginning of time. I'll bet even your mom had to do it on occasion."

"Sure, but she had Dad and my grandparents. Josh doesn't have anybody."

On second thought, fuck that. He had Cameron.

Whatever theater business was waiting for him would have to wait a little longer. Cameron made his way back through the theater to the parking lot. He hopped in his car and quickly got to Josh's house. He knocked on the door. When no one answered, he banged even louder. He was about to pound on the door a third time when the curtains opened and Jackson and the dog peered out. "Open the door," Cameron said.

Jackson looked at him uncertainly. "We're not supposed to open the door to strangers."

Cameron fought the urge to roll his eyes. "Jackson, I'm not a stranger. I'm Mr. Cameron."

Jackson looked at him again. "Oh." He disappeared into the house and reappeared a moment later. "Uncle Josh said to tell you he's sick and to come back later. You don't want to catch what he has."

Cameron bit back a curse. "Jackson. I've already been exposed. Let me in, please. Your Uncle Josh needs me. Doesn't he?"

"I…I guess so."

He opened the door and Cameron walked into the living room. He surveyed the scene and grimaced. The place was a wreck. Dirty dishes and empty takeout cartons covered the coffee table. Toys were scattered all over the living room. A brief detour into the kitchen turned up more of the same. Cameron peeked into the laundry room to find two big baskets of dirty laundry, some of which was beginning to smell.

This was worse than bad. Josh was obsessive about his laundry.

Speaking of. He went back into the living room to find Josh swaying in the middle of the room, with Jackson holding Pepper and hovering nearby and Beth watching him anxiously. Josh was pale under a fever flush and had huge circles under his eyes. He had three days of beard on his cheeks and his hair stood up in spikes. "This is the last place you need to be," Josh croaked.

"You need help." Cameron reached Josh in two steps and took hold of his arm. "You need to be in bed." Josh's arm was hot. Fever. Several degrees.

Josh opened his mouth to answer but was overtaken by a coughing jag that seemed to go on forever. Cameron turned to the boy. "Jackson, where does your Uncle Josh keep his sheets?"

"Hall closet."

"Would you get a set and leave them on the bed?"

Jackson headed down the hall. "You need to leave. You'll catch this shit," Josh protested.

"Don't worry about what you think I need to do. You're sitting down until I can get the sheets changed and then you're hitting the sack. I can stay a few days until you're feeling better."

"What about your job?"

"That's the beauty of owning the company. I can come and go as I please." He felt his face soften. "I'll go in after I get the kids to school, and I'll work until I have to pick them up." He looked at Josh in alarm. "You haven't been driving in the shape you're in, have you?"

"What choice did I have?"

"Oh, sweet Jesus. Or is that sweet Moses in this house?"

Josh laughed weakly. He steered Josh to the sofa. Josh sat and looked up in confusion. "Why are you doing this?"

Because I love you and you need me.

Cameron blinked. He couldn't tell Josh the truth. "Because you need the help. Besides, I've already been exposed," he added dryly.

"Oh. I guess you have." Josh leaned his head back and shut his eyes.

"Sheets are on the bed," Jackson announced.

Cameron looked around the room. "How long has it been since you picked up your toys?"

Jackson and Beth looked at one another. "Two days? Three? Not sure," Jackson said.

"Uncle Josh didn't say we had to," Beth added helpfully.

"Tell you what. I'll get the sheets changed and your Uncle Josh into bed, and you guys pick up your toys so we don't step on them and break them," Cameron instructed.

"If Uncle Josh goes to bed, we won't get any supper," Beth protested.

"So? We didn't get any last night," Jackson said.

Cameron looked at them in alarm. "Uncle Josh too sick to cook for you last night?"

"We ate up the last of the cereal," Jackson said. "Uncle Josh was asleep at suppertime and didn't get anything delivered."

What the fuck? Josh should've called him.

"Well, I'm not nearly as good a cook as your Uncle Josh, but I bet I could put together some hamburgers. Think that would work?"

"Sure." Jackson pulled the toy box out in the middle of the room and started filling it.

Cameron found the sheets and changed Josh's sweaty bed. Josh tried to object, but Cameron gave him no choice as he escorted him to the freshly made bed. "You need something else to sleep in. No arguments," he added when Josh started to protest.

Josh managed to change into fresh pajama bottoms and a loose t-shirt. Cameron coaxed him into finishing a glass of water after he took his acetaminophen, and tucked him in. Josh turned over and was asleep before Cameron got out of the room.

He returned to find the toys mostly picked up and Pepper curled up on his bed in the corner. Beth and Jackson were looking at him uncertainly. His mind raced, not sure what they were supposed to be doing. He spotted their backpacks thrown in the lounge chair. "You two have homework?"

Jackson looked at him warily. "No?"

"Really?" Cameron tilted his head.

"Yes, I do," he said in his most put-upon voice.

"Where do you sit to do it?"

"We work at the kitchen table," Beth said. "I have homework too. We always have homework." Jackson shot her a dirty look.

"Then that's next."

It took him a few minutes to get the mess cleared from the kitchen table. The kids settled in and spread out their papers. He started a load of laundry and cleared the coffee table of pizza boxes and takeout cartons, and then loaded the dirty dishes in the dishwasher. He added the cartons and boxes from the kitchen to the garbage sack. He checked the fridge and threw out the half-eaten takeaway. He checked the freezer and the pantry. Hmm. They were mostly empty, as was the only sack of dog food.

Josh had been too sick to shop.

Cameron hated grocery shopping. He sure wasn't doing it with two kids in tow.

Still, if they were going to eat, he had to get food somehow. He went online and almost jumped up and down with joy. Several of the major grocery chains delivered. Two of them later this evening if he got his order placed in the next few minutes. He looked uncertainly at the children sitting at the table. "Jackson. Beth. What do you like to eat?"

"Pizza," Jackson said.

"Chinese. Only I'm tired of pizza and Chinese," Beth added.

Cameron thought about all the empty pizza boxes and takeout cartons. "I'm sure you are. What do you like that we can fix here?"

Jackson and Beth looked at one another. "Hamburgers. You said you could make those," Jackson ventured cautiously.

Cameron wrote down the ingredients for a hamburger.

"Mac and cheese. That comes out of a box," Beth said.

Cameron added boxed mac and cheese to the list.

"What about fried chicken?" Jackson asked.

"We'll do that takeout," Cameron said quickly. "What else?"

It took a little while, but he finally had five meals the kids liked he could cook. The children returned to their homework and he ordered groceries, which would be there in ninety minutes. Great, more time to get the mess cleaned up and another load of laundry in the machine.

Chapter Nineteen

Cameron breathed a sigh of relief when the doorbell rang. Ninety minutes had turned into almost two and a half hours. An hour ago he'd been forced to give the kids small bags of Fritos to hold them over until he could get dinner on the table. The chips had stopped the whining and after a short squabble, a Disney movie was agreed upon, getting them out from under his feet so he could work on the kitchen and the laundry. He was already on his third load of wash and a pile sat on the edge of the sofa waiting to be folded. He started to ask the children to fold them but looked at the big towels and the smallish kids, and changed his mind.

He could do a better job himself.

He rummaged through the bags until he found the package of hamburger patties. He got those started and kept one eye on them while he put away the rest of the groceries. The burgers were about done when Beth stuck her head in the door. "It smells good," she said.

"Thanks. Where does Uncle Josh keep the knives and forks?"

"In here." She opened the drawer. "I'll set the table."

"Thanks," he murmured.

She looked at him hopefully. "Is Uncle Josh eating with us?"

"I don't think so. He's sick."

Beth's bottom lip started to quiver. "Is he gonna die like Mommy did?"

Cameron reared back and looked at her in horror. "Good grief, no. Where did you get an idea like that?"

"Mommy was sick and then she died. People die when they get sick."

Cameron's heart broke for the frightened little girl. "Not from the flu, Beth. Your mother had cancer. That's a whole 'nother ball game."

"Are you *sure*?"

"Yeah, I'm sure," he said gruffly. "Josh is gonna be fine. You only need to set three places." He watched her count out three of each utensil and place them on the table exactly where they needed to be. He stared at the set table. She got it perfect. He hadn't expected a six-year-old to be that competent.

The hamburger patties appeared to be done, He placed each on the bottom side of a bun. He stuck his head in the living room and called Jackson before turning back to Beth. "What do you like on your hamburger?"

"I like it plain. Jackson likes lettuce."

"Don't like lettuce," Jackson said from the door. "I like tomatoes."

"Ya didn't like 'em last week," Beth said indignantly.

"He can eat his burger however he wants to," Cameron said quickly. "Do you need help washing your hands?"

"She does. I don't." Jackson pulled the stepstool to the sink and washed his hands.

Cameron looked at Beth. "Uncle Josh picks me up. But you don't have to," she added quickly when he took a step backward.

"It's okay. Come here." He motioned her to the sink and turned on the water. She turned away from him and he hoisted her up. *She sure doesn't weigh much*, he thought as she held her hands under the spray. He put her down and eyed her critically. She didn't seem thin or anything.

On the other hand, he'd never picked up a six-year-old girl. He had no idea how much one weighed. Yeah, he was clueless.

The kids sat down at their places and dug into their burgers. Cameron took a minute to pile his high with all the fixings before sitting down with it at the table. Beth swallowed a big chunk of burger. "You forgot something to drink," she complained.

Cameron swore to himself and got them each a glass of water. "We'll do milk tomorrow," he said when the kids eyed the water doubtfully.

The children didn't say much and by the end of supper they were visibly drooping. Cameron glanced at his watch. Damn, it was no wonder they were tired. It was already after nine. He looked at them. "It's late. Can you manage your own baths or do you need help?"

"I can manage," Jackson informed him. "She needs her water run. Oh, and she always goes first."

Beth shot her brother the same look Vivi would shoot Cam when they were kids. "Okay. Put your dishes on the counter and we'll do baths. Then it's off to bed with you. It's late."

He ran Beth's water, and then spent fifteen minutes looking for pajamas, until she said all her jammies were in the dirty clothes. *Oh hell.* He offered, "You could sleep in a shirt and your underwear."

"Oh, but I *couldn't*. You might see my panties."

Cameron looked down at the horrified child in consternation. She had to sleep in something. "How about you wear one of Uncle Josh's t-shirts? Nobody can see your panties then."

She nodded and he slipped into Josh's room. Josh was thrashing in his sleep and burning up with fever. Cam swore under his breath. They were going to have to get his fever down somehow. He found an old Durango tee and handed it to Beth through the bathroom door. She emerged a moment later, looking unexpectedly cute in Josh's old shirt. "Okay, into the bed," he said as he pulled back the covers. "I need to go tend to Josh."

"I want a story," Beth protested.

"Tomorrow," he said firmly. She crawled in and he pulled up the covers. After a detour by the bathroom—the water was on and Jackson was splashing behind the shower curtain—he hunted down a plastic basin and filled it with cool water. He found a washcloth and towel and positioned himself next to Josh, who was moving about restlessly, mumbling in his sleep as sweat poured off his body.

Cameron pulled up the footstool and pulled the covers off Josh. "No, it's cold," he protested, grabbing for the covers.

"Josh, we've got to get your fever down."

Cameron pulled up the t-shirt and said, "Hands up." He pulled off the soaked shirt to find Josh's chest and arms gleamed with sweat and his entire body shook. Josh looked at Cameron with eyes that were bleary. "It's not really you. I'm dreaming."

"No, it's me," Cameron said quietly. He wet the washcloth and started running it down Josh's chest. Josh protested for a minute before lying back, too exhausted to fight, and let Cameron wipe him down with the cool cloth. There was nothing sexual about what he was doing. Far from it. But his cock still jumped at the sight of Josh's beautiful body. The body that figured in Cameron's dreams too many times to count.

He spent long minutes bathing Josh's upper body. When he'd done all he could for the time being, he found another shirt and helped Josh get it over his head. He dumped the water down the sink and went in search of Jackson. The boy's room was empty and Cameron found him in the kitchen spooning vanilla ice cream into his mouth. "I was still hungry," he said defensively when Cameron put his hands on his hips.

"You should have said something. You and Beth could have both had ice cream."

Cameron snagged a bowl and spoon and dug into the carton. "This is good, but I like Rocky Road better," Jackson volunteered.

"Wish I'd known that. I like it better too." He took a big bite of the vanilla. "But this isn't bad."

They sat eating the ice cream in silence. "Is Uncle Josh gonna be okay?" Jackson blurted suddenly. He looked at Cameron with worry on his small face.

"Yeah. Josh is going to be fine. Like I told Beth, your mom died from cancer. Flu is not cancer."

"Okay." He looked a little relieved as he took another bite of ice cream. "It's just that if Uncle Josh died, we'd have to go to Bradford and live with Uncle A.J. and Aunt June. They don't like us any more than you do."

Cameron raised his brow. "Who says I don't like you?"

"That time you came to dinner. You didn't want to talk to us, and you didn't say anything. You didn't like it when Beth's milk spilled on you."

Cameron sighed. "Jackson, I like you and your sister. The milk wasn't that bad. I've never been around kids. It's not that I didn't want to talk to you. It's that I don't know how to talk to you."

Jackson looked puzzled. "Why is it any different from talking to an adult?"

Cameron felt his mouth drop open. *The kid had a point.* "You're right. I guess it isn't." He looked at Jackson curiously. "Did your uncle and aunt not want to talk to you?"

"Uncle A.J. didn't. He and Aunt June always looked at us funny. They called us bad names when they didn't think we could hear them."

Cameron remembered the conversation he'd overheard. He wasn't surprised. "I'm sorry."

"If Uncle Josh dies, we'd have to go up there. *Bubbe*'s too old for us to live with her."

"Jackson, Josh is going to be fine. You won't have to go to Bradford."

The relief on Jackson's face was heartbreaking.

"Don't worry. I like you fine. When I talk to you, it's gonna be like I'm talking to a grown-up. I don't know any other way to talk."

"That's all right. I don't mind being talked to like an adult. Can I talk like a grown-up to you?"

"Sure." Cameron was glad that was settled.

They finished their ice cream in companionable silence. Jackson said Cameron didn't have to tuck him in and scurried off to bed with the dog in tow.

Cameron spent the next two hours working on the kitchen and living room, using disinfectant wipes on the table and the chairs, the counters and appliances, and what he could in the living room.

He ran two more loads of clothes, including Josh's sweat-soaked sheets and his pajamas, and did his best to clean and disinfect both bathrooms. He checked Josh and over Josh's objections wiped his feverish body down again, and got more Tylenol and water down him. It was after midnight when he kicked off his shoes and took off his shirt and belt, and curled up on the sofa.

Morning came all too soon. He came awake to the sound of his phone alarm buzzing on the coffee table and Pepper licking his face. Beth stared at him from a couple of feet away. "I'm hungry. Are we going to eat here or at school?"

Cameron blinked. "Where do you usually eat?" He pushed the dog away.

"Sometimes here and sometimes there. Uncle Josh decides. Why don't we ask him?" She ran for the bedroom before he could stop her.

Cameron swung his legs off the sofa and sprinted after her. "Beth, let's not wake Josh. He still feels really bad."

Beth skidded to a halt in the door of Josh's bedroom. "He's still asleep."

"He is. And we're gonna leave him that way. We'll eat here this morning. Where are your school clothes?"

Beth made a face. "My uniforms are all in my second drawer. Or you could let me wear something else," she added helpfully. "We could say you didn't know about the uniforms."

"Nice try, kid." They went in her bedroom and Cameron found the uniforms. "Get dressed and I'll get breakfast ready."

Cameron made a cup of coffee and a big pile of toast for him and the kids. He gulped his down in three bites, and while they finished he checked on Josh. His forehead didn't feel quite as hot, and he was resting comfortably. Cam debated for a minute, but decided to leave Josh sleeping. He left a full glass of water and a bottle of Tylenol on the nightstand and a note in the bathroom. "Kids to school. Will pick them up after school and get them here. Go back to bed. All is under control."

As he locked the front door, he realized he didn't know where they went to school, and that he didn't have car seats for them. Cursing under his breath, he went back inside and found Josh's phone and car keys. A quick call to Mrs. Goldstein's number solved the first problem. *Bubbe*'s beloved Ella offered to transport the kids herself, but it was already late and he didn't want the kids to be tardy. She told him what time school let out and he set his phone alarm to go off in time to pick them up. Pinching Josh's car keys solved the second problem, and soon he and the kids were on their way.

He took them to school first and then made a quick pit stop at his own place for a shower and a duffel bag. The Heiser Steel parking lot was almost full, and he was glad he had his marked parking spot up against the building. Their new office manager was at her post and Cameron's emails and paperwork were mostly caught up, so he spent the morning re-bending the rods he'd screwed up so badly yesterday. Two of them were salvageable, but the third was beyond saving. He got another rod and went to work. At lunchtime, he had a quick taco from the café next door for lunch and was bending another rod for the chandelier when his phone buzzed. School let out in a half hour and he was filthy and covered in sweat.

He would have to shower and change when he got to Josh's.

He turned off the forge and left the hot iron cooling. It felt like he'd just gotten there and he already had to leave. It made him wonder how Josh juggled it all. He hadn't cut down on his hours at the Durango and was handling all his commitments as a parent as well. It was a wonder Josh had managed to go out on a date at all.

He should've cut Josh a little more slack.

But that would have involved being around the children. While last night and this morning had gone all right, he wasn't convinced he was all that good with them. Or for them.

Which was sad. Being around Beth and Jackson wasn't nearly as trying as he'd thought it would be.

He navigated his way to the elementary school and got in line with the rest of the parents. Jackson and Beth ran for the crossover, followed by a teacher holding a clipboard. She lowered her head and her smile morphed into suspicion. "You're not their Uncle Josh."

"I'm Cameron Heiser. Josh is sick, and I'm helping out."

She looked down at the clipboard. "You're not on the authorized list to pick them up."

Cameron sighed. "Josh is down with the flu and too sick to drive. Call either him or his grandmother's number and get their authorization."

"I'm afraid I can't do that," she said stiffly.

Cameron's eyes narrowed. "You can do that. Or you can take the kids back inside while I call his grandmother's house and drag a ninety-one-year-old's elderly caregiver out to pick up two children who are probably covered with flu germs, thus exposing both little old ladies to the flu. This will most likely take the better part of an hour, piss off everybody involved, and make you late to your pedicure. Josh is too sick to be safe behind the wheel. What'll it be?"

The woman squinted her eyes, and then marched over to some other woman with a clipboard. She made a phone call and nodded her head. The first woman brought the children back and handed him a paper through the window. "Fill this out and bring it back in the morning," she said officiously.

"You betcha." He winked and saluted her.

"Wow, Mr. Cameron, you're a smart-ass," Jackson crowed as he climbed in the car. "You're an awesome smart-ass."

"Why, thank you, Jackson. That's the nicest thing anyone's said to me all day."

***

They found Josh sitting on the sofa munching on soda crackers. His eyes were still glassy, and he was wrapped in a blanket. "What are you doing out of the bed?" Cameron demanded.

"I was gonna go get the kids, but I found your keys instead of mine." He looked up at Cameron, puzzled. "What's going on?"

"You're sick as a dog and need help." He felt Josh's forehead. "You still have a fever. You need to get some food in your stomach and go back to bed."

"But the kids—"

"Jackson and Beth will do their homework and eat their dinner like they did last night. You'll eat a bowl of chicken noodle soup and drink a lot of water, and take your Tylenol, and then go back to bed."

"But it's Friday."

"Friday. Does that mean they can wait on their homework?"

"No. It's Shabbat. They need to go to synagogue with *Bubbe* and Ella."

"Ella called me earlier in the day, and she and I made an executive decision. Your *bubbe* doesn't need to be exposed to you or the kids. Ella said we can take care of Shabbat here. She said you have a book written for children around here somewhere. Is it where I can put my hands on it?"

"Over there. On the bookshelf beside the television."

He found a well-worn Jewish children's Bible and another chock-full of stories, some of which were from what he called the Old Testament, and others he didn't recognize. Josh flipped through the book of stories and zeroed in on the story of Noah's Ark. "I figure you know this one."

"It's in my Bible too," he said dryly.

"You can read it to them tonight. We can get them back to the synagogue when I'm well again."

"Okay. Noah's Ark it is."

Josh looked at him again. "Why?" he croaked. "Why are you taking care of us?"

Because I love you and you need me. Because I want you to get well. He couldn't come out and say that. Not after the way things ended between them.

"Because you need help," he said instead. "And you don't have anyone to help you. Does that work for you?"

"Yeah. That works for me."

Chapter Twenty

Cameron shut off the blowtorch and wiped the sweat off his forehead. The metal components of the chandelier had all been shaped and he was in the process of welding together the pieces. It would be finished in the next couple of days, especially since Josh had recovered enough he could take over at home.

Young sure beat old when it came to getting well. With a chance to rest and heal, Josh had recuperated quickly. His fever was down, and while he was weak and would be off work for a few more days, he could take care of the children again. Cameron would pick them up this afternoon from school and take them home. He would then pack his stuff and leave things in Josh's hands.

The thought of it sucked.

He made a swift run by his desk. A stack of invoices sat in his inbox and emails waited for him. He should probably deal with them today, but he didn't want to be late and piss off prune-face again, who glowered at him every afternoon when he went through the line. He could stay late tomorrow. He could come in as early and stay as late as he wanted. He was going back to his usual routine of doing what he liked when he liked. The thought of which should have had him jumping for joy.

Should have. But didn't.

Refusing to think about why, he hopped in Josh's crossover and drove to the elementary school, preparing to get the teacher's goat one last time. This afternoon her usual scowl was gone, replaced by an expression of concern as she ushered the kids to the car. "Mr. Heiser, neither of the children are feeling well."

"What's wrong?"

"They said their throats hurt and they both feel like they have fever. We would've called, but they didn't land in the nurse's office until it was almost time to go."

"Okay." He hopped out and felt of their foreheads himself. "Definitely fever." He knelt in front of Jackson. "How do you feel?" he murmured.

"Like shit," Jackson said dolefully.

Cameron choked. He didn't dare look up at the teacher. Instead he turned to Beth. "Like him," she rasped.

He hustled them both into the car and called Josh. "The kids are both sick. Do I take them to the doctor?"

Josh muttered a swear word. "We use the same pediatrician Vivi does. Bring them here and I'll make an appointment."

Josh had an appointment for the children in the next hour. He was freshly showered and shaved when he came out to the car and Cameron grimaced at his own dirty, sweat-stained work clothes. "They won't care," Josh said, reading his mind. "Their only worry will be the children."

Thankfully, the waiting room was empty. The children were coughing badly and not happy to be at the doctor's office. "They're gonna give us a shot," Beth griped.

"They may," Cameron admitted. "I don't know." He looked over at Josh, who was dealing with insurance and paperwork. "Did they get flu shots?"

"Not yet. Damn it."

Dr. Ramirez was a grandmotherly woman with gray hair and a comforting smile. She swiftly scanned the paperwork. "You're getting over it yourself?" she asked Cameron.

"Not me. Their uncle." He pointed his thumb at Josh.

"I'm not surprised. It's highly contagious."

No shit.

The doctor examined both children and declared them flu victims. She prescribed an antiviral in liquid form and advised them on the use of Tylenol in children this young. "Push fluids. They're going to be sweating off a lot and it needs to be replaced."

They carried the feverish children to the car and swung by the neighborhood pharmacy on the way back to Josh's place. They took the children to their bedrooms and Josh turned to Cameron. "Thanks for all the help," he said quietly. "I can take it from here."

Cameron arched an eyebrow. "Can you? Taking them to the doctor wore you out."

"I'll be okay. Besides, you've taken enough time away from your business for us. You need to get back to your company."

Cameron crossed his arms in front of him. "I can take a few more days and help you until they feel better. You're still weak as a kitten and they're going to need tending twenty-four seven for the next little while. Go park yourself on the sofa while I run a load of laundry." He laid his hand on Josh's arm. "I've got this, Josh."

Josh nodded weakly and sank down into the sofa. Cameron headed to the utility room. He was nuts. It was time for him to go back to his own life. But Josh needed help. Taking care of sick children was no picnic, especially with a long-legged dog thrown in. Not that he'd ever done it himself, but he'd heard stories.

Josh wasn't well enough to do it on his own. Cam loved Josh and didn't want him getting sick again. That was the only reason he was staying. He was staying for Josh. Only for Josh. He wasn't staying because of the children.

Maybe if he told himself that often enough, he might believe it.

***

Josh put his dirty plate in the dishwasher. "Thanks for the omelet. It was delicious."

Cameron shrugged. "It was an omelet. No big deal."

"It is if you haven't had one since the holidays. They're a little sophisticated for the kids. We do lots of scrambled eggs and mac and cheese around here these days." He sank back into his chair.

"Nothing wrong with those." Cameron put his own plate in the dishwasher. "How much sleep did you end up getting last night?"

"A lot more than you did. I crashed after sponging Jackson down at one. I sorta heard you up with them later."

"I sponged them both down about four."

Josh winced inwardly. The kids had been awake since seven, which meant Cameron had gotten damned little rest. They had refused Josh's offer of a cooked breakfast and opted for bowls of cereal instead, which he filled with extra milk he insisted they finish. Neither would go back to bed, so he put on the original *Toy Story* with a promise if they sat quietly and didn't move around, they could watch the entire trilogy.

So far it was working, with Jackson curled up on one end of the sofa and Beth on the other, both clutching a stuffed animal. He could tell from their flushed faces that they were still running fevers. He was about to take the Tylenol and the prescription antiviral to them when Cameron's phone beeped and he got up from the table. "Time to go be Dr. Heiser." He scooped up the meds and got a couple of spoons out of the drawer. "Bring them some water."

Josh filled two glasses and followed Cameron to the sofa. "Aw, do we have to take some more of that stuff?" Jackson groused. "It tastes awful."

"It tastes like candy," Cameron said dryly.

"You gotta be kidding. It tastes like sh—"

"Pretend," Cameron said firmly. Without giving Jackson a chance to argue, he popped a dose of the antiviral prescription in his mouth. "Now for the Tylenol."

"Why do I have to take two?" the kid complained.

"It's like this. See this stuff?" Cameron held up the Tylenol. "This will make you feel better. And this one?" He held up the prescription bottle. "This one actually helps you get better. You need them both."

"Okay." Jackson swallowed the second teaspoon and took the water from Josh. It took a little coaxing, but he downed the entire glass.

Cameron turned to Beth. "Your turn."

Beth nodded weakly and took her meds without protest. She put her head down on a sofa pillow and shut her eyes.

"Boy, she must feel bad," Cameron murmured. "Her pajama pants and shirt don't match and she didn't even notice."

Josh snickered. "I see you've had dealings with my fashionista already."

"I had no idea it could matter that much to a six-year-old." Cameron carried the medicine back to the kitchen. "Jackson's I did myself. The combinations he comes up with would make a straight man cringe."

"That would be Jackson."

They cleaned up the kitchen together. Cameron insisted Josh join the children in the living room. "You're still not well. Rest while you can."

"Don't you have to go to work?"

"I'm going in for a short day. It's okay," he said when Josh started to object. "I own the place, remember? I'll get some laundry started first."

Josh nodded and sank into the armchair. Cameron disappeared into the laundry room for a couple of minutes before picking up his keys. "Don't kill yourself over lunch. There's canned soup for them, and sandwich fixin's for you. I'll be back in time to clean up, and put dinner on the table. Keep your ass parked in a chair as much as you can. You're still not one hundred percent. Far from it."

Josh popped a snappy salute as Cameron sauntered out the door.

Long after Cameron had left, Josh stared at the front door. He didn't get it. He understood why Cameron was helping. Even though they were no longer a couple, Cameron still cared enough to take care of him. If it were Cameron sick, he would be doing the same.

What he couldn't understand was why Cameron was convinced he wasn't good with kids. He was fine with them. He wasn't gushy. He was brisk and matter-of-fact. He told it to them like it was. He certainly wasn't "bad" with them. Far from it. A lot of kids would love to have a parent like Cameron.

Josh knew better than to argue. Cameron's mind was made up. He wouldn't have walked away from Josh and their relationship otherwise.

He got out his laptop and spent most of the morning taking care of Durango business. He emailed Rachel to bring him his mail and paperwork only to learn that she too had gone home with the flu. Maggie wasn't back yet, and Cameron had closed the offices until someone was well enough to go back to work.

Josh breathed a sigh of relief. Catching up later would be a bitch, but he really didn't feel like working right now, even from home. Beth and Jackson got restless about eleven, so he deep-sixed the third movie and let them play on the floor with their Legos until lunchtime. Neither was particularly hungry, but he managed to get a bowl of soup down each of them.

By the time they were finished eating they were flagging. He put on the last movie and turned it off ten minutes later when they were fast asleep.

The sandwich fixin's he found in the fridge were all his favorites, and tears stung his eyes as he put together a thick, savory treat. The carefully stocked fridge was another testament to Cameron's thoughtfulness.

The children napped for a couple of hours while Josh rested. Beth's face was increasingly flushed and she began to move around restlessly. He put his hand on her forehead and swore as he held the forehead thermometer to her skin. A hundred and three.

Damn. He needed to do something.

Or maybe not. He didn't know the first thing about taking care of a sick child. Maybe it was all right for her fever to be that high.

He put in a quick call to Dr. Ramirez and was assured that while not wonderful, the fever wasn't all that bad and that her regular Tylenol and a sponge bath would help. He carried Beth to her room and was in the process of giving her a cool sponge bath when he heard the front door open. "Josh? Where are you?"

Josh went to the door. "Back here. Her fever's up and I'm sponging her off."

Cameron was in the room a moment later. "Back in executive mode, I see," Josh said. Cameron had been in his work clothes for the last week and it was jarring to see him in a coat and tie.

"Kiwanis meeting." He shucked the coat and bent over the bed. "How's she doing?"

Josh held the thermometer to her forehead. "Better, but not great."

He started to lean down again but Cameron edged him out of the way. "You go sit. I've got this." He rolled up the sleeves of his dress shirt and wrung out the soggy washcloth.

Josh watched as Cameron slowly and gently wiped the child's chest and face. *The same way Cameron had tenderly bathed his fevered body a few nights ago.*

Josh's face flamed as he backed out of the room. There had been nothing remotely sexual in Cameron's touch that night. He'd been about making Josh feel better. But there had been love and caring in his touch as he'd wiped Josh down, and there was the same caring in his touch this afternoon as he ran the cool washcloth over his sick Beth. Cameron had it in him to care about the kids. He *did* care, which was all the children really needed.

He didn't know why in the world Cameron couldn't see that for himself.

***

Josh watched as Cameron gathered up the last of his clothes and toiletries and stuffed them in his duffel. It had been five days since the kids had gotten ill, ten days since Josh had come down with the vicious strain. Ten days Cameron had been an intimate part of their lives. Today that would end. Cam agreed Josh was strong enough to care for the children, and that they were on the mend to the point that they didn't require day-and-night tending. Which meant that it was high time for Cameron to return to his own life. Cameron zipped his duffel and they traded car keys. "I never even got to drive that smokin' hot Shelby," Josh teased as he handed the Mustang keys to Cameron.

"Do you miss the Miata?" Cameron asked as he stuffed his keys in his pocket.

"When have I had time?"

"Good point." He looked around the room for the last time. "I think that's everything. If you find something else, you can bring it to me at the theater."

"I will." He glanced at the sofa. "I guess you'll be glad to get back to your own bed."

Cameron shrugged. "I will. As sofas go, it wasn't bad."

Josh bit his lip. Cameron could have had the other half of his bed if he'd wanted it. But Cameron didn't ask, and under the circumstances, he didn't know if he should make the offer.

Cameron glanced down at the children, who were building yet another Lego house from scratch. "They really love those things."

"They do. They're good at it."

"They are." He paused for a minute. "Should I tell them good-bye?"

"Sure."

Cameron approached the children hesitantly. "Beth. Jackson." They looked up at him. "I'm leaving now."

"I know. You're going to work. What are you cooking for supper?" Jackson asked.

"No. I mean I'm not coming over this afternoon."

"You're not?" Beth leapt to her feet. "Who's cooking supper then?"

Jackson looked up with a scowl on his face. "Did you decide you don't like us after all?"

"*No*. It's nothing like that. Your Uncle Josh is all better and he can take care of you now."

"Oh."

"But you'll come see us, right?" Beth gave him a pout smile.

Josh couldn't interpret the expression that flitted across Cameron's face before he looked down at her and smiled. "Yep. I'll come see you." He gave her a quick hug and put out his hand for a high-five with Jackson. "I'll see you both."

Josh swallowed back the lump clogging his throat. It was all he could do not to throw his arms around Cameron and beg him to stay. It was wrong, so wrong for Cameron to be leaving like this. They belonged together. All of them. Why in God's name couldn't Cameron see that?

Begging wasn't going to change anything. Cameron's mind was made up. Instead he schooled his face into a semblance of a grateful smile for the man he loved so much. "Thanks again for all you did."

Cameron smiled crookedly. "My pleasure." He gave Josh a jaunty salute, squared his shoulders, and walked out the door.

Josh waited until the front door was closed. Then he fled to his bedroom so the children wouldn't see the tears pouring down his face. He'd lost Cameron again, and he felt this loss even more keenly than he had before.

It'd been easier when he could tell himself Cameron was right, he was hopeless with kids and they'd be better off without him.

So not true.

Cameron did fine with the kids, even when they were sick. He'd be a great parent or step-parent. There was no reason for him not to be a part of their lives.

The only obstacles were the ones in Cameron's mind. Sometimes, though, they were the ones hardest to overcome.

Chapter Twenty-One

Cameron parked in his covered space at the condo and dragged himself up the stairs. It was nearly eight in the evening and even then he'd left a mountain of work undone. It'd been two days since he'd moved back home, and free to put in the long days to be caught up by now. But work had been like swimming through molasses. He tried to focus on his job, but his thoughts kept returning to the precious family he'd left behind in that little house in the Deco District. He worried about Josh and whether he was really ready to take over like he said he was. He worried about the children and whether they would return to school too quickly. He worried Josh would try to put in too many hours at the theater and get sick all over again. His head wasn't in the game.

It didn't help he'd woken up with a cough this morning and continued to worsen as the day progressed. By the middle of the afternoon he had the muscle aches from hell. He tried all day to deny what was happening to him. He was tired. It was allergies. It was the cedar trees out in the Hill Country.

He had the flu.

Cameron cursed and collapsed onto his sofa. A violent shiver tore through his body and his face felt hot. He dug an old thermometer out of the bathroom cabinet. Shit. A hundred and two. Definitely one sick puppy. It was time to stop trying to deny it.

So much for playing catch-up at work.

He put in a call to his internist, who called in a prescription to a twenty-four-hour pharmacy that delivered. His head was swimming, but he managed to get into and out of the shower and put on pajama bottoms and a loose tee. The thought of food turned his stomach, but he got down a couple of cans of carbonated water, his prescription, and a dose of Tylenol. His dizziness had him stumbling into his bedroom and collapsing on the bed without even pulling back the covers.

The next few days were a blur. He alternated between chills and sweats. A cool shower would have been nice, but he was too unsteady to risk it. His mother and Vivi both offered to take care of him, but Vivi was needed at the office and he didn't want her to catch it a second time. He told his mother and his Aunt Jane, both looking at sixty-five in the rearview mirror, do not come over. If it was making him this sick, it could land one of them in the hospital or worse. Although he wanted to, he resisted the urge to call Josh, who was struggling to get his kids back on their feet.

It sure would've been nice to have the kind of tender caring Cam had given them.

Besides, he and Josh were no longer a couple. Sure, he'd taken care of them, but Josh was firmly in the *ex* category.

Because Cameron had put him there.

He dozed and he thrashed about, freezing one minute and sweating the next. Every muscle in his body ached, and no matter how much water he downed, he was always thirsty. His sleep was erratic and when he did manage to doze off, he dreamed of Josh and the kids.

He dreamed of things they'd never done together, and never would because he wasn't the kind of man the kids needed in their lives.

A single tear snaked down his cheek as he contemplated his lonely existence without them.

Even having the flu would've been better with them around.

It took four days for his fever to break. When he hit the shower, his legs weren't steady. He donned fresh pajama bottoms and a t-shirt, stripped his bed, and put his sheets in the washer. He'd done nothing strenuous, but he was bone tired and collapsed on the sofa until he could drum up the strength to open a can of soup for lunch. Fresh sheets went on the bed and he was back in it, sound asleep for the rest of the day.

The next few days were slow going, but he felt better each morning. The better he felt, the lonelier he became. He had been with Josh and the kids for ten short days. Yet they'd wormed their way into his heart. Seeing Josh in action with the kids made him love Josh more. He poured out love and caring on Jackson and Beth. Whatever her mistakes in life might've been, his sister had done a wise thing in bringing her children to Josh to raise.

What'd surprised him the most was he found himself caring for the kids, as people with distinct personalities.

He could love them easily. So easily. He could be part of a loving family, rather than enduring this lonely, miserable existence without them. He had the balls to man up and take his place beside Josh and the children. He knew how to be the man they needed him to be when they were sick. He had it inside him to be that guy every day.

He had to be, or he'd never be where he wanted to be, by Josh's and the kid's sides for the rest of his life.

***

Josh parked *Bubbe*'s huge new crossover in her driveway under the portico and retrieved her walker from the back. "It was good to be back in synagogue," he said as Beth and Jackson came bouncing out of the backseat.

"It's a shame you have to work so many Friday nights," *Bubbe* muttered as he helped her from the passenger seat to her waiting walker. "Especially now that you have the children."

"It is what it is," he said. "There's always the Saturday morning service." The children raced to the door. "I'm glad we're between shows right now and I could bring you since Ella's out of town." They had a substitute in for the weekend who would've taken *Bubbe*, but it was a good excuse for him and the children to spend a little time with her.

She squeezed his hand. "I'm glad too." She lowered her voice. "I hope there's something decent to eat waiting for us. The agency said this lady's a good caregiver, but not much of a cook."

"At least they're honest."

The food was okay at best, but the children didn't seem to notice and polished off their dinners without coaxing. Pinch-hitter Lydia settled them in front of the television and cleared the table while *Bubbe* and Josh lingered over store-bought cheesecake. They talked about inconsequential things mostly. *Bubbe* had something on her mind and Josh knew if he gave her long enough, he would find out what.

It took a while, but she asked offhandedly if she needed to keep the children for him anytime soon. "For you to have an evening to yourself. Or to go out with your friends," she added.

Sly old dog. "Or to go out on a date." He tried to smile but couldn't. "I'm not going out on dates these days."

"I thought you and your young man were seeing one another again."

"We gave it another go, but we bombed out the second time. I doubt we'll try for a third."

Her forehead creased into a frown. "I thought he took care of you and the kids the whole time you were sick."

"He did." Josh felt a lump form in his throat. "He took wonderful care of us. He's a good and caring man. He loves me. I know it down to my bones. I love him just as much. He's got it in his head he won't be a good parent, that he's not good with kids, and they need a better man in their lives than he is. He's worried he can't raise them right because he's not Jewish. Way down deep I think he believes gay folks shouldn't try to raise a family, even though he swears he doesn't think that anymore." He cleared his throat and swiped under his eyes. "I didn't mean to sit here and do this."

"Uncle Josh cries a lot since Mr. Cameron left," Beth said from the door. She ran in the room and hopped up onto Josh's lap. "He does it where he doesn't think Jackson and I hear, but we do. I'm sorry, Uncle Josh. I miss Mr. Cameron too." She put her arms around his neck and patted his back.

"Yeah. He promised to come see us and he hasn't." Jackson sounded angry and sad. He pulled out the chair beside Josh and clambered up. "I guess he didn't mean it."

Bubbe's lips tightened. "I'm sorry he let you down." She looked over at Beth. "I'm sorry you miss him. Was he good to you, *kindelah*?"

"He made nice suppers, and took us to school, and read to us on Shabbat."

"He talked to us like we were grown-ups," Jackson volunteered. "He let us talk to him the same way."

"I see." She looked from Beth to Jackson. "Do you miss him?"

"Like a son of a bitch," Jackson said.

"Jackson," Josh and *Bubbe* snapped in unison.

"Well, I do," he said defensively.

Bubbe's lips twitched and she shook her head. "I wish I could wave a magic wand and make it all better. Since I can't, maybe you two can enjoy some of the chocolate chip cookies Ella left behind."

***

Cameron aimed the blowtorch at the thin strip of metal and applied the right amount of pressure as the iron heated to a red glow. To his relief and satisfaction, the metal bowed into the exact shape it needed to make a smaller version of the elaborate chandelier he'd designed for the steak house. The owners had been so pleased with his work they'd commissioned another, smaller version for their rustic retreat north of Fredericksburg. He was behind on the project though, and unlikely to catch up anytime soon. It was only his second day back on the job, and he still looked and felt like shit. Unlike Josh, his body was taking its sweet time healing. Another strip, two at the most, and he was going to have to call it a day and go home to the empty, lonely condo where his only companions were his regrets and memories.

Maybe he would do three more strips before calling it a day.

He cut another piece of metal and was about to apply the torch when he spotted Vivi coming through the door from the office suite, her stylish business suit and heels a sharp contrast to his sweaty work clothes. Safety goggles were perched on her impeccably made-up face. She came straight to him and signaled him to take out his earplugs. "You have a visitor," she shouted over the screeches and whines of the factory floor.

"I have a what?" he yelled.

"A visitor. Someone wants to talk to you." She had an indecipherable expression on her face.

"Take care of them yourself," he tried to say, but she was gone before he could finish his sentence.

He swore and turned off his blowtorch. "What an afternoon for a visitor," he mumbled. He was hot and sweaty, and hardly dressed for whoever this was who hadn't called to make an appointment. Since customer service could make or break a company, he'd disguise his irritation and do his best to please whoever was waiting.

He wiped the sweat off as best he could and opened his office door, and froze in his tracks. Clara Goldstein was sitting in the chair across from his desk with a steaming cup of coffee in front of her and a displeased expression on her face. She was the last person he expected to pay a visit, especially the way he and Josh parted. Unless she was here about metal work.

Which he seriously doubted.

He wiped his grubby hand on his work pants and offered it to her. "How are you, Mrs. Goldstein?" he said. "Sorry for the state I'm in. I was welding together a chandelier."

She shook his hand despite its grimy state. "I didn't realize you worked on the factory floor. I thought you owned the place."

"Vivi and I own it. I do custom pieces."

"Charge dearly for them, I imagine."

"I do." He sat down behind his desk. "I doubt you came here to discuss chandeliers. What can I do for you this afternoon?"

Her eyes narrowed. "It's not what you can do for me. It's what you can do for my heartsick grandson and his equally devastated children. You broke their hearts, Mr. Heiser. You need to make it right." She looked at him imperiously and he felt himself shrink down into his chair.

This woman was ninety-one years old but had a backbone made of steel. She'd reigned over her family's business for seventy years, and no one in San Antonio would dare take her on. They'd lose, and lose badly.

On the other hand, she was here on a mission of love and deserved his honesty. He sat up and looked her in the eye. "Ma'am, Josh and the kids aren't the only ones hurting. I miss him, *Bu*—Mrs. Goldstein. I miss all three of them. I don't know what to do to make it right."

"Let's talk about that, then. Starting with why you left. Don't bother me with that you're-no-good-with-the-kids malarky. You were fine with them, according to the experts."

Cameron felt his brows go up. "What experts?"

She looked at him as though he wasn't too bright. "Beth and Jackson, of course. They think you're wonderful. Well, Beth does. Jackson's angry because you promised to go see him and haven't." She pinned him with a glare. "Which you shouldn't have done, if you didn't mean it."

"Sorry. A walloping case of the flu made that a little hard. This is only my second day back to work."

"Oh." She didn't look entirely mollified. "Does Josh know?"

"Not unless he heard it at the theater. He has his hands full with his job and his kids. He didn't need to worry about me."

"Maybe he would've wanted to worry about you," she said tartly. "Maybe he would've wanted to take care of you the way you did him." She leaned over the desk. "That's what people who love one another do, Mr. Heiser. They take care of each other. They take care of the *kindelah* God gives them. Unless you don't want to be bothered?"

"It's not a matter of being bothered. It's a matter of getting it right. I want to with all my heart. I don't know if I can. With any child, really, but especially with Jackson and Beth."

"Because they're Jewish."

"Because they're Jewish. What I know about Judaism and raising Jewish children would fit on the head of a pin. They need a Jewish father to do that for them."

"They have a Jewish father to do that." She looked at him appraisingly. "Unless you'd consider converting."

"I'd have to bury my mother."

"Never mind. It was worth asking."

"There's still the question of getting the rest of it right. I have a lot of doubts about that."

"Why?"

He let out a deep breath. *Here goes nothing.* "It probably started with my father. He never thought gay men should raise kids. He knew I was gay. I always thought everything he said about being gay was meant for me."

She waved her hand in front of her. "I met your father a few times. He was a homophobe. Didn't like Jews much, either."

Cameron winced. "I know." He leaned forward. "But it wasn't only Dad. I've seen some gay families, who... let's say their picture's beside dysfunctional in the dictionary and let it go at that."

"True of some straight families as well."

"But for gay families it seems worse." He looked at her helplessly. "What if I give it a go with Josh and then mess it up?"

She looked at him unblinkingly. "What if you give it a go and don't? At least you care enough to be worried about it. Cameron, may I call you Cameron?" He nodded and she continued. "Children don't come with a set of instructions, and the baby books are balderdash. We learn it as we go. You relearn with every child. Josh is doing that with the children. You would too. I think you would do fine. More importantly, Beth and Jackson think so. As does Josh. Their opinions are the only ones that really matter. Except for yours."

"I never thought about it. How somebody learns to be a parent. I never expected it to be an issue."

"You probably haven't. You've never been around kids much, I'm willing to bet, and had no idea whether you were good with them. But you've been around Josh's kids, and those children gave you their seal of approval. Maybe it's time for you to think about learning to be a parent, and whether you have it in you to do that," she said firmly. "It wouldn't hurt you to do a little homework while you're at it. That's what the Internet's for. You're not the first gentile to want to make a family with Jews, and you won't be the last. See what other people have to say about it."

Cameron nodded. "If you say so."

"I say so." She looked at her watch. "I've taken up enough of your time. Before I go, some food for thought. My grandson loves you and misses you. You were good to his children and they miss you. I want you to think about this. Coming here wasn't easy for me. Given the choice, I would have wanted Josh to love and marry a nice Jewish girl. You're neither. But you seem to be the missing piece in that little family. The piece they need."

"The piece they need? Mrs. Goldstein, I certainly hope so."

"Let me ask you three questions, and then I really do have to go. First off, do you love Josh?"

Cameron swallowed. "I love that man with all my heart."

"Question two. Can you see yourself loving the children?"

"Yes…yes, I can," he stammered. "Actually, I do."

"Question three. Can you see yourself being good to them and taking good care of them for the rest of your life?" Cameron said nothing. "That's going to be the clincher. If you can rid yourself of the seeds of doubt your father cruelly planted in you, and see yourself with those children as the good and loving man Josh says you are, there's nothing stopping you from being with the man you love and making a family with him."

Cameron dipped his head. "You make it sound easy."

"Easy? Dream on. It's hard. Very hard. But it's other things too, if you want it to be. Rewarding. Satisfying. Gratifying. Joyous. Loving." Using the lip of the desk, she pulled herself up from the chair, and magically her caregiver appeared with a walker. "Thank you for your time," she said as she turned to put her hands on the walker.

"Thank you for yours."

Slowly, and carefully, Mrs. Goldstein left his office, followed by her caregiver. Vivi saw them as far as the door before making a beeline back to his office. "What was that all about?"

"It was a 'come to Jesus' talk."

"From a Jewish lady?"

Cameron shrugged. "Nothing I haven't already heard."

Vivi looked at him with narrowed eyes. "Did any of it sink in this time?"

He sat back. "Maybe it did."

He went out to the factory floor and bent two more rods before calling it a day. He was deep in thought as he drove home. Before he realized where he was, the hot water from the shower drenched his tired shoulders. He couldn't shake what *Bubbe* had said to him.

He pulled on sweatpants and a tee then parked his ass in his favorite spot. He stared out the huge picture window at the San Antonio skyline, consumed by his thoughts as the sun set in the west and the lights of the city winked on.

He re-reviewed Clara Goldstein's questions. Absolutely, he loved Josh. He could love the kids. Probably already did. But could he be good to and for them, and take care of them for the rest of his life? He got up and poured a sparkling water, and went back to the living room, where he sipped his drink while he mulled things over.

He thought about the ten days he'd spent with them. Sure, he'd taken care of them, but it was a temporary situation and they all knew it. If he and Josh got back together, his relationship with them would have to be forever, or why bother. The big questions were: Could he be good for them for the long haul, and raise them the way their mother had wanted them raised?

A much harder question to tackle.

He finished his drink and left the sofa, powering up his computer. He needed to know more before he could answer. He found a treasure trove of advice and knowledge, and spent hours reading everything he could find, from handbooks on raising Jewish children to bulletins from the local synagogues.

He read several articles written by non-Jewish parents raising their children as Jews. What it pretty much boiled down to was Josh would have to do the heavy lifting. There were some things out of their shared scripture he could teach them. The moral values were common to both faiths, as were a number of basic tenants. It would require effort on his part, but not much more than it would if he were instructing them in the ways of his own faith.

He let himself picture what life would be like if he were with them all the time. Living with them and the little dog in Josh's house. Maybe later in a bigger house in the Deco District or a two-story in one of the tony suburbs. Getting the kids dressed and to school on time and helping them with their homework. Taking them shopping for school supplies. Cooking them healthy meals. Going with Josh to parent-teacher conferences and Open House. Cheering them on at soccer and baseball and football games. Clapping and beaming with pride as they performed on the Durango stage. Having the inevitable talks about love and sex, and booze and drugs, and always about being decent people.

Giving them hell for breaking the rules. Teaching Jackson to drive and giving Beth's boyfriends the stink eye. Choking back tears as they waved good-bye from the steps of the college dorm. Breathing a sigh of relief when they landed their first job as an adult.

Holding Josh's hand as Jackson stood under the canopy with the love of his life. Holding Beth's newborn child in his arms.

Standing under the canopy with Josh as they said their vows to one another.

Hell, why couldn't he do it? He'd done fine with them when they were sick. Why couldn't he do fine with them all the time?

He'd been wrong. So wrong. It might take a little getting used to, but the role of husband and father looked mighty damn fine on him.

He looked at the time with surprise. He'd spent hours surfing, learning, and thinking. It was too late to go over to Josh's tonight. He'd go tomorrow. He'd take them dinner. He'd feed Josh and the kids and try to make things right with the man and kids he'd come to love.

He hoped it wasn't too late.

***

Josh sank tiredly into his desk chair and stared at the mountain of paperwork facing him. He had finished a stroll through the Academy classes in progress, which was usually a surefire pick-me-up, but today had done nothing to snap him out of his funk. He'd been back to work for nearly a week and there was still a backlog. It didn't help Rachel had caught the same damned flu, or that Maggie's sister's entire family was sick with it and she was trying to take care of them. He was trying to do the work of three people. From the pile of papers and mail in Cameron's cubby, it didn't look like he'd been by any time recently. If Josh didn't hear from him in a day or two, he'd call or email and see what was going on. Either Cameron was avoiding him, or Cameron had come down with the flu along with everybody else.

Both possibilities sucked.

He checked the time. The kids would be in their Academy classes for another couple of hours. He had to decide whose work to tackle first. Maggie had been out the longest, so he turned to the half-finished grant proposals she had emailed him and was slogging through one and wishing to hell Maggie had finished it when Vivi stuck her head in the door with Julie on her hip. "She's outgrown her baby carriers, I see," he said.

Vivi plopped down in a chair and heaved a sigh of relief. "She's getting heavier by the day. We're shopping for another stroller this weekend. Something small and lightweight. The monstrosity we got at the baby shower's too much for short jaunts."

"Then you'll be carrying two strollers, not one."

"Says the man with two car seats in his backseat."

"At least Julie doesn't argue about it. Jackson's convinced he doesn't need one."

"What did you tell him?"

"To talk to me in eight inches and fifteen pounds."

Vivi laughed. "Wait 'til he thinks he's ready for beer."

Josh held up his hand. "Not helping, Vivi. You're here to hang out?"

"Maybe for a little while, but not really." She held up a beat-up canvas bag. "I came by to get Cameron's paperwork, if you would be so kind. He's feeling better and can deal with it now."

"Aw, shit. He caught that crap from us."

"He did. It knocked him on his ass."

"I was afraid that would happen." Josh ran his fingers through his hair. "I wish he would've called me. I could've taken care of him."

"At what risk to you and the kids?"

"We've already had it. We're not going to catch it again that fast."

"I wish he'd called you too." She looked at him with exasperation. "You two are a couple of fools."

"Yeah, we are. Kind of like that other Durango couple. You know, the ones who married for money and then decided they wanted love instead." Josh tried and failed to hide his smirk.

Vivi stuck out her tongue.

He leaned forward. "I love your brother. I would take him back in a heartbeat, but he can't get past Jackson and Beth."

"Maybe he will." She looked at him with an expression he couldn't decipher.

She handed the bag to Josh and he emptied Cameron's cubby. "Thanks for taking this to him."

"Glad to help."

Vivi left, and Josh returned to work on the grant proposal until his office door burst open, and this time Beth barreled in. "I learned to do a time-step." She did a respectable version of the dance step across his office floor.

"Wow. Way to go. You're gonna be dancing across the Durango stage before you know it."

Beth beamed as Jackson wandered in. "I acted out the part of a snake," he announced before Josh could ask.

"Okay."

"Down on the floor and everything."

"Not sure where else a snake would be." Josh was careful to keep his face serious.

Jackson shot him a withering look. He gave them each a hug. "Are y'all about ready to go home and get some supper?"

They nodded and followed him out to the car, chattering incessantly until he pulled into his driveway beside a familiar Shelby Mustang.

The one he hadn't gotten to drive.

What the fuck?

The kids fell silent mid-sentence. "Is that Mr. Cameron's car?" Beth asked.

"What's he doing here?" Jackson asked.

Good question.

One he needed the answer to before he got his hopes up, or his heart broken again.

He hopped out of the car, the kids on his heels. The front door was unlocked and the house was filled with a delicious aroma coming from the kitchen. "Cameron?" he called out.

"In here."

Beth squealed and ran for the kitchen. "Mr. Cameron, I missed you." Josh hit the kitchen as she threw her arms around Cameron's knees, almost knocking him to the ground.

Cameron bent down and kissed the top of her head. "I missed you too, little one." He straightened and Josh sucked in a breath. Cameron's face was pale and dark shadows rode under his eyes. "You're still sick. Beth, let go of him so Cameron can sit down." Without giving him a choice, Josh steered Cameron to the kitchen table and pulled out a chair. "Sit."

Cameron sat.

Jackson peered at Cameron's washed-out face. "Man, Mr. Cameron. You look like shit."

Josh flinched. "Jack-son…"

"It's okay, Josh. Jackson and I talk to each other like grown-ups," Cameron said solemnly.

"Maybe Jackson could be a little less grown-up," Josh suggested firmly. "Now, you two get out of your uniforms and come back to the kitchen. The pizza I smell in the oven and the salad on the counter says dinner's ready."

The kids took off. Josh sat down across from Cameron. "What's going on?" he asked quietly.

"More than I have time to tell you before the kids get back." His smile was crooked.

"But… but—"

Cameron leaned over and placed a gentle kiss on his lips. "We'll talk after they go to bed. Now, since you shoved my tired ass into a chair, will you get dinner to the table?"

Josh nodded, a tiny seed of hope sprouting in his heart.

The kids were back in a flash. Josh helped them wash their hands and Beth set the table while Jackson fed Pepper. Josh gave everyone plenty of pizza and salad. They let the children carry the conversation during dinner. They were eager to tell Cameron about going back to school and their classes at the Academy. "Today I learned to do a time-step," Beth announced proudly. "Uncle Josh, can you do a time step?"

"Your Uncle Josh can do a lot more than a time step." Cameron smirked and Josh choked on the pizza.

"How about you?" Jackson asked Cameron.

"No, but my sister can. Vivi's a terrific dancer. I can sing, though, and act a little."

Jackson launched into a description of his experience as a snake. Josh watched Cameron interact with his child. *Please, please let this be what it looks like,* he prayed silently as they finished dinner and loaded the dishwasher. Their discussion might take a while, and Beth and Jackson needed to be in bed first.

Maybe Josh and Cameron needed to be there as well.

Cameron looked really wrung out. Josh parked him in the living room with the remote. The children were wound up, probably from Cameron's unexpected appearance, and took longer than usual to get to bed. "I want another story," Beth whined as he shut her book and handed over her stuffed bunny.

"Nope, that's it for tonight. I'll read you one tomorrow."

"Or maybe Mr. Cameron can read it to me," she said slyly.

"We'll see."

He left Jackson reading his own bedtime story and shut his bedroom door. Cameron was sitting on the sofa with his shoes off and his feet on the coffee table. "You need a footstool in here. Or a recliner. Or something," he announced as Josh plopped down across from him. "No, come sit by me." Cameron patted the sofa beside him.

Josh eyed the sofa. "Why?"

"Because it's easier to tell you I'm sorry and I love you, and beg you to take me back if I'm holding your hand." Fear warred with hope as he sat beside Cameron, who took his hand. "Is it too late? Have I blown it entirely?"

"No. Of course not. But I have questions."

Cameron squeezed his hand. "Fire away."

"I don't know how to ask you. Is this a change of heart, or am I still supposed to keep you separate from my kids?"

"You're a package deal. You, Jackson, and Beth. I'm fine with that."

"Okay," Josh said slowly. "You're willing to spend time with the kids."

"I am."

Josh tamped down the hope soaring through his veins. "I guess my next question is, to what do I attribute this change of heart? I've tried to talk to you, and I know Vivi has. She told me she has. What happened to make you change your mind?"

Cameron's lips twitched. "A visit from an imperious lady who was *not* happy with the way I treated her grandson and his children."

Josh felt his jaw drop. "*Bubbe* talked to you?"

"She did. Remind me not to get on her bad side again. It's not a pleasant place to be."

"Wha…what did she say to you?"

"Before I tell you, you need to know. My decision was made before *Bubbe* talked to me. Hearing her opinion was a boost, but it wasn't the deal breaker."

Josh smiled. "Okay. Go on."

"She told me the business about me not being good with children was, let's see if I remember her word…balderdash, and that the experts—the kids—thought I'd been great. She'd rather you wanted a Jewish girl, but excepting that impossibility, I'm the missing piece in your family. She said to go home and do a little digging about being a non-Jew in a Jewish family. So I did."

He cracked his neck like a prize fighter entering the ring. Josh saw it before Cam said another word. His man was all in. "I figured when you and Vivi tried to convince me I had what it took, it was because you loved *me*. Your grandmother talked to me because she loves *you*. You and the kids. I want to try. I want to try so damn bad. I love you, and I love them."

"You do?" Josh cursed the squeak in his voice.

"Of course I love you." Cameron smiled. "You I expected to fall for. The kids?" He shrugged. "They kinda snuck in there, ya know? They're easy kids to love."

"They are."

Cameron leaned in. "The most important thing is, I can see myself being something good in their lives. What do you think? Is it too late for you and me?"

"Really? You know I love you." He ran his hand down the side of Cameron's face. "What you don't know is how much the kids care. They missed you. They missed you bad, and told me so."

"Well, they won't have to miss me anymore. I'm all in." He leaned forward and squeezed Josh's hands. "How do we do this? Date? Go out with the kids in tow?"

Josh felt his smile split his face. "You could move in here until we need something bigger. Unless that's going too fast."

"It'd be a hell of a lot easier than trying to date. Unless you'd rather…. No, my place is too small. Here it is. We'll look for something bigger later. Maybe, I don't know, make us a permanent thing." He looked at Josh with hope.

"I can see us standing under the canopy. *Bubbe* would be good with that."

"Then we won't wait forever." He scooted closer. "Come here. I want to kiss you, and I need you to be close." Cam's cheeks were flushed and they were both gasping for breath by the time they came up for air. "God, I've missed you," Cameron said as he stroked the hair back from Josh's face. "I want you so bad I can taste it."

"Are you still too sick? Do we need to give it a few more days?" Josh asked.

Cameron took Josh's hand and put it over his rock-hard erection. "Does it feel like I need a few more days?" He glanced toward the hall. "The kids are here."

"They're here all the time. They're going to be here for the next ten or fifteen years." Josh snickered. "I doubt it stops Miguel and Vivi. Or Jessica and Brian. I can't see it bothering Letti and Kevin. I bet Wade and Owen—"

Cameron cut him off with a hard kiss. "I hear ya." He stood and held out his hand and together they half-ran to the bedroom. They stripped and suited up in record time and sank onto the bed in a tangle of arms, legs, and desire. They gasped in mutual delight as they became one. Josh pumped hard, his need for Cameron overtaking any tenderness he might've shown, and in a matter of seconds exploded in an orgasm that shook him from his head to his toes. Cameron's need proved to be just as great, and in a matter of minutes he too was arching in ecstasy.

They came down to Earth slowly, holding one another as the sweat cooled their feverish bodies. "So much for the slow, sensuous buildup," Cameron said dryly.

"It's what we needed. We've been apart too long for it to be anything else." Josh curled up next to Cameron. "We have the rest of our lives for those slow, sensuous buildups."

Cameron's face lit up. "We do, don't we? The rest of our lives. Damn. That sounds good."

"It does, doesn't it?"

Epilogue

Production manager Miranda Jenks stood at the back of the Durango Theatre with her clipboard in hand and watched as the opening act of *West Side Story* unfolded. It had been a hard eighteen months. Brutally hard. First the pandemic and then a severe lack of city funding shutting down the theater for months after they'd been closed for over a year. They were finally open again; the curtain had gone up on *West Side Story* and the young actor playing Tony was singing "Something's Coming."

Despite the long absence from the theater, the actors slipped back into the roles they were rehearsing when the theater shut down. Tonight, they were knocking it out of the ballpark. She breathed deeply, at last freed from nearly two years behind a mask. The aroma of popcorn and beer almost, but not quite, disguised the odor of the powerful disinfectants used by the professional cleaning company Josh and Cameron persuaded to donate their services.

Her eyes drifted toward the happy couple. They'd always been good at their roles as executive director and chairman of the board. But now that they were married and raising a family together, they were a force to be reckoned with. They were sitting in the back row with Jackson between them, Beth having been judged too young to understand the production's powerful story. Miranda looked at Jackson wistfully. He had dark hair and blue eyes, and as cute as he could be. Ten now? Eleven?

Older than Tommy had been when he died.

Miranda jerked her thoughts back to the present. She spotted a couple of concerns during a scene change and jotted a note to mention it to the crew chief after the show. Likewise with a sound system delay the audience most likely didn't notice, but she did. All part of her job. Along with everything else that went on during a performance.

Few people outside the theater world had even heard of a production manager, much less understood what one did. They thought the director was in charge. Which they were. But the nitty-gritty details were handled by the production manager, even during rehearsal. At the first performance, the director bowed out and patted himself on the back for a job well done, and the production manager took over the supervision of the production. She oversaw every single performance, from making sure the curtain went up on time to catching and noting glitches that needed to be corrected before the next show, to smoothing the feathers, which inevitably got ruffled when highly creative and artistic people worked together.

She loved her job.

She stood beside the sound booth for a few more minutes and watched the beginning of the Dance at the Gym ballet sequence between the Sharks and the Jets. As always, she marveled at Jessica's talented choreography. Things seemed to be running smoothly, and she decided to take a bit of a breather in her favorite hidey-hole.

She moved aside the stand with the velvet ropes and climbed the steep, carpet-covered stairs to the freshly cleaned balcony, deserted but for the musical director and the orchestra members cloistered in the small individual rooms in the sound booth.

Tonight the balcony wasn't completely deserted. A lone figure sat in the back row with a ball cap pulled low. Whoever it was appeared to be watching the stage intently. Miranda wondered who the person was and, more importantly, why they'd chosen to sit in the back row of the balcony rather than in their purchased seat downstairs. But the man...or woman, she couldn't tell in the dark, wasn't hurting anybody. If she was still up here after the show, Miranda would make it a point to find out what was going on.

She wandered about halfway down and took an aisle seat as the Dance at the Gym scene finished. She caught another glitch during a scene change, which she jotted down. The actor playing Tony sang the iconic "Maria." The scene changed again and she sat up straighter.

Emma's first song was coming up.

She watched with pride as Emma Ellis, her blonde hair covered by a dark wig, took her place on the stage as Rosalia sang "America," a newcomer's sarcastic take on American life.

Emma was a recent alumnus of the Academy and a little young for the part, but the decision to cast her had been unanimous. In the two years since she'd moved in with her grandparents, Emma had blossomed, finishing high school and attending a local college online. Miranda watched as Emma performed and held her own with the older actor playing Anita. Leaving her asshole father's house and moving in with the Summersets was the best thing that could have happened to her. It was what Miranda's closest friend Renee would have wanted for her daughter.

Which was why Miranda had reached out after Renee's death to the lonely girl, mired in grief and trapped in the house with her alcoholic father. She had enlisted the help of Renee's influential grandparents, and the Summersets had overridden Ross Ellis's objections and gotten Emma involved in the Academy. Miranda's involvement in Emma's life went far beyond the theater.

Emma and Tommy had gone to nursery school together and had been in the same grade in school. Emma had been there for her son while he fought for his life and lost, and she'd laid a bouquet of sunflowers on his casket before they lowered him into the ground.

The same sunflowers she'd laid on her mother's casket eight years later.

Miranda made herself shake off her sad memories. Tonight wasn't a night for sadness. It was a night for joy and pride, and new beginnings. Emma was rockin' the stage, and Miranda couldn't have been prouder.

The story moved along. Intermission came and went, and the mysterious figure had not moved from the back row. Miranda was becoming truly curious. She continued taking notes on what was working and what needed attention, and before she knew it, Tony and Maria were singing "There's a Place for Us" as Tony died in Maria's arms.

It was time to go downstairs.

She stood and climbed the steep balcony steps. The song finished and as applause began to echo around the auditorium, the house lights winked on slowly and the figure in the ball cap raised his head and graced her with a piercing glare.

She froze on the steps, not trusting her vision, as she stared into blue eyes staring at her with disdain. *Ross Ellis.* Renee's widower. Emma's father. Her neighbor one farm over. The man who'd neglected her best friend for years. The drunken asshole Josh had thrown out of the theater.

What the hell was he doing at the Durango?

TURN THE PAGE FOR A BONUS NOVELLA
SAUL AND CLARA'S STORY

FUTURE'S EMBRACE

Chapter One

San Antonio, 1948

Saul got off the San Pedro Avenue bus and walked up the sidewalk toward the ornate, imposing synagogue. A cool November wind ruffled his hair and the fine fabric of his impeccably made suit—a suit he'd finished late last evening. He'd almost put it to the side with the rest of the suits he'd tailored over the past months, but if he was going to be a walking advertisement for his talent, he needed to wear his best efforts for potential customers to see. Especially the men he saw at Shabbat services. They, and the wealthy gentiles of San Antonio, would be his customer base when he opened his clothing store a few months from now. Some of the men from temple came to him for custom-made suits and shirts, but that was a sideline. He hoped it would become full-time once his store opened, and his beloved Elise was running it for him.

He straightened the *yarmulke* on his head, climbed the steps and spoke to a few fellow worshippers, then sat in the back pew for Friday evening Shabbat services. He glanced around the sanctuary, spotting a number of familiar faces. After thirteen years in the city, he knew, or at least recognized, many members of San Antonio's small Jewish community. But he wasn't all that close to any of them. Between the long hours he put in as a tailor, and his innate reserve, he'd never taken the time, or made the effort to get more than friendly. He'd found the community to be unfailingly kind to him and to the other lonely souls who came their way. The temple's members had been especially warm and welcoming when the hollow-cheeked, dead-eyed Holocaust survivors began to trickle into their community.

The cantor had already started toward the lectern when the back door opened and a young woman slipped in and sat in the pew across from his. Saul glanced in her direction, then looked again at the delicate blonde across the aisle. Her outfit, a two-piece suit, caught his eye first. The fabric wasn't of the finest quality, but it was well-cut and stylish, and suited the girl's small frame perfectly. Her shoes, scarf, and handbag coordinated nicely as well. That kind of impeccable taste and flair was rare in San Antonio, especially in a girl who looked like she was still in her teens. His gaze traveled up to her finely boned face, lush but unsmiling lips, and bright blue eyes. A pretty package, whoever she was. Saul shifted on the pew. Under other circumstances, he might've found her appealing, but she was too different from Elise. His tall, dark-haired sweetheart had become the standard by which he judged other women. By those standards, this girl was too short, too blonde, and too young to ever interest him.

Besides, it wasn't an Elise look-alike he was looking for. He was waiting for Elise herself. It didn't matter if he hadn't seen her for thirteen years. It didn't matter if he hadn't heard from her for eight. It didn't matter if the entire family he'd left behind in Leipzig had been wiped out in the camps. She had survived it all somehow. She was out there somewhere, and come hell or high water, he would find her, and then she would take her place by his side. To believe otherwise was unthinkable.

But that didn't stop him from sneaking looks at the blonde when he should've been paying attention to the service.

After the closing prayers, the cantor invited them all to the social hall for the Oneg Shabbat. Saul considered skipping it, but the alternative was to return to the lonely room he'd rented for years in Mrs. Blum's downtown boardinghouse. Even though these days he could afford better than a single room, he wanted to save his money for his store.

He shuffled along with the rest of congregation and stood patiently during Kiddush and the Hamotzi. He was balancing a plate of food on his knee and chatting with Sam Ackerman, the elderly owner of a local ranch supply store, when the girl from across the aisle approached, looking at them uncertainly. "Which of you gentlemen is Saul Goldstein?" she asked haltingly.

"I am," Saul said. "May I help you?"

She replied with a half-smile. "I hope so." Her accent was German, layered with something else. British, maybe.

"Here. Sit beside young Saul." Mr. Ackerman stood swiftly. "My Mamie's going to want to leave about now. I need to go find her."

"No, it's—" She looked after the older man helplessly.

"It's all right," Saul said. "*Nehman sie platz.*"

"English is fine," she said as she took the vacated chair.

He tried to smile encouragingly. "What can I do for you?"

She glanced over at the rabbi. "Rabbi Shulman said I should talk to you. He said you were opening a clothing store soon and thought you might be able to offer me a job."

He looked at her eager expression. "Actually, no. Not at this time. It will be months before the store will be ready to open." *Not until Elise is here.* "I won't need a sales staff until then."

The girl's face fell. "I see," she said quietly. "Thank you for your time."

Saul's heart twisted at the sight of the disappointment on her face. "No, wait," he said as she stood to leave. "Please. Sit. Sit." Reluctantly she sat. "Please, tell me a little about yourself."

The girl took a deep breath. "My name's Clara. Clara Ehrman. I've been in San Antonio for only a month. I'm staying with my best friend Jennie Kirby—who's Jennie Rodriguez now—but I need to find a job and a place to live. I have some experience in retail that might benefit you if you're opening a new business." She fell silent.

Now Saul's curiosity was piqued. She couldn't be more than eighteen or nineteen, so he doubted if her so-called experience amounted to much. It was what she wasn't saying he wondered about. Not that he couldn't guess a good bit of it. *Jewish, German accent, by herself in America.* It wasn't hard to draw a few conclusions from that. She didn't have the gaunt features and broken health that cloaked the typical concentration camp survivor. Her cheeks were rosy, her complexion healthy, her hair thick and lustrous, and while she was small, she wasn't underweight or thin. Wherever she'd spent the war, whatever she'd been doing, she'd had food to eat. But her lips were unsmiling, and in her eyes he could see the same loneliness, the same desolation shared by the other survivors, many of whom were the only ones in their family to live through the horror of the Holocaust.

It was the same loneliness he saw in his eyes every time he looked in the mirror, on days when common sense prevailed and despair overcame hope. Which was happening more and more often as time went by.

Clara was as alone in the world as he was, best friend Jennie or no. She needed a job if she was going to build a new life in a new country. It wouldn't hurt for him to hire someone to get things organized for when he opened his new store. "Actually, Miss Ehrman. I might be able to use you after all. I might be interested in hiring someone to help me get ready to open. It would mean working out of a room in the boardinghouse where I live downtown, and helping me order and organize merchandise."

Her eyes widened. "I'm supposed to work out of your room?"

"No, no," he said quickly. "I've rented a couple of empty rooms from Mrs. Blum downstairs from where I live. You'd be working out of those. Mrs. Blum is there all the time. There would be nothing improper about your working there."

"Good to know." Her face cleared. "When do I start?"

Saul fought back a snicker. "Don't you even want to know what I'm paying you?"

"Mr. Goldstein, I need a job. Anything you're willing to pay me is more than I have now."

"True." Nevertheless, he named a number that was more than fair. She nodded and thanked him. He wrote his address on the temple's bulletin and handed it to her. "Monday morning. Nine. For now, dress practically. Not in your synagogue best. You won't be meeting the public."

"You won't be in that beautiful suit?" Her face turned red and she blushed becomingly.

"No. This is for Shabbat." *And to wear for Elise.*

She nodded. "Monday morning. Dressed for work. Thank you, Mr. Goldstein. You won't regret hiring me. I promise."

She offered her hand and they shook on it. Her fingers in his were small and warm, her grip surprisingly firm and businesslike, yet soft and feminine at the same time. Something inside Saul stirred, something that hadn't stirred since he'd gotten on the train in Leipzig and ridden away from Elise.

Something that had no business stirring when he touched Clara Ehrman.

He watched with hooded eyes as she made her way to the exit and wondered if he'd made a mistake in agreeing to hire her. His curiosity getting the best of him, he turned around to seek out Rabbi Shulman only to find the venerable old cleric standing at his elbow with a faintly satisfied expression on his face. "I gather from the smile she sent my way that you agreed to hire her," Rabbi Shulman said quietly. "Good move on your part."

"I don't know about that. I'm not planning to open for a while yet." He looked at the rabbi. "What's her story?"

"It's the same story we've heard way too many times since nineteen forty-five," the rabbi said quietly. "Her family's gone. She's alone in the world, but for the little gentile friend she followed here."

"I figured as much. She wasn't in the camps. She's too healthy for that. Where was she, and what was she doing?"

"I don't know. She wasn't all that forthcoming. You know as much as I do. But the girl's eager to work, and I think she'll be an asset now as well as later when you get your store open. Which is when? Some of the wives are kvetching. They want you to outfit their husbands."

"I don't know. I was hoping it would be after Elise gets here. The day the door opens, I want her by my side."

The old rabbi looked at him with sad eyes. "Saul, we've talked about this. You know as well as I do, at this point the chances of finding your beloved Elise alive are slim and becoming slimmer by the day." He held up his hand when Saul started to object. "It's been three years. Over three really, since the camps were liberated. Elise knows, or knew, where you are. She knows how to contact you. You've checked list after list and never found her name among the survivors."

"I never found her listed among the dead, either," Saul said stubbornly. Unlike his parents and two brothers, who he'd learned died at Bergen-Belsen in 1942. "Until I find out for sure, I'm not giving up on her. Elise deserves better than that from me."

"I understand. But, Saul, you've had your life on pause ever since you immigrated," Rabbi Shulman said. "First you were saving to bring your family over and claim your sweetheart. Then, when the war started, you were waiting to hear they were still alive. You're still waiting for Elise. You're thirty-what? Three? Four? It's time to stop living for something that may or may not happen down the road and start living your life in the here and now."

"What about Elise? Do I give up on her?" Saul asked tightly.

"No, *menschnik*. Don't give up on her. You may well get that miracle you want so badly. But don't keep living your life waiting for it. Go ahead, Saul. Open your store." The rabbi gave his arm a gentle pat. "It's time."

***

Clara strode briskly to the bus stop on the corner of the main artery in front of the synagogue and sat down on the bench to wait for the bus. She breathed a huge sigh of relief at the weight that was off her shoulders. Mr. Goldstein had agreed to hire her. She had employment and an income. Presumably, this meant she could get her own place to live, a room in a downtown boardinghouse or something equally modest that would be hers.

Maybe this meant she hadn't made a colossal mistake in coming to Texas.

The bus pulled to a stop. She paid her coins and sat down halfway to the back. The lights of the city shone through the bus windows and fell across her inexpensive suit. She looked down and repressed a stab of embarrassment. She had been so proud of the outfit when she'd picked it out in the shop in Swindon. But compared to the exquisite clothes worn by the worshippers in temple tonight, it was cheap and looked it. It had looked particularly bad next to Saul Goldstein's suit. His outfit was made of the finest fabric and perfectly tailored, probably by Saul himself. He wore it with panache. Like he'd been born to wear only the finest.

It didn't hurt he had the perfect body to show it off. Or if his body was less than wonderful, the tailoring of the suit hid the flaws. Tall, broad-shouldered, and narrow-hipped, he made the suit look good. Her outfit had looked downright shoddy in comparison. On the other hand, once she had a place to live, with the salary he'd offered, maybe she could afford to buy a nice outfit or two of her own.

The bus stopped and started through San Antonio's downtown, first through the area where the nicer shops were located, and then into the shabbier section, where the goods were secondhand or inexpensive, and many of the shop signs were in Spanish. She got off at the corner where several lines connected, and onto another bus, which lumbered past downtown and into the neighborhood where Jennie and her young husband lived. Known locally as the Westside, or less kindly, Meskin Town, the neighborhood consisted of tiny houses, many of them not much more than hovels, crammed together on miniscule lots. Clara had been taken aback when Jennie had brought her here for the first time, with a whispered apology as they walked up the sidewalk. "I thought Jesse and I would have our own flat by now," she'd said under her breath as she'd ushered her inside. "Or I would've waited to write."

Clara would've waited to come.

She was here now, staying with Jennie's in-laws in a house that was bursting at the seams, and it was either make the best of it or go back to England and the heartache she lived with day in and day out in the town where she'd spent the war.

She rode patiently until it was her stop and walked the two blocks to the tiny house Jennie and Jesse shared with his widowed mother, his grandmother, and his teenaged sister. Jennie was waiting for her on the front porch, sitting on the steps smoking a cigarette. Her friend smiled tiredly as she blew out a plume of smoke. "So, did you meet any good-looking Jewish chaps to take you out tomorrow night?" Jennie teased.

"I did better than that. I got a job."

"A job?" Jennie sat up straighter. "Tell me about it." She patted the step next to her. "You wanna fag?"

"No." Clara sat down. "Saul Goldstein, one of the men at synagogue, is opening a clothing store in a couple of months. He hired me to help him get it all put together."

"That's good. You'll be able to use what you learned working all those years for Mrs. Formby in the shop in Swindon." She took another puff of her cigarette. "Lucky you."

She patted Jennie's arm. "Something will come along that's better than cleaning houses with Mrs. Rodriguez."

"I don't know." Jennie threw down the rest of her cigarette and ground it into the sand. "The minute I say my last name's Rodriguez, I get the same treatment every other Mexican in this town gets. They decide I'm not worth giving a chance. Never mind the blue eyes and freckles. Geez, I had no idea it would be so bad. Jesse tried to tell me, and I didn't believe him. I couldn't imagine this kind of prejudice. Not in America."

"At least they haven't built death camps," Clara said dryly. "Not yet, anyway."

Jennie winced. "There is that. Still. There are days I wish I'd stayed in England."

"Oh Jennie, no," Clara said. "You have Jesse. He loves you."

"He does. But the rest of it's awful. It's hot and dusty most of the year. Jesse and I can't get a decent job, and he has to take care of his mother and grandmother, which means we're stuck living here. I don't even have anybody to talk to. They don't know English and I don't know Spanish."

Clara was quiet for a moment. "You have good food to eat and plenty of it. They're still rationing food in England, and will be for the foreseeable future. You're lucky. You have a darling young husband and two families who love you, one in England and one here. That is, if you'd give the Rodriguez women a chance. *Two* families who love you. Do you even realize how blessed you are?"

"Oh Clara, you're right," Jennie said, chagrined. She threw her arms around her friend. "I need to stop my whining and count my blessings, don't I?" She gave Clara a swift hug. "I know it's not the same, but I love you so much, and so does my family."

"I know that. It means a lot to me."

The girls fell silent. Jennie didn't realize what Clara carried around in her heart. Even though she'd been beside Clara on that awful day in Vienna, clutching Clara's hand when Clara found her entire family listed among those who'd perished at Mauthausen, Jennie had no real understanding of how alone Clara felt in the world, despite the love the Kirby family had for her. The loneliness she felt for her family, and being separated from her culture, her heritage, most starkly, the hunger she felt to be with others who shared her Jewish roots.

Jennie took a breath. "Okay. I'm done. Sob story over. Tell me about this Mr. Goldstein. Young? Old? Fat? Skinny? Any hubba-hubba there?"

Clara let out with a crack of laughter. "Jennie, there was no hubba-hubba anywhere in the synagogue. Most everybody there was old. There weren't any good-looking chaps my age anywhere to be found."

"But what about your new boss?"

Clara considered Saul for a minute. Tall but not overly so. Thick, curling brown hair. Chiseled cheekbones and chin. Lush, full lips. Soft gray eyes, with lines in the corners that gave away his age as something over thirty. Eyes with the same haunted devastation in them she had. His German accent was beginning to fade, overlaid with the twang she was beginning to associate with San Antonians. "If I were thirty and not nineteen, he'd probably be hubba-hubba. He's too old for me, and way out of my league. You should see him. He has *money* written all over him."

"Money? All the better, my dear," Jennie teased.

"No, really. Besides, he's my boss. I need this job too badly to mess it up with any funny business."

Jennie sobered. "Yes, you do."

The front door opened and Jennie's good-looking husband stepped outside. He leaned over and planted a kiss on Jennie's head. "*Querida*, you wanna walk down the block to the icehouse for a little while? We can get a little food, a *cerveza* or two, and do some dancing, maybe? They have a band playing tonight."

Jennie was up like a flash. "Sure. Clara?"

Clara looked from Jesse to Jennie and shook her head. "Thanks. But I ate a plate at synagogue. I'm fine." Jesse and Jennie had little enough time to themselves. They didn't need her tagging along.

Jesse took Jennie's hand and practically pulled her down the sidewalk. Clara fought a smile as she went inside the tiny house. Mama and *abuelita* were already asleep in the bedroom they shared, and Jesse's sister was working the night shift cleaning at the local hospital. Clara curled up on the end of the sofa and opened the latest Agatha Christie she'd taken out yesterday from the library. She tried to concentrate on the words on the page, but her thoughts kept drifting to the turn her life had taken—hopefully for the better—this evening.

Thanks to Saul Goldstein's job offer, she'd no longer be dependent on the kindness of others. She'd no longer be living in the spare bedroom of the Kirby family's country estate in southern England where she'd lived for the last ten years, or sleeping on the Rodriguez family's sofa in San Antonio where she'd been for the last month.

Tomorrow first thing she would find her own place to live and start to build a new life here with a new job, new friends, and a new congregation. Maybe, at some point, a new family of her own in this hot Texas city. A husband and children, and a new life with them.

Maybe then she wouldn't feel so utterly, completely alone.

Chapter Two

She was going to kill Saul Goldstein. Kill him dead and tell God he died.

A cold gust of December wind blew through the door as Saul shut it behind him. Clara stared at the closing door in consternation. Honestly, the man didn't know the first thing about retail, and he was totally oblivious to the hints she'd kept dropping for the last two weeks. She picked up a stack of underwear that had come in and looked at it with disgust. Shoddy. There was no other word for it. Shoddy and poorly assembled and wouldn't last through a season. She turned a pair of boxers inside out and groaned. They were even worse from this angle. She had no idea what had prompted Saul to order them. The man knew quality; the suits and shirts he tailored were proof of that. This load of merchandise was anything but quality. The only thing about them that said otherwise was the ridiculous price the manufacturer suggested charging for them.

If Saul thought savvy shoppers were going to pay that much when they could get better at the five and dime, he had another think coming.

Clara shoved the offending underwear back in the box. She would point out the problem when Saul returned from wherever he'd gone and hope that for once he would listen to her. Which he probably wouldn't. Despite her years in retail, which Rabbi Shulman had told him about, he hadn't listened to a thing she said. He acted like she was an *iung meydl* fresh out of the schoolroom.

She shook her head in disgust. He had made more mistakes than she could count. If he kept on at the rate he was going, his business wasn't going to make it past the three-month mark. Which would be a crying shame.

From what their landlady, Mrs. Blum, had said one night over hot tea, Saul had been working and saving his money for thirteen long years, living in a single room on her top floor when he could have afforded far better. All this time, he'd been using public transportation when he could've owned a car. Instead, he'd put away his money so he could open a store. Despite ignoring her suggestions, he'd been as kind and decent to her as anyone she'd met in San Antonio. He'd arranged for her to rent a room in Mrs. Blum's all-ladies house next door to the boardinghouse where he lived, and given her an advance toward her first month's rent. She wanted with all her heart for the store to succeed, for his sake as well as her own.

If he only he would listen to her.

She opened another shipment. These weren't so bad, so she put price tags on them and returned them to the box, so that they could be quickly displayed for sale when they had a store and a counter upon which to display them. She was working on a box of ties when Saul came sailing in, a huge smile on his face. "I found the space I want to rent for the store. It'll be perfect."

"Where?" she asked eagerly. His enthusiasm was catching.

"On Broadway. A couple of miles north of downtown. Close to that Catholic girls' school."

Oy. A million miles away from a boatload of potential customers.

Clara almost groaned out loud. She had been down Broadway once or twice and had a good idea where he was talking about. It was in the middle of the toniest neighborhoods in San Antonio, which would be fine for the wealthier customers, but it was in a part of town the Mexican community shied away from unless they were mowing a lawn or cleaning a house. No way would the Rodriguez family or any of their neighbors come anywhere near Saul's store. She doubted if any of the less-than-prosperous Anglos would, either. Either deliberately or unintentionally, Saul had excluded the vast majority of the shoppers of San Antonio. Shoppers he was going to need if his store was going to get off the ground.

She looked at Saul hesitantly. "That's a pretty fancy-schmancy neighborhood, isn't it? Are you sure that's where you want to open?"

He looked somewhat taken aback. "Where else would I want to open? I'm carrying only the best. I want to appeal to the customers who want only the best. That would be the people in those neighborhoods." He looked at the box of underwear. "Did you get that box labeled?"

"I wanted to show it to you first," she said. "I wanted to be sure you wanted it in your store before I labeled it. The quality isn't nearly as fine as the price tag."

He looked at her doubtfully. "What do you mean?"

It took her nearly a half hour to convince Saul that the undergarments weren't worth the money he'd have to charge for them. By then it was time for lunch. Saul said he had a few hours of work to do at the big department store downtown. He left her with instructions and would see her later in the day before leaving her to her own devices.

Clara did a quick calculation in her head. The work he'd left to do wouldn't take anywhere near all afternoon, and she had her lunchtime on top of that. She could take an hour or two to look around downtown and see if she could find space for lease that would be a better location for the store.

She swallowed a peanut butter and jelly sandwich in three bites while she told Mrs. Blum what she was up to. "He's making a mistake," she assured the older lady. "Maybe I can steer him to a better location."

She boarded a bus and rode south a few blocks, away from the old homes and boardinghouses and into the retail section of downtown. She hopped off the bus and started walking down Houston Street, one of the two major arteries running through the downtown retail district. Christmas decorations festooned the storefronts and spanned the street, reminding Clara that they were in the middle of America's busiest retail season. The sidewalks were teeming with San Antonians of every possible variety, shopping, taking lunch breaks, and enjoying the beautiful afternoon. Well-dressed Anglos rubbed shoulders with Mexican *abuelas* and shopgirls, and the stores were clogged with Christmas shoppers, eagerly spending their hard-earned dollars on gifts for family and friends.

Clara looked long and hard at the shops lining Houston Street. The stores carried a variety of goods. Some of the shops were high-end; others carried less expensive merchandise. But it was the shoppers in those stores whom Clara studied closely. There were a few stores with only wealthy customers inside, but most of the stores were serving a broad spectrum of the city, and the less-affluent

Anglos and Mexicans were forking over their money as cheerfully as the rich.

This was what Saul needed, she thought as she came to the end of the storefronts on Houston Street. She walked a block south and started up Commerce, with her eyes peeled for a "For Lease" sign. She stopped and peered into a window or two. Too big. Too small. Too much renovation would be needed. She was almost back to her bus stop when she spotted a sign across the street. She looked both ways and ran against the light, earning a severe look from an older lady in a DeSoto. Clara peered into the gloomy space and took a deep breath as a smile broke over her face.

It was perfect.

Not too big. Not too small. There were already counters for shirts and underwear and racks to hold pants and suits. It would need a thorough cleaning, but otherwise seemed to be in good shape. There were shops lining the entire block, but not another menswear shop in sight. The sidewalk outside was thronged with potential customers.

This location would work. It would be so much better than the one Saul found this morning. She could hardly wait to tell him about it.

It was nearly six before Saul reappeared. His eyes were tight and his shoulders were tense, the way they were when he'd spent the afternoon bent over a sewing machine. "You still working?" he asked as he rolled his shoulders, the muscles in his chest and arms straining the fabric of his shirt. Shoulders Clara suddenly itched to rub for him. She quickly shook off that thought. "I'd have thought you'd be finished by now."

"I took a long lunch," Clara said. She felt her face light up. "I found a place for you to open your store. It's downtown on Commerce—"

"Why'd you waste your lunch hour looking for a storefront? I told you this morning I found one. You should have been out looking for a pretty blouse to wear."

Clara firmed her lips, determined not to let his dismissive attitude stop her. "I can find a pretty blouse later. Finding a good location for the shop is more important."

"I've already found a good location for the shop," Saul said patiently. "It's in a wealthy area, close to where my target customers live."

"Which is exactly what's wrong with it," Clara persisted doggedly. "You won't reach—"

"I said I'd found a location," Saul broke in. "A good location. All right?"

"No, it's not all right. If you'd just let me—"

"Clara, I don't know where you think you found and I don't care. I don't know what business you think you have inserting yourself into my decisions regarding the store. It's my store, and my call to make."

"I'm inserting myself because you don't have the first idea what you're doing," Clara snapped. "You're an amateur, Mr. Goldstein. A well-meaning amateur who doesn't know the first thing about retail besides sewing a straight seam. I'm inserting myself because somebody better, or you're going to lose everything you've spent years working your *tuches* off for. If you lose this business, I lose my job and have to move back in with Jennie, and I don't want to do that. So yes, I went out and found you a better place to open your store. So please, *please,* listen to me."

"Amateur? I'm an *amateur*? You're nothing more than a *kinder*, a girl barely out of school. I don't know what you think you know, but I promise you, you're merely a child who doesn't know what she's talking about."

"And you're a hardheaded fool who's about to lose everything you've spent years saving up to do," Clara shot back. "To hell with this. If you lose it all, so be it."

She shouldered past him and stormed out of the room. Tears of anger stung her eyes. *Kinder*? A child? She'd worked for Mrs. Formby for five long years, absorbing everything she could during her tenure in the shop at Swindon. Saul might be a fantastic tailor, but he didn't know the first thing about running a shop.

She made it as far as her room before the tears began to fall. It probably didn't matter whether the shop succeeded. He was going to fire her. No business owner was going to put up with that kind of impertinence out of an employee.

Her eyes were still red when she went down to dinner an hour later. The table was half-empty. Besides her, Saul, and Mrs. Blum, there were only two other boarders at dinner. Stewart McGill was a young goy who lived there because it was inexpensive, and Anna Kempler was a young history teacher who was fascinated with her and Saul's stories. The girl meant well but occasionally made a pest of herself with her incessant questions. Clara said as much to Mrs. Blum, who encouraged her to talk to the teacher anyway. "You need to tell your story. You and Saul both. How else will the world learn what was done, so that it doesn't happen again?"

Tonight was no exception, except Anna wanted to talk about Saul's store. "So, have you found a place to open your store?" Anna asked eagerly.

"Yes, I did," Saul said. "The perfect place." Clara felt him glance her way but she kept her eyes down.

"Good, good. You listened to Clara then," Mrs. Blum said, smiling brightly. "Clara, I'm glad you could help him."

Saul's mouth dropped open. "No, I didn't help him. Mr. Goldstein is quite convinced he knows what he's doing," she said tightly. "He's not interested in my suggestion."

"Really? With all the experience Clara brings to the table? Why would you not be interested?" Mrs. Blum looked at him disapprovingly.

Saul's ears turned red but he said nothing.

Anna looked from Saul to Clara, her eyes bright with curiosity. "Where is the storefront you like?" she asked Saul.

"Up Broadway. Close to Brackenridge Park. It's close to Terrell Hills and Alamo Heights. Not too far from Olmos Park."

Anna turned up her nose. "Oh. Close to the rich goyim. I hope there's enough of them to keep you in business."

"Up Broadway? Man, I wouldn't shop that street on a bet," Stewart popped up. "Too pricy for my wallet."

"Neither would I," Mrs. Blum said.

Saul looked around the table. "But aren't the wealthy going to want to shop where it's convenient?"

"And miss all the fun of going downtown? Not on your life." Anna laughed. "Saul, those rich families where I teach like to go downtown and make a day of it. Shop a half dozen stores, go to lunch, see the sights, take the kids to Santa, be part of the excitement. Especially this time of year."

Stewart grinned. "Yep. The lights and the Christmas trees are half the fun. Even if I can't afford much."

Mrs. Blum and Anna laughed, and Mrs. Blum changed the subject. Saul was quiet, but he kept looking at Clara curiously and she wasn't particularly surprised when he banged on her door an hour later. She yanked open the door. "Yes?" she asked crossly.

"How did you know all that and I didn't?" he demanded.

"You know the answer to that. I told you I had experience in retail."

"How much experience? As young as you are, it couldn't amount to much."

She raised her chin. "I have *five years* in the business. I worked in a fancy men's clothing shop in Swindon from the time I was fourteen."

"I see."

"Do you really? Do you have any idea how much I learned in those five years?"

"No, but I have a feeling you're dying to tell me." He pointed to the jumper lying on her bed. "Put on your sweater and take a walk with me. I'll buy you a hot chocolate and you can tell me what all you learned."

Clara grabbed her jumper. She put her key in her pocket and together they left the house and started down the sidewalk. "I get why the shop on Broadway maybe isn't such a good idea. Anna and Stewart pretty much spelled it out. Tell me where you think I should open and why you think your spot would be better," he said.

She gestured to the bus coming up the street. "Why don't I show you?"

Saul nodded and they ran for the crowded bus. There was only one seat left and they sat down together. This close, she could smell his aftershave and feel the warmth from his body so close to hers. Despite her aggravation at his stubbornness, she felt drawn to him. *Stop thinking like that,* she admonished herself. It didn't matter how she might feel about him. He would never be interested in a teenager who was little more than a refugee, even if he did need her expertise to make a go of his store.

They took the bus all the way to Commerce Street. The stores were open late and the sidewalks were every bit as crowded as they had been earlier in the day. They walked briskly down the block and Clara pointed out the vacant property. "You can't see as much tonight as I did today. But there are counters and racks, at least enough to get started. Except for needing a thorough cleaning, it looked like it was in good shape."

Saul peered in the windows. "It looks like it's about the right size." He turned around and leaned against the glass door. "All right. Tell me why this location's so much better." He folded his arms in front of him.

She gestured to the crowd on the sidewalk. "They are. There are your customers, S... Mr. Goldstein."

"If you can yell at me and tell me I'm an amateur, I think we can be on a first-name basis," he said dryly.

"Okay, uh, Saul. There they are. Your customers. They're already down here, making a day or an evening of it. They've got a few quid in their pockets and are ready to spend it. It's not only the wealthy people. Look at them. Anglos, Mexicans, soldiers from the military bases, ranch families from out of town. Rich, poor, and everyone in between. *Everybody's* down here. I know you're thinking of your custom suits, and the wealthy men who will buy one. But San Antonio's not rich enough for those to be your only patrons. There aren't enough moneyed people to keep you in business. You need to cater to a broader clientele. Maybe hire some apprentice tailors to make a less pricy line of suits, or order some to sell off the rack. Have something a soldier stationed at Fort Sam can buy for his wedding. Or Jesse can buy for his sister's *quinceanera* coming up in April."

"But they won't be repeat customers," Saul argued. "I'll be lucky to sell them one suit every five or ten years."

"That's right. But they show up looking good in one of your suits, the other chaps will want to know where they got the suit, and before you know it all their friends will be making their occasional suit purchase from you as well. Along with their shirts and their underpants. You'll have more customers than you know what to do with. It worked in Swindon. You should have seen the way the soldiers lined up to buy their first civilian suit after they got out of the service. No reason why it wouldn't work for you as well."

"I see." He got out a piece of paper and jotted down the phone number on the "For Lease" sign. "Why don't we walk down the street for a bit? You can tell me a little more about your years in the British shop."

He offered her his arm and together they strolled down the street. "How did you happen to end up working in Swindon?" he asked conversationally.

"I was in England with my mother's childhood friend and her family when Kristallnacht destroyed so many lives. My parents asked if I could stay in England until things got better, and the Kirbys kindly gave me a place to live. They never made me feel unwelcome or asked me for anything, but they needed help with expenses, so Jennie and I both got jobs in the shops. She learned as much as I did."

He didn't ask anything more and she didn't volunteer. It was obvious what had happened to her family. "So what other nuggets of wisdom would you share with your amateur employer?" he asked dryly.

Her face flamed red. "I'm never living that down, am I?"

"Probably not," he said cheerfully. "But the question's serious."

Clara thought for a moment. "We already talked about the less-than-wonderful underwear this morning. Be careful not to assume if something comes from a fancy company, that it's automatically fine quality. Check it carefully before you offer it for sale. The wealthy tend to be savvy shoppers. They know the best when they see it and that's what you better offer them."

"And?"

"If you're going to reach out to everyone in San Antonio, you need at least one salesclerk who's bilingual. Preferably more than one. A lot of the people in Jesse's neighborhood don't speak English. Even if they do, it's comforting to be able to converse in their native language."

"I know. When I first came, I'd go to Fredericksburg to hear German spoken on the street."

"Where?"

"Fredericksburg. It's a German community up the road a bit," he said when she looked puzzled. "So, how do I manage this something-for-everyone and still make the wealthy feel like they're experiencing exclusivity?"

"That's easy. Make everyone feel special. Give them all the exclusivity experience. Make them all feel like they're enjoying the fanciest shopping out there, even if they're buying a suit off the rack or a sack of underpants."

"I suppose you know how to do this?"

"I do. So does Jennie."

"Was that a hint?"

Clara looked at him in surprise. "It wasn't meant to be, but if you want to take it as such, go ahead. She would love working for you."

"The husband. Does he speak Spanish?"

"His first language."

He took a deep breath. "Okay, then. Lots to think about." He pointed to a café across the street. "I believe I promised you chocolate. I'll bet they make a good one."

They did. It was flavored with cinnamon and had a bit of a bite and Clara loved it. Saul insisted she try something called *bunuelos*, a fried fritter dusted with brown sugar. She took one bite and her eyes flew open. "Saul, this is *delicious*," she breathed.

"I know. I fell in love with them the first time I ate Mexican food. Have you tried any yet?"

Clara laughed. "I stayed with the Rodriguez family for weeks. That's what they cook. I love it."

"Then you moved to the right town."

She was beginning to think so as well.

They enjoyed their cocoa and *bunuelos*, and after, he again offered her his arm as they strolled down the street toward the bus stop. Clara couldn't help but notice the warmth of his tall, strong body as they walked close to one another on the crowded sidewalk. Although Christmas wasn't their season, the excitement of the holiday sent little shivers down her back. Or maybe it was walking next to Saul, with her hand tucked in his arm and her body pressed close to his. She liked walking this close to him. She liked talking to him, exchanging ideas about his new store. She plain liked *him*.

Saul Goldstein. Her much-older boss. The man who signed her paycheck. The man who was completely and totally out of her league.

This was not good. It was not good at all.

But she'd be damned if she knew what to do about it.

Chapter Three

Clara got prettier by the day.

Saul shook off the thought and forced himself to concentrate on the custom suit he was putting together. He needed to get this outfit finished so he could get it fitted in time for the Ackerman grandson's bar mitzvah. He needed to quit thinking about his appealing employee labeling dress shirts one room over. How pretty her hair was or how terrific her new suit looked on her, or how excited she'd been to wear it for Shabbat services last Friday. He needed to stop thinking about her at all.

He was being disloyal to Elise. He couldn't do that. He *wouldn't* do that. When Elise joined him, he wanted to be able to tell her that he'd thought of no woman but her. If he kept daydreaming about Clara, then he couldn't in all honesty tell Elise any such thing.

Even if thinking about Clara was the nicest part of his morning.

He redoubled his efforts and had the pants finished by noon. The jacket would take the remainder of the day, so he decided a meal was in order and ran next door, where Mrs. Blum was putting out a deli-style lunch of cold cuts and homemade bagels, which Jesse and Jennie had both learned to love. Clara was seated at the table, along with Jennie and Jesse Rodriguez. He'd approached hiring the young couple with the same doubtfulness with which he'd taken Clara's other advice, and had been pleasantly surprised by both of them.

Jennie, a typical English rose, was every bit as knowledgeable as Clara, and Jesse had a strong back and a pleasing disposition, and was eager to learn the ropes. Saul had wrestled with the choice of location for a few days. Who wanted to admit a teenage girl knew more about retail than a man his age did? Finally, bowing to her superior knowledge, and to her visible delight, he rented the space on Commerce Street. They were due to move in tomorrow, which would give them two short weeks to clean the place, and get the merchandise on the counters and racks for sale. Most of that work would fall into his employees' capable hands, while he hired a couple more clerks and whipped up some moderately priced suits to have ready for sale on the first day.

Jesse and the girls greeted him with big smiles. "Are we ready for tomorrow?" he asked the three of them as he sat down at the end of the table.

"We are," Clara said, her smile lighting up her face. "Can I make you a bagel?"

"I've got it." He piled thinly sliced roast beef between bagel halves and added mustard. "Mmm, that's good," he said, devouring half the sandwich in one bite. "Jesse, you need another of these?"

"Don't mind if I do," he said.

Jennie jumped up and put together another sandwich. He stifled a laugh. The young couple wasn't shy about food, that was for sure. They were paying Mrs. Blum a small fee for their lunches, but Saul had been slipping her more money to cover their ravenous appetites. No doubt though, they were working it off. They'd be working even harder for the next few days, as they cleaned the store and packed and unpacked Jesse's ramshackle old truck with merchandise. A frisson of excitement ran down Saul's back as he regarded his three employees.

He was opening a store in two short weeks. Thirteen years of hopes and dreams were coming to fruition. Things were almost perfect.

They would have been perfect had Elise been here to open it with him.

He shook off the thought and instead went over his checklist in his head, listening with half an ear to the young people at the table with him. Determined to get Mr. Ackerman's suit finished, he gave instructions to the three and closeted himself in his sewing room for the afternoon. It was after six when he finally emerged, his shoulders stiff and his eyes burning. He had a beautiful suit sewn, pressed, and ready, but for last-minute alterations.

He went to the room next door, expecting to find it empty, and instead found Clara marking a box of dress shirts. "These came in about an hour ago," she explained. "I thought it would be good to go ahead and get the price tags on."

"You could've taken care of that tomorrow," he said. "You've put in a long day."

"So have you. How's the suit coming?"

"All done. Mr. Ackerman's coming in the morning for a final fitting. Now that I'm not working at the department store anymore, I'll have to do the fitting here."

She looked around the room. "It's not so bad. He won't mind." She smiled. "It'll be nice to get moved into the store."

Saul stood transfixed by the sight of Clara's smile. She didn't smile all that often. Not that he blamed her. Life had been sad for the girl. But that smile. It positively transformed her, took her from simply pretty to spectacularly beautiful. Beautiful, and everything a man could want.

Everything Saul could want.

He stared into her eyes for a moment as her smile of joy took on an element of interest, of desire, of invitation. He had a wow moment. *She's interested in me.* She was attracted to him. Apparently as attracted as he was to her. He couldn't deny it any longer, he was attracted to her. He wanted to take her in his arms. Touch her and hold her. Kiss the life out of her until she was moaning.

He wanted to do the things with her that a man does with a beautiful, desirable woman.

He hoped by the glint in her eye and tilt of her head, she wanted the same.

He took a step toward her, and then another. She held out her arms and he melted into them, his kiss hard, hot, and hungry as he possessed the young woman who'd changed his life. He held her tight against his body, her nipples rubbing against his chest, and her fingers tangling in the back of his shirt. He could hear her moan deep in her throat. Or was that his own moan he heard? He couldn't be sure. All he knew was he was like a starving man devouring a feast, a thirsty man drinking from a well.

He'd been alone for so long. He needed this. The touch of a woman's arms and lips, and her body next to his. Clara wasn't shy about her needs. She held him tight against her warmth and seemed to welcome the feel of his desire poking into her stomach.

Her kisses and caresses weren't all that experienced, but she had all the heat and desire a man could want. Right here in his arms, warm and willing.

Kissing him with everything she had in her.

They clung together for long moments, their lips on fire and their tongues fighting a duel that neither of them could lose. She felt right at home in his arms, and it had been so long, so damned long since he'd held a woman. Thirteen long years since he'd kissed a woman with everything he had in him. Since he'd held Elise in his arms and met her lips with his.

Elise.

What had he done?

Saul thrust Clara from him and looked at her in horror. Clara blinked. "Saul?" she asked uncertainly.

"I...I'm sorry," he stammered. "I...I never meant for us to do that." He scrubbed his hand across his mouth. "*Oy vey.* What kind of a bastard am I?"

Clara looked at him in dismay. "Was it that awful?" she asked quietly. "Was I that bad?"

"No, of course not." He looked at her with irritation. "But we shouldn't have done that."

"It doesn't seem so wrong to me." Clara reached for his hand. "It seemed rather nice, actually."

Saul jerked his hand away. "You don't understand," he said harshly.

Her face froze. "Then I suggest you explain it to me."

"I love someone else."

"You *what?*" Her eyes widened, and then narrowed as she waited for him to speak.

"I love someone else. Elise Meitner. A...a girl I left behind in Leipzig." He gestured around the room. "That's what this is all about. Her father doesn't...didn't think I'm good enough for her. I've been saving for years to open my own store and show *Herr* Meitner I'm good enough for his daughter."

"I see." Clara folded her arms in front of her. "I thought you'd been over here a long time. I didn't realize you only came over here a year or two ago."

"I've been here thirteen years. I came over when I was twenty."

Clara was silent for a minute. "Thirteen years. Since 1935. When did you last see Elise?"

"The morning I left Germany."

Her lips firmed. "When did you last hear from her?"

"I got her last letter in the spring of 1940. She was hoping to get out soon."

"And nothing since."

"No, but—"

"But nothing. You're telling me that you practically threw me across the room out of some misguided loyalty to a woman you haven't seen in thirteen years and haven't heard from in eight? You have to be kidding me."

Saul felt his back go up. "Why would I be kidding you?"

"Actually, you're not kidding me. You're kidding yourself if you think she's out there after all this time."

"Why wouldn't she be out there somewhere?"

"For the same reason the rest of the German Jews are gone. She was exterminated, Saul. Like my family, and like yours."

"Her name hasn't been on any of the lists."

"So? Lots of names didn't make it to the lists. Has she been on any of the survivor lists?"

"No, but—"

"But nothing. If she were alive, you can bet the first thing she would've done would be to write you. The fact that you've heard nothing speaks volumes."

"She has to be out there somewhere," he insisted stubbornly.

"If she is out there, which is seriously doubtful at this point, then she doesn't want to get in contact with you."

"Why wouldn't she want to get in contact with me?"

Clara shook her head. "She's found someone else."

"*What*? No. She wouldn't do that," he snapped.

Clara shrugged. "She might. You can protest all you want, but I know better. I saw it all the time. It's called 'Dear John.' It usually came in the form of a letter. The Brits and Yanks got 'em all the time. The I'm-sorry-but-I-found-somebody-else letter. Kept the local pub in business, those letters did."

"She wouldn't," Saul insisted hotly. "She loves me, and I love her." He glared at Clara angrily. "You're angry because I don't want to kiss you again."

"No, I'm not angry. No way am I going to be a stand-in for your precious Elise." Her face softened. "I'm sad. Sad a man who ought to be smarter than that is pining over a woman who's nothing more than a lovely memory."

"She's more than a memory. She's my sweetheart and she's going to come here and take her place by my side," he insisted.

She looked at him in disappointment. "You go on thinking that if it makes you feel better." She squared her shoulders and walked out, slamming the door behind her.

Saul sank down into the chair. It couldn't be, he assured himself. Clara was wrong.

Elise was out there. She was alive. She still loved him. She wasn't dead and she hadn't fallen in love with another man. She was out there and she would join him soon, taking her place by his side. He would be reunited with his lost love.

Any other outcome was unthinkable.

***

Clara sat on a park bench in the dark with her hands stuffed deep in her coat pockets. It probably wasn't the safest thing she could do, sitting by herself in an almost deserted park, but it was quiet and private, with no chatty landlady or nosy boarder to interrupt her solitude. In the distance she could hear the bells of San Fernando Cathedral tolling the hour. It was almost Christmas and although it wasn't her holiday, she could appreciate the peace and goodwill associated with the season. Under other circumstances she might have even enjoyed the feeling. But tonight she was feeling anything but peaceful. Saul had destroyed any semblance of goodwill in her heart.

The man was *dummkopf*, a *nar*, a stupid fool. Thirteen years and he was still hanging on to the memory of a woman who was most likely dead. If she wasn't dead, she was dead to him, or more likely, he was dead to her. Clara couldn't understand it. Why a man so handsome, so virile, who had so much going for him, was stuck in the past, especially when he had so much to live for in the here and now.

Was she any smarter? She was falling for a man who was nearly fourteen years older than her, and was clinging to the memory of a ghost. There were plenty of reasons why Saul and Clara were a bad idea. Tonight had brought them to light one more. She needed to quit thinking about him and daydreaming about him. Not that it would be easy with the kiss of a lifetime to think about. She didn't know what to do. The best thing would be to leave his employ and work somewhere else. But she would have to move, since he lived in the boardinghouse next door and they ate at the same table, and she would never find another employer as generous as Saul. So she was stuck for the foreseeable future.

She would have to find another way to get him out of her mind.

***

Saul stood behind the counter of his new store and looked around with a deep sense of satisfaction. Tomorrow was it. Opening day. The culmination of thirteen years of hard work, scrimping, and saving. The doors would open, and within a few days or weeks he would learn if his dream would come true, or if the years of effort had all been a waste. It was a heady feeling, heady but scary at the same time.

He'd done everything he knew to assure his venture would be a success, and when Elise joined him, he wouldn't only be a tailor of fine suits, he'd own the business that sold them to the wealthy patrons of San Antonio.

And the not-so-wealthy. He glanced over at Jesse and Mario, the other young man from the *barrio* he'd hired last week. They were still coming into the shop in their work clothes, but tomorrow morning they would be on the sales floor attired in suits Saul had fit to them that showed what an off-the-rack suit could look like if properly altered. Jennie and Clara had a couple of lovely suits he'd made. Most of the time he only tailored men's clothes, but he'd made an exception for them, and the ladies looked great, if he said so himself.

Jennie had been effusive in her thanks and praise. "Would you look at me? I look rich," she'd crowed. "Thank you, thank you, thank you!" Clara had been less forthcoming, thanking him quietly, but she'd smiled to herself when she thought he wasn't looking, pleased in spite of her ongoing irritation with him.

Irritation he'd certainly earned. He'd had no business kissing her. Then spurning her the way he had. It was a wonder she hadn't walked off the job. She'd stayed on, but they had yet to return to the easy working relationship they'd had before. Maybe given a little more time, the tension would ease. He sure hoped so. Having Clara angry with him was damned unpleasant.

They managed to finish up a little after six. Jesse and Jennie took the bus in one direction, and he and Clara braved the cold January rain until they could get on the bus that would take them to the boardinghouse. Saul was bursting with excitement and saw no reason to hide it. He chattered all the way to their stop, ignoring Clara's noncommittal responses, finally falling silent as they walked in the boardinghouse.

Mrs. Blum met them at the door with a handful of envelopes she handed to Saul. "You're an important man," she teased as Clara disappeared into the house next door. "You've got mail from all over. Mostly here and New York."

"Invoices, most likely."

"That would make sense. You have one that's from overseas. It looks like somewhere in Germany." Her expression was troubled, yet hopeful.

Mrs. Blum knew exactly what a letter from Germany might mean.

"Th-thanks," he stammered. He ran inside and took the stairs two at a time. His hand trembled and it took him three tries to get the key in the lock. He threw the mail down on the bed and pawed through it until he found a beat-up-looking letter. It wasn't Elise's handwriting or her usual stationary, but that didn't mean a thing. It had to be from her. Or about her.

The return address was the name of the Meitner family's next-door neighbor, *Herr* and *Frau* Gunther. They weren't Jewish, but Elise had written of their tremendous kindness to the Meitners when the persecution started. He sat down on the bed and carefully removed the letter, and read it three times before the horrible truth sank in.

Es tut mir so sehr leid Ihnen zu sagen dass Elise gestorben ist.
I'm sorry to tell you that Elise has died.

He read through the rest of the letter, stained with *Frau* Gunther's tears. She was sorry she hadn't written sooner. They'd had to flee when the bombing started and had only recently been able to return to what was left of their home in Leipzig. Elise's father and brothers had been taken into custody in June of 1940 and Elise and her mother a month later. Nothing had been heard of them until another neighbor's teenage daughter, who had miraculously survived the camps, said she'd been in Buchenwald with Elise and her mother. According to the neighbor, Elise held on for two long years until starvation and disease had finally taken her. *She tried, Saul. She tried to stay alive for you. It was just too much.*

Thirteen years of hard work for nothing. Thirteen years of effort down the drain. Without Elise, the store didn't mean a damned thing. None of it did. It had all been in vain.

The woman he loved and longed to share his life with was gone from this world, and with her she'd taken everything he had to live for.

Saul cursed sharply. He started to wad up the letter but thought better of it and instead tossed it on the dresser. He beat the wall, beat it until his fists bled. He cursed the despicable Nazis, and cursed the camps, and cursed *Herr* Meitner for not letting him bring Elise to San Antonio. He cursed his new country and city. The country and city that Elise would never share with him.

When he'd exhausted himself, he opened a bottle of whiskey, filling a water glass almost to the brim. He finished half the glass in a single gulp and topped it off. He hadn't had a drink in months, but tonight he was going to by-God drink away the pain. Drink until the horror faded. Drink until oblivion rescued him from the sorrow engulfing him to the point of paralysis.

He drank the second glass down, the whiskey burning all the way to his empty stomach as he waited none too patiently for the numbing to start.

He got out his wallet and stared at the last picture he and Elise took together before he'd kissed her good-bye at the train station and promised to send for her. To his grief, her image was fuzzy, faded, and indistinct despite the picture in his hand.

Sometimes she was tall and dark with soft brown eyes and a gentle smile. Other times she was small and blonde with lush but unsmiling lips. He tried and failed to picture her clearly in his mind. He didn't know if his memory was playing tricks on him, or if it was the alcohol talking.

He was well into his second bottle when a key turned in his lock. He looked up with eyes he couldn't quite focus to see a small woman with blonde hair looking at him with concern. "Saul? Are you all right?" He looked at her through squinted eyes. *Elise? No.* It was Clara looking back at him.

"Me? Fucking ducky, as they would say in Jolly Old England." He waved his glass in front of him. "Why?"

"You didn't come down to dinner and Mrs. Blum was worried. She sent me up here to check on you."

He waved the glass around some more. "As you can see, I'm fine. *Vunderlekh.* Hunky-dory. Swell." He could feel himself sway as he rose to his feet. "You can get lost. Or better yet, come here and let me screw you. I haven't had a woman in waaaay too long, and you'll do. You're not her, but you'll do." He lurched toward her and grabbed her by the shoulders. "You smell good."

He bent his head and his lips met hers, hard and angry. He felt her freeze for a minute before she thrust him away from her and slapped him soundly across the face. "You *chaszzer.* Pig. To kiss me like that when it's another woman you want. I wouldn't screw you if you were the last man on Earth."

His eyes blinked as he looked at her. "What? Why would I want to kiss you or screw you? You're not Elise."

She looked at him with contempt. "No, I'm not Elise. I'm Clara."

He collapsed down into the chair. "No, you're not Elise. Elise is dead." He gestured to the dresser with his bloody knuckles. "Elise is dead. *Frau* Gunther said so. She's dead. *Dead.* The woman I'll love for all time is dead." He felt his eyes fill with tears. "I'll never kiss her again. I'll never touch her hand, or make love to her, or watch our babies grow. She's *gone.* Gone forever."

His tears overflowed and he was wracked with loud, noisy sobs he had no control over. For a good half hour he cried, helpless to stop, sobbing out his heartbreak. He was vaguely aware of Clara sitting down across from him on his bed. Her arms were folded across her middle and she watched him impassively. She probably thought he was a *nebbish,* a wimp. A real man wouldn't cry like this. He was beyond caring what Clara or anyone else thought. His sorrow was too deep for words. The only way he could express it was through his tears.

His sobs finally tapered off. For a long time he stared down at the bloodied fists in his lap. He picked up the glass and swallowed the rest of the whiskey in one gulp, but when he would've poured another, Clara swiped the bottle before he could pick it up. "You've had enough." She put the bottle out of reach on the shelf in his closet.

"No, I want—" He lurched for the bottle but fell across the bed instead.

"You know, you're right where you need to be." She picked up his feet and put them on the bed. He was vaguely aware of her taking off his shoes and his tie and covering him up with a blanket. He blinked and shut his eyes.

Mercifully, he passed out.

Chapter Four

Now he knew for sure, and he hadn't taken it well.

Not that she'd expected him to. Saul was deeply and irrevocably in love with Elise. His learning of her death wasn't going to change that.

Sighing, Clara tugged the belt off the snoring man and tucked the blanket around him. She'd already spotted the empty bottle on the floor beside his chair. Sheesh. He'd consumed nearly two bottles of whiskey. She hoped since it was early enough, he'd sleep it off by morning. Sorrow or no, they still had a store to open, a grand opening that every influential Jew at temple had promised to attend, along with their rich goyim friends. Saul would have to be on his feet and alert.

She had her work cut out for her.

She started to leave, but the letter on the dresser caught her eye and beckoned. She reached out and picked it up. The handwriting was beautiful, but her written German was rusty and it took her a while to pick through the tearstained pages. The paper was dry, so the tears were probably shed by the author.

The starkness of the message was in sharp contrast to the emotion expressed by the tearstains. The writer minced no words. Elise had died in a concentration camp six years ago. She'd tried to stay alive for Saul but it had been too much for her. The writer was shipping a small chest Elise left behind for Saul, to be sent to him if she didn't survive. The letter included the combination to the lock on the chest.

It was the same story that had been repeated countless times in the last three years.

The same story of the Ehrman family's fate.

Clara stared down at the letter as her own eyes overflowed with tears. So many gone. So many fallen victim to an inexplicable hatred. A hatred no civilized society should feel, but yet somehow had. She thought of her own sweet mother, her young, handsome father, her pesky little brother. Gone, every one of them, along with the baby sister born after Krystallnacht she never even got to hold. Aunts, uncles, cousins, all gone.

It wasn't only the Ehrmans who were gone. Rudi, the quiet little bookworm who lived across the street. Gone. Heidi, the loud-mouthed girl up the block who was already boy-crazy at twelve. Gone. Her beloved *bubbe*, who made the best brisket and latkes ever, and kissed her grandchildren with overwhelming affection. Gone.

Her entire past. Gone.

The love of Saul's life. Gone.

Six million people, the papers were now saying, whose only crime was being Abraham's issue. Gone.

Millions of others, who for whatever reason were deemed unworthy by the Nazi regime. Gone.

It was simply too much to fathom.

Her tears fell and she didn't try to stop them. Now that Saul was asleep, she could cry without his knowing. He didn't need to cope with her grief. He had enough sadness and loss of his own.

She cried for a long time, her tears joining *Frau* Gunther's on the pages of the letter. She cried for the dead, those she knew, and those she didn't. She cried for the life in Austria lost to her forever. She cried for herself, because she'd fallen hard for a man who loved another.

She loved Saul. Against her better judgment she'd fallen for him. A man who would never love her back. A man who loved a woman who left this world years ago. He loved her, and he always would.

Finally, when she'd cried out her sorrow, she wiped her eyes and went back to her own room. She didn't really expect to sleep much, but the crying had worn her out and she'd barely put her head down when the alarm jangled in her ear. She took the shortest shower on record and dressed in one of the beautiful new suits Saul had tailored for her. She pinned up her hair in a victory roll, painted her lips a vivid red, and donned her stylish pumps.

Giving a nod to her appearance, she grabbed her handbag and headed to the house next door. She hoped against hope Saul was up and about, but her hopes were dashed when she heard his snores all the way from the staircase at the end of the hall. "*Oy vey*. I was afraid of this." She got out the key she'd never returned to Mrs.

Blum, and let herself in his room. She gaped at the man who was spread-eagled on the bed, stark naked but for a thin pair of boxers that hid absolutely nothing from her startled gaze.

She blinked and stared for a minute. Beautiful. Absolutely beautiful.

His chest was well-muscled and strong and covered with a generous sprinkling of hair the same color that graced his head. His arms and legs were muscular and solid. But it was the schlong between his legs that drew her attention.

She didn't know much about men's private parts, but from what little she did know she'd bet that he was considerably blessed in that department. A part of her wanted to reach down and touch it through the thin boxers he wore, to see what it felt like as it hardened in her hands.

Thrusting those thoughts away, she reached out and shook his shoulder. "Saul. It's time to get up," she said quietly. "You have a store to open."

He slapped at her hand and turned over. "Saul, get up," she said firmly. Still no response. "Saul," she snapped. *"Get up."*

He pulled the pillow over his head.

Okay, enough was enough. Desperate times called for desperate measures. She went out to the hall and opened the closet holding cleaning supplies. *Aha.* Just what she needed. She carried the bucket to the bathroom and barged in, hoping she wasn't disturbing one of the other boarders. Thankfully the room was empty. She half-filled the bucket with cold water and marched it down the hall. "Last chance, Saul," she said loudly.

His answer was a loud grunt.

"Don't say I didn't warn you."

She raised the bucket and threw the entire contents on his nearly naked body, jumping back when he jack-knifed up with a roar. "What in the hell?" he yelled as he clawed at the cold water on his chest and stomach.

"You have a store to open in an hour," she said calmly. "You need to get ready."

"I-uh-what?" he sputtered.

"You have a grand opening happening in an hour. You need to be dressed in your best suit at the door greeting your customers."

She looked him up and down. "You have a way to go, so I suggest you get cracking."

He looked around the room and down at his practically naked body. "What happened?"

"You went on a bender and got knackered. Get moving."

He looked around the room and his eyes stopped on the letter she'd returned to the dresser. "Elise is gone. I got drunk." He looked at her with eyes that weren't quite focused. "I think I tried to kiss you or something."

"Or something," she snapped. "Damn it, Saul, *get moving*. Your store opens in an hour." It was more like two but he didn't need to know that.

"Why?" he asked morosely. "Elise is gone. Everything I worked for was for her. Why should I give a damn now?"

Clara's temper snapped. "Because you're not the only one depending on that damn store to succeed. I need a job or I'm going to be homeless and hungry. Jennie and Jesse need their jobs so they can get their own place, and she doesn't hightail it back to England. Mario's wife just had a baby. Those two tailors coming on board this morning quit their other jobs to go to work for you. Pull your damn self together, and get your butt down the hall into the shower before I haul you down there myself."

"Like you could," he said sullenly.

Without quite knowing how she did it, she yanked him up and practically pushed him down the hall. Stewart was coming out of the bathroom wrapped in a towel and under other circumstances she would've been embarrassed. This morning there was too much at stake. "Help me get this *yutz* in the shower," she snapped.

Stewart started laughing. He took Saul by the arm and frog marched him into the bathroom. "I got this," he assured her as he shut the door in her face.

Saul returned to the room ten minutes later with only a towel around his hips. He was freshly shaved and except for the bloodshot eyes didn't look too bad. "Are you going to be all right?" Clara asked coolly.

"I guess so." He picked up the boxers on the bed and turned his back to put them on. Clara stifled a gasp as the towel dropped. *My God, what a* tuches, she thought as she took in Saul's hard, firm butt.

What a body, period. A body that would never be hers to touch, she thought before she could stop herself.

What a waste.

He yanked up the boxers and turned around to glare at her. "You can leave now."

"Forget it. I don't trust you. Get your clothes on and let's go."

He gave her a pointed glare and put on the rest of his clothes. "Do you want something to eat before you go?" she asked.

He shook his head. "I'd puke it up."

"Okay then. Let's go."

The morning was cold and clear and by the time the bus delivered them to Commerce Street he had a little color in his face. Jennie and Jesse were right behind them, and Mario and the two tailors were there a few minutes later. She and Jennie laid out trays of cinnamon rolls and *pan dulce* and made a big urn of coffee. By the time the store opened, they were all ready to go.

Saul unlocked the doors at ten and customers rolled in. Clara recognized many of their faces from temple. Saul recognized even more and spent the morning shaking hands and accepting the well wishes of the mostly well-heeled crowd. Some were there to window shop, but plenty brought their checkbooks or a wad of money. She and Jennie stayed busy at the cash register, while Jesse and Mario spent the morning helping the men try on the off-the-rack suits.

The crowd thinned out a bit after lunch, but picked up again once the soldiers and the rest of the base employees got off work. They were still ringing up sales thirty minutes after the official closing time.

Saul disappeared into the back with the cash register receipts. The sales staff, Clara included, headed for the bus stop. She boarded the bus and leaned her head against the window, exhausted down to the tips of her toes.

The store was going to be a success. With her help, Saul had nailed it and managed to have something in the store to sell to nearly everyone. Under other circumstances, she would've been thrilled, but today's victory was hollow. She'd helped the man she loved achieve the success he'd dreamed of for so long, but her heart had paid a high price for doing it.

She'd finished her dinner and was sitting in the communal living room trying to get interested in *Kon-Tiki* when Saul dragged himself across the threshold. She looked up and nodded her head toward the kitchen. "Mrs. Blum put away a plate of food for you." Her eyes returned to the printed page.

He nodded but headed for the chair next to hers. He sat down and looked at her with his chin dipped to his chest, and his voice a raspy whisper. "I am so, so sorry for my behavior last night," he said softly. "There is absolutely no excuse for what I did." He paused a minute. "I wouldn't blame you if you quit."

She met his gaze with a frank one of her own. "If I could afford to, I would."

He flinched. "It would serve me right if you did, but I hope you won't. You saved the day this morning. You're absolutely right. I'm not the only one whose future depends on the success of Goldstein's. From now on I won't forget it."

"That's good."

They sat in silence for a few minutes. Saul stared at the floor. Gone was the happy man who'd been so excited to be opening his store. Today he was quiet, his grief a cloak around him. Clara's heart clenched painfully. She couldn't keep working for him. It would be the end of her. She'd suffered so much grief and so much loss already. To be around him day in and day out, loving him with all her heart while he grieved the loss of the woman he loved—she couldn't do it.

Sooner or later it would break her spirit entirely. It would be too much to bear.

She'd stay on for a month or two. Long enough to help him get the store off the ground. By then she should have another job lined up, and could only hope he would give her a good reference.

Reference or not, job or not, she would be gone.

For her own piece of mind, she had to go.

***

Saul sat for a moment looking at the tally on the strip of paper coming out of the adding machine. Nice, very nice. Exactly as every tally had been this week. Shirts and underwear were selling well. The off-the-rack suits were moving briskly as the town ramped up for next month's Easter and Passover celebrations. He'd spent the day doing what he loved best—making custom suits that were going to be his signature item, even if the other merchandise actually earned him more money.

Carefully, he transferred the cash and checks to the bank bags and locked them in the safe until he could get them deposited on Monday morning. Clara and Jennie had left the store in perfect shape, ready for tomorrow morning. All he had to do was lock up and head to the bus stop.

He looked at his watch. It wasn't all that late, and he hadn't been to Shabbat services in a couple of weeks. He hopped the bus that would take him to the synagogue. Really, it was time to go shopping for a car, he thought as the bus lurched to its tenth stop in as many blocks. If he had a care, he'd have to move somewhere that had parking. Maybe it was time to do that as well.

The store was making a decent income and he no longer had any reason to save for the future. The future he'd dreamed of for so long was gone to him forever. All he had was the present, and maybe it was time he started living in it.

He ran in the door as the cantor stepped to the lectern. He sat down in his usual place and glanced across the aisle. Clara was in her seat across from him, but she wasn't alone. Seated next to her was a young man he'd seen here a time or two. He was talking quietly to her, nothing improper, and she didn't appear all that interested in the conversation. Still, Saul's gut burned at the sight.

Who the hell does the shmendrik *think he is, sitting with Clara like that?*

Saul wrenched his attention away and managed to pay a little attention to the service. He felt himself sigh with relief when services were over and the young man took his leave. Clara's gaze flicked over to Saul as she nodded at him on the way out, her expression every bit as cool and detached as it had been since the debacle back in January.

She'd been the model employee, and more than once had gone the extra mile to help. But that was the extent of her involvement with him or the store these days. Which was a shame. They'd had such a lovely relationship before he'd screwed it up royally. Now she was angry and had one foot out the door.

He followed the crowd out to the reception hall. Having missed both lunch and dinner, he piled his plate higher than usual and was balancing it on his knees, plowing through the finger sandwiches, when Sam Ackerman wandered up and sat down beside him. "Miss lunch?" he asked sardonically as he eyed the pile of sandwiches on Saul's plate.

"How'd you guess? Lunch and dinner both. I was going to stop at the coffee shop at the end of the block, but these looked wonderful."

"I remember those days. Mamie and I worked so hard that first year we forgot to eat dinner half the time. So how's it going? Sales good?"

Saul nodded. "It started off good. We had a couple of slow weeks in February, but then it picked up again. Men are getting outfitted for Easter and Passover."

"You'll make a lot off Easter duds in this town. A thought. Next year, have a few Western-style shirts for Rodeo week in February. It will keep 'em coming in."

"Good idea. I'll do that."

Sam's expression softened. "How are you doing with the other?"

Saul shrugged. "It's taken the shine off the store opening, that's for sure. I was looking forward to it so much, but now it's kind of hollow. Without someone to share it with. Without her by my side."

"Without your sweetheart, you mean."

"Exactly."

"But you have others to share that success with." Sam looked at him sternly. "You have a store full of employees who have thrown their hearts and souls into making Goldstein's a success. Have you celebrated your success with them?" He glanced across the room where Clara was putting finger sandwiches on a plate. "That young lady has turned herself inside out to help you succeed. Have you celebrated with her? She's certainly been by your side."

"It's not the same," he said quietly.

"It's never going to be the same." Sam looked over at Clara again. "But it could be as lovely. Different, certainly. But equally wonderful."

Sam was talking about more than the store.

Saul looked over at Clara. He *was* sharing Goldstein's with someone. He was sharing it with her. He had shared a lot more with her than the store. She had been by his side for months. His feelings were so tangled. He didn't know what to think.

Elise's death had changed nothing. He loved her. He'd loved her since he was a boy of sixteen, and a part of him would love her until the day they shoveled dirt onto his box. Yet, he had feelings for Clara. What those were, he couldn't say. He couldn't define them exactly. But he definitely felt something for the lovely young woman.

Not that his feelings for her would do him a bit of good. She was young and vibrant and beautiful. She deserved a young man like the one she was sitting with tonight. Fresh-faced and happy with nothing tragic in his past, who could love her with all his heart. She would never be interested in a man fourteen years her senior whose heart would always belong to another. Who was torn between the past and the future.

She could do a lot better than him.

Chapter Five

The time had come for Clara to go.

She glanced over at Saul as he carefully covered the custom suit he'd made for the president of the biggest bank in San Antonio. Mr. Winters had finished trying on the suit for the last time, and he and Mrs. Winters were positively beaming.

"Mr. Goldstein, I don't believe I've ever purchased a suit this nice here in San Antonio. It's such a relief not to have to go all the way to Dallas for one."

"It was my pleasure, sir," Saul said modestly.

"Have you considered branching out to women's clothes?" Mrs. Winters asked. "Not that I don't love shopping in Dallas, but it would be nice not to have to go that far."

"No, but I have a friend at temple who's thinking along those lines. I'll be sure to mention your interest," Saul said diplomatically.

Saul rang up the sale and ushered the couple to the door. Clara looked around the store. It was positively hopping with Saturday afternoon shoppers. The store was solidly in the black and busier by the week. Saul had taken on two more saleswomen and was interviewing for another next week. He was working well with Jennie, who could step into Clara's shoes at any time. She would give him two weeks' notice, of course. She'd reached out to a few stores and a couple of office jobs and been offered interviews by three. She hoped by the time the two weeks were up she would have another job lined up. It didn't matter if she hadn't. She was leaving anyway.

Working with Saul every day was breaking her heart.

She waited until the store was closed and the rest of the employees had left. Most of them were in a hurry to go. Rushing home to dye eggs or, in Jesse and Jennie's case, prepare a huge Easter picnic to eat in the park. Saul was finishing up with the register receipts when she knocked on his door.

"Are you still here?" he asked.

"Where else would I be?"

"Maybe getting ready to picnic with the Rodriguez family?"

"No. They go to church first." She stepped in the office. "We need to talk."

Saul's smile disappeared. "What do we need to talk about that we can't talk about on the bus?"

"This." She pushed a handwritten letter toward him. "It's my letter of resignation. I'm giving you my two weeks' notice." She took a deep breath. "I hope you'll be kind enough to give me a favorable recommendation."

Saul reached for the letter and read through it. "You're quitting? Just like that?" He looked at her with a scowl.

She raised her chin. "I told you back in January I'd quit if I could afford to. I'm to the point I can't afford not to. Besides, you don't need me any longer. The store's a success and if you have questions, Jennie knows as much as I do."

Saul sighed. "I've already apologized for my abominable behavior and will do so again every day if it'll keep you here. I'm as sorry as I can be I behaved the way I did. I know you're angry, and with good reason, but I swear there will never be a repeat."

She swallowed. "It's not that. Not exactly."

"Then what is it? Do you need more money? I can afford to pay you a bit better if that's what the problem is."

"It's not money," Clara said quietly. "You've been more than generous."

"Then what is it? Shorter hours? An office? What can I offer you to get you to stay?" He looked a bit panic-stricken.

Clara felt her eyes fill with tears. "You can never offer me what I really need from you. Please, please accept my resignation and let me go."

She jerked up her handbag and ran out of the office. The sidewalk wasn't overly crowded and she sprinted toward the bus stop, cursing the dress shoes, which hampered her movement. Jennie and Jesse were still waiting for the bus. Jennie took one look at the tears on Clara's face and opened her arms. "Did you tell him?" she asked.

Clara nodded. "He wants me to stay but I can't. I just can't."

Clara's bus lumbered to a stop. "Come spend Easter with us tomorrow," Jennie said as Clara left her embrace.

"But I'm not Christian."

"A picnic's a picnic," Jesse said.

"Pretend it's a Passover picnic," Jennie said. "We'll come for you about noon."

Clara nodded and got on the bus.

She'd done it. It hadn't been easy, but she'd taken the first step in getting on with her life. She would miss Saul. She would miss everyone at the store, but if she was going to make a new life for herself, working at Goldstein's and mooning over a man who could never return her love wasn't going to help her move on.

***

Saul had been right. Clara was angry enough to leave.

And now she had.

He cursed out loud, and he zipped the money bag shut with a vicious yank before throwing it in the safe. He locked the front doors, not bothering to check on the condition of the shelves or racks, and stormed down the street to the bus stop, where he spotted his bus pulling away, presumably with Clara on it. Jennie and Jesse were sitting on the bench. Jennie's expression cooled considerably and her smile faded when she spotted him. He smiled at them nevertheless. "Don't the two of you usually take a bus down at the other bus stop?"

"Usually, but we're headed to Brackenridge Park tonight. We're holding a picnic table until my cousin Diego can get there," Jesse said.

"Your cousin gets to pull the all-nighter," Saul said jokingly.

"He doesn't have an *esposa* to go home to. I do." Jesse leaned over and kissed Jennie's cheek.

Saul sat down beside them. "Jennie, I have a question for you. You and Clara are close friends, yes?"

"You could say that," Jennie answered slowly.

"Then you know that she handed me a letter of resignation this evening."

Jesse reared back in surprise. "She did what?"

"She quit. Resigned. Gave me two weeks' notice. She didn't give me much of a reason."

"I'm not surprised," Jennie murmured.

"You knew she planned to quit," he said.

"I did," Jennie admitted.

"So maybe you could tell me why?" Saul pressed.

Jennie looked hesitant. "I think that's her story to tell."

"All she said was that I could never offer her what she really needed. Please tell me what that is. I'll offer it to her, I promise."

"I agree with Clara. You can't offer her what she needs most," Jennie said.

"Yes, he could," Jesse broke in. "If he wanted to."

Saul looked at Jesse, surprised. "What is it she wants?" he demanded. "What can I offer her?"

Jennie looked at her husband accusingly. "You've been eavesdropping."

"You and Clara talk too loud." Jesse turned to Saul. "Mr. Goldstein, Clara fell for you. Hard. She loves you and knows you're carrying a torch for the dead girl in Germany. It hurts her to be around you knowing you'll never love her back."

Saul felt his mouth drop open. "She couldn't love me. She's only a girl. She doesn't know about love."

Jennie's eyebrow flew up. "How old were you, sir, when you fell for the girl in Germany?"

Saul winced. "Okay. Maybe she's old enough. It doesn't make sense, though. Why would she love me? I'm a lot older than her, I have a sad history, and I love Elise. She should love a young man like Jesse, who can love her back with no reservations."

Jennie looked at him with exasperation. "Mr. Goldstein, the heart wants what the heart wants. For whatever reason, she loves you."

"You could love her back if you wanted to," Jesse added. "I don't mean to be cruel, sir, but your sweetie in Germany is dead. Are you gonna spend the rest of your life pining for what will never be, or are you gonna build a new life with somebody else?"

"Jesse," Jennie snapped.

"No, he's right," Saul said thoughtfully. "I know I should move on. I don't know if I can."

His bus pulled up and Saul bid the Rodriguezes good evening. He was deep in thought as the bus lumbered down the street. Jesse thought he could move on. Jennie wasn't so sure. Obviously, Clara had given up on him, or she wouldn't have quit. He'd be damned if he knew which of them was right.

He got off the bus and ambled down the street, the April breeze warm on his face. He would've gone straight to his room, but Mrs. Blum waved at him from the women's front door. "A trunk came for you today," she said quietly. "From Germany."

He gulped and nodded. "Elise's trunk."

"I had Stewart carry it up the stairs and put it in your room."

"Thank you."

His steps were leaden as he climbed the stairs. He shut the door behind him and stared for a moment at the small trunk sitting at the foot of the bed. An entire lifetime stashed into that small box. He was tempted to put the trunk in the bottom of his closet and forget about it, but Elise, or someone, had gone to the trouble to fill it, and *Frau* Gunther had sent it to him. The least he could do would be to look inside. He found the letter with the combination and after two tries had the lock open. With a mixture of anticipation and dread he lifted the chest and looked inside.

His fingers trembled as he removed the Meitner family's menorah. He was amazed that they had packed it for him. Her parents had been vocal in their disapproval, saying their daughter could do better than to marry a tailor. Next was a yarmulke that had probably belonged to her brother. Then he found a tallis, which looked brand new, and a sterling silver kiddush cup. Next was a mezuzah with the scroll inside, and at the bottom he found the Jerusalem olive wood box he'd given Elise for her nineteenth birthday. Hesitantly he opened the box and with tears in his eyes he lifted the sterling silver Star of David necklace he'd given her the morning he left Leipzig. It wasn't an expensive piece, but she had loved it and promised to wear it every day until they were together again.

Beneath the necklace he found a stack of letters tied together. His breath caught as he ran his finger across the return address. They were all the letters he'd written to her. He smiled even as tears formed in his eyes. He had the matching stack in the bottom drawer of his dresser. He put those aside and looked down in the box again. There was one more letter. It was addressed to him in Elise's handwriting with no address or postage. It was tucked rather than sealed shut and not on her usual feminine stationery. It was on simple tablet paper in a plain envelope. From the scrawl with which it was addressed, it appeared to have been written in a hurry.

His fingers shook as he fumbled to open the letter. He smoothed out the rough sheet from a simple tablet and stared down at the words.

Mein schatz,

If you are reading this, then you probably already know I didn't make it out alive. I hope you never get this letter, of course, but things are bad here and getting worse. I am leaving this chest with Frau *Gunther to send you in case the unthinkable happens. I hope she never has to send it, but I no longer trust all will be well. They came for Papa and my brothers last night. Mama and I are afraid we're next. They're taking everyone, putting them on buses and trains to who knows where. Rumors have it that we're being taken to the camps. We don't know for sure. All we do know is that nobody who has been taken has returned.*

I love you, Saul. I have worn your necklace every day and dreamed of you every night. I know you have done the same. In a perfect world, we would be together now. But our world is not perfect. Far from it. And if you're reading this, it means that you must go on without me. I know you love me, and I know you will grieve me. But I want you to go on. I want you to find another woman to love. I want you to love her with the same depth and intensity you've loved me. I want you to stand under the canopy with her, to stomp the glass and kiss her while your new friends in America clap and cheer. I want you to hold her hand as she gives birth to your children and stand beside her as you open the store you've dreamed of all these years. I want you to live, Saul. Live the life with her that you didn't get to live with me.

That will be the greatest thing you can do to honor my memory.

She's out there, Saul. Now go find her.

All my love,

Elise

Tears poured down Saul's face as he read the letter through for the second time, and the third. She had known him well, his Elise. She had known he would grieve her to the point of paralysis. That he would cling to her memory. That he would dwell on what could have been and not look at what might be. A small smile touched his lips even as tears fell from his eyes. If ever a letter had been written with love, it was the one he held in his hands.

What now? He returned the beloved keepsakes to the chest, all but Elise's letter, and packed it away in his closet. It was well past Mrs. Blum's dinnertime, so he took off down the sidewalk to a little Mexican food place a couple of blocks down and ordered a sack of tacos to go. The park was busy tonight with couples and families enjoying the warm April weather, but he found an unoccupied bench and sat down to eat his tacos and mull things over.

He still loved Elise. More accurately, he loved her memory. She'd given him his marching orders. It was time he moved on. He had a new life here in San Antonio, a new business, and a new opportunity to find love. He had a lot to offer a woman. Maybe it was time for him to open himself to loving someone else, to caring for her, to having the things he'd wanted so much to share with Elise.

He finished the last of his tacos and watched a young couple walk down the sidewalk holding hands. The girl was visibly pregnant and they were both smiling. Could he see himself doing that with Clara? Could that be them?

He thought back over his relationship with the prickly young woman. She'd been part of his life for months, sharing meals with him at Mrs. Blum's table, riding the bus downtown together, working side by side with him in the store. He'd come to rely on her. He turned to her innumerable times every day, sometimes for her expert advice, and sometimes to talk to her, and sometimes to watch her when she didn't know it.

He looked forward to her presence in the morning, and talking to her at the dinner table at night. It wasn't always roses with her. If she was irritated with him, she didn't bother to hide it. But he could count on her for the truth when he needed it, and a smile when he'd pleased her. The thought of losing her, of her leaving his store and moving away from Mrs. Blum's house, scared him to death.

He'd come to depend on her that much.

But what about the idea of him and Clara, going through life together as a couple? As he watched the young people walk together toward the bus stop, he smiled. He could see them being together. He could picture them clinging to one another in the dark of the night as he made sweet love to her. He could see them holding hands in the park on a sunny afternoon, standing under the canopy making their vows, picking out a home together, having a family, building the business into something to be proud of.

It wouldn't be a repeat of his relationship with Elise. Far from it. Clara was a different woman altogether. Blunt, forthright, no-nonsense with a heart of gold. A heart she'd apparently given to him.

He gulped. He'd given his heart to her as well, he realized in shock. He didn't know how the hell it had happened, but somehow the precious young woman had made her way into his heart. She'd snuck in while he wasn't looking and taken her place as the woman he could love for a lifetime.

It shouldn't be a surprise. Not really. She'd earned his love in so many ways. She pushed him to be a better version of himself. She supported him in the store and out of it. Thanks to her, he walked into Goldstein's every morning with confidence, knowing with her guidance he would make the right decisions for the business he wanted to grow.

She was his friend and his confidante. She was honest, smart, good, and decent. She was kind and caring, but unrelenting if he was headed in the wrong direction.

She had his best interests at heart.

And she understood. She'd lost her family too. She knew the same loneliness, the loss, and the wrenching emptiness down to the depths of her soul. She would treasure her husband and her children even more because of it. He understood that about her because he would too. He would love his wife and his children with everything he had in his heart.

He wanted Clara to be his wife. He wanted her to have their children. She'd given him no choice but to love her.

Here he'd been consumed with grief for a woman he hadn't seen in thirteen years, and was forced to examine his heart because she urged him to with all her heart. He would love Clara with all his being until he drew his last breath.

He could do it, he realized with a sense of wonder. He could love her deeply and intensely. Not as he'd loved Elise, but with a different depth and intensity. God knew, Clara would demand no less.

Clara could be his new everything, and he could be hers.

They could have a wonderful life together.

He'd have a tough job convincing her, but he'd use everything he had in him to make her believe.

Chapter Six

Clara looked at herself in the mirror and made a face. There wasn't much to the shorts, she thought ruefully as she looked at the perky sailor suit in the mirror. She had never shown this much leg in her life. England had been too cold to wear something this skimpy, and the Kirbys wouldn't have approved anyway.

When she and Jennie went shopping last week, she'd given in to her friend's persuasion. "Come on, Clara. It'll be hot for months and you have the legs to get away with it." So here she stood, wearing less than she'd ever worn in public in her life, waiting for Jesse and Jennie to take her to the Rodriguez family picnic. She could only hope Jesse's mother and grandmother weren't too shocked by her outfit.

She was putting on her lipstick when Mrs. Blum called for her to come down. She took the stairs two at a time and froze in her tracks to find Saul, not Jesse and Jennie, waiting for her at the foot of the stairs. He had a bouquet of spring flowers in his hand and an unfathomable expression on his face, at least until he got a look at her legs in the revealing shorts. At that point his gaze ran out on stalks and his mouth flew open. "Here." He thrust the flowers at her. "These are for you."

She took the flowers from him, dumbfounded. "I-uh-thanks," she stammered. "I don't have a vase to put them in."

"Not a problem," Mrs. Blum said cheerfully. "I have a vase. I'll put them in water and leave them on your dresser."

She whisked the flowers away and disappeared into the kitchen. Clara looked at Saul in confusion. "Flowers? For me? What's this all about?"

He threw his head back and looked her in the eye. "For millennia men have been known to bring flowers to their sweethearts. I'm merely following tradition."

"What? I'm not your sweetheart."

"Something I hope will change soon. By the way, I took the liberty of sending Jesse and Jennie on to their picnic without you. I hope you will do me the honor of having your picnic with me instead. Ah, here it comes now," he said as Mrs. Blum bustled out of the kitchen with a picnic basket.

"But I-you… What's going on, Saul?"

"We need to have a talk. A long talk. I figured we could have it over a picnic in the park. I'm glad you're already dressed for it. Love the shorts, by the way."

"Thanks," she said dryly.

"Now, would you rather get on the bus and go out to one of the suburban parks, or picnic somewhere close? No, you're not going to turn me down," he added when she started to object. "You're going to come with me and eat a sandwich and hear me out. Please, Clara. It's important. To both of us."

"I don't know," she said hesitantly.

"Come with me, please. Come with me and listen. Would you rather go to a park close to here or somewhere else?" He took her arm before she could object and ushered her toward the door.

"The park down the street is fine."

The park was packed and they ended up taking the bus out to Woodlawn Lake, a small lake and park in a fashionable neighborhood full of art-deco-style homes. Saul snagged a picnic table and set the basket between them. "Shall we eat before we talk?"

"That's fine."

Her curiosity burned and she could barely appreciate the roast beef sandwiches and Mrs. Blum's macaroon cake. She finally gave up and pushed her plate to one side. "What did you want to talk to me about?" she asked quietly.

"A lot of things." Saul came around the table. He sat down on the picnic bench beside her and took her hand. "I ran into Jennie and Jesse at the bus stop yesterday. I asked them if they knew why you want to quit. Jesse was quite forthcoming."

Clara felt her face turn red. "Jesse has a big mouth."

"For which I am grateful." He turned to her. "I had no idea you felt that way about me."

"There was no point in letting on. You love Elise. You've loved her for years and always will. I can't compete with that. Besides, you're out of my league. You're older and sophisticated."

Saul threw back his head and laughed. "You think I'm out of your league? You think I'm sophisticated? That is not true. If anything, it's the other way around. A beautiful young woman like you deserves better than crusty, set-in-my-ways old me, I promise you. We can work that out later. We need to talk about Elise." Clara tried to slip her hand free but he held on tightly. "Elise is gone, Clara. I want to move on."

"Wanting to move on and actually doing it are two different things. I saw you the night you found out she was dead. I was there, remember? You said you would love her for all time. You were horrified you'd kissed me. You asked why you'd even want to." She took a breath. "That hurt. It cut me to the quick."

"I said a lot of things that night. Most of them I didn't mean, even then. I sure don't mean them today." He got something out of his pocket. "Here. I want you to read this. It was in a chest of Elise's things *Frau* Gunther shipped to me."

"No, I—"

"Read it. Please."

Clara unfolded the letter. She read through it twice and handed it back to Saul. "She loved you very much to write you a letter like that knowing she was probably going to die."

"Yes, she did, and she was right. I want to move on, Clara. She wanted me to."

"You think you want to move on with me." She managed to tug her hand free. "I'm flattered, I truly am. But no."

"Why not?" he demanded. "Jesse said you love me. Do you?"

Clara lifted her chin. "Saul, it's not about whether I love you. I do and you know it. It's that you don't love me and never will. You love her."

"Yes, I do love her," he said slowly. "I guess it would be more accurate to say I love the memory of her."

"There you have it. Think what you're asking of me. Saul, I lost everyone in the Holocaust, the same as you. *Everyone* who loved me is gone. Now you're asking me to be a stand-in for your lost love. To live my life with you knowing you don't return my love. That you really want to be with her. The answer to that is no. I won't be a substitute for Elise or anybody else. I don't want to be a replacement. I deserve to be loved for who I am. I deserve to have a man love me the way you loved her. You can't do that."

"What makes you think you'd be a stand-in for Elise? You couldn't stand in for her if you tried."

She wanted to slap him. "You don't think I can even do that. I'm not as good as she was, right? So why are you asking me to?"

He ran his hand around his neck. "That's not what I meant. You wouldn't be replacing her. You're different, as is my relationship with you. She was sweet, gentle, always tried to make everyone around her happy. She wouldn't stand up to her father and marry me because she was trying to keep her family from getting upset. You wouldn't do that. You say what you think and do what you think's right, even if it ruffles feathers. If you wanted to marry me, you would, unhappy family be damned."

"All well and good. But you said you'd love her forever." She looked at him and felt her insides wither.

"Tell me. Your family's gone now. Do you still love them?"

"Of course I do. I will always love them."

"Now tell me this. Can you love again? Will you love your children someday?"

"Like you wouldn't believe. What does that have to do with us?"

"Plenty. I'll love Elise forever the same way you'll love your family forever. Like you, I can love again. I love her memory, but it doesn't mean I can't love you as well."

"You don't love me."

"How do you know? Have you given me a chance?" He took her face between his palms. "Damn it, girl, I do love you. It's like you snuck into my heart while I wasn't looking. I swear, Clara. I can give you the love you want so badly. Give me a chance. Please."

He leaned forward but she pulled her head away. "You want to kiss Elise."

"Damned if that's so." He put his hand behind her head and pushed her toward him. "I want to kiss *you*, Clara. Not her. Not anybody else but you."

His lips weren't gentle as they came down on hers. Seeking, demanding, Saul wrapped his arms around her and pulled her up onto his lap. His lips were hot and hungry, his chest strong against her pebbling nipples, and his thighs hard beneath her legs as they clung to one another.

Clara couldn't resist. She knew she should. A kiss would resolve nothing, but it felt so right, so perfect to be in his arms, kissing him and clinging to his masculine warmth. She gave herself over to his embrace, returned his kisses and ran her fingers down his strong back, reveling in the strength of his body. She would give herself over to the moment, savor it and milk it for all it was worth as she kissed the life out of the man who held her in his arms.

They kissed for a long time, oblivious to their not-too-private surroundings. Finally, he pulled his lips away from hers. "My eyes are open, Clara. I know who I'm kissing."

She looked at him with bemusement. "What does that have to do with anything?"

"I'm kissing you. You, Clara. The woman I want to be kissing. Not anyone else."

He pulled her close and continued his sensual assault. Hotter, deeper, even more passionate, he took possession of her lips again and again, kissing and tasting and nibbling until she was a puddle in his arms. "My eyes are open, Clara," he said against her lips. "My eyes are open and I'm kissing the woman I love. From the way you're kissing me back, I'd say you love me too. Have I convinced you yet I love you?"

"No."

"Then I'll have to kiss you again. And again, and again, and again, until you can feel the love I have for you. It's there, Clara. Reach out for it. Touch it. Feel it. My heart…it's yours now."

His lips came down on hers again, hard and insistent, and as she returned his embrace, as she opened herself to his emotions, she could feel there was much more than passion in his touch. *She could feel it.* She could feel the love in his arms cradling her close and his lips on hers. She could feel the tenderness and the caring mixed with his desire. She could also feel his need, a need for her that transcended the physical. The need of a man alone in the world, who was alone like her, who needed her love as badly as she needed his. A man who needed her in the dark of the night and the bright light of day, to go forward with him into the future, a future that held a wealth of promise for bright and happy tomorrows.

If that was really love she felt.

They held on to one another for long minutes. When he raised his head, his eyes were shining as he looked into hers. "Have I convinced you I love you?"

"If I say no, will you kiss me again?" she asked softly.

"I'll kiss you every morning, noon and night for the rest of my life if that's what it takes."

"I'm convinced, I think, but I'd like that. To be kissed morning, noon, and night for the rest of my life."

He kissed her again, hard and sweet. "Does this mean you're now my sweetheart?"

"I suppose so. So how are we going do this?" she asked as she looped her arms around his neck.

Saul settled her on his lap. "First off, you're going to keep working for me. I need you at the store, Clara. Not merely as my employee. I need you there by my side. As my support, my partner, my anchor. If we steal a few kisses in the back, all the better. All right?"

"All right." Besides, if he loved her, she had no reason to leave, and every reason to stay.

"We're going to do what sweethearts have done since the beginning of time," he continued. "We're going to get to know one another. We're going to go on dates. Movies, picnics, fancy dinners, and tacos in the park.

"We'll go roller-skating. Ride a Ferris wheel and a roller coaster. I'll take you dancing. We're going to have the fun neither of us has had the chance to have before. We'll make some beautiful memories. You'll become accustomed to the ways of this older man and I'll get used to keeping up with a beautiful young woman.

"Most important, I am going to convince you beyond a shadow of a doubt I love you deeply and dearly, and will for the rest of my life. When I've done that, when the time is right, we'll stand under the *chuppah* together, take our vows and stomp on the wineglass, and spend the rest of our lives as man and wife.

"You and me and whatever children and grandchildren we're blessed with. We'll treasure every minute we're given. We'll embrace the future together and make it ours. How does that sound?"

It sounded wonderful.

***

When Saul held his baby son in his arms for the first time, he closed his eyes and told God, "We will never forget. Our children and our grandchildren and their grandchildren will never forget. I promise this, as will they."

ABOUT THE AUTHOR

The author of over forty romance novels, Emily Mims combined her writing career with a career in public education until leaving the classroom to write full time. The mother of two sons, she and her husband split their time between central Texas, eastern Tennessee, and overseas visiting their kids and grandchildren. For relaxation Emily plays the piano, organ, dulcimer, and ukulele for two different performing groups, and even sings a little. She says, "I love to write romances because I believe in them. Romance happened to me and it can happen to any woman—if she'll just let it."

Connect with Emily:
facebook.com/emily.mims.756
twitter.com/emilymimsauthor
instagram.com/mims_emily
website: emilymims.com

www.BOROUGHSPUBLISHINGGROUP.com

If you enjoyed this book, please write a review. Our authors appreciate the feedback, and it helps future readers find books they love. We welcome your comments and invite you to send them to info@boroughspublishinggroup.com. Follow us on Facebook, Twitter and Instagram, and be sure to sign up for our newsletter for surprises and new releases from your favorite authors.

Are you an aspiring writer? Check out www.boroughspublishinggroup.com/submit and see if we can help you make your dreams come true.